A PEN & DAGGER NOVEL

NOVEL THREAT

A PEN & DAGGER NOVEL

NOVEL THREAT

TRACI HUNTER ABRAMSON

SHADOW
MOUNTAIN
PUBLISHING

Library of Congress Cataloging-in-Publication Data
Names: Abramson, Traci Hunter, author.
Title: Novel threat / Traci Hunter Abramson.
Description: Salt Lake City : Shadow Mountain Publishing, 2025. | Series: A pen & dagger novel | Summary: "Brandon Hale, a CIA officer ready to resign and start a publishing career, is pulled back into undercover action after a source's murder links a New York publishing house to terrorism. Kimber Seidel, an aspiring novelist and CIA finance officer, meets Brandon, unaware of his true role. Their growing connection is tested as they face increasing danger and unraveling secrets"—Provided by publisher.
Identifiers: LCCN 2024039802 (print) | LCCN 2024039803 (ebook) | ISBN 9781639933846 (hardback) | ISBN 9781649333551 (ebook)
Subjects: LCGFT: Spy fiction. | Novels.
Classification: LCC PS3601.B76 N685 2025 (print) | LCC PS3601.B76 (ebook) | DDC 813/.6— dc23/eng/20240830
LC record available at https://lccn.loc.gov/2024039802
LC ebook record available at https://lccn.loc.gov/2024039803

Printed in Canada
PubLitho

10   9   8   7   6   5   4   3   2   1

*For the many dedicated individuals
I worked with during my years with the CIA.*

You weren't just friends. You were family.

PROLOGUE

FINLAY GRIPPED THE wheel of his Mini Cooper, the windshield wipers swishing back and forth in a fruitless battle against the steady rain. The flash of headlights illuminated his rearview mirror, and his heartbeat quickened. Had he been found out?

He scanned the dark, narrow road for a pullout, his knuckles turning white as he traversed the next several miles, the car behind him now too close for comfort.

Finlay finally spotted a place where the road widened enough for a car to pull over, and he took advantage of it, hoping and praying that the car behind him would pass.

It did, and he let out a sigh of relief.

Everything was going to be okay. Maybe if he kept telling himself that, it would be true.

He wished now that he'd never gone into Asadi's office, that he'd never seen what the man was planning: death-toll numbers in the hundreds, if not thousands. Innocent people would be lost, including women and children.

Finlay couldn't let that happen.

The drive from Anglesey would have been best made during the day, but he'd needed to wait for his wife and children to go to bed before he'd slipped away. He'd needed to make sure no one knew where he was going. And in the dark, this late at night, he could be sure no one was following him from the island off the northern coast of Wales.

He checked his rearview mirror again, relieved to see only darkness.

Maybe he should have brought his wife and daughters with him, but he'd feared they might alert the neighbors. And if the neighbors knew they were going on a trip, Asadi or someone else in the Labyrinth organization was bound to find out too.

Even the suspicion of betraying the organization would be grounds for Asadi to order Finlay's death and the deaths of his entire family. No, Finlay had to be careful. And he was.

Tonight, he would meet the man who could protect him, the man he trusted to keep him and his family alive.

CHAPTER 1

BRANDON HALE HUDDLED against the honey-colored stone building, his gaze sweeping the darkness, the trees and open space beside the stream barely visible beneath the overcast sky. The rain cascading into the water flowing under the bridge a short distance away intensified the noise.

Brandon's body tensed with each passing moment. It was eerily quiet. Too quiet. Then again, this little English village in the Cotswolds, quaintly named Castle Combe, could have been plucked right out of the 1600s, except that the light spilling out of a nearby window was fueled by electricity rather than lamp oil.

He'd already taken a walk around the grassy area where he would soon meet his informant and was relieved that he hadn't spotted any sources of concern.

A drop of water trickled down the back of his neck, somehow finding its way past the collar of his trench coat. He'd grown accustomed to the wet and cold, working in the UK, but his time with the CIA was quickly coming to a close. Tomorrow was the day he would turn in his resignation, and he would finally take a step toward the career he had always dreamed of.

Next month, he would put his degree in literary arts to work. He could hardly wait. He rather looked forward to editing thrillers instead of living them. But for tonight, he had a job to do, and that job included collecting information from Finlay and making sure the man wasn't identified as Brandon's source.

Brandon considered walking through the area again, but a check of his mobile told him he didn't have time. Two minutes until midnight.

Only a few seconds passed before Finlay's stocky figure emerged on the narrow walkway nearby. A light flashed twice in rapid succession, followed by a third flash of longer duration. Contact.

Brandon did another quick scan of the area before striding across the bridge. He reached the older man's side. "What do you have?"

"You have to get me out of here," Finlay said, his words coming quickly. "Me and my family."

Not the start Brandon had hoped for. His best contact within Labyrinth was in danger or had cold feet. It was up to Brandon to determine which. "What happened?"

"I found something I wasn't supposed to see." Finlay shivered, and his voice trembled. "I think Asadi knows."

Asadi Mir, the man believed to be the head of Labyrinth. Brandon's already active senses heightened further. "What did you see?"

"This." Finlay stopped and held out a business card. "The money trail leads back to New York."

Though Brandon was tempted to use the flashlight on his phone to read the card, he pocketed it instead. He wasn't going to draw attention to them and potentially risk his asset's safety.

"My car is this way." He urged Finlay toward the roadside not far from them.

"What about my family?"

"My priority is to keep you safe," Brandon said.

"But—"

"I'll come back for your family as soon as we have you out of sight," Brandon said, cutting off whatever protest Finlay had planned.

"No one would think to look for me here."

The words were barely out of his mouth when a single gunshot pierced the air, overshadowing the sound of the storm and rushing water. Finlay grabbed at his chest and fell to his knees before collapsing onto the grass.

"No!" Brandon's protest caught in the wind even as his training kicked in. He drew the pistol holstered at his waist and fired two shots into the woods. Exposed to the shooter and with no place to take cover, Brandon dropped beside Finlay, the moisture of the damp ground seeping into his trousers.

He peeked over Finlay's prone body and waited for the shooter to fire again to help him pinpoint the assassin's location. A second shot never came. Instead, the faint crunch of footsteps on frozen leaves carried in the wind. Brandon lifted his weapon again and fired once more.

• • •

I'm not getting paid enough for this. And no matter what Asadi thought, Darragh wasn't working with Labyrinth because of some grudge against the US and the UK. He was in this for the money.

With his sniper rifle gripped in his hand, he placed his foot at the base of the tree, where the ground was still firm despite the rain. Had visibility been better, he would have set up out of range, but instead, he'd been forced to shoot from the edge of the woods.

Another shot fired, and Darragh ducked. Bark splintered off a nearby branch.

His heartbeat quickened. He was the one who was supposed to be doing the shooting. This being-fired-at scenario wasn't in his plans.

He lifted his rifle and peered through his scope. The man with the gun had taken cover behind Finlay, the top of the man's head barely visible.

Darragh slid his finger onto the trigger, but before he could fire, the man popped up and squeezed off two more shots.

Darragh jumped behind the tree, but not before a bullet ripped through his coat and caught the fleshy part of his upper arm.

No, he didn't like people shooting back at him. Not one bit. And certainly not another pro.

That thought caused him to pause, and Darragh's chest tightened. If Finlay was meeting with someone who was not only armed but also had the training to clip Darragh despite the lack of visibility, Finlay may have caused more damage than Asadi realized.

Faced with the choice of confronting his opponent and exposing himself to more gunfire or fleeing to ensure Asadi understood the dangers, Darragh chose the safer option. He darted from one tree to another amid another blast of gunfire.

Without looking back, he picked up the pace and sprinted toward his waiting car. He would settle up with Finlay's friend another time, and when he did, Darragh would make sure he was paid handsomely for the privilege of eliminating the man who had shot him.

•   •   •

Brandon scanned the woods for any additional movement, any other sign of life, but the footsteps quickly faded, the shooter never passing into Brandon's field of vision. A minute stretched into two. Keeping his head low, he reached out and checked Finlay's neck for a pulse. Nothing. He tried again, but only the steady rhythm of the falling rain beat against his skin.

Dropping his head, Brandon fought against reality. He had taken so many precautions, yet the one moment he'd worked so hard to avoid had happened on his watch. He had lost his asset. Labyrinth had silenced their mole, the CIA had lost their source, and the man's death was Brandon's fault.

Finlay had tried to stop the deadly terrorist group by sharing information, and that decision had cost him his life.

His heart jackhammering in his chest, Brandon lowered his weapon and pulled out his mobile. He retrieved the emergency contact he had put into his phone on the fourth day of the CIA's new-employee orientation—the number he'd never had to call before tonight.

After working through the verification process to secure the call, he was finally patched through to an operations officer.

"My asset was killed," Brandon whispered. Just saying the words caused bile to rise in his throat.

"Are you safe?" the woman on the other end asked.

"I don't know." Brandon described the situation and his current position.

"A clean-up crew is on the way," she said. "I need you to take cover. Your only job right now is to stay out of sight and to make sure no one takes the body."

"What if the authorities show up?"

"Then, you'll use your MI5 credentials to take over."

Another tool the CIA had given Brandon that he'd never had to use before. He hoped he wouldn't need them tonight.

• • •

Kimber Seidel highlighted another line on her spreadsheet. Three separate incidents they believed Labyrinth had orchestrated in the past four months, and she had yet to find a single clue as to where their money was coming from. Even the reports from her contacts within the underground diamond trade had come up empty.

Her friend Mark appeared in the doorway of her cubicle. "Are you ready to go?"

"If I say no, does that mean I can stay home?" Kimber tried to muster some enthusiasm for her weekend plans that most people would envy. A flight to London tonight and three days with her sister at Fashion Week. Kimber let out a sigh. A weekend pretending to be something she wasn't.

She held up her copy of *The Rise of Theodore Roosevelt*. "I could order Chinese food, sit by the fire, and read a book."

"You can read on the plane, and you don't have a fireplace," Mark said.

It was true. Her living room was little more than four walls, six bookcases, and a sofa. "My next apartment is going to have a fireplace."

"Good luck with that." Mark tilted his head toward the door. "Come on. You and Tessa will have a great time."

Maybe, assuming Kimber survived the complete change in her wardrobe and the thirty-minute makeup routines needed to fit into her sister's world. Tessa's job as the personal assistant to one of the top talent agents in the US was a dream for her, but Kimber preferred jeans and T-shirts over Chanel and Gucci.

Kimber grabbed her suitcase and headed down the passageway between the rows of cubicles.

Mark fell into step beside her. "I'll come with you if you want."

She glanced at him and nearly laughed at the hopeful expression on his face. "You're still hoping Tessa will go out with you."

"Can't blame a guy for dreaming."

She'd introduced Tessa and Mark at the CIA's family day last year, and he'd been obsessed ever since. "I guess I could think of worse people to have for a brother-in-law."

"Exactly. We should totally double date." He cast a glance at Logan as they passed him.

Kimber lowered her voice. "I'm not going out with Logan."

"Why not? He's a nice guy." Mark reached the vault door and pushed it open, waiting for her to pass through.

"He is a nice guy," she agreed. "And he can speak six languages, has his pilot's license, can defuse nine different types of explosives, and is a black belt in aikido." Kimber didn't mention that she knew about the explosives because she and Logan had undergone that particular training together.

Mark waved a hand in the air. "Don't tell me you aren't giving him a chance because he's an operative."

"I've been down that road before. I don't plan to go there again."

"You're being stubborn again," Mark said. "He's CIA; you're CIA. It totally works."

Memories of a dark street in Georgetown surfaced, and she fought against them. "Logan's undercover. I'm not. It totally *doesn't* work."

"Don't let what happened with Daniel get in the way of your social life." In a brotherly gesture, he put a comforting hand on her shoulder and intensified his gaze. "It's time to move on."

Logically, she knew he was right, but that didn't stop the turmoil of guilt from churning inside her. She lifted her hands in exasperation. "He nearly got killed because I couldn't figure out how to lie about my job. I still get nervous every time I meet new people." A new challenge shot panic painfully into her chest. "What am I supposed to do if someone on the airplane asks me what I do for a living?"

They reached the elevator, and Mark pressed the Down button. "Put in your AirPods and ignore everyone. You'll be fine."

"And if there's a little old lady sitting by the window who insists on talking to me?" Kimber asked. It had happened before.

"Tell her you're a writer."

"I'm not a real writer." Sure, she had written a book. Three actually. She'd even gone through the process of having her manuscripts cleared by the CIA's Publication Classification Review Board so she could share her work with her critique group, which she had yet to attend, but it wasn't like she'd ever been published. This was just a hobby that allowed her to dive into fictional worlds when she needed to escape her real one.

"You *are* a writer," Mark insisted. "I've read your stuff. It's good."

"You're just saying that because you're hoping to be my brother-in-law someday."

"I'm saying it because it's true."

The doors opened, and she led the way inside.

"Let's practice." Mark turned to face her. "Hi, I'm Mark. I'm a financial analyst. What do you do for a living?"

She shook her head. "This is silly." She punched the button for the fourth floor.

"Answer the question," Mark insisted. "What do you do for a living?"

"I'm a writer?"

"You can't answer a question with a question." Mark lifted one finger as he made his point. "Say it like you mean it."

"I'm a writer."

"Good." The doors opened, and Mark walked out of the elevator in front of her and headed toward the new headquarters building exit. "Now you just need to believe it."

CHAPTER 2

ASADI MIR STOOD on the beach in Rhos-on-Sea, his mood reflected in the stormy clouds above. He had grown rather fond of this spot in North Wales, of the slow pace and the locals' friendly dispositions. At times, he could almost pretend his brother and sister were still alive and that the United Kingdom and the United States weren't responsible for robbing him of his family.

He shoved both hands into his jacket pockets and fisted them there as he fought for calm. So many plans were in motion, and one rogue employee could interfere with far more than the day-to-day operations.

The tide rolled onto the wide stretch of sand, the water nearly reaching his boots. He had relocated to his flat overlooking the Irish Sea yesterday after learning of Finlay's betrayal. With only two bridges connecting Anglesey to the mainland, he could hardly afford to get caught on the island in this weather when helicopter travel was less than ideal.

A burning ignited inside him, starting in his chest and slowly creeping outward. The Brits and the Americans would pay for what they'd done, and this time, the world would take notice.

Footsteps approached, and Asadi waited until his man stepped beside him before speaking. "Any problems?"

"Finlay was with someone," Darragh said. "I don't know who."

Asadi slanted a look at the assassin. "Is he still breathing?"

"Finlay's not. The other man is."

Fury rose inside Asadi, and he turned to face the man who had been one of his best hired guns since Asadi had created the Labyrinth organization four years earlier. "Why didn't you take them both out?"

"He was armed." A wave rushed onto the beach, and Darragh stepped back to keep his shoes from getting wet. "I couldn't get a clean shot without risking being seen."

"Your job was to eliminate the threat."

"I did. They were only together for a minute before I took out Finlay. He didn't have time to tell him anything."

"In the intelligence world, a minute is an eternity."

"I have the number plate of the car Finlay's friend was driving," Darragh said, his icy blue stare now focused on Asadi. "I tracked it to London."

"Then, I suggest you make your way to London. You have one more threat to eliminate."

"You know my fee."

"I'll transfer it today."

Darragh nodded. "I'll leave today."

• • •

Brandon opened his eyes to sunlight streaming through his bedroom window, the London traffic audible through the glass.

Cars moving at a decent speed cut through his consciousness. Morning rush hour outside his flat was never more than a crawl. He reached out his hand and checked the time on his phone. Eleven thirty.

He shot up in bed. He'd overslept. It was Friday, wasn't it? The memories of Finlay pressed to the forefront of his consciousness.

For a brief moment, he convinced himself last night had been a dream, a horrible nightmare that would fade with time. Then he sat up and spotted the clothes he'd discarded when he'd arrived home. The bloodstained overcoat, the rumpled shirt and trousers.

Brandon's chin dropped to his chest. Finlay Addington was dead, and it was Brandon's fault.

The sharp blade of failure tore through him again, the single gunshot ringing through his memory with alarming clarity. Brandon's mind raced with everything he could have done differently. A meeting inside a car or at a pub or in a hotel room. He'd let his asset dictate the terms of the meeting, and that decision had cost Finlay his life. And for what? To pass along a business card?

Pushing out of bed, Brandon crossed the room and retrieved the card from his trouser pocket. He'd read the contents last night, but the words didn't make any more sense now in the light of day. Monroe Publishing. Why would a business card from one of the largest publishers in the world warrant assassinating Finlay?

He set the card on his dresser beside his offer letter from a London publishing house. He was supposed to resign from the CIA today. Whether he could drum up the nerve after such a colossal failure remained to be seen.

• • •

Brandon walked into the CIA's London office at half past noon, indecision and doubts still plaguing him.

The secretary by the front door looked up from the computer monitor on her desk. "I don't know what happened last night, but Langley has called four times in the past hour." She picked up a message and handed it to Brandon.

He furrowed his brow. "It's only seven thirty in the morning there."

"I know. They've been calling since six their time."

"Sorry." Brandon took the message slip and read the name and title: Grayson Yarrow, the deputy director of operations.

Brandon's fingers tightened on the paper he now held, and dread filled him. If someone at that level was calling him, it couldn't be good. Then again, what did he expect? He'd lost a valuable asset in the field. His one error in judgment would likely overshadow the previous seven years he'd spent with the agency that had gone incident-free. And on the eve of his planned departure, no less.

He made his way to his cubicle and dialed the phone on his desk.

The phone rang only twice before a man's voice came over the line. "Yarrow."

"This is Brandon Hale."

That was as far as he got before the DDO said, "I read your report from last night."

"I'm sorry, sir. I cleared the area. The shooter must have slipped in behind me."

"Can you ID them?"

"No." Yet another failure. "I only caught a glimpse of him when he took off." Brandon's heart pounded in his chest. "I'm sorry, sir. My asset was nervous about meeting, and I let him choose the time and the place."

"It wouldn't have mattered where or when you met," Director Yarrow said. "Forensics found tracking devices in your asset's watch, in his shoe, in the lining of his coat, and in his car."

"I don't get it. The only thing he had for me was a business card for a New York publishing house."

"That's the reason I called. I want you back here in the States. You fly to New York on Monday."

"Fly back, as in a quick trip? Or as in move back?" He was supposed to start his new job in London in less than three weeks.

"This will be a permanent assignment. It's time we put that Ivy League education of yours to work," he said. "You're going undercover at Monroe Publishing starting Tuesday."

This day kept getting more surreal. He supposed that was one way to get a job, but he had different objectives for his future. "I actually have a job offer from a publishing house here in London. I planned to turn in my resignation at the CIA today."

"Brandon, we need you. You have the knowledge on Labyrinth, and you have the pedigree we need to insert you without anyone raising an eyebrow."

The CIA needed *him*. That phrase hadn't ever been used before with him. "Like I said, I was planning to resign today."

"Don't let one bad incident scare you off," Director Yarrow said. "You've done good work since you've been with us."

Another unexpected compliment. Brandon weighed his options: the future he wanted against the deep guilt stewing inside him. The need to bring Finlay's killer to justice combined with his inherent desire to ensure Finlay's death hadn't been in vain. "How did you pull off getting me a position there? Their offices aren't even open yet this morning."

"Our computer hackers have been working through the night," Director Yarrow said.

"What position would I be taking?"

"Turns out the managing editor needs a new assistant," Director Yarrow said. "They were going to fill it internally, but your background will justify HR bringing someone in from outside."

An assistant. So much for working in the editorial field, where he belonged. "Don't you think people will notice if I'm hired without meeting the managing editor first? Surely he'll want a say in who gets the job."

"She. Amelia Franklin. And she's been in Hong Kong for the past two weeks," Director Yarrow said.

"What about jurisdiction?" Brandon asked. This was FBI territory. He should know. He'd spent two years on loan to the FBI, four months of which had been spent going through the FBI Academy so he could operate as a field agent instead of office staff.

"The FBI is in the loop. You'll meet with Special Agent Ebeid on Tuesday night," Director Yarrow said. "And, Brandon?"

"Yes?"

"What happened last night wasn't your fault."

Brandon's insides twisted. He wished he could believe that.

CHAPTER 3

MARK HAD BEEN right. Kimber had had a great time with her sister, even though the majority of her time had been spent at parties, wearing high heels, trendy clothes, and far more makeup than usual. She'd been amazed at how efficiently Tessa had helped her talent-agent boss keep track of the million moving pieces of Fashion Week while also socializing with dozens of people.

In the seat beside Kimber, Tessa leaned forward and opened the minibar in the back of the limo her boss had hired. She pulled out a sparkling water, poured some into a glass, and held it out. "Do you want some?"

"Sure." Kimber accepted the glass and took a sip while her sister poured the rest into another glass for herself. "You know, it's pretty sad that we have to fly to London to see each other."

"I know," Tessa said. "I'll be back in New York at the beginning of March. You should come up and visit me for a weekend."

"Or you could come down and see me."

"Hmm. A weekend going to clubs and parties or a weekend hanging out in our PJs, streaming *NCIS* episodes?"

"Hey, I love that show." Kimber glanced down at her current outfit: fitted white dress pants, a flowing black-and-white-striped blouse, and an orange blazer. "And PJs are a lot more comfortable than what I'm wearing now." Their driver pulled up in front of Heathrow Airport. "I can't believe I'm all dressed up to fly across the Atlantic."

"Greta's limo, Greta's rules." Tessa's eyes sparked mischievously. "Besides, she let me arrange a little surprise for your flight home."

Kimber furrowed her brow. "What kind of surprise?"

"You'll see." Tessa reached out and hugged her. "Travel safe."

"Thanks. You too." Kimber gave her one last hug as the driver opened the back door. She stepped onto the sidewalk, where her suitcase already waited for her. "Thank you."

The driver nodded in response.

Kimber grabbed the handle of her bag and strode into the airport, the heels of her boots clicking against the linoleum.

She got as far as the security checkpoint and stopped. She'd given herself nearly three hours to reach her gate, but she waited in the security line for well over two hours. Three passengers in front of her had ignored security's warning about liquids in their carry-ons. Another dozen passengers underwent bag searches for various reasons, ranging from drugs to the silverware a patron hadn't wanted to check despite the inclusion of a set of steak knives.

By the time Kimber finally made it through, she had only a few minutes until the plane was supposed to board.

She turned the corner toward her gate. Maybe if she hurried, she would have enough time to use the bathroom stall to change into jeans and a T-shirt.

The gate agent announced that her flight was preparing to board, and a line of people waited near the check-in counter. Kimber scanned the wide corridor between the gates on either side of the terminal in search of a restroom, but none were visible. So much for changing her clothes.

Resigned, she retrieved her cell phone from her computer bag and pulled up her boarding pass. She glanced at her boarding group, surprised to see the code for first class.

Less than a minute passed before the gate agent's voice sounded over the intercom. "First-class passengers are now welcome to board."

Kimber fell in line with the handful of other first-class passengers and made her way to her seat. As soon as she stowed her carry-on in the overhead compartment, she set her backpack in front of her and dialed her sister's number.

Tessa answered a moment later. "Did you make your flight?"

"I just boarded," Kimber said. "You upgraded me to first class?"

"Yep. Now you have no excuse not to use the next few hours to work on your book."

"I could have done that in coach."

"True, but this will make up for having to fly through JFK." Tessa's smile came through in her words. "Plus, Greta said I could use some of her points to make it happen."

"Well, thank you. And thank Greta for me."

"I will. Talk to you soon."

Kimber ended the call and pulled her laptop from her bag. It wouldn't hurt to skim over her latest story idea. She opened the detailed spreadsheet that included her character sketches, scene summaries, and plot points. It was far easier to dive into creating a new fictional universe than to think that she was never going to get published if she didn't submit.

Within minutes, she was in a different world, a place where her characters faced adventure with daring and finesse, a place where insecurities became endearing instead of crippling, a place where love was possible.

For the next fifteen minutes, the words flowed. She barely noticed the man who approached until he sat beside her and slid his soft-sided leather briefcase beneath the seat in front of him.

Kimber glanced up. The man appeared to be a year or two older than her, maybe twenty-nine or thirty, his light-brown hair cut short, his angular face clean-shaven.

He straightened and glanced at her with a guarded expression, his blue eyes meeting hers. "Sorry. I didn't mean to disturb you."

"It's fine. I'm sure I'll have to put this away soon anyway." Kimber powered down her laptop and slipped it into her backpack.

The flight attendant approached. "Would you care for something to drink before we depart?"

"Water would be wonderful." Kimber looked at the back of the seat in front of her, but there wasn't a tray to put down. "Where's the tray?"

"In the arm handle." The flight attendant gestured to where the tray was concealed in the thick arm rest.

The man beside her also opened his tray. "I'll take a water as well."

"Yes, sir." The flight attendant disappeared into the forward galley and returned a moment later with two glasses of water on a tray. She handed Kimber a napkin and a glass of water.

Water in a real glass on an airplane. She could get used to this. "Thank you."

"You're welcome." The flight attendant set a napkin down for the man next to her. When she went to set his glass on it, someone bumped her from behind, and the water sloshed over the rim.

"I'm so sorry, sir," the flight attendant said, her embarrassment evident in her expression.

"It's fine." He dabbed his napkin on the wet spot on his slacks. "It's just a little water. It'll dry." A hint of British upper class slipped through his American accent. "Do you have another serviette?"

"Of course." The flight attendant passed him several more napkins. "I really am sorry."

"Don't worry about it." He finished wiping the moisture off his clothing and set his water on his tray. After the man assured the flight attendant that he was fine for a second time, the woman returned to her duties.

He took a sip of water, his firm grip on his glass a sure sign of stress.

The urge to dispel his tension rose inside Kimber. "Are you on your way home?"

"Yeah." The muscle in his jaw twitched. "You could say that."

Trying another tactic, she offered her hand. "I'm Kimber."

"Brandon." He put his hand in hers. He stared at her a moment before he released her hand and motioned toward her bag. "What were you working on?"

"I was just playing around." The question of what he did for a living burned on her tongue, but she swallowed it. If she didn't ask any questions, she likely wouldn't have to answer them either.

· · ·

Brandon was surprised when Kimber fell silent. She exuded a friendly vibe, but she didn't overshare details about her reasons for being in

London, and whatever questions she might have asked him remained unspoken. Thank goodness. Brandon didn't think he could handle idle conversation while his emotions were still in turmoil.

It was too bad. Normally, he would have loved to find himself sitting next to an attractive woman with a quick smile and kind eyes. Her dark hair hung loosely past her shoulders, and while she was dressed like a fashion model, she had a refreshing warmth about her. She was exactly the sort of woman he would choose to date given the opportunity. Today, however, his mood didn't lend itself to flirting.

A man was dead—a man he had promised to protect—and even though the director claimed it wasn't Brandon's fault, Brandon had been there. The director hadn't. And no matter what anyone said, Finlay was no longer breathing because Brandon had failed to protect him. That meant it was undeniably his fault. Even his mandatory counseling session after the incident hadn't helped dispel his guilt.

Kimber crossed her legs, the simple movement distracting him.

Focus. He had to be missing something about Labyrinth in the information Finlay had fed him during the last few months. Over the past three days, he had read through everything Finlay had shared with him, reviewed the autopsy and forensic reports, and studied the corporate structure of Monroe Publishing.

Now he was flying across the Atlantic to take a job he was overqualified for, with the entire sum of his possessions packed in two suitcases, a carry-on, and his briefcase. Too bad he'd had to leave most of his books behind.

The flight attendant spoke over the intercom, instructing everyone to power down their laptops and place other electronics in airplane mode. Brandon checked his email one last time before following the directive. Then he slipped his phone into his bag and pinched the bridge of his nose in the hope that he could combat the headache forming there.

"Are you okay?" Kimber asked.

"Just a bit of a headache," Brandon said.

"You look like you have a lot more on your mind than just a headache."

She was right, and her perception was a bit disconcerting. "It's been a rough couple of days."

"I'm sorry." Kimber studied him, and Brandon braced for the follow-up questions that were sure to come. To his surprise, her next question had nothing to do with ferreting out the cause of his mood. "Do you like to read?" she asked.

"Yes." He furrowed his brow. "Why?"

Kimber pulled a book from her bag and held it out. "I don't know if you'd be interested in this, but you look like you could use a distraction."

Brandon glanced at the book cover. It was the recent biography on Theodore Roosevelt that he'd been meaning to read. He'd been meaning to read a lot of things but rarely had the opportunity. "You're lending me your book?"

"You can keep it. I finished it yesterday morning." Kimber passed it to him. "It's good. Definitely worth your time." Her cheeks flushed as though she had somehow misspoken. "Not that I know how you value your time, but I enjoyed it."

At the moment, he'd enjoy anything that would keep his mind off Finlay. "Thank you." Not sure what to think of the impromptu gesture, he flipped through the first few pages. An editorial mark caught his attention, and he studied that particular page closer. "You wrote in it."

"Oh, sorry. I can't resist correcting mistakes when I find them."

Brandon's mood lightened. "That's one way of dealing with typos." He closed the book. "Are you sure you won't want this back? You might want to read it again."

"I don't read books twice, at least not nonfiction."

Curious that she made the distinction, he asked, "Does that mean you reread novels?"

"All the time." Her expression brightened. "It's fascinating to see how authors use tools to evoke emotions, to make readers feel by drawing on relatable experiences."

He couldn't have said it better himself. At the moment, he wouldn't mind diving into a fictional world that included a happily ever after for everyone involved. "What's your favorite genre?"

"I don't know that I have a favorite. I mostly look for books that are well written and that have compelling characters."

Even though Brandon had planned to avoid conversation with anyone, Kimber included, something pushed him to press the issue. "When you walk into a bookstore, what section do you head for first?"

"Romantic suspense."

"So, you do have a favorite."

"Yeah." A little line formed between her eyebrows. "I guess I do."

CHAPTER 4

KIMBER'S LAPTOP REMAINED in her bag for the full eight hours of the flight. Her conversation with Brandon had morphed from their favorite books to favorite movies to favorite music to so many other topics. They had discovered, thankfully, that they both preferred the Mets over the Yankees and the Giants over the Jets.

Brandon's initial reservations had eased during their time together, although Kimber didn't miss the occasional flash of tension, as though some bad memory kept surfacing that he didn't want to face. Though he didn't say as much, Kimber suspected Brandon was either leaving trouble behind or heading toward it. Kimber couldn't help but wonder if that trouble came in the form of an ex-girlfriend or perhaps a current girlfriend.

The pilot's voice came over the intercom, announcing their impending arrival into JFK.

"I can't believe we talked this whole time," Kimber said.

"Me neither." He looked at her with an odd expression, as though not quite sure whether he was confused or relieved.

The plane touched down, the jolt of their sudden decrease in speed pulling their bodies forward.

As soon as the plane slowed, Kimber reached into her bag and pulled out her cell phone. The moment she switched it out of airplane mode, it buzzed with several incoming text messages, the most recent of which was from Mark, telling her that he would meet her in the pickup lane.

"A message from your boyfriend?" Brandon asked.

Was he probing to find out if she was in a relationship?

"No, just a friend. He's picking me up from the airport in DC." Kimber tried to imagine what it would be like if Brandon were interested in her. They had gotten along so well, and never once did he press about what she did for a living or ask details about her family that she didn't want to answer. It really was too bad that they didn't live in the same city. She would have loved to get to know him better.

She pushed that thought aside. Guys who looked like Brandon didn't ask her out.

The Fasten Seat Belt sign chimed as it turned off. Kimber texted Mark a quick message before storing her phone in her bag again.

Brandon unfastened his seat belt. "I'm really glad I met you."

Kimber smiled. "I'm glad I met you too."

Almost reluctantly, Brandon stood and retrieved his carry-on bag. "Which one is yours?"

"The blue one with the purple luggage tag on it."

He lifted it down for her. "Here you go."

"Thanks."

The airplane door opened, and the few people in the rows in front of them exited. Brandon remained in the aisle and waited for Kimber to go first.

She walked up the Jetway, Brandon right behind her, until they passed through the line at customs and emerged from the kiosks at the same time. When Kimber reached the main passageway beyond, she stopped and checked for her gate number. She was disappointed when she looked at the signs and saw that her gate was in the opposite direction of baggage claim.

Brandon stopped beside her. "I guess this is goodbye."

Even though Kimber was tempted to ask for his number, she couldn't quite get the words out. After all, for all she knew, he really could have a girlfriend. "I guess so."

"Have a good flight."

"Thanks."

Brandon took a step back, and then with a last look, he turned and moved toward baggage claim.

Unable to resist, Kimber watched him until he was swallowed by the crowd of other travelers making their way to and from the various gates. With a twinge of disappointment, she headed the other direction. Time to get back to reality.

. . .

Kimber was still on his mind when Brandon climbed out of the cab in front of the high-rise apartment building. If he'd had the energy, he would have looked up at the dizzying height of the ridiculously tall structure, but at the moment, such a gesture might be more than he could handle. Knowing that he hadn't asked for Kimber's number was a clear testament to his diminished mental faculties.

Working on autopilot, he hauled his three suitcases and briefcase inside. The expansive lobby was brightly lit, the walls freshly painted. A cluster of leather chairs occupied the center of the open space, with an arrangement of flowers situated on the glass table in the center. He had to admit, he hadn't expected to be housed in a building this nice.

When he reached his floor, his footsteps were nearly silent on the plush carpet in the hallway. He parked his luggage beside apartment 819, surprised to find a standard lock rather than a keypad mechanism. No one had given him a key or mentioned how he was supposed to obtain one. Mentally and physically exhausted, he debated whether it would be easier to track down the building manager or grab a cab to the nearest hotel.

One look at his overly full suitcases answered that question for him. He didn't want to haul all his stuff back downstairs. With a sigh, he searched for the secure email that had included his new address. Surely someone had given him instructions on how to get inside.

He skimmed to the bottom and located a phone number to call to gain access to his new flat. He dialed, and the ringing sounded both in his ear and from somewhere nearby.

A woman's voice answered. "Yes?"

"This is Brandon. I was told to call this number to get the keys to my new flat."

"Which apartment?" she asked.

"Eight nineteen."

The door behind him opened, and a woman with wavy silver hair opened the door, a set of two identical keys in one hand and a plate of cookies in the other. "Welcome to New York." Rather than hand him the keys, she walked past him and unlocked his door for him. "I'm Gertrude Evanston, but you can call me Trudy."

"Brandon Hale. Nice to meet you."

She pushed the door wide and walked inside, holding the door open to make it easier for him to pass through. "The sheets and towels are clean, and there are extras in the linen closet in the bathroom." Trudy dropped the keys on the kitchen counter and set the plate of cookies beside it.

"Thanks." Brandon set his suitcases inside the furnished living room. "Are you the building manager?"

"No, just a friend who was asked to give you your keys." She motioned to the cookies. "I made these this afternoon. I thought you might need a snack while you settle in."

"I appreciate it."

She gave a satisfied nod. "You're welcome." She moved toward the door. "Let me know if you need anything. You have my number."

"Thanks again, Trudy."

She waved and pulled the door closed behind her.

Brandon flipped the dead bolt and looked down at his luggage. He debated for half a second whether to unpack his bags tonight. Opting for the path of least resistance in his quest for getting to bed, he grabbed his carry-on, hauled it into the single bedroom, and tipped it on its side. He changed into a pair of pajama pants and a T-shirt. Then with barely a thought to his new surroundings, he brushed his teeth, turned off the lights, and flopped onto the queen-sized bed in the middle of the bedroom.

He peeked briefly at the open suitcase on the floor before closing his eyes. He'd unpack tomorrow.

• • •

Kimber pulled her carry-on behind her, her backpack hooked to the handle. She'd forced herself to spend the hour-and-a-half flight between JFK and Washington National airport working on her manuscript. Over the course of her return home, her hero had taken on several Brandon-like qualities, right down to his angular facial features and love of reading.

She strode through the automatic doors and crossed to the outer curb where cars were fighting for space as they waited for passengers. She spotted Mark's blue Mustang and crossed to him. After loading her suitcase into the back seat, she climbed into the passenger seat and clipped her seat belt into place. "Have you been waiting long?"

"I only had to circle once." Mark glanced over his shoulder and pulled into traffic. "So, how was your trip?"

"Amazing."

"See? I told you you'd have fun." Mark navigated through the passenger pickup area and moved into the through lane leading to the George Washington Parkway. "Did Tessa ask about me?"

Kimber laughed. "I'm afraid not."

"You know, we could always go up and visit her when she gets back to New York," Mark suggested. "I'll be your personal bodyguard."

"You know that I have more martial-arts training than you do, right?"

"Yeah, but I'm bigger and scarier looking." He glanced at her and wiggled his eyebrows.

She took in his slender frame and laughed. "Right."

"Did you get any writing done on the plane?" Mark asked, changing the subject.

"A little." Kimber thought of the reason she hadn't written on her first flight. She couldn't say why, but she kept the memory of Brandon to herself.

"You should send me your new pages. I need something good to read."

"I would think you'd be tired of reading my stuff by now," Kimber said, "especially considering how many times I have you go over everything."

"You have some great books. One of these days, you need to trust me and submit them." Mark merged onto the parkway before he glanced at her again. "I know what I'm talking about."

Even though Mark had graduated from college with a finance degree, he'd started out as an English major and had proved to be an amazing editor for her over the past few years. "You always tell me you know what you're talking about, but I haven't seen you write anything new in at least six months."

"I'm a better editor than a writer." Mark took the turn toward her apartment. "So, about this trip to New York . . ."

She laughed again. "Maybe we can convince Tessa to go to a show with us. That would give you a reason to come with me without looking like you're stalking her."

"That could work." He pulled up to a stoplight. "I could see if Logan wants to come, and we can double date."

"I already told you, I'm not going out with Logan." If she were going to start dating again, she'd much prefer to go out with someone like Brandon, someone who didn't have any ties to the CIA.

"Have you ever considered that you may be a little too picky when it comes to your social life?"

She cocked an eyebrow and shot him a knowing look. "So says the man who is hung up on a woman who doesn't even live in the same city as him."

"Yeah." He pulled up in front of her apartment complex. "We both have problems."

"Right now, my only problem is remembering what time zone I'm in and getting some sleep before my alarm goes off in the morning."

"Good luck with that."

"Thanks." Kimber climbed out of the car and retrieved her suitcase from the back seat. "And thanks again for picking me up."

"No problem." Mark flashed her a grin. "I like it when you owe me."

She simply shook her head. "I know you do."

CHAPTER 5

BRANDON SAT IN a conference room with the personnel director and the three other new employees at Monroe Publishing, the remains of their boxed lunches spread out before them. He'd been rather proud of himself for winning the battle against jet lag this morning as he'd filled out endless paperwork, but the lengthy briefings that had followed about protocol and confidentiality had zapped his energy. Now, with his paperwork and briefings behind him, he was eager to settle into this new job and evaluate his access to the rest of the staff.

He still wasn't sure if it was luck, his new boss's need for him to start right away, or the CIA's meddling, but the HR director had informed him that he would start work this afternoon while the rest of the new employees would undergo two more days of training.

A woman in a chic gray business suit entered the conference room, her short, blonde hair perfectly styled.

Brandon stood instinctively.

"Which one is my new assistant?"

The woman from HR pointed at Brandon. "Brandon Hale."

"Come with me."

"Yes, ma'am." Brandon grabbed his briefcase from where he'd tucked it beside his chair and followed her into the hall.

Without breaking stride, she said, "I have Rebecca Hamilton at two. Order in some Thai for me. And run up to legal. They haven't sent down the contracts."

Brandon opened his mouth to ask for her specific order, but the woman—he assumed she was Amelia Franklin—stepped into a large office with a glass wall separating it from the hallway.

As though it were an afterthought, she motioned to the desk outside her door. "Oh. That's yours. The password is in the top drawer. Be sure to change it."

"Yes, ma'am."

She slipped a key from the pocket in her blazer and handed it to him. "This is the key to the executive elevator. It's reserved for the top execs and a select few assistants. Unless you're arriving or leaving for the day, I expect you to use it. You won't have time to wait around for the other ones."

"Understood."

"Good." Amelia put her hand on the door. "Oh, and pick up the food yourself. I want you to make sure the order is right before you bring it back to the office."

The order she had yet to give him. He opened his mouth to ask for details, but before he could, Amelia closed the door in his face.

Brandon turned toward the open area filled with cubicles.

A woman at the desk beside Brandon's stood. She was about his age, her eyes sharp, her clothes trendy. "So, you're the new assistant."

"Yes." Brandon extended his hand. "Brandon Hale."

"Mary Driscoll." She shook his hand, her gaze raking up and down the length of him as she did so.

Brandon pulled his hand back. "I don't suppose you know what Amelia likes when she orders Thai? Or where she orders from?"

"I don't think she cares where you order from, but the spicier, the better."

Brandon caught the little lift in Mary's eyebrows and the flicker of deceit in her expression. "Thanks." He took a step toward the door. "Can you also tell me who handles petty cash?"

"Sheila. Ninth floor."

Still gripping his briefcase, Brandon headed for the elevators. When he found them, he figured out which was the keyed executive one he had been instructed to use and hit the button for the ninth floor. The finance office was thankfully right beside legal.

A woman with gold-rimmed glasses looked up. "Can I help you?"

"I'm looking for Sheila."

"I'm Sheila."

Brandon extended his hand and introduced himself. "Any chance I can get copies of the receipts for the past month of Amelia's expense account?"

"I can do that. And while you're here, fill this out so I can issue you a company credit card." Sheila handed him a piece of paper and a pen.

Brandon filled out the information, pausing to check his phone for his new address.

Sheila clicked on her mouse. A moment later, the printer beside her whirred to life.

Brandon handed the credit card form to her. "Here you go."

Sheila unlocked her top desk drawer, pulled out a credit card, and typed something on her computer. She then retrieved the pages from her printer and handed them to Brandon.

"Here are the receipts and your corporate credit card. It's for official use only."

"Understood." Brandon held up the receipts. "And thank you for this."

"Good luck." The way she said it, Brandon suspected figuring out Amelia's Thai order might be the least of his challenges in this job.

He walked out of the finance office and flipped through the receipts until he found one for a nearby Thai restaurant. As he hoped, the detailed order was included on the receipt. He had to flip only to the next page to find another identical receipt.

Brandon called the restaurant and put in Amelia's order before moving down the hall to the legal office.

Not comfortable with carrying legal documents while running errands, he delivered the contracts to Amelia first.

When he reached her office, he knocked on the door before he entered. "Here are those contracts you requested."

She looked up from the two computer screens situated on her desk and stretched out her hand. "And my lunch?"

"I'm going to pick it up now. Is there anything else you need while I'm out?"

"My dry cleaning." She reached into her purse and handed him a claim ticket.

Brandon fought back his frustration. He hadn't earned a degree from Brown to pick up someone's dry cleaning. But this was a cover assignment, and he needed to excel at it if he wanted to find the person responsible for Finlay's death. The sooner he could complete this mission, the sooner he could step away from the CIA and find a job more suited to the work he was trained to do.

Using his best subservient voice, he said, "I'll be back shortly."

Brandon headed for the elevator and made his way outside. Time to run some errands.

• • •

Kimber was only a quarter of the way through her inbox when Mark appeared at her cubicle. "Can you take a look at this?" Mark handed her an account printout over a quarter of an inch thick. "We're missing almost half a million dollars in the operations budget for East Asia."

"What's the exact amount we're off?"

"Four hundred fifty thousand dollars." Mark leaned against the edge of her cubicle wall. "It happened yesterday, and I can't, for the life of me, figure out where the money went."

"Four hundred fifty thousand even?" Kimber asked.

"Yes. This is everything that posted when the money disappeared yesterday."

With a possible solution in mind, Kimber scanned the first page of the report and then the second. She made it all the way to page fourteen before she spotted the likely source. "Pull the backup documentation on this one." She highlighted the entry and handed the report back to Mark. "My guess is the seven and two are reversed."

Mark looked down at the paperwork. "Which would be a difference of four hundred fifty thousand dollars."

"Yep."

"How did you figure that out so fast?"

"It wasn't that complicated." She shrugged. "The amount was divisible by nine, which meant it was likely a number reversal, and I only had to look at entries that were at least six figures."

Mark held up the printout. "Thank you."

"No problem." Kimber turned back to the stack of work on her desk and processed three travel claims before her phone rang, interrupting her flow.

She plucked up the receiver for her secure line. "This is Kimber."

"This is Jeanine from Deputy Director Yarrow's office. He'd like to meet with you at your earliest convenience."

Startled by the oddity of the request and curious to know why she would receive it, Kimber said, "I can come up now."

"Good. I'll let him know you're on your way."

Kimber ended the call and wove through the maze of cubicles to leave her office. After passing through the glass-encased hallway connecting the new headquarters building to the original one, she made her way to the correct floor and found the DDO's office.

The woman at the desk in the reception area looked up. "Kimber Seidel?"

"Yes."

"Go right in." She motioned to the door behind her. "He's expecting you."

Kimber knocked on the door and waited for the corresponding "Come in" before she opened it.

The man behind the desk looked up, his blue gaze intent. The sense of scrutiny intensified as though she were standing on the runway at a fashion show rather than in an office at CIA headquarters.

"Sir, I'm Kimber Seidel. I was told you wished to see me?"

"Yes." The older man motioned to one of the chairs across from him. "Please sit down."

Kimber sat and fought the urge to fidget.

"I understand you've written several manuscripts that have been reviewed by the PCRB."

PCRB. Alphabet soup for Publication Classification Review Board. She clasped her hands together and swallowed. "That's right."

"I have an assignment that's perfectly suited for your talents, but it would require you to relocate."

Kimber was due to rotate to a new position this year, but she hadn't expected it to occur until summer, at the earliest, and she certainly hadn't anticipated it coming with a move. A flutter of anticipation rippled through her. "Where would I be going?"

"New York."

New York, where her sister lived. Where Brandon lived. She pushed that thought aside. The odds of her seeing Brandon again were astronomical even if they did end up living in the same city.

She reined in her thoughts. "What exactly is the assignment?"

"Have you heard of Labyrinth?"

"The terrorist group?"

"Yes."

She nodded. "I've been researching their funding methods for several months now. We still haven't determined how they're moving money."

Director Yarrow leaned back in his chair. "Until last weekend, we assumed Labyrinth was using cash to fund their operations."

That information was consistent with her research. "What happened last weekend?"

"We received a tip that they're funding their operations through a New York publishing house." He straightened and rested both arms on the edge of his desk. "That's where you come in. We want you to publish with Monroe Publishing."

Kimber unclenched her hands and gripped the arms of her chair. "Me? Publish a book?" She shook her head, and a wave of panic washed over her. "My manuscripts aren't ready." She wasn't sure they would ever be ready.

"That's not what our reviewers at the PCRB said." Director Yarrow tapped a file on his desk. "I asked them for their recommendation of who would be best suited for publication, and your name topped the list."

Kimber absorbed his comment, her disbelief nearly overshadowing his compliment. "I appreciate the reviewers' confidence in my work, but getting published takes months of preparation. I don't even have an agent."

"You do now." Director Yarrow picked up a manila envelope from his desk and extended it to her.

She reached out a trembling hand to take it.

"Patricia Banik has agreed to represent you and broker the deal with Monroe. She hopes to have negotiations underway within the next week or two."

"What happens if Monroe isn't interested in any of my manuscripts?" Kimber asked.

"Then, we try for the next qualified candidate on the PCRB's list." He held up the file on his desk. "After browsing through your latest submission, however, I suspect we can help you be successful."

Her stomach jumped. She had dreamed for years about seeing one of her books in print, but that dream had been firmly placed in the "someday" category. Trying to realign her personal timeline for a potential writing career, she said, "Let's say I am successful. Then what?"

"We'll relocate you to New York, where you'll do everything you can to insert yourself into the literary scene," Director Yarrow said. "We have an inside man at Monroe, but his position won't likely gain him access to the parties and the upper levels of management. We need you to fill that gap."

"Why does it matter if I have access to upper management?"

"Because we believe someone high up in the company is funding Labyrinth."

"And you want me to find out who?" First, he wanted her to jump into her dream career without warning, and now he wanted her to be an operative? Kimber shook her head. "I'm a finance officer, not field personnel."

"The main reason you came to our attention was the quality of your submission to the PCRB, but since you've been through operations training and you've achieved expert status in self-defense and firearms, you are a viable candidate for this assignment. Add to that your qualifications on bomb disposal and you're the ideal person for the job."

Kimber didn't mention that she'd studied martial arts because of a crush on Benjamin Nichols in the third grade or that her firearms training had come from her grandfather, who'd been a game warden. Her work with the CIA had landed her only the bomb-ordnance training, and even that had occurred more by happenstance when she'd been working for security. "Do you anticipate me needing those skills on this assignment?"

"No, but it's always wise to send in operatives who are prepared for whatever might come their way."

Kimber couldn't argue with that, but she hardly considered herself prepared to use her self-defense skills against someone trying to harm her.

"What do you say?" Director Yarrow continued. "Are you willing to explore a new career to help us gather intel?"

She'd joined the CIA to make a difference, but she'd never anticipated doing it in this way. Despite the nerves and doubts racing through her, she nodded. "Anything I can do to help."

"Good." The director stood. "One more thing."

"Yes?"

"Your new pen name will be Kimber Frost." He motioned to the thick envelope in her hand. "And no one can know that Kimber Frost and Kimber Seidel are the same person. We can't risk anyone learning you're CIA."

"I'm going undercover?"

"You're simply changing your last name for anyone outside your family and those here at the agency who need to know."

"My sister lives in New York. I'll have to tell her."

"You can tell her that you've stepped away from the agency to pursue your writing career," Director Yarrow said. "And advise her that you need to keep your previous career private."

Keeping secrets from her sister. That would be a challenge. "I'll do my best."

Director Yarrow handed her a single piece of paper. "This is your schedule for the rest of the week. You'll be off-site tomorrow, and on Thursday, you'll have a briefing with our analyst working on the Europe desk. That's where our most recent incident with Labyrinth occurred."

Incident. Far too often that word equaled death.

"You should have just enough time to make that meeting before you leave for the airport," Director Yarrow said as though turning her life upside-down were no big deal. Maybe it wasn't for him. "We'll have you sign your paperwork with your agent today, but she wants to meet with you in person," Director Yarrow continued. "You'll also meet with the special agent in charge of this case from the FBI."

"I need to let my boss know."

"It's already been taken care of. Officially, you gave your two weeks' notice today." Director Yarrow rounded his desk. "Your office has already been informed."

"Why would I need to lie to my friends here at the agency?" Kimber asked, confused. It was standard procedure to transfer to a new assignment every two or three years. Surely pretending to quit the CIA was overkill. "My coworkers are used to people going undercover."

"It's for your protection," Director Yarrow said. "This isn't a typical undercover assignment. You're about to go into the public eye, which means we need to distance you from the CIA as much as possible. That includes severing ties between you and those you know here at headquarters."

Cut her off from her friends and her colleagues. She clasped her hands together. He was yanking her entire support system out from under her. Her insides withered, and her mind raced. She gathered her composure, and then, with a deceptively calm voice, she said, "I understand."

She understood, but this wasn't going to be easy.

CHAPTER 6

ASADI CALCULATED THE time in New York. Seven in the morning. He stood and paced to the window of his Rhos-on-Sea flat before he pulled up his contact's number and hit the Call button.

The call took a moment to connect, and Asadi focused on the rise and fall of the waves on the beach two floors below him. Another storm was coming in, leaving Asadi banished from his main home on Anglesey. He was ready for Finlay's contact to be eliminated so he could go back to business as usual.

It finally rang three times before the familiar voice came over the line. "What is it?"

"I have an order coming with a quick turnaround," Asadi said.

"Give me the details."

Asadi passed along the funding amounts, both the fee the buyer would pay and the amount they would need to pass to the supplier.

"This amount will take at least a week to push through."

"We have four days," Asadi said. "Make it happen."

A sigh followed. "I'll do what I can."

Asadi ended the call and moved to the next transaction, this one for an assortment of weapons bound for Syria.

A knock sounded at his door. Asadi checked the app on his phone to identify who was on the other side before he answered it. Darragh rushed inside and closed the door behind him.

"We have a problem." Darragh took several steps into the flat before he whirled to face Asadi. "The guy Finlay met with works for the US government."

The implications crashed over Asadi. If Finlay had managed to contact someone from the US government, the likelihood was that Finlay had already had the man's number long before he'd learned of their funding methods. "How sure are you?"

"I tracked his car to a rental company, but the payment was made on a government credit card." Darragh's eyes darkened. "I checked the documentation myself."

"Any idea who he is?"

"No, but I got a good look at him. I'll know him if I see him again."

"What about the guy's driving license?" Asadi asked. "Rental car companies don't let you take their cars without having a copy on file."

"The person who rented it was some secretary at the US embassy. From the looks of it, she rents cars all the time."

"They must have a system in place to protect the identities of their employees to keep them from coming to anyone's attention." Employees who were likely CIA. "It's time for you to stake out the US embassy."

"I have been. No sign of him yesterday, and he hasn't shown up today." Darragh lifted both hands. "He's either working out of another office, or he's not in London anymore."

Asadi let the implications sink in. If Finlay had shared what he knew about Labyrinth, their entire operation was at risk. "Keep looking for Finlay's friend." Asadi slipped both hands into his pockets and gripped his car keys. "In the meantime, I need to pack. We're moving our offices."

"Do you already have somewhere in mind?"

"I have some ideas," Asadi said. "Contact me as soon as you complete your assignment. If Finlay's contact isn't still in London, someone has to know where he went."

"So, you want me to chat with the secretary who rented the car."

"Yes. That's exactly what I want."

"And if she doesn't talk?"

Asadi narrowed his eyes. "You know what to do."

• • •

Brandon walked out of Monroe Publishing at six o'clock, exhausted both mentally and physically. Who knew that keeping up with one woman could be so taxing or that it would require intelligence training to do so.

The lingering dregs of adrenaline pumped through him as if he'd just sprinted a mile with someone chasing him the entire way.

No one had been chasing him, but he'd certainly had plenty of obstacles thrown in his path throughout the afternoon.

Not only had Mary tried to sabotage him with Amelia's lunch order, but Regina, the woman who sat in the cubicle on the other side of him, had tried to send him to the wrong coffee shop too. As though he wouldn't notice the Starbucks cup in Amelia's trash can and her standard order on her petty cash receipts.

Brandon buttoned his overcoat, pulled out his phone, and looked up the address where he was scheduled to meet Special Agent Ebeid. An eleven-minute walk or a ten-minute subway ride. He opted for the walk.

He moved down the bustling sidewalk that was crowded with more people than he could count, mostly businessmen and -women making their way home from work. He tugged on his gloves to fight against the chill in the air.

Free of the confines of the office and the less-than-ideal environment within, Brandon's thoughts turned to how much had changed in the past week. One week ago, Finlay was still alive and Brandon had still had his flat in London, where he had expected to remain indefinitely as he'd begun his new career in publishing. Now, here he was, working in a job that would challenge him at every turn, but not in the way that he was accustomed to.

He stifled a yawn and tried not to think about what time it was in London right now. He should be in bed rather than thinking about dinner. At least he'd managed to stay awake on his flight from London to help him start adjusting to the new time zone.

He smiled, the warmth of the memory washing over him.

The wind picked up, dropping the wind chill by several degrees. Brandon quickened his pace, and nine minutes later, he entered the dimly lit French restaurant.

A man standing beside the door stepped forward. "Brandon." He extended his hand. "I'm Rafi Ebeid. Glad you made it."

Brandon shook his hand. "Sorry I'm a bit late."

"It's fine." Rafi signaled to the hostess, who directed them to a table in the back corner of the restaurant.

Brandon waited until the hostess handed them both menus and left them alone before he spoke. "I'm surprised you wanted to meet here." Brandon glanced at the other patrons scattered throughout the restaurant. Thankfully, the two tables closest to them remained empty.

"If we're spotted here, you can say you were eating dinner with a friend," Rafi said. "You wouldn't be able to explain if you were caught leaving my office."

"True." Brandon opened the menu, barely glancing at it before he turned his attention back to the FBI special agent across from him. "Do you have any new information for me?"

"Patricia Banik, a well-known literary agent, is going to be sending a manuscript over tomorrow. I need you to put it at the top of Amelia Franklin's to-be-read pile."

"What's the book?"

"It's called *Words Unspoken*," Rafi said. "It's a spy thriller by an author who has agreed to let us use her work to gain access to the social events and upper management of Monroe Publishing."

If they had an author planted, what was he here for? "Is this author already with Monroe?" Brandon asked.

"No. She's a debut author."

Not a promising start to the FBI's plan. "Is the book any good?"

"It's supposed to be," Rafi said. "The more you do to push this author into the upper echelons of the publishing house, the better. We need her to be one of their stars so she has easier access."

"You should know that a lot of what happens in the publishing world is more luck and timing than anything else." Far too many of his former college classmates had tried their hand at getting published only to have their work fall flat, while authors with seemingly no training in the literary field flourished. "And publishing houses rarely expect their debut authors to become immediate stars."

"I'm aware of that, which is why I'm hoping you can give this author a little help," Rafi said. "Patricia has already set up some buzz that she has a few offers on the table for this particular manuscript."

"Does she?" Brandon asked. "The publishing world is pretty tight-knit. Word will get out if she's spinning lies to try for a better offer."

"The possibility of a movie deal is real enough and so is the offer from London Press."

The pieces of the plan fell into place. "Let me guess. The government is backing both offers."

"Promising a few million that we likely won't have to pay is an easy venture," Rafi said. "But having those numbers floating out in the industry will make this particular manuscript worth snatching up before it goes to auction."

"I'll do what I can to help it along, but so far, I haven't done much beyond fill out paperwork and run errands."

"That will change soon enough."

The confidence with which Rafi spoke made Brandon suspicious.

He narrowed his eyes. "What do you know that I don't?"

"The submissions editor is going to be out sick tomorrow. You're going to field the call from Frost's agent."

"I have no idea how you're planning to pull that off, but I'll be ready."

"Good."

A waiter approached and introduced himself. "Can I get you started with something to drink?"

"Just water." Brandon stopped himself before specifying that he wanted still rather than sparkling.

"I'll have a Coke."

The waiter nodded. "I'll give you a few more minutes to look over those menus."

As soon as they were alone again, Rafi opened his briefcase and pulled out what appeared to be a folder over an inch thick. "Here's the manuscript that will be coming your way. Familiarize yourself with it."

"Why didn't you just email it to me?"

"I don't want to take the chance that anyone could trace this manuscript back to a government entity," Rafi said.

They were taking precautions as though they were worried about someone doing a deep dive into his email accounts. Curious, Brandon held up the thick file folder. "Where did you find this author anyway?"

"I didn't. Your people did." Your people—as in the CIA, not the FBI. "Her manuscript went through the vetting process and caught a reviewer's attention."

Which meant the author was an agency employee. Relieved that Brandon wouldn't be responsible for managing a civilian, he said, "I'll start reading it tonight." He didn't have anything better to do anyway.

He tucked the manuscript into his bag and looked at the menu in earnest. He was starving.

•   •   •

She was moving to New York. Maybe.

Kimber walked into her apartment and dropped her keys onto the kitchen table.

Her conversation with Director Yarrow still seemed like a dream rather than reality. Ending up in a one-on-one meeting with him in the first place fell into the surreal category, but that was far easier to comprehend than the idea of her novel being pitched to a well-known publishing house.

After a meeting with legal, she had signed her contract and authorized Director Yarrow to forward her approved manuscript to her new literary agent, Patricia Banik. Of course, the moment she'd signed the document, he had admitted that all three of her manuscripts had been sent to Patricia last Friday.

Kimber dropped onto her couch. She had an agent. One of her manuscripts would be submitted this week. It really was unbelievable.

At least she'd been lucky that Mark had already left for the day when she'd returned to her office after all her meetings. Side-stepping the news about leaving the CIA would be hard enough, but outright lying to her best friend was not something she looked forward to. She wasn't even sure she *could* lie to him successfully.

Her cell phone rang, and she retrieved it from her purse. A smile formed when she read the screen: Tessa.

Kimber checked the time. Nearly eleven o'clock in London. She hit the Answer button. "Hey there. What are you doing, calling me in the middle of the night?"

"It's not quite midnight," Tessa said, the buzz of voices carrying in the background. "And I wanted to make sure you got home okay."

"I did. Sorry, I should have texted you, but I didn't want to risk waking you up."

"It's fine. I just had a break between parties and figured I'd call."

"Sounds to me like you wanted an excuse to get away from Greta," Kimber said. "Or are you avoiding one of the male models?"

"A little of both," Tessa admitted. "Enough about me. How was your day?"

"Interesting." Though Kimber didn't want to open the door to lies and deceit, she let one fact slip. "I found out today that I might be moving to New York."

"Seriously?" Tessa asked, excitement filling her voice. "How? Why?"

"I can't say much on the phone, but if everything pans out, I'll give you the details when you get back home."

"I hate it when you can't tell me things, but that would be amazing if we were both living in the same city," Tessa said. "When will you know?"

"I'm not sure. There are still a lot of details to work out." That was true enough. "If all goes well, I could know within the next couple weeks."

"Selfishly, I hope it happens."

"I do too. Honestly, it could open a lot of doors for me." Not only for her writing career but also to find the information the CIA hoped she could access.

The flutters of excitement transitioned into stabs of panic, and she drew a deep breath. She could do this. It wasn't like she was being asked to carry a gun or face terrorists. She was simply the means to access the people who worked with those terrorists.

"Whatever happens, I'll make sure we see each other when you get back," Kimber said.

"Great. And if you need to stay at my place while I'm gone, feel free. I'll text my landlord to let him know it's okay to give you the key."

Kimber jumped on the opportunity. "Actually, I'm supposed to go up this weekend."

"I'll call him tonight, then, and text you his number so you can make sure he's there to let you in."

Perfect. She'd much rather stay at her sister's place than a hotel. "Thanks, Tessa. I appreciate it."

"No problem." The buzz of voices increased in volume. "I'd better go, but just so you know, I'm totally hoping you end up in New York."

"Me too."

CHAPTER 7

BRANDON'S SECOND DAY working for Amelia was even busier than the first. With his body still fighting against the change in time zones, he'd awakened far earlier than he would have liked, but that had given him the chance to arrive at the office early and plant a listening device beneath his desk. It likely wouldn't amount to anything, but at least he had one little corner of Monroe Publishing covered in case anything happened when he wasn't around.

He rubbed his eyes. He might have had an easier time today had he not gotten caught up reading Kimber Frost's manuscript last night.

Her first name had caught him off guard. He'd never met a Kimber before his flight from London, and now he knew two. Sort of. He didn't know anything about Kimber Frost except that she was CIA and had agreed to help infiltrate Monroe Publishing. Now it was up to him to pave the path. The woman was seriously talented.

The brief notion that the two Kimbers could be one and the same had flitted through his mind, but the likelihood that the author had been in London the same week he'd been moving home was nearly impossible. Not to mention the Kimber he knew didn't seem like the operative sort. She was far too friendly. Unlike the women he currently worked with.

He lowered into his chair after his latest trip to Starbucks. Now if he could just spend enough time at his desk to connect Kimber's agent with Amelia, this plan might actually work.

Mary and Regina approached from the break room, each of them casting evil stares in his direction. They must have really wanted his job. Although why, he had no idea. From what he'd gathered, Mary worked for Margaret, the art director, and Regina was the personal assistant to the marketing director. Both of those positions were equal to his own. At least, he assumed they were.

Maybe the two of them had aspirations to move into the editorial department and saw his job as a step toward that endeavor. Regardless of the reasons, the two women were not making any effort to hide their dislike for him.

Amelia returned from her meeting and settled into her chair in her office. Hoping she would stay put for a while, Brandon sent an email to Patricia Banik to request her to call now. How long it would take her to see his note remained to be seen.

To his surprise, less than a minute passed before Patricia called.

"I'll let her know you're on the line," Brandon said. He hit the button to transfer the call and resisted the urge to cross his fingers. He needed Amelia to take this call.

"What is it?" Amelia asked in lieu of a greeting after she picked up.

"I have Patricia Banik on the line for you."

"What does she want?"

His heart sank. That wasn't the reaction he was hoping for. "I think she's calling about the Kimber Frost manuscript."

"Who's Kimber Frost?"

"She's a new author a lot of people have been excited about," Brandon said. "I skimmed through her manuscript before you came in this morning. It's really good."

"Please don't tell me you're using your job to help some girlfriend get her manuscript published."

"No, ma'am." A fellow CIA operative's manuscript, yes, but not a girlfriend's. Brandon kept that thought to himself. With sincerity in his voice, he added, "I've never met this author or her agent."

A heavy sigh carried over the line. "I don't have time to deal with this right now. Take a message," Amelia said. "And go pick up my lunch. I want the soup and salad."

A stone dropped into the pit of Brandon's stomach. "Yes, ma'am." Not only had she not taken the call, but he also had no idea what restaurant she wanted her soup and salad to come from. He swallowed hard and tried to keep his voice calm when he switched over to speak to Patricia. "I'm sorry, Ms. Banik. She asked me to take a message."

"Text me the next time she's not on the phone," Patricia said. "And mention that there's a potential movie deal on the table."

"I'll pass that along."

As soon as he hung up, Mary stood and folded her arms on the top of the cubicle partition between them. "You'd better be telling the truth about not knowing this Kimber girl."

"I am." Brandon swiveled in his chair to face her. "Why would it matter anyway?"

"Let's just say, Amelia doesn't appreciate people using their positions to help their friends get their foot in the door."

Which was exactly what Brandon needed to do, even if the "friend" was actually a fellow operative. Frustrated and not in the mood to deal with Mary's games, Brandon lifted his eyebrows. "Is this the same as you telling me Amelia likes her Thai food spicy or Regina saying she prefers the café across the street instead of Starbucks for her coffee?"

"I don't know what you're talking about." Mary gave him an innocent look before adding, "I'm just offering you some friendly advice. Amelia's last assistant tried to fast-track her sister's manuscript. It didn't end well."

"I don't have a sister," Brandon said. "And I'm telling the truth about Kimber Frost."

"That's good for you, then." She straightened before resting her hand on the partition again. "How did you find out about the Thai food and coffee?"

"Sorry." Brandon shrugged. "I never reveal my sources."

The corner of Mary's lips twitched. "Right."

Brandon checked the petty cash receipts and identified the most likely restaurant for Amelia's lunch order. After calling it in, he headed out the door. When he returned thirty minutes later, he delivered Amelia's food and Patricia's message.

Amelia set the message aside.

"Ms. Banik asked me to mention that the Kimber Frost manuscript has a potential movie deal on the table."

Amelia's left eyebrow twitched slightly, but rather than comment on Patricia's message, she retrieved her salad from the takeaway bag and set it on her desk. "Get Jamal Gibson on the line."

He nodded and left Amelia's office. After connecting Amelia with Jamal, Brandon ate his own lunch at his desk while watching for the moment when the call would end. As soon as Amelia hung up, he texted Patricia to let her know Amelia was currently available.

He answered Patricia's call thirty seconds later.

"Ready to try again?" Patricia asked.

"Yes, ma'am." Brandon hit the button to ring Amelia's office.

"What?"

"Patricia Banik is calling again."

"Tell her I'm at lunch." Amelia hung up before Brandon could respond.

Brandon switched over to Patricia. "I'm afraid she's eating lunch right now."

"Amelia always has been stubborn," Patricia said.

Brandon was finding that out for himself. With Amelia's reaction to Patricia's last two calls, he suspected any future ones would only irritate her further.

He glanced at Amelia's open door. Not wanting to risk his conversation being overheard, he pulled out his cell. Despite still being on the phone with Patricia, he sent her a text message. *I can't speak freely right now, but will you be in your office for the next hour?*

Patricia answered by speaking into the phone rather than texting back. "I'll be here until five."

Brandon texted her again. *I'll see if I can get her to return your call.* As soon as he sent the text, he spoke into his office phone, "I'll make sure Amelia gets your message."

Determined to plant the idea that Amelia needed to take Patricia's call, Brandon hung up and texted Rafi. *I need you to call me at my office number. Untraceable.*

He probably didn't need to make that final note, but it was better safe than sorry. This operation would be dead in the water if the call were traced back to the FBI.

As soon as he ensured the text went through, he deleted it.

The phone on his desk rang a moment later, and Rafi's voice came over the line. "Why am I calling you?"

"The Frost manuscript?" Brandon's voice rose at the end to make his reply sound like a question.

"No luck getting Amelia to take Patricia's call?"

"Yes, Ms. Banik did mention the possibility of a movie deal."

Disbelief carried in Rafi's voice. "Don't tell me you need me to pretend to be a movie producer."

"Yes, sir. That's correct."

"I'm not sure I can be convincing in that role," Rafi said.

"I don't believe I can share that information, but I'd be happy to give Amelia a message," Brandon said. "Would you like me to have her call you back?"

"I shouldn't have to answer that question," Rafi grumbled. "Get Amelia and Patricia connected today. We need this to happen soon."

"I understand," Brandon said and ended the call. He crossed to Amelia's office again. "Amelia, I'm sorry to bother you, but that was someone inquiring about the movie rights for the Frost manuscript. Is there another book by Kimber Frost that's already been published by Monroe?"

"No." Amelia's eyebrows furrowed. "I've never heard of Kimber Frost before today."

"That's what I thought. I told him I didn't know of any we had under contract. He said he would check back with Patricia Banik."

"I thought she was making up stories about a possible movie deal. This almost never happens." Amelia blew out a frustrated breath and pointed at Brandon's desk. "Get Patricia on the line. We might as well get to the bottom of this."

"I'll call her right now." With a sense of victory, Brandon made the call, and Patricia picked up on the second ring. "I have Amelia Franklin calling for Patricia Banik."

"Good work," Patricia said.

"Thank you. I'll put you right through." Brandon transferred the call and resisted the urge to let out a sigh of relief. Connecting Amelia and Patricia was only the first step. Now Patricia needed to convince his new boss to accept the manuscript and make Kimber Frost one of Monroe's lead authors. Not an easy feat.

Fewer than five minutes passed before Brandon's phone rang again, but this time, it was Amelia asking to see him.

Brandon walked into her office.

"You said you skimmed through the Frost manuscript?" she asked.

"I did."

"Good. Let's see if you have an eye for talent," Amelia said. "I want you to read through the rest of it tonight and give me your impressions."

"Me?"

"Yes, you. Going through the typical eval process will take a few weeks, and I don't know if we have that much time," Amelia said. "Patricia already has offers for movie rights and foreign distribution. I want to know if this is a project worth fighting for before it goes to auction or if I should let it pass."

"I'll do my best."

She motioned toward his desk. "There's an evaluation form on the server. I want your assessment first thing in the morning."

"Yes, ma'am."

"And stop calling me ma'am. You make me sound like I'm fifty years old."

Amelia was fifty years old. Or more precisely, she was fifty-one. Brandon kept that tidbit of knowledge to himself. "What would you prefer I call you? Ms. Franklin?"

"Amelia." She placed her fingers on her keyboard. "If you were able to get my lunch and coffee orders right on the first day, I suspect you'll last much longer than my last three assistants."

Brandon lifted his eyebrows. "They didn't last long?"

"No." Amelia stared at him for a moment. "They didn't."

CHAPTER 8

FOR THE FIRST time since receiving her new assignment, Kimber made the turn onto Chain Bridge Road and pulled into the left-turn lane that would take her to the CIA headquarters main gate. She'd spent all of yesterday out of the office. A virtual meeting at her apartment with her new agent had been followed by an afternoon at the FBI learning all the information they had on Labyrinth's domestic activities, most of which was speculation on possible sleeper cells and the potential funding of extremist military groups.

The more information the FBI offered, the more convinced Kimber was that no one really knew what resources Labyrinth had in the States or if they even posed a domestic threat.

The real damage thus far had occurred overseas: an embassy bombing in Yemen, the assassination of a top US news correspondent in Madrid, a gas leak that killed a CIA operative in Ankara. Her stomach turned at that one. Not only had the intelligence operative died, but so had his family, including his wife and four children ranging in age from eight to sixteen.

On the surface, the incidents all looked like accidents. Even the news correspondent's death could have been explained away as him getting caught in the crossfire of someone else's altercation, but each of these deaths had one thing in common: Every one of the victims had been investigating Labyrinth.

Fear rippled through her. She was admin support, not an operative. Was she putting herself in danger by accepting this assignment? Never before had she worked undercover, nor had she spent any time working in the field.

Gripping her steering wheel tighter, she shook her head in an attempt to push away her fear and doubts. If she followed Director Yarrow's instructions, no one would know she was associated with the government.

She flashed her badge and passed through the gate, circling to the parking structure by the new headquarters building. She parked her car and stepped out into the frigid February air. Stuffing her hands in her pockets, she climbed the stairs to the main walk.

A meeting with the European Division this morning and then a trip to New York. With how her schedule was playing out, she wouldn't have to face her coworkers in her office until next week. Thank goodness.

Her relief was short-lived. She didn't even make it halfway to the entrance before Mark was by her side, a look of disbelief on his face and accusation carrying in his tone.

"What's going on, Kimber?" he asked, his voice low. "There's no way I'm buying the story about you resigning from the agency."

"Where did you hear that?" News did travel fast.

Mark grabbed her arm with his gloved hand to stop her forward progress. Several employees passed by them. Mark waited until they were out of earshot before he spoke again. "Don asked me how long I'd known about your plans to leave."

"I'm sorry, Mark. I meant to tell you," Kimber said. "It all happened so fast."

"What happened so fast?"

"Me getting an agent and a publishing contract." Maybe a publishing contract.

"You got an agent and didn't tell me?" He stepped in front of her so they were face-to-face. "Yeah." He shook his head. "Not buying it. Last week you were still afraid to show your work to anyone besides me."

"I do have an agent."

"Since when?"

"Since Tuesday."

"And you're already planning to quit?" He shook his head again. "You're the most practical person I know. You would never quit until you were sure your book had sold and you had a nice little nest egg saved up." He studied her face, and his eyes widened. "You aren't quitting. You're going undercover."

Her stomach dropped, and her doubts multiplied. She hadn't even made it into the building before she'd been found out. "How in the world did I think I could do this? I barely said anything, and you already saw through my cover story."

"I'm your best friend. I'm supposed to figure things out."

The wind whipped over her, and she shivered. "This is going to be a disaster."

"Tell me what's really going on."

"I can't say much, but I've been asked to use one of my novels as a way to gain access to the publishing world." She let out a sigh. "No one is going to believe I'm resigning, are they?"

"Sure they will." Mark shifted to her side and started forward. "And I'm going to help you sell it."

Kimber matched his pace. "You're going to lie for me?"

"You got it." Mark pulled his badge from his pocket as they approached the glass doors leading to the fourth-floor lobby. "If I'm the one telling people why you're leaving, you won't have to."

He reached for the door, but she grabbed his arm before he could pull it open. "What happens when I get to New York and people ask me why I quit my job?" A new bubble of panic rose within her. "You won't be there to lie for me then."

"No, but people in New York won't know you're CIA," Mark said. "Rely on the truth as much as you can, and don't tell people anything they don't need to know."

"You make it sound so simple."

"It is simple." Mark pulled the door open. "Trust me."

"I do trust you. It's me I'm not so sure about," Kimber said. "There's a reason I avoid undercover situations."

"And dating case officers," Mark said, a hint of disapproval in his voice. "What are you doing tonight?"

She pulled her badge out of her pocket. "Actually, I'm heading to New York this afternoon. Why?"

"Monday, then. We can get together after work and practice your cover story."

"It's worth a try." She waited until they passed through security before she spoke again. "Of course, first I have to report to Director Yarrow that I've already blown my cover."

"Sometimes inadvertent disclosures happen." Mark shrugged.

She stopped and tilted her head. "I wouldn't know. I've never been undercover before."

"Okay, me neither, but we'll both put in our reports, and we'll be fine."

They'd put in their reports. Code for telling on themselves for knowing or sharing too much information.

"You can do this," Mark continued. "In the meantime, you need to remind yourself of one very important thing."

"What's that?"

"You're a writer."

. . .

Brandon read through his evaluation of Kimber Frost's manuscript one last time. He'd tackled the delicate balance of providing both constructive criticism and praise. Amelia needed to know he wasn't simply rubber-stamping the project, but she also had to be excited enough about it to make a bid on the manuscript before it could go to auction.

With the inflated offers the CIA had orchestrated, the manuscript had the potential to bring in a good paycheck, significantly higher than if the author had tried to submit it on her own. As for how long Amelia would sit on the project, he had no idea.

Eager to move the process along, he drafted an email to Amelia, attached his evaluation, and clicked Send. The decision was in her hands now.

With that task off his to-do list, Brandon took care of the few emails that had come in this morning and skimmed over Amelia's appointments for the day. An editorial meeting at nine thirty, a marketing meeting at eleven. Her lunch meeting would be over Zoom, which suggested he would be making a run to pick something up from one of her favorite restaurants.

Anticipating it wouldn't be long before Amelia sent him on some errand out of the office, he answered the basic correspondence Amelia had already delegated to him and took the time to fill out his expense reports for the week. All the while, he recorded his observations of the habits of his coworkers, using a combination of the notes app on his phone and the little notepad he now kept inside his jacket pocket. Unfortunately, nothing he'd seen so far appeared to be anything beyond business as usual.

He was in the middle of noting the packages Margaret had received when his cell phone buzzed with an incoming text from Amelia.

In my office. Now.

Brandon pushed back from his desk and crossed into her office. "What can I do for you?"

"Call Ramon and tell him I need to meet with him this afternoon," Amelia said. "And reach out to the board of directors. They're meeting on Tuesday, and I need to add an item to their agenda."

Ramon was the chief financial officer. He would certainly have the right access to funnel money through this company for Labyrinth. Brandon typed Amelia's instructions into his notes app. "What do you want added to the agenda?"

"The Frost manuscript."

Brandon fumbled his phone. "The Frost manuscript?" he repeated.

"The advance on it will likely be high enough to need their approval, and the author will be in town next week." Amelia tapped her finger on her desk. "I don't want to wait for other publishers to go after her."

Brandon had only sent her his analysis an hour ago. As much as he wanted this deal to go through, he asked, "Don't you want to have someone else read the book before moving forward?"

"I read it last night, and I agree with your evaluation," Amelia said. "It's a solid manuscript. With the possible movie deal and international distribution, it has the potential to be quite profitable."

"I agree."

"When you reach out to the board, do what you can to move this item to the top of the agenda," Amelia said. "They're more likely to say yes when they aren't tired."

"I'll do what I can."

"Good." Amelia gave him a dismissive nod. Brandon took a step back, but before he left, she added, "Good job on the analysis, by the way."

Surprised by the compliment, Brandon pocketed his phone. "Thank you."

"Let me know if you run into any problems with the board," Amelia said. "And don't let Ramon's secretary put me off until tomorrow. I have no problem crashing whatever meeting he's in if he doesn't agree to meet with me."

Brandon believed her. "I'll make sure to emphasize that point."

"See that you do."

CHAPTER 9

WHEN KIMBER HAD flown through JFK on Monday, she'd never envisioned she would be back in New York again so soon, but here she was on a Friday afternoon, meeting with her new literary agent. How much life had changed in a few days.

Kimber followed the receptionist down the carpeted hall until they reached an open door.

"Here you are." The receptionist motioned her inside, where Patricia sat behind a desk.

Patricia stood. "Kimber, it's so nice to finally meet you in person."

"You too." Kimber shook Patricia's outstretched hand.

After the receptionist left, Patricia closed the door and waved at the two chairs facing her desk. "Please, sit down."

"Thanks." Kimber took the chair closest to the window and gazed out at the view of the skyscraper across the street. To Kimber's surprise, Patricia opted for the seat beside her rather than returning to her spot behind her desk.

"Special Agent Ebeid will be stopping by to meet with you in a few minutes, but I wanted to take a minute to chat about your work and what will happen in the next few weeks."

Her work, which Patricia had read. "I appreciate that. This is all new to me."

"It won't be for long," Patricia said. "You're a very talented author."

Heat rose to Kimber's cheeks. "Thank you."

"I assume you already had this professionally edited."

"No, but my friend Mark has been reading it for me, and he gives great feedback."

"Clearly. I did make several editorial changes before submitting your manuscript, but overall, your writing is solid."

Someone changed her words on her behalf? This would take some getting used to. "What sort of changes?"

"Nothing too significant. I just deepened the characters a bit and enhanced the climax," she said. "Normally, I would send those suggestions back to the author for corrections, but with the short turnaround time, that wasn't possible."

"Wouldn't it have been wise to wait to submit until the manuscript was ready?" Kimber asked. "If the agency wants me to become a lead author for Monroe, rushing may sabotage those plans."

"The manuscript is ready," Patricia insisted. "I may have tweaked a few things that I would normally have given to the author to fix, but your employer was very insistent that we move forward as quickly as possible." She pulled out some paperwork and passed it to Kimber. "Here's the paperwork for your DBA. I need your signature at the bottom, and then I'll have my assistant file it with the courts."

Kimber glanced over the "doing business as" paperwork that would allow her to legally operate under her pen name. She signed it, then passed it back to Patricia. "I still don't know how they expect a debut author to command enough attention to be invited to the top-level events."

"I do." Patricia gave a warm smile. "Your agency has agreed to commit several million dollars toward a movie adaptation of your book."

Kimber blinked several times as she repeated Patricia's words in her mind. "I'm sorry. They're doing what?"

"Five million dollars, to be precise." Patricia shrugged. "If I do my job right, they'll be the low bidder, and another production company will swoop in and purchase the movie rights."

Five million dollars? For *her* book? Kimber shook her head. This was all part of the government's plan. She may have written the words, but CIA dollars would be the reason for her apparent success. "I've done enough research into the book business to know that movie rights don't normally go for that much."

"The five million is the seed money for the production costs. With the first money already in, the likelihood is that a studio will partner, which will be enough to garner a lot of attention and drive book sales to an elite level."

Kimber's entire body tensed. The CIA was trying to make her out to be something she wasn't. Her words surely weren't worthy of such attention.

A tidal wave of inadequacy crashed over her, and she had to take a moment to find her voice. "I can't believe the agency would commit so much money to making my manuscript attractive to Monroe."

"It's a small price to pay if they can achieve their goals."

Patricia's easy mention of the agency's goals caused Kimber to pause. As far as she knew, Patricia had simply agreed to represent her. "How did you end up involved in all this?"

"My brother works for the agency. Has for years." Patricia reached out and put her hand on Kimber's arm. "And no, I don't have a security clearance, which I'm sure you'll check when you get back to whatever computer tells you such things. I just know enough to understand the importance of your success." She glanced at the door before lowering her voice and leaning closer. "And I know my objective is to place your manuscript with Monroe Publishing."

"That's a tidbit we both need to keep to ourselves."

"My brother emphasized that several times during our initial conversation." She stood and retrieved a paper from her desk. "I took the liberty of opening social media accounts on your behalf. Here are your usernames and passwords."

"I haven't been on social media since joining the agency."

"That's about to change. I know how you CIA types like to stay low-key, but to be successful as an author, you need to be the opposite." Patricia plucked her cell phone off her desk and tapped on the screen. "This is your new Instagram account."

An old-fashioned typewriter filled the circle where her photo would typically be, and several posts had been created over the past few days, the photos ranging from images of pens and blurred manuscripts to shots of the city, as though she were visiting for the first time.

"I already have over four hundred followers?"

"It always helps when someone with a strong following tags you. I've had my coworkers helping me with that, along with a few clients."

"Thank you."

"If this deal goes through the way I hope, I'll be thanking you. It will bolster my career and yours."

A knock sounded at the door.

Patricia rose and opened it. A man in his early thirties stood on the other side, his dark suit tailored, likely to conceal a holstered weapon beneath his jacket.

"Patricia Banik?" the man asked. As soon as Patricia nodded, he said, "I'm Rafi Ebeid. I believe you were expecting me?"

"Yes. Please, come in." Patricia waited for him to enter, then closed the door. "Have you met Kimber?"

"No." He shook Kimber's hand. "But if plans go as we hope, I suspect we'll be seeing a lot of each other."

A daunting prospect. Kimber kept that thought to herself. She waited until Patricia took her seat behind her desk and Special Agent Ebeid sat beside her before she asked, "What exactly is my role in all this, Special Agent Ebeid?"

"Please, call me Rafi. We don't want you to inadvertently refer to me as FBI when others are around."

"That's smart," Kimber said, especially since those nuances were ones she rarely had to deal with. "What happens now?"

"Assuming Ms. Banik can get a deal to go through, we want you to socialize as much as possible with the employees at Monroe. Meet with your editor and the marketing staff as often as you can, make friends with the people in the office, take them cookies to say thank you for their help. Anything you can do to be a constant presence will help them see you as nonthreatening."

"You hope someone will say something in front of me that will tie their activities to Labyrinth?"

"Yes."

"It sounds like any author could do that. Why is the government going to such lengths to make me a big name?" Kimber asked.

"Because you have the talent and the background to gain the access we need in this investigation," Rafi said. "The more money the publisher invests in you, the more they'll want you in the spotlight."

"And the more they want you in the spotlight," Patricia continued, "the more access you'll have to the top execs."

"It sounds like we're still dealing with a lot of 'ifs.'" Not her favorite way to operate.

"We are, but those should be sorted out in the next few weeks," Rafi said. "In the meantime, we've secured an apartment for you. It won't be ready until next Wednesday, but here's the address in case you want to check out the neighborhood and see the building." He handed her an envelope. "The key is in there with your new secure cell phone and the combination to the safe in the closet. Your firearm and encrypted laptop will be inside."

"Firearm?"

"It's standard procedure."

Kimber's head was spinning. "I thought I would have to find my own place if this move actually happens."

"The FBI maintains a few apartments in the city. We prefer that you stay in a location where we've already vetted the neighbors." He handed her a business card. "If you have any questions, that's my cell number. Call me anytime."

"Thank you." Kimber slid the card, the envelope, and her social media information into her laptop case.

Patricia leaned back in her chair. "Now that Rafi is here, I think we need to talk about what we can and can't put on social media."

As Rafi and Patricia discussed the best ways to get Kimber noticed by the public, Kimber could only envision how quickly her life was about to spin out of control.

CHAPTER 10

DARRAGH MATCHED HIS footsteps to the woman's in front of him. He'd spent three days determining the American secretary's typical routine to find her vulnerabilities and to search for the man who had shot him. That search had ended today—not because of his success but because of his failure.

He didn't know who had spotted him outside the US embassy, but Darragh had no doubt the Americans had identified him as a threat. With surveillance no longer an option, he had to take more direct measures, and he would start by having a chat with Susan Turner, the US secretary who had rented the car last weekend.

The woman retrieved her keys from her purse and entered her apartment building. Darragh rushed forward and grabbed the door before it could close.

She turned as he slipped inside, a hint of concern flashing in her eyes. Her footsteps quickened as she crossed the narrow lobby and approached her ground-level flat. Darragh waited until she was at her door before he closed the distance between them.

"Susan Turner?" he asked as though he didn't already know the answer.

She took a step back. "Who are you?"

"I'm a man who needs information." Darragh pulled his pistol from his holster and took aim. "And you're just the woman who can give it to me."

Fear filled her expression, but her focus remained on his gun. "I don't know anything."

That was what they always said. He waved his gun toward the door to her flat. "Maybe a little time together will help refresh your memory." Darragh pushed her against the wall and grabbed the key from her hand. Pressing the gun barrel to her temple, he unlocked her door before ushering her into the cramped apartment.

A chair and a sofa were tucked in the area to the right of the door, and several plants were arranged beside the window. Every available space along the wall had furniture pushed up against it, from plush chairs to bookshelves.

The woman stumbled and immediately grabbed a vase off a nearby table. She turned and hurled it at him.

Darragh ducked, but the vase clipped him in the shoulder, the same arm where he had taken a bullet only a week before. He cried out in pain and responded by shooting the secretary in the leg.

She gasped and stumbled backward.

She grabbed for the lamp, and Darragh took aim. "I don't recommend that," he said sternly. "You can either cooperate, or you can die. The decision is yours."

She lowered her hands.

"That's more like it." Darragh took a step forward. The woman would die before the night was over, but she didn't need to know that. At least, not yet.

• • •

Brandon had survived the week. Barely. He couldn't count the number of times Mary and Regina had given him bad information or tried to sabotage his new position, but he was quickly learning that his predisposition to suspect that everyone at this company was out to get him was closer to the truth than he cared to admit.

He pushed his way through the revolving door in the lobby of the office building and stepped into the flow of pedestrian traffic on the sidewalk. He pulled on his gloves and headed to the subway. All around him, groups of friends and couples chatted as they waited for the train and then boarded when it arrived.

A spurt of envy surged through him. Friday evening and he had nothing to do. He couldn't even claim a single friend or coworker he could talk to since moving to New York.

His contact with Special Agent Ebeid needed to remain at a minimum to avoid anyone connecting him with the FBI, and he certainly didn't have any interest in spending time with the other assistants at Monroe, which didn't bode well for him trying to gather information. Even talking to his mom was complicated by time-zone challenges since her move to Singapore with her new husband.

Brandon reached his stop and headed up to the street level. The scent of Italian food wafted from a nearby restaurant, and the buzz of conversation carried outside when the door opened and a couple walked in. Maybe he should eat out tonight instead of his usual takeaway. It would be nice to be around people who weren't against him, for a change.

It was pretty sad that the prospect of speaking with a waiter or waitress was the potential highlight of his weekend.

Brandon approached his building, a sense of familiarity washing over him when he caught a glimpse of a woman heading his way—dark hair, a white coat that stood out against the darker colors most people on the street wore. She moved closer, and recognition dawned. Kimber?

She must have seen him at the same time he had spotted her because she slowed and narrowed her eyes as though she weren't sure she believed he was right in front of her. "Brandon?"

Brandon took several steps forward, closing the distance between them. "What are you doing here?"

"I was just checking out the neighborhood." She gestured with her hand, nearly hitting a woman who rushed by them. She winced and called out, "Sorry."

"I thought you lived in Virginia."

"I do, but there's a chance I'll be moving here to New York."

"New job?" Brandon asked.

"That's the hope."

Delighted to talk to someone not related to his work, Brandon said, "I hope it works out."

"Me too." She glanced down for a moment before looking back up at him. "What about you? Do you live around here?"

"Not too far," Brandon said, automatically keeping his answer vague. "Where are you heading now? Do you have plans with your sister?"

"No. She's out of town until next week, but she's letting me stay at her place," Kimber said. "I was going to grab a bite to eat."

The prospect of spending time with Kimber instantly brightened his already improved mood. "Do you mind if I join you?"

Kimber shot him a skeptical look. "You don't already have plans?"

"No. I haven't met many people since I moved here." Brandon motioned toward the restaurant he'd passed a moment ago. "Do you like Italian?"

"I love Italian."

"Come on." Brandon reversed his course and started toward the restaurant entrance. "I've been wanting to check this place out."

Kimber followed him inside and waited until Brandon gave his name to the hostess before she spoke again. "I can't believe I ran into you here. What are the chances?"

"There are over eight million people in New York City, so the odds are probably about a million to one."

"I'm glad the odds worked in my favor," Kimber said. "I wasn't looking forward to eating alone."

Brandon's gaze met hers. "Me neither."

• • •

The dark cloud that had hung over Brandon the first time they'd met on the plane was gone, or perhaps it had moved farther into the distance. All throughout dinner, Kimber had waited for some mention of a girlfriend or an ex who had broken his heart, but their conversation had been delightfully absent of such topics.

The waiter arrived at their table and cleared their empty dishes away.

"Can we have the check, please?" Brandon asked.

Kimber pulled her cell phone out of her purse to check the time. "Oh my gosh. We've been here for over two hours?"

Brandon glanced at his watch, and his brow furrowed slightly. "I didn't think it had been that long."

The waiter returned with the check, and Brandon paid using the credit card device the waiter held and then pocketed his card and receipt before Kimber could retrieve her wallet from her purse. After thanking the waiter, Brandon stood as Kimber did the same.

"You didn't have to pay for me," she said.

"It's not a problem."

She slipped on her coat and walked with him to the door, her thoughts racing. Would she see Brandon again, or was this another wonderful time together that would never repeat itself?

Brandon reached past her to open the door for her, a blast of cold air rushing over them.

As soon as they reached the sidewalk, he asked, "Which way to your sister's place?"

Kimber motioned to her left. "You don't have to walk me home."

Brandon shrugged. "It's what the men in romance novels would do."

Kimber stopped on the sidewalk, and she couldn't stop the smile from spreading across her face. "Are you secretly a hopeless romantic?"

"Maybe."

She laughed. Had she known him better, she probably would have let him walk her home, but even though Brandon seemed safe enough, showing him where she was staying, especially since he knew Tessa was out of town, went against her natural instincts. "Tell you what. You can walk me as far as the subway."

"Fair enough." He walked beside her. "What do you have planned for tomorrow?"

A shiver of anticipation rushed through her. Was he asking because he wanted to spend more time with her?

"I haven't decided yet." She stopped at a red light, several other pedestrians crowding around them. "I usually try to go to the library's main branch while I'm here."

"Why would you go to the library when you don't live here?"

Because it was one of the most peaceful places to write. She swallowed that answer and chose another. "I love the architecture of the Schwarzman building. It's one of my favorite libraries in the world."

"I've never been there."

"Seriously?" Kimber grabbed his arm and stared. "You've never been?"

"This is my first time living in New York," Brandon said. "And I haven't been here that long."

"We have to fix this." Kimber released his arm and motioned in the general direction of the library. "You should come with me tomorrow." Belatedly, she realized how her words must sound. "That is, if you don't have plans."

"My only plan was to go grocery shopping, but I can do that first thing in the morning." The light changed, and Brandon put his hand on her back as though making sure he didn't lose contact with her as the crowd of pedestrians rushed forward. As soon as they reached the other side, he asked, "What time do you want to go?"

"How about we meet up around ten?" Kimber asked. "That's when it opens."

Brandon nodded. "Sounds good. And afterward, we can grab some lunch, maybe stop by a bookstore."

"Why are we stopping by a bookstore if we're going to the library first?"

"Because I need to add to my personal library. I had to leave a lot of my books behind when I moved to New York." Brandon reached out and touched her arm briefly. "I thought maybe you could help me pick a few out."

Goose bumps rippled across her skin. "I'd like that."

"Great. It's a date."

A date. She had a date with Brandon.

"I just realized; I don't know your last name," she said.

"Hale." Brandon looked down at her. "What's yours?"

"Seidel." She gave him the truth before she thought better of it. Should she have said Frost? No, that was a pen name. Surely it was okay to keep using her real name in situations like this. She hoped.

"Now that we've been formally introduced, does that mean I can have your number?" he asked.

His request shouldn't have sent a kaleidoscope of butterflies fluttering in her stomach, but it did. Thankfully, she managed to keep her voice calm when she said, "Sure."

Brandon smiled at her response.

The butterflies took flight.

He was just asking for her number. It wasn't a big deal. But it was for her. She hadn't dated anyone since Daniel, and the prospect of going out with someone who didn't have to worry about hiding his career from the world was liberating.

But she would have to hide her true employer from him. That gave her pause. She'd have to take Mark's advice: stick to the truth and simply neglect to share that she worked for the CIA.

She pulled her phone from her purse while still protecting the rest of the contents inside.

Brandon waited for her to unlock her screen and create a new contact before he held out his hand to take it from her. Though she preferred not to give anyone access to her phone, she doubted Brandon wanted to announce his personal information with so many people walking by them.

She stepped beside him so she could see her screen while he inputted his name and number. She half-expected him to text himself, but instead, he handed her phone back to her.

"Now you can text me so I have your number."

Still amazed that he wanted to stay in touch, Kimber opened her text messages and typed her name before pressing Send. "There you go."

"Great. Thanks."

Kimber returned her phone to her purse.

"You know, I should have asked for your number on Monday," Brandon said.

"I had the same thought." Needing clarity in where their relationship was heading, she added, "But I thought you might have a girlfriend."

"No girlfriend." Brandon shook his head, but instead of his gaze returning to her, he hesitated as though focused on something or someone to his left.

They reached another red light, and Kimber glanced around. A man in his early twenties with stringy brown hair stared at her, but he quickly averted his gaze when he caught her looking at him.

Kimber used her free hand to grip her purse, adjusting it so it was in front of her hip. When the light turned green, she squeezed Brandon's hand and stayed where she was.

He looked down at her, his eyebrows raised, but rather than question why she hadn't moved forward, he glanced at the man who'd been eyeing Kimber's purse a moment ago.

They remained where they were while the crowd flowed past them. The stringy-haired man hesitated a moment before he stepped into the crosswalk.

As soon as he was halfway across the street, Brandon leaned down and whispered, "You saw him too?"

"Yeah." Kimber started forward. "We should be fine now that he's in front of us."

"Are you sure you aren't a New Yorker?" Brandon asked.

"I'm not a New Yorker, but I've traveled in enough cities to notice when someone's footsteps are mirroring mine." And her CIA training had reinforced those skills. She kept that thought to herself.

"I'm impressed."

"Don't be. I'm sure there are all sorts of safety tips I haven't learned yet."

"That's probably true for all of us."

Kimber slowed as they approached the subway station.

"Should I pick you up in the morning, or would you rather meet at the library?" Brandon asked.

"We can meet by the library's main entrance." Kimber lifted her gaze to meet his. "Thanks again for dinner."

"It was my pleasure." He took her hand in his and lifted it to his lips.

The gesture was so old-fashioned, yet she couldn't deny that the kiss had caused her stomach to flip-flop and sent a fresh wave of goose bumps rippling over her skin. "You really are a hopeless romantic."

"Guilty as charged." Brandon released her hand. "I'll see you tomorrow."

"See you then." Kimber gave a last wave before she headed down the stairs toward the train station. She made it all the way to Tessa's apartment before the surrealness of tonight caught up with her. Brandon Hale was intelligent, interesting, handsome, and kind, and she had enjoyed every moment she'd spent with him. His phone number was now in her phone, and he seemed interested in her. Was this all for real? Or was it possible that he was too good to be true?

CHAPTER 11

BRANDON STRODE DOWN the street, the light snowfall dampening his coat and hat. He should have called a taxi, but he hadn't had the chance to work out this morning, and he needed to get his body moving. And walking always helped him organize his thoughts, like about who in Monroe Publishing had access to the bank accounts. Sheila in finance, Ramon, the chief financial officer, and John, the CEO, currently topped Brandon's list.

He passed the restaurant where he and Kimber had eaten last night, marveling at how she had shown up right when he'd needed a friend. She really was too good to be true.

That thought had rolled through Brandon's mind repeatedly since their chance meeting last night. She shared so many of his interests; she didn't push for information he couldn't give. She was even beautiful but didn't seem like the type who obsessed over her appearance.

The idea that some enemy intelligence agency had planted her in his life had popped up with annoying frequency over the last fourteen hours, enough that he had checked his belongings for tracking devices. He'd found none, nor had he been wearing any sort of electronics that she could have tapped into when they'd been on the plane on Monday. Even his phone had been traded out for a new one when he'd reached the States.

His deep dive into her social media accounts hadn't revealed anything, all of them showing no activity since she'd been in college. Her having a history that went back that far gave him some comfort. A new account would have screamed alias.

Now, walking toward the library, Brandon had to face a new fear. What if Kimber did move to New York? He'd want to see her, to spend time with her, to see if this connection between them could turn into a real relationship. Juggling his cover story with reality was never easy, but he suspected she might be worth the effort.

What would it be like to have someone to talk to at the end of the day, someone to spend time with, someone he could simply enjoy being around without worrying about a sniper hiding in the shadows or someone overhearing the secrets they shared?

Brandon turned the corner and got his first good look at the Schwarzman building. The three archways in the center were illuminated, and two matching lion statues flanked the wide stone steps leading to the building. Kimber stood beside the statue nearest him, only her jeans and shoes visible beneath her long, wool coat.

She spotted him, and her face lit up. The brightness in her eyes, the lift of her eyebrows, the quick smile—either Kimber truly was happy to see him, or she was best actress he'd ever met.

She hurried toward him. "Good morning."

"Morning." Unable to resist, he leaned down and kissed her cheek.

A faint blush tinted her skin. "You have perfect timing. I just got here too." She headed up the steps. "How did the grocery shopping go this morning?"

The shopping he would have done had he not been stalking Kimber on social media. "I never made it to the store."

"Maybe after the library, we should do that for you," Kimber suggested. "Tessa will love me forever if I pick up a few things for her. She gets back on Tuesday."

"If Tessa's your sister, won't she love you anyway?"

Kimber laughed. "Yes, she will."

Brandon tried to envision Kimber and him shopping together. He couldn't remember the last time he'd done that with someone else. It probably hadn't been since he'd taken his mom to the grocery store the last time he'd visited her in Arizona. That had been before she'd moved two years ago.

Kimber hurried toward the entrance, her footsteps steady despite the snow accumulating on the steps.

Eager to get out of the cold, Brandon kept pace, relieved when they passed through the doorway.

He stepped inside and stared at the soaring space before him. Marble floors, a ridiculously high-arched ceiling, two sweeping staircases leading to the upper levels. "Wow."

"This is just the beginning." Kimber tugged off her gloves and continued forward. "Let me show you some of my favorite spots."

"We aren't here to just look at books, are we?"

"No, but we'll look for those too."

• • •

Kimber tucked her scarf a little tighter around her neck as she emerged from the subway with Brandon. The snowfall had continued throughout the two hours they'd explored the architecture and browsed the stacks of books at the library as well as during their lunch at a little café afterward. Now they were on their way to one of Kimber's favorite bookstores located in Carnegie Hill. She couldn't tell how much snow had fallen; most of it was little more than a slushy mess on the roads and sidewalks.

"Which way?" Brandon asked.

She motioned down the street. "We just go up to Madison and then down a few blocks."

"How close are we to Central Park?"

"Three blocks." She narrowed her eyes. Little snippets of memory flashed through her mind: his use of British terms and phrases, the occasional wisp of a British accent, the way he angled his silverware on his plate when he finished eating a meal. Those details combined with Brandon's clear lack of familiarity with the city created an unexpected realization.

Kimber started down the street. As soon as they were both settled into a comfortable rhythm, she asked, "How long ago did you move from the UK?"

"How did you know—" He broke off as though not ready to confirm she'd guessed correctly.

"You have a few Britishisms you haven't lost yet," Kimber said. When Brandon continued to stare at her with a stunned look, she expanded on her comment. "You call pants trousers and napkins serviettes. And since you have a few words that sound more British than American, I assume you were living there for a while."

"Almost three years." Brandon glanced up at the Walk sign before crossing Park Avenue. "And to answer your question, I moved here on Monday."

"The day I met you."

He nodded.

She hadn't expected that answer. She'd assumed he'd been coming home after visiting London.

They reached the opposite curb, and Kimber asked, "How do you like it here so far?"

"Until today, my world has revolved around going to work, going home, and ordering takeaway."

"Does that mean you moved here for a new job?"

"Yes."

She wanted to ask more, to find out what he did for a living, but asking that question would mean she'd likely have to answer it in return. Yet not asking it might make it seem like she was avoiding the topic. She forced the question out. "What do you do for a living?"

"I'm pretty much just an office jockey. Lots of paperwork to push," Brandon said.

"You moved from London to push around paperwork?" Kimber asked.

"It feels like it." Brandon shrugged. "My new position is working for someone pretty high up in my company. Lots of responsibility, a lot of confidentiality."

Confidentiality. She understood that concept well.

"What about you?" Brandon asked. "What do you do for a living?"

Kimber tensed. She'd opened the door to the question, and now she had to walk through it. Mark's words replayed through her mind: give the truth you're comfortable with.

"I work in finance." There. She'd done it. She'd told him without mentioning that she was CIA and would soon be working undercover.

"It sounds like we're in a similar field."

"I definitely have a lot of paperwork to push," Kimber said, although her thoughts weren't on spreadsheets and ledgers. They flitted instead to the pile of printed manuscripts she had tucked away in her closet.

They reached Madison Avenue, and Brandon motioned forward. "Would you be up for a walk in Central Park before we go to the bookstore?"

"Sure." More than happy to draw out their time together, she asked, "Have you ever been?"

"No, but if I'm going to live here, it would be nice to be familiar with the sites."

"I agree." Kimber continued toward Central Park. "How do you like your new job? Is it better than what you left behind?"

Brandon's eyes clouded briefly. "I'm not sure yet. It has potential."

"That's good," Kimber said. "How about the people you work with?"

"Let's just say there isn't anyone from my office who I'd want to spend the afternoon with."

"That's lucky for me, but I'm sorry you haven't found any friends at work yet."

"What about you? Do you have a lot of friends you'll be leaving behind if you move here?"

More than she cared to admit, but Mark was the one she would miss the most. "I do, but DC isn't that far away. I hope I'll be able to keep in touch with them; plus, my sister is here, so I'll have someone I already know."

"You know me too."

"This's true." She couldn't deny that having Brandon here would be a welcome bonus to her move to New York, assuming she could figure out how to live the lie without compromising her actual reason for being here.

When they reached the park, Brandon asked, "Now where?"

"It depends on what you want to do. We can walk along the reservoir or go to one of the museums. Then there's Belvedere Castle."

"What about ice skating?"

"That's on the other side of the park. If you want to do that, we'll want to cross over to Central Park West and catch the train."

"How did you get to know this area so well?"

"I visited my sister a lot when she first moved up here," Kimber said. "I think I have the map of Central Park memorized."

"Where's your favorite place to go?"

"I love just walking around, but if you want to get out of the snow, we could stop in one of the museums." She tilted her head to her left. "The Metropolitan Museum of Art is that way, and the city museum is about the same distance in the other direction."

"Do you mind if we just walk for a bit?" Brandon asked. "Or is it too cold?"

She was cold, but with the fat snowflakes drifting down, she couldn't resist taking advantage of nature's beauty. "I could walk for a while."

They entered the park, and Brandon slipped his arm around Kimber. The warmth of his body beside hers chased away the worst of the winter chill, and Kimber's steps matched his. They looked like a couple. She supposed they were a couple, sort of. How this had happened when she hadn't even expected to see him after they'd said goodbye at the airport was yet another unexplained miracle.

Brandon tilted his head to look down at her. "When do you go back to Virginia?"

"I fly back tomorrow morning." She wished she could stay longer, especially if it meant spending more time with Brandon.

"I know this probably sounds strange, but I'm going to miss you."

The unexpected connection flowed through her. "It's not so strange," she said. "I'm going to miss you too."

• • •

Brandon and Kimber had spent the entire day together, all the way through dinner in Chelsea and a trip to the grocery store.

Juggling the four bags of groceries in his hands, he approached his apartment. The door beside his opened, and Trudy peeked out.

"I was wondering if that was you." She glanced down at the load he was carrying. "Oh, good. You found the store."

"I did."

Brandon set two bags beside his door and dug out his key.

"I have something for you." She held up a hand, motioning for him to wait. "Hold on a minute."

Brandon opened the door and carried the first two bags into his apartment. He grabbed the ones he left in the hall as Trudy returned with a loaf of bread in her hand. "I hope you like banana bread."

"I love banana bread." He accepted the offering. "Thank you."

"Enjoy the rest of your weekend." She disappeared back inside.

With the loaf in one hand, he hauled the rest of his groceries inside and locked the door behind him. He set the banana bread on the long counter that separated the galley-style kitchen from the rest of the living room.

His new home still looked the same as the day he'd arrived, except for the single glass sitting beside the sink.

Though the space had a certain charm and elegance, the bare walls and his unpacked suitcase in the bedroom prevented it from feeling like anything beyond a simple safe house. Not exactly the kind of place he could bring a date, even if it were just to watch a movie or share a meal.

Brandon checked the clock on the stove: ten forty-two. For twelve hours, he'd enjoyed Kimber's company and the sense of normalcy she brought with her. He really hoped she'd move to New York. Beyond the much-needed companionship, he suspected that given the chance, they could become much more than friends.

He put away his food and unwrapped the banana bread—might as well try some while it was fresh—and retrieved his laptop from the safe. He took a bite of the sweet bread, humming his approval. He hoped Trudy had a habit of baking. He rather liked eating something he didn't have to make or dish out of a takeaway box.

Settling at the desk, he pulled up his secure email and browsed through the activity from today. As was typical for a Saturday, the correspondence was light, but an email from the security office in London caught his attention.

He opened it and read the brief message. *Suspect identified surveilling the US embassy in London. Darragh Byrne, suspected ties with Labyrinth. Current location: unknown.*

Brandon read through the detailed incident report in which one of his coworkers had spotted the same man near the embassy several days in a row, always watching from a different position. That tidbit alone emphasized the suspicion that the man wasn't simply a local resident who was curious about the goings-on at the embassy. When someone had tried to approach him, the man had fled the area.

Brandon opened the attached file, which included a rap sheet with a photo from Interpol.

Darragh Byrne, thirty-four years old, originally from Belfast, wanted on suspicion of murder, last known location: London.

A list of murder cases followed. The first two were both suspected murders for hire, but the rest of the victims all had one thing in common: a tie with Labyrinth. The name at the bottom of the list stood out. *Finlay Addington, killed February 19.*

Brandon gripped the edge of his laptop, and his chest tightened as the memory of that night replayed in slow motion, right down to the doubts and guilt that had followed Finlay's murder.

Brandon fought against the emotional storm brewing inside him and focused on the assassin's image: light-brown hair, deep-set green eyes, a squared-off jaw with a day's worth of stubble. He was the sort who would easily blend into a crowd, someone who wouldn't be noticed until it was too late.

Yet he had been noticed.

A chilling question needled through Brandon's brain: Why had Darragh Byrne been watching the embassy for so many days in a row? Or more precisely, who had he been looking for?

The answer to both questions came with alarming clarity and a streak of fear. Brandon was the only person who had recently associated with someone from Labyrinth. And if his suspicions were correct, when Director Yarrow transferred Brandon to New York, he had inadvertently saved Brandon's life.

CHAPTER 12

ASADI SCROLLED THROUGH the emails on his phone, confirming that his plans were moving steadily forward.

He leaned on the stone railing of the balcony overlooking the water. This little spot outside Valencia, Spain, was more convenient when it came to overseeing the day-to-day of Labyrinth's arms-trade operations, but Asadi much preferred living where he didn't have to deal with language barriers and he was already recognized as a local. At least this location also boasted an unobstructed view and a private dock. And the weather was considerably warmer than on Anglesey.

The light breeze ruffled his dark hair and rippled over his light jacket. Maybe it wouldn't be all bad if he had to stay here.

His phone rang, and his heartbeat quickened when Darragh's name flashed on his screen. If he had good news, perhaps Asadi could return home. He hit the Call button. "Did you find him?"

"No. He isn't there."

Asadi bit back a sigh. Whether he remained in Spain or returned to Wales, Asadi needed Finlay's friend to die. "Keep watching for a few more days."

"That's not possible. Someone spotted me, and I was careful not to be noticed," Darragh said. "The guy who came after me had to be CIA."

Asadi clenched his jaw, irritation rising inside him. All the intercepted shipments, all the clients who were arrested suddenly made sense. "Finlay must have been feeding the CIA information for a while."

"That's what my source said. She also indicated his handler is now in New York."

"Then, that's where you need to go." New York. London. Asadi didn't care where the man died as long as it happened soon. He couldn't risk any loose ends this close to the day when his plans would finally come to fruition. Soon, his brother's and sister's deaths would be avenged.

"Finding this guy will be a needle in a haystack."

"Maybe not." Asadi paced the length of the balcony before turning back and returning to where he'd started. Up until two weeks ago, Finlay's access to information had been limited to the *when* and *where* of shipments going in and out of the UK, but if Asadi's suspicions were correct, which they usually were, Finlay had seen the financial statements for Monroe Publishing, which had corresponded with their shipments.

If Finlay had been working with the CIA and had learned about Labyrinth's association with Monroe, he had not only shared that information, but the CIA would also be quick to send someone into the publishing house to investigate.

"I'll call you back," Asadi said, "but for now, get yourself to New York."

"It'll take me a few days. With the CIA looking for me, I'll have to get out of England before I can fly over."

"Get there as soon as you can." Asadi ended the call and pulled up another contact. The phone rang only twice before it was answered.

"What is it?"

Asadi strode across the balcony again. "I need a list of every new employee Monroe Publishing has hired in the past week."

"That's easy enough. I'll pull that for you when I get to the office on Monday. Any particular reason you want this?"

Asadi could share his concerns, but that would create unneeded resistance when it came to the upcoming shipment. "Just taking some precautions."

"Should I be worried?"

"No, but I'm sending one of my people over to keep an eye on things for a while. I need you to find a suitable position for him."

"What kind of experience does he have?"

Asadi's lips curved slowly into a smile. "Security."

. . .

Kimber's cheeks burned as she replayed the same conversation for the twentieth time today. Yes, she was planning to leave the agency. No, she didn't know yet when her book would come out. Yes, she had an agent. No, she hadn't signed a contract.

She understood her coworkers' innate curiosity, but she was surrounded by people skilled in the art of interrogation and who used those skills at every opportunity. Eager to make her escape, Kimber excused herself from her latest grilling and went in search of Mark. As she'd hoped, he was in his cubicle.

He glanced up. "How's it going?"

"Considering that no one but you had any clue that I write novels, it's been a bit crazy today."

"We knew that would happen." Mark checked his computer screen. "I didn't realize it was so late. Are you about ready to go?"

"I'm past ready."

He powered down his computer. "Come on. Let's get out of here before you get cornered again."

They made it past only three cubicles before Logan stepped into their path.

"Hey, Kimber. Did I hear correctly that you're leaving?"

"Yeah, you did." Kimber took a step to the side in the hopes of moving past Logan without having to tell even more lies.

"We should get together before you leave, maybe this weekend."

"Thanks for the offer, but it's going to be pretty crazy packing."

Mark nudged his way past Logan, opening a narrow path for Kimber to follow.

"See you later, Logan." Mark guided Kimber to the door.

Kimber lowered her voice. "Thank you."

"You're welcome."

They made their way outside, the sun beating away the chill of the morning.

Leaving her gloves in her pocket, Kimber strode toward the parking garage. "Are you still up for getting together tonight?" she asked. "Everyone may believe I'm leaving, but I think that had more to do with you telling the story than my reaction to their questions."

"I'll meet you at your apartment," Mark said.

"Thanks." Kimber headed down the stairs of the parking garage to her car. As soon as she slid behind the driver's seat, she unlocked her glove compartment and retrieved her cell phone. Four missed calls. Three from unknown numbers and one from Brandon.

Not sure how Brandon would react if he knew she was spending the evening with Mark, she started the car and waited for the Bluetooth to engage so she could call him back.

Her call went unanswered. Too bad.

She drove out of the parking garage and to the back gate. She'd already merged onto the George Washington Parkway when her phone rang, and Brandon's name lit up her screen.

A flutter of excitement rose inside her. She pressed the button on her steering wheel to answer. "Hey there. Are you still at work?"

"I'm just leaving the office. It sounds like you're driving."

"Yeah. I'm heading home, but I saw that I missed your call."

"That was from when I was out running errands. I thought you might be on your lunch hour when I was."

"Today was one of those days when my lunch hour barely lasted five minutes."

His deep laugh carried through the speakers. "Any word yet on that new job you were talking about?"

"No, but I don't think I'll hear anything for a couple weeks."

Brandon fell silent for a moment before he asked, "So, who is the job with anyway?"

Kimber gripped her steering wheel a little tighter. She'd already told him she worked in finance. So did she lie to him about who she was interviewing with? Or did she lie and tell him she was a writer when she wasn't yet? Preferring to stick with the familiar, she chose the former. "It's with American Express." Everyone knew that company. And surely they had to have an office somewhere in New York. Hoping to avoid any follow-up questions on what kind of position she was hoping to get, she asked, "What about you? What company do you work for?"

"Monroe Publishing."

Kimber's jaw dropped open. Thank goodness they weren't on a video call.

What were the chances that the guy she was interested in just happened to be working for the company she had been asked to infiltrate? And what would she do if she saw him there? Her chest tightened, and her anxiety rose. She was proving to be the worst undercover operative ever.

Realizing that Brandon was probably expecting her to respond, she asked, "How are you liking your job so far?"

"It pays the bills. Mostly, I run errands and deliver publishing contracts from one office to another," Brandon said. "I really hope you end up getting the new job."

"Me too."

They talked the entire thirty-nine-minute drive from Langley to Kimber's apartment in Alexandria. Though she didn't want their conversation to end, she dug for an excuse so she wouldn't have to introduce Brandon to her friendship with Mark quite yet. Far too often, the men she dated mistook their friendship for something more.

Another call beeped through, this time from her new literary agent. "Hey, I'm sorry, but I have a call I have to take. Can I call you later?"

"Sure. Talk to you soon."

Still reeling from Brandon's revelation on where he worked, Kimber switched the call. "This is Kimber."

"Kimber, it's Patricia. I have good news."

Kimber's fingers tightened on the steering wheel again.

"The managing editor of Monroe Publishing wants to meet you."

Patricia said this was good news, but now that Kimber knew where Brandon worked, it was anything but good. "Is that normal?"

"It's not uncommon when a publisher is considering signing a significant contract," Patricia said. "I'm sure she wants to size you up to see how you present yourself."

"Why would that matter?"

"Because it makes their job easier if you're comfortable interacting with people, especially if you can translate that on camera."

"On camera? You mean, like, on talk shows?"

"Talk shows, podcasts, online book clubs . . ."

Kimber couldn't imagine it. Okay, so maybe she had dreamed of being that kind of author, the type who was showcased on the popular podcasts and talk shows, who had huge lines for every book signing and needed three pens at the table to make sure she didn't run out of ink. But that was all a pipe dream.

"Our meeting is a week from Friday, but I'd like you to come to New York the day before. We'll spend a few hours practicing for the meeting and making sure you present yourself in the best possible light."

"Sounds good." But it would sound better if she earned this without the CIA's help.

"Also, this particular editor we'll be meeting with is very conscientious when it comes to public image. We'll need to talk about what you're going to wear—clothes, accessories, makeup. The works."

"My sister can help with a makeover," Kimber said. "She sent me home with three new outfits from Fashion Week in London."

"Take photos of you in them and text them to me. I'll see if they'll work."

"I'll do that tonight after I get home." Kimber parked in her usual spot at her apartment complex.

"We'll talk soon," Patricia said. "And congratulations. If I'm right, by the time we walk out of Monroe Publishing next week, you'll be well on your way to becoming one of their lead authors."

"I can't even imagine."

"You don't have to as long as you keep putting words on the page about your imaginary world. That's the secret to success—always working on the next book."

"I'll remember that." Kimber ended the call and turned off the engine. She climbed out, not surprised that Mark was already waiting by the stairs leading to her apartment.

Though her news burned inside her, she swallowed it. If all went well, she would have even more amazing news to share with both Mark and Brandon by the end of next week. Or it would be if she could figure out a way to explain to Brandon why she'd lied to him.

• • •

Brandon entered his apartment, his briefcase in one hand and a bag of Chinese takeout in the other. Despite the grocery run he'd made on Saturday night, he didn't have the energy to cook tonight, not after another grueling day trying to keep up with Amelia while also avoiding Mary's and Regina's attempts to get him fired. And he had no doubt that was exactly what they were trying to do.

Today's efforts had included answering his phone for him while he'd been picking up Amelia's lunch order and telling whomever it had been that Brandon no longer worked there. Brandon had never considered that he'd need to use the listening device he'd planted to protect both his cover and his job. And since he still had no idea who'd been on the other end of the call, for all he knew, the aftermath was still yet to come.

Determined to shake off the irritations of the day, Brandon retrieved a bowl from the cabinet and sat at the serving bar. At least he'd had the chance to talk to Kimber tonight, although he was starting to wonder if she was going to call him back.

His phone buzzed with an incoming text. He read the message from Rafi. *Check your email.*

Brandon retrieved his secure laptop from the safe in his bedroom. After carrying it back to the kitchen counter, he turned it on and accessed his email.

The message from Rafi topped his inbox, the subject line reading simply *Maze.*

He opened it and skimmed the contents. Asadi Mir had disappeared from his home base in Wales, and his bank accounts were all closed. More concerning was the new chatter intel had picked up, something about a new target. Labyrinth was up to something, and the CIA no longer had an inside source.

Another email popped up, this one from the London station chief. Brandon skimmed the message sharing the news that Susan Turner had died over the weekend in a house fire. Brandon felt the shock set in first, then disbelief. She'd been the one who had arranged for his travel from London to New York. What were the chances that she would die so soon after Finlay's murder? Suspicion erupted, and a knot of despair formed in the pit of his stomach.

He opened a new tab on his internet browser and did a quick search about the fire. The details were sparse at best.

Needing a distraction, he browsed through the latest world news. Nothing screamed terrorist attack or assassination, nor did he uncover anything in the secure CIA correspondence overseas that indicated where Asadi Mir had gone.

Mir hadn't passed through any kind of border control, suggesting that he'd either relocated within the UK or had left by boat. From what Brandon had seen of Labyrinth's resources, either was possible.

He took a bite of cold Chinese food and debated whether he should warm up the rest in the microwave.

When his phone rang and Kimber's name popped up on the screen, he closed his laptop. There was no additional indication of what Labyrinth was up to or whether the organization had been involved in Susan's death, but surely he could ignore work for a few minutes and pretend to have a normal life.

He answered the phone. "I was hoping that was you."

"Sorry it took me so long to call you back. The call I got was about the possible job in New York."

Hope rose within him. "And?"

"It's looking promising," Kimber said. "I have a meeting in New York this Friday. If it goes well, I could move as early as the following week."

"That's great." The mere prospect of her moving to New York lifted his spirits. "It's hard to believe you could be here that soon."

"I know. Everything is happening so fast," Kimber said. "Of course, my sister will be thrilled if it actually happens."

"That makes two of us," Brandon said, not bothering to hide his excitement. "Do you think your sister would mind if I took you out to dinner Friday night?"

"I think she would understand, but I should probably warn you, if things don't go well at my meeting, I doubt I'll be much fun to be around."

"We'll plan to celebrate that night," Brandon said. "And if things don't go the way we hope, we'll commiserate together."

"I hope we'll be celebrating."

Brandon paced across the room. "Me too."

CHAPTER 13

KIMBER AND BRANDON talked every night, and with every conversation, Kimber prayed a little harder that her possible move to New York would actually happen. She still had reservations about what she would do if she ran into Brandon at Monroe, but from everything he'd told her, she suspected he spent most of his time out of the office. And she was meeting with the managing editor, not someone in the legal department.

If she did get the publishing contract, she could come clean—sort of. Surely he'd understand if she told him she was too afraid to talk about her writing until she was sure she had a contract. That much was true.

She stacked several shirts on top of her bed and rolled them together to prevent wrinkles. With her large suitcase now full of clothing, she zipped it and set it beside her door. She didn't know if she would really be moving, but the opportunity to take a few things that she would want to her sister's made sense. And Kimber didn't have a return ticket yet. Who knew how long this trip would last.

Her phone rang with an incoming video call. She smiled when she saw that it was Brandon, then sat on her bed and accepted the FaceTime request. "Hey there," she said as soon as his image appeared.

"How's it going?" Brandon asked. "Is that a suitcase behind you?"

"Yes. I've been trying to decide what to bring with me this weekend," Kimber admitted, eyeing the bookshelf across the room.

His gaze shifted to her suitcase again. "You're trying to decide how many books to bring, aren't you?"

"Maybe."

Brandon laughed. "Why doesn't that surprise me?"

"I don't know, but it's kind of scary that you guessed what I was thinking." Especially since they'd spent only a few days together in person.

"It didn't take long to figure out your reading material is a priority." Brandon shifted off his bed and moved across his room, revealing bare walls. "Just pick out a few of your favorite books to bring with you now. We can always go to the library to get you more."

"I'd like that." Kimber crossed to her bookshelf, her phone in hand.

Brandon continued forward until his kitchen came into view. "I have a feeling we're going to become permanent fixtures at the library."

"I have no doubt."

•   •   •

Asadi paced the concrete deck, his mobile phone in his hand, his bank information on his screen. His contact at Monroe had pushed through the funding in time for this latest arms deal, and with the profits they'd received, Labyrinth now had the cash they needed for their next strike. Or rather, strikes.

Anticipation flowed through him. They had the money. They had the bombmaker on contract. They had the date. They had people in place at both targets.

Originally, his subordinates had thought small: the US embassy in Lisbon, a train station in Budapest, a café in Vienna. The list went on, but none of them had had a guarantee for American and British casualties.

Asadi had morphed the plans into a much bigger scheme, and people throughout the Western world would feel the ripple effects of his efforts. But first, he needed this New York problem put to rest. Darragh should have arrived by now, but Asadi had yet to receive an update.

He closed his banking app and dialed Darragh's number.

Darragh answered on the fourth ring. "I'm still looking."

"What's the problem?"

"The information on the four new employees is coming in bits and pieces," Darragh said. "It took me a day to get all their phone numbers and another day to track the first two down at their offices."

"What about the other two?"

"One is no longer working there," Darragh said. "The other works in the warehouse in New Jersey. I'm heading out there tonight. Considering you already have the date set, I want to be well out of this city as soon as possible."

"That would be wise." Asadi stared out at the peaceful view of the water. That peace would remain with him once the Brits and Americans truly suffered as he had. "This event will be memorable."

"I'm sure it will be," Darragh said. "I'll call you as soon as I check out the guy at the warehouse. I should have something by morning."

"Good. I'm tired of waiting."

"And I'm tired of New York."

CHAPTER 14

THE SCENT OF corned beef and pizza carried through the office, evidence that multiple lunch orders had been delivered during the half hour Brandon had been out picking up his and Amelia's lunch. He delivered Amelia's Caesar salad to her along with her water and fresh lemon before settling at his desk. He pulled his sandwich out of the takeaway bag, not quite able to contain the smile that tugged at his lips. Kimber was arriving today. In fact, she was probably already here.

Unable to resist, he retrieved his phone from his pocket and pulled up his favorites. He wasn't quite sure how she had ranked into that category so quickly, but it had made sense to add her number there since he called her more frequently than anyone else.

He hit the Call button, and she answered on the second ring.

"I'm so nervous," she said, skipping her traditional greeting. "If this meeting doesn't go well, there's no way I'll get the new job."

"If it's meant to be, it'll happen." Brandon really hoped it was meant to be. He unwrapped his sandwich. "Just be yourself, and everything will be fine."

"Be myself." Her voice trembled slightly. "I'd need to stop shaking to do that."

He set his lunch aside. "Breathe."

He could hear her inhale before she let out a heavy sigh.

"I'm not sure it's helping," she said.

He couldn't help but laugh. "Trust me. Breathing is essential."

A woman's voice sounded in the background.

"Who's that?" he asked.

"My sister. She's telling me to relax too."

"Take her advice," he said. "Also, do you want me to pick you up tonight, or would you rather meet me at the restaurant?"

"I'm not sure how late my meeting is going to go. How about I meet you there?"

"Sounds good." He took a sip of his water bottle. "I'll text you the address."

"Okay. I'll see you tonight."

"And remember, keep breathing."

"Right."

With a smile still on his face, Brandon ended the call and took a bite of his lunch. He looked up the address to the restaurant where he'd made reservations and texted it to Kimber. He hoped she'd have good news to share. Already, he had come to rely on talking to her every night. The possibility of exploring a deeper relationship felt like a fairy tale, one that always seemed to elude him.

He finished his lunch and worked through the latest correspondence Amelia had assigned to him. When he sent the last email, he checked the time on the wall clock across the office. Five more minutes until Kimber's meeting. Within an hour or two, he would find out if she was staying.

His office phone rang, and he answered.

"Kimber Frost and Patricia Banik are on their way up," Amelia said. "Show them into my office as soon as they arrive."

"Of course." Brandon stood as the elevator dinged. He stepped out of his cubicle as two women emerged. His eyes widened when he spotted Kimber. *His Kimber.*

She wore the same white slacks and orange blazer as the day he'd met her, but today, her hair was pinned up into a sleek bun. What was she doing here? That thought had barely formed before two and two added together to equal four. Kimber Frost and Kimber Seidel were the same person. The next realization followed in a flash: Kimber was CIA.

His thoughts still reeling, he adopted his best neutral expression and moved forward to greet them.

Kimber spotted him, and her expression lit with surprise.

Though Brandon wanted to greet her properly, the presence of Mary sitting in a nearby cubicle was enough to deter him.

Before Kimber could speak, Brandon extended his hand to the older woman. "You must be Ms. Banik."

"Yes, and this is Kimber Frost," Patricia said. "We're here to meet with Amelia Franklin."

"I'm Brandon, Amelia's assistant." He shook hands with Patricia before offering his hand to Kimber. "It's nice to meet you both."

Surprise again reflected in Kimber's eyes, and she hesitated slightly before putting her hand in his. "It's nice to meet you, too, Mr.—"

"Hale."

Kimber nodded, her expression no longer readable.

"Please, follow me. Ms. Franklin is expecting you." Drawing upon every ounce of energy to appear calm, he led them to Amelia's office and made the introductions.

He fought to keep his attention on Amelia rather than Kimber. "Is there anything else I can get for you?"

"Would either of you care for something to drink?" Amelia asked Kimber and Patricia.

Kimber shook her head.

Patricia took her seat. "We're fine. Thank you."

Taking his cue, Brandon left the room and closed the door behind him. He returned to his desk and dropped into his chair. This was the job Kimber had been talking about? She'd never mentioned she was a writer. Then again, he'd never mentioned he was with the CIA, not that he could have shared that information even if he'd wanted to. Apparently, they'd both been keeping secrets.

• • •

Kimber's butterflies were gone, replaced by a heavy pit in her stomach. She'd lied to Brandon, and now he was acting like he didn't even know her. Her little white lie couldn't have been worthy of this reaction.

She'd been so excited at the prospect of living in the same city as him. But now she had a new possible problem: He knew her as Kimber Seidel. He knew her real name.

Maybe this move wasn't such a good idea after all.

"I've looked over your terms." Amelia flipped open the folder on her desk. "I have to say, a seven-figure advance is quite a stretch for a debut author, regardless of how much I enjoyed the book."

"We both know you'd pay at least that if we take this book to auction, particularly with the interest we've already received for the movie and international rights." Patricia crossed her legs and leaned back in her chair as though she were perfectly content to take Kimber's work elsewhere. "Kimber's dream has always been to be a Monroe author, but I have advised her that we'll need to entertain other offers unless your price is right."

Amelia focused on Kimber. "What's the latest Monroe novel you read?"

"*Dark Night* by Sarah Ryker."

"That only came out last week."

"Yes. I finished it last night," Kimber said. "It was very well done."

"I agree." Amelia tapped a glossy red fingernail on the paperwork in front of her. "I am concerned that Kimber doesn't have any social media presence to speak of. That's a huge drawback."

"Her website has already been created, and my office is working with her to establish a stronger network online."

Reminding herself that she had a job to do, Kimber forced herself to enter the conversation. "I'm sure my sister can help me with setting up influencers as well. She's Greta Meyer's personal assistant and handles all of Greta's social media accounts."

"Do you have a personal relationship with Greta?"

Kimber nodded. "She's the one who chose this outfit for me." It was true, even though Greta hadn't specifically suggested she wear it today. When Kimber caught a hint of disbelief on Amelia's face, Kimber added, "I was with Greta and my sister in London for Fashion Week earlier this month."

"Having access to people of influence will certainly help, but this price is not something we agree to lightly, particularly for a debut author."

"A million dollars for a two-book deal, which includes Monroe keeping the international distribution," Patricia said firmly. "This book has blockbuster potential, and you know it." She motioned to Kimber. "Besides the manuscript in your hand, Kimber already has two additional books written. You would have your choice of them."

"With an option for the third," Amelia said without missing a beat.

Patricia cast a quick glance at Kimber before nodding. "Agreed."

Kimber goggled at the other two women in the room. Had that just happened? Had Amelia just agreed to pay her a million dollars for writing books? She shook that thought out of her head. The money had to ultimately funnel back to the government somehow, especially if they were fronting the funds for a movie deal.

Almost as soon as the agreement was reached, a man from the legal department joined them. Amelia introduced him as Conrad, and he appeared to be in his late thirties and as slick as his alligator shoes. For the next hour and a half, Patricia argued contract points, negotiated the value of movie and foreign rights, and hashed out editing deadlines and release schedules. They also set up appointments to meet with the marketing team and to sign the final contract.

By the time Conrad left them alone with Amelia again, Kimber's head was spinning.

"One more thing I should mention is that it would be beneficial for Kimber to remain in New York for the next few weeks," Amelia said. "Is that going to be a problem with your current job?"

"No," Kimber said. "Patricia suggested I take the next few weeks off so I'd be available for whatever you need."

"For now, I suggest the two of you get started on your social media campaigns and polishing the next book." Amelia stood. "We're going to do great things together."

Kimber's heartbeat quickened. This was really happening. Two of her books were going to be published.

Kimber stood and shook Amelia's hand. "I look forward to it."

Patricia opened the door and led Kimber into the space between Amelia's office and the cubicle opposite it. Brandon looked up from his desk, his eyes meeting hers.

"I'll see both of you next week," Amelia said. "Brandon, would you walk them out?"

"That's not necessary," Kimber said before Patricia could speak. "We can find our way."

Kimber nodded a farewell to Amelia and then headed down the hall without a backward glance.

•　•　•

Brandon pulled out his mobile phone the moment the elevator doors closed. He'd text Kimber and apologize for pretending he didn't know her.

Amelia motioned to him before he could pull up his favorites list. "I need to see you."

His heart sank. He slipped his phone back into his pocket and grabbed a notepad and pen before following Amelia into her office.

"Close the door and sit down."

Brandon did so. "Did your meeting go well?"

"Yes, and because of that, we have a lot of work to do." Amelia put her hand on the manuscript on the corner of her desk. "I need you to set up meetings for me with marketing this afternoon. Once you do that, draft an email to the board of directors to inform them of the pending contract with Kimber Frost." She handed him a piece of paper with bullet points of the main contractual details.

Brandon's eyes widened when he noted the amount of the advance. Kimber was about to earn a million dollars on her first book deal. At least, he thought this was her first contract under her pen name. He'd already done a deep search on the internet to see if she had other publications under her real last name, but Kimber Seidel barely had any presence online. Then again, maybe Frost was her real name. Either way, the CIA had clearly created one of her identities. He looked forward to finding out what was truth and what was fiction.

"As soon as you draft that email, get down to legal," Amelia continued, breaking into his thoughts. "Conrad should know to expedite Kimber's contract, but tell him I want it no later than the end of next week."

"I'll take care of it." He added legal to his to-do list. "Is there anything else?"

"That'll do for now."

He left the room and returned to his desk. As soon as he sat down, he made the call to the marketing director and set up the meeting for three o'clock. He then opened a new document on his computer. Though he itched to pull out his mobile to text Kimber, he focused on his current task. This email to the board of directors was his first writing assignment since starting this job, beyond the evaluation Amelia had delegated to him. If he wanted to continue earning Amelia's trust, the email needed to be perfect.

Brandon stared at the blank document for a full minute before placing his fingers on the keyboard. Short and succinct. That was what Amelia would want. He hoped.

He crafted the message and read through it three times before he copied and pasted it into an email to Amelia.

He clicked Send, then pushed back from his desk and crossed to Amelia's office. "I'm heading down to legal. I'll be back in a minute."

"What about the email to the board of directors?"

"It should be in your inbox."

"That was fast." She opened her email and skimmed over it. "I'll have my edits for you when you get back."

Brandon nodded. He had secretly hoped Amelia would take his draft email as written. He should have known better. After all, her job was to constantly look for ways to improve other people's words.

As soon as he reached the elevator, he pulled out his phone and texted Kimber. *Sorry about today. I'll explain later.*

He stepped out on the ninth floor and debated whether he should add an explanation now, but when one of the legal secretaries walked into the hall, he hit Send and pocketed his phone.

"Is Conrad in his office?" he asked.

"Yes, but he's busy working on a new contract."

"I know." Brandon moved past her. "That's why I'm here."

CHAPTER 15

HE WOULD EXPLAIN later. Kimber paced the length of her sister's living room and read Brandon's text for the twentieth time.

She sidestepped her suitcases stacked at the end of the couch, her body trembling from the adrenaline still coursing through her. She'd told one little white lie about who she hoped to work for here in New York. That couldn't have been reason enough for him to treat her like she didn't exist. They'd been talking every day for the past week. Sure, that didn't mean they were officially dating, and they were a long way from exclusive, but she'd thought they were at least friends. And friends didn't pretend they didn't know each other. Well, except for her friends from the agency, but that was only because she could never be sure if they were undercover or not.

Brandon was hardly a CIA operative. He worked at a publishing house, for heaven's sake. Not to mention, she had no interest in dating anyone at the agency, undercover or not.

The events of the day rushed through her mind, from the moment she'd seen Brandon to her meeting with Amelia. A seven-figure, two-book deal. Even with the government backing her, she hadn't expected that. Dreamed about it, yes, but only in her wildest imaginations, the ones she kept tucked in the secret part of her heart that she didn't share with anyone.

The door to her sister's apartment opened, and Tessa walked in. Her brow lifted. "Well?" She closed the door. "How did it go?"

Kimber stopped circling the room, not sure how to answer.

Tessa studied her, sympathy blooming on her face. "You're upset. What happened?"

"I saw Brandon."

"The guy you've been talking to?"

"Yeah." Kimber dropped onto the couch. "He's the managing editor's assistant."

"And?" Tessa set her purse on the coffee table and sat beside Kimber.

"And he acted like he'd never seen me before."

"Is it possible he didn't recognize you?" Tessa asked.

"We went out on Friday night and spent all day Saturday together." Kimber motioned at the orange blazer hanging off a kitchen chair. "I was even wearing the same outfit as when we met." She furrowed her brow at that thought. "Which is kind of embarrassing actually." Kimber lifted her hand and waved that thought away. "Besides, we FaceTime as often as we talk on the phone. He saw me on his screen a half dozen times this week."

"I'm sorry." Tessa put her hand on Kimber's knee. "I wonder why he acted like that."

"I have no idea." Unless he really was holding a grudge against her for misleading him.

Tessa leaned back on the couch and tucked one leg underneath her. "What about your meeting with the publisher?"

"With Brandon's boss?" A fresh wave of wonder washed over her. "It looks like I'll be staying in New York for at least a couple weeks."

"What about work?"

Phrasing her comment carefully, Kimber said, "If everything goes well, I won't be working at my current job much longer."

Tessa's eyes widened. "They offered you a contract?"

Kimber couldn't help but smile. "My agent hammered out the details today."

"Oh my gosh!" Tessa squealed and threw her arms around Kimber. "I can't believe this!"

"I can't either." Kimber hugged her sister for a moment before easing back. "Patricia thinks we could have the contract finalized in the next two to three weeks."

"And you're going to stay in New York that whole time?"

"Amelia mentioned that it would be helpful." Kimber shrugged. "I'm not sure why." That much was true.

"If you don't mind the couch, you can stay as long as you want."

"Thanks, but Patricia has an apartment she said I can stay at. I can move in on Wednesday."

"That's great, but are you really going to quit the CIA?" Tessa asked, disbelief carrying in her voice. "You love your job."

"I know." Find a grain of truth. "I do love working for the CIA, but I've always wanted to be an author."

"I guess the CIA probably wouldn't be crazy about you trying to get famous while working for them."

That was exactly what they wanted her to do. Focusing on more important issues, Kimber said, "I do need a favor from you."

"What's that?"

"The CIA knows about my meeting today and what happened. They don't want me to tell people that I worked for them."

"Why not?" Tessa asked. "I thought you were allowed to tell people that."

"I was, but it's for my protection and yours."

"Why would I need protection?"

"You travel overseas a lot. If my books do well, I could end up with some overseas tours too," Kimber said. "The CIA doesn't want us to become targets for people who might take advantage of my association with them."

Tessa crinkled her nose in disbelief. "You don't actually think someone would try to kidnap one of us, do you?"

"I'm sure my old bosses are just being overly cautious, but if keeping this secret will ensure our safety, I think it's worth it."

Tessa shrugged. "If that's what you want, but it really is too bad. I mean, you writing spy thrillers and working for the CIA is kind of cool."

"Trust me. The day-to-day life at CIA headquarters isn't nearly as exciting as people think it is."

"You're just saying that because you have to."

Kimber laughed. "Maybe."

"Don't worry." Tessa slipped off her shoes. "You can trust me."

"Thanks." Kimber's stomach twisted uncomfortably. Kimber could trust her, but she couldn't tell her the truth.

. . .

Brandon stood outside the restaurant, and with every passing minute, his concern increased that Kimber wasn't going to show. She was already ten minutes late.

A hollowness started in his chest and expanded outward. He still couldn't believe she'd walked into his office today. What were the chances? And how many times had that exact thought flowed through his mind? First, they sit next to each other on the plane, in first class no less. Then they randomly run into each other in the middle of Manhattan. And now this. Whether this was divine intervention or fate, somehow, they had been destined to meet. Now if he could just talk to Kimber to explain why he'd acted the way he had. Surely she would understand once she learned who he really was and that his behavior had been rooted in the same reason she had neglected to tell him her meeting today was with Monroe.

All around him, people rushed by, some couples walking arm in arm, other people hurrying to or from work. The scent of fresh bread and grilled meat wafted from the restaurant behind him.

Someone bumped into him as they passed by. Brandon glanced at the man in the dark overcoat and did a quick assessment. Just a businessman paying more attention to his phone than where he was walking. Brandon stepped closer to the restaurant entrance and tapped his screen. *Are you coming? We need to talk.*

Yes, we do. I'm almost there.

Relieved beyond words, he entered the restaurant. Red-and-white-checkered tablecloths covered round tables in the center of the dining area, booths lining the walls. Low candles flickered behind red-glass globes, and nearly all the tables were filled.

He gave his name to the hostess and turned his attention to the wide window and the busy Manhattan sidewalk beyond.

He'd been here only two weeks, but already, he could pretend he'd opted to follow his original plans: graduate from Brown, land a job with a publisher, eventually work his way up to become an editor.

He shook those thoughts away. After his dad died, the CIA had given Brandon the money to pay tuition along with a new sense of purpose. Maybe someday, he'd learn if that particular stroke of fate had been as his recruiter had claimed—Brandon coming to their attention through an article he had written—or if there was more to it than that. He'd long suspected it was the latter, just as he suspected his father had been far more than an analyst working for a Tucson communications company.

Brandon spotted Kimber approaching, and he moved to open the door for her. The instinct to take her hand and kiss her cheek swept over him, but he fought against it. The firm set of Kimber's jaw told him neither gesture would be welcome.

"Thanks for coming," he said instead.

Kimber simply lifted her eyebrows as though expecting him to explain regardless of the others crowded by the hostess stand, waiting for their tables.

He lifted his hand to signal to the hostess that his date had arrived. The woman retrieved two menus and motioned for them to follow. They wove past the crowded tables in the dimly lit room to a booth in the corner.

They took their seats and accepted the menus the hostess handed them.

"Your server will be with you shortly," she said.

"Thanks." Brandon waited for the hostess to leave before he set his menu aside.

"Look, I'm sorry I lied about who I was interviewing with," Kimber said without preamble. "I know I should have told you the truth, but I was afraid to talk about my writing in case today ended in disappointment."

"I understand."

"Then, why did you act like you'd never seen me before?"

"Because I read your manuscript." He didn't miss the flush in her cheeks, nor did he understand it. "I pushed it to the top of the pile. I went to bat for it." Brandon paused as he let those details sink in.

Awareness lit her eyes. "Wait, are you saying . . . ?" Her voice trailed off.

Brandon put his hand on hers and leaned across the table. Whispering in her ear, he said, "The publishing house isn't our only common employer."

He leaned back, Kimber's expression transforming from disbelief to acceptance.

"You're the—" Again, she stopped herself midsentence.

Brandon nodded. "I can't lose this job," he said. "Not to mention, I told Amelia I'd never met you."

"You didn't know we'd met," she said, an odd sort of resignation in her voice. "I was using a pen name."

"I know that now, but I couldn't let Amelia or anyone in the office think I'd pushed your book because of our relationship, especially since they're planning for it to be one of next year's lead titles."

"So, you pretended we'd never seen each other before."

"Yes."

Kimber picked up her purse. "I should go."

"Amelia's eating on the other side of town. There's no chance she'll see us. And you're already here," Brandon said. "Let me buy you dinner."

"Thanks, but no." Kimber slid out of her seat and leaned down so only he could hear her. "I'm not a risk taker, and this is too much of a risk." She straightened. "It was good seeing you again." She turned and left, and Brandon could do nothing but watch her go.

• • •

Kimber still couldn't believe it. What were the chances that two CIA employees would end up sitting next to each other in first class, accidentally meet again in the middle of Manhattan, experience a connection, and then end up working together? The odds had to be somewhere north of astronomical.

She pushed her way through the crowded subway platform as the train on the track opposite her screeched to a stop.

Maybe it was a good thing she hadn't told Mark about Brandon. He'd be the first to insist she not discount Brandon as potential boyfriend material because of his job, but how could she not? As much as she loved talking to Brandon, the man was, in essence, her partner. He wasn't just someone who had a cover story she needed to protect. He was the person whose cover story was helping protect her.

Someone bumped into her, and she automatically grabbed her purse. Her fingers grazed against a man's hand.

Instinct kicked in, and she grabbed the man's thumb, twisting it before she identified who that particular appendage belonged to. The man standing behind her yelped in pain.

Ignoring him, she yanked her partially open purse in front of her so she could make sure her wallet was still inside. Once she caught a glimpse of red leather, she used her available hand to zip her purse back up.

"Let go of me!" the man demanded.

The situation caught up with her in a rush. Someone had tried to steal her wallet. And she had stopped him.

Anger and frustration rose inside her, in part from the situation with Brandon and in part from the man who had tried to rob her. She turned to face the culprit, a lean man in his late twenties. She twisted his thumb a little harder. "Next time you try to steal my wallet, I'm going to break your thumb."

The man nodded, his Adam's apple bobbing up and down.

Kimber released him, and immediately, he took off through the crowd.

A woman standing beside her spoke. "That was impressive, but you might want to invest in a purse that doesn't have a zipper on the top. Too easy of a target."

"Thanks for the advice."

"No problem." The woman turned to face Kimber, her perfectly manicured hand gripping the top of her own purse, a black Kate Spade worn cross-body. "I'm Evangeline."

"Kimber." Kimber narrowed her eyes. The woman appeared to be a few years older than her and had an awareness about her common to those living in large cities, but in Kimber's experience, New Yorkers didn't typically introduce themselves on the subway. "Do you work here in Manhattan?"

"Work here. Live here," Evangeline said. "I moved here after college and never left. What about you?"

"I'm visiting my sister." That much was true, even if the visit would end on Wednesday when Kimber moved into her new apartment.

"Fun. How long are you here for?"

"I haven't decided yet." Or rather, the CIA hadn't decided for her yet.

Their train approached, and the doors whooshed open. Passengers spilled out, and more crowded into the already packed train. Keeping her hand firmly on her purse, Kimber maneuvered to a grab bar by the door. Evangeline ended up beside her.

"Have you visited New York before?" Evangeline asked.

"A few times." Enough times to know this wasn't normal.

The train wheezed to a stop. More people got off and on. Kimber maintained her position near the door. She had only two more stops to go.

"Are you doing anything fun while you're in town?" Evangeline asked as the train started moving again.

"Just hanging out." Kimber glanced up at the map on the side of the train that listed the upcoming stops.

The CIA protocols she'd learned when first joining the agency echoed through her thoughts. When the train stopped the next time, Kimber hesitated long enough to see if Evangeline was getting off. When she didn't move, Kimber slipped past the people coming on the train. "Have a good night."

Without waiting to see if the woman followed, Kimber strode quickly down the length of the platform. She glanced over her shoulder then, not spotting Evangeline but not sure she'd be able to see the woman through the sea of people anyway.

Kimber had two choices. She could wait here for the next train, or she could exit here and walk the rest of the way to her sister's apartment. Of course, once Kimber arrived at her sister's place, Tessa would want to know why she'd cut her date short.

Not prepared for that conversation, she made her way to the exit. Maybe she could find a quiet spot to eat dinner and call Mark. With any luck, he could talk her through a way to tell Tessa the truth without giving away the real reason she was about to have a publishing contract and why her budding relationship had come to a screeching halt. Of course, she'd have to admit to Mark that she'd been talking to Brandon in the first place and hadn't ever told him about it.

A heaviness pressed in on her as she considered the loss of Brandon's friendship and what life would be like now that he was no longer part of her daily routine.

She reached street level and headed in the general direction of her sister's apartment. She passed one restaurant after another, each as busy as the next. So much for finding a quiet place to talk. Only a few more days. Then she would have her own place, where she would hopefully find some peace and solitude.

With no easy diversion to avoid going back to Tessa's apartment, Kimber continued down the sidewalk. She would have to face her sister eventually, with or without a pep talk on how to lie about why Brandon was no longer someone she could feasibly date.

A tightness formed in her chest that could be described only as heartache. She sighed. She barely knew Brandon. It wouldn't take long to get over him.

She reached Tessa's apartment and used her key to let herself in.

Tessa looked up from where she sat on the couch, the remote control in her hand. Sympathy instantly shone on her face. "Oh no. What happened?"

What happened? Kimber fumbled for words. "Let's just say Brandon isn't who I thought he was."

"Are you going to explain that to me?"

Kimber shook her head. "No." She set her purse down and dropped onto the couch beside Tessa. "What are we watching?"

"*The Devil Wears Prada*."

"You've seen that movie a dozen times."

"I know, but it's a good one." Tessa shrugged. "And I didn't have anything better to do tonight."

Kimber cocked an eyebrow. "How many invitations did you turn down?"

"Only three." Tessa stretched her legs out to reveal her feet clad in fuzzy pink socks. "But tonight my feet needed a break from high heels."

"Maybe we should focus on your love life for a while instead of mine."

"Or better yet, we can work on your social platform." Tessa picked up her phone and turned it toward Kimber. "I've been planning your social media campaign."

"I haven't even signed my contract yet."

"It doesn't matter," Tessa insisted. "Patricia said you need to create a stronger online presence, and that's exactly what we're going to do this weekend."

"That sounds exhausting."

Tessa's eyes brightened the way they always did when she was planning something Kimber wouldn't like. "Oh, you have no idea."

CHAPTER 16

AN ENTIRE WEEKEND wishing he could talk to Kimber and knowing she was determined to keep her distance from him. Brandon had tested his theory that she wouldn't answer his calls twice on Saturday and once on Sunday. The handful of text messages he'd sent had also gone unanswered.

Now, here he was, back at the office, where news of Kimber's contract and the endless potential of her manuscript was buzzing about. Hardback, paperback, digital, audio, movie deals, international distribution, media tours. Every department was working overtime to make sure the contract went through and that they were all ready for when the deal hit the papers. And it would hit the papers. That would be the first wave of media hype for Kimber's manuscript now slated to come out a year from October.

Monroe Publishing was moving fast to secure their new rising star, and Brandon was trying not to think about her. Trying and failing.

She really had been too good to be true: smart, beautiful, easy to talk to. Their shared interests had created a bond between them, and now their shared employer had frayed that bond.

He hated that she'd stepped away from the potential simmering between them, but he couldn't deny that she was probably wise in doing so. Someone connected to Finlay's death worked in this building, and that someone would likely kill again if he or she perceived a threat to Labyrinth's funding stream.

A stone dropped in his stomach at that thought. Finlay was dead because Brandon had failed to protect him. Even though Kimber was also CIA, part of his job was to keep her safe. Doing that while pretending they barely knew each other was a challenge he would soon have to navigate.

Of course, if he could figure out who was involved with Labyrinth, he could ensure her safety as well as his own, but thus far, his access to the various departments had been limited to making appointments for Amelia. Rarely did he get the opportunity to see the top execs, much less speak with them.

Amelia walked out of her office. "Brandon, grab your laptop. I need you to take notes."

Take notes at the department head meeting? This was a first. A welcome one at that.

Brandon retrieved his laptop and fell in behind Amelia as she strode down the hall toward the conference room. When they walked in, three people were already seated at the oval table in the center of the room. Amelia took her spot beside Haseeb, the director of marketing. Across from them, Savannah, the sales director, already had her laptop open on the table in front of her, a thick stack of papers beside her. Two seats down was a man Brandon hadn't yet met, but based on the staff portfolios the agency had provided for him, he was Ramon Alvarez, the CFO of Monroe Publishing and one of the men at the top of Brandon's suspect list.

Not sure how many people would be at the meeting, Brandon moved to one of the chairs lining the wall behind where Amelia now sat.

"Brandon, sit here at the table." Amelia motioned to the spot next to her.

Brandon pulled out the chair she'd indicated, but he didn't miss the little lift of Ramon's eyebrow, a subtle show of his surprise.

Brandon set his laptop on the desk and opened a new document to take notes.

He started by listing the individuals present, adding to it as new arrivals walked in: Jamal, director of new products; Conrad from legal; Margaret, the art director; and Whitney, the social media manager.

"I have some good news." Whitney took her seat and lifted her phone. "Kimber Frost already has over fifteen hundred followers on Instagram."

"How?" Amelia asked. "She only had four hundred twelve when she came in on Friday."

"She probably bought followers." Savannah shook her head in disapproval.

"I don't think so," Whitney said. "She was tagged on Greta Meyer's account twice, and she posted a reel from the New York City Library that has several hundred likes. Her engagement is way too high for her followers to be bought."

Amelia tapped a red, polished fingernail on the table. "She mentioned she was connected to Greta Meyer, but I didn't expect this much traction so quickly."

Neither had Brandon. Somehow, he'd imagined Kimber spending the weekend mourning the loss of their budding relationship, much like he had. Based on the picture Whitney painted, Kimber hadn't had time to miss him.

He pulled out his phone and checked Kimber's Instagram page. Six posts since Friday night, all of them featuring Kimber front and center as she explored the city she hoped would become her new home.

"If her social media efforts are any indication of what we can expect from her, this amount on her advance might be justified after all," Conrad said. He picked up the stack of papers beside him and passed them to each person at the table except Brandon. "The movie deal alone will cover our initial outlay, and if we're smart on how we price our preorders, the initial sales on the first book should recoup a good portion of our second payment."

"In that case, let's talk marketing." Jamal pushed his glasses more firmly onto the bridge of his nose. "The sooner we can line her up on the top podcasts and talk shows, the better."

Haseeb opened his laptop and tapped on the keys. "I've already reached out to Top Shelf about featuring Kimber on their podcast when this deal hits the trades."

"That's a good start," Jamal said. "Keep at it."

"How soon will the contracts be ready?" Amelia asked.

"The review copy will go out to all of you this afternoon." Conrad tapped his fountain pen on his leather portfolio. "As soon as I have everyone's comments, we'll need a day for a final review."

"I want this contract signed by the end of the week," Amelia said. "Everyone, send your comments back to Conrad by noon on Wednesday."

"It's been a while since we've moved a contract through this quickly." Ramon leaned back in his chair. "Are you sure we shouldn't take some more time with this?"

"With the movie deal looming, we need to act fast." Jamal scrawled something on the notepad in front of him. "I'd like to have those rights go to auction next month."

"Why are you sending it to auction?" Ramon asked. "We already have a lucrative deal on the table."

"Yes, but I think we can get more for it," Jamal said. "We've already heard rumors that Seaswept Studios and Knight Entertainment are interested too."

Ramon tilted his head. "They're only interested because they heard about the existing offer."

"Which pushes up the price tag for us," Jamal said.

Brandon listened to the possibilities bounce back and forth, typing the various points on his laptop as he did so. The CIA had expected to front millions of dollars in their efforts to take down Labyrinth. Based on what he was hearing, the buzz they created would take over the financial burden for them.

"Movie deals are all fine and good," Savannah said, "but we need to line up our international distribution. Since we lost David Unger, we have a serious gap in our market in the UK."

"What are we thinking when it comes to foreign translation?" Conrad asked. "Our exports to Finland, France, and Germany could use some bolstering."

"Let's get the contract signed before we worry about that," Jamal said.

The meeting morphed into editorial and production timelines, Brandon struggling to keep up with all the dates they threw around the table. By the time the meeting ended, Brandon's head was spinning.

Amelia pushed back from the table. "Brandon, email those timelines to me and Conrad. We'll need those to put the deadlines in the contract."

"I'll send them to you as soon as I get back to my desk." And as soon as he cleaned up his notes so they were decipherable to someone other than him. Even with the jumble of information, one thing was certain: Based on the deadlines and marketing schedule, Brandon didn't know how Kimber was ever going to find time to write another book.

CHAPTER 17

KIMBER ROLLED OVER on the couch and cracked her eyes open when footsteps padded across the hardwood floor. She'd stayed up way too late last night reading the latest Jack Carr thriller and even later trying not to think about Brandon. Now, with her latest revisions emailed back to Patricia, she needed something new to distract her.

Despite spending Saturday night at a party with Tessa and her boss, Kimber's mind kept replaying that moment when Brandon had whispered to her who his primary employer was. She still couldn't quite believe it. Why did he have to be CIA? And undercover CIA, at that.

Kimber sat up as her sister lowered into a kitchen chair to put her shoes on.

"Sorry," Tessa said. "I didn't mean to wake you."

"It's fine. What time is it anyway?"

"Almost six." Tessa stood and grabbed her purse and keys off the table. "Greta wants me to escort one of her clients to an appointment for a fitting."

"This early in the morning?"

"The client is up for an Oscar."

"Ah." Secrecy. Kimber could relate to that.

Tessa headed for the door. "See you later."

Kimber lay back on the couch, debating whether she should get up or try to go back to sleep. Technically, she didn't have anything to do today. She hadn't had anything to do yesterday either, but after spending all of Monday pacing Tessa's apartment and studying images of the key executives at Monroe, she needed a change of pace.

If she was going to play the part of author, maybe it was time to write another book. Or at least keep working on one.

She kicked off her blankets and reached for her laptop, which was charging on the end table. She'd barely opened her latest manuscript when her phone rang. Mark.

She answered. "Why are you calling me so early?"

"I'm on my way to work, and this is the first time I could call when you weren't with your agent or your sister."

She hadn't been with Patricia or Tessa on Friday night.

Mark's words caught up with her. "How did you know that I've been with Tessa and Patricia since I've been here?"

"I'm tracking the locations of their phones."

"That's disturbing. And probably illegal."

"You know me better than that," Mark said. "I got the FBI to sign off on the traces."

"Why would they do that?"

"Because after I reported to Director Yarrow that I found out about your assignment, he pulled me into your circle of need to know. I'm now working the finance side of the Monroe case."

That got her attention. "How did that happen?"

"Director Yarrow wanted someone to coordinate with the FBI, and since I already knew about your cover, I got the job."

"That's great. Have you found anything yet?"

"No. I spent all day yesterday searching for funding streams between Labyrinth and Monroe, but the only large payments we've found on Monroe's side besides advances to their authors and royalties twice a year are the payments to marketing firms and printers. So far, everything looks legit."

"Let me know if anything does pop up. I hate not having access."

"From what my FBI contact said, you'll have secure access once you move into your new apartment."

"They said I could move in tomorrow," she said.

"Are you sure that's a good idea? No one is going to believe you leased an apartment before you have your contract signed," he said. "Least of all Tessa."

"I already told her Patricia offered to set me up with an apartment to use while I'm here."

"Quick thinking." A touch of admiration carried in his voice when he added, "You're finally getting the hang of this lying thing."

"No, but I'm learning to stretch the truth the way you taught me. Patricia was in the room when Agent Ebeid talked to me about the apartment."

Mark laughed. "Like I said, you're getting the hang of this."

"I'm not sure that's a good thing." Had she been worse at lying, maybe Brandon would have learned the truth about her sooner. She missed him. And she missed Mark. "I don't suppose you want to come up and visit this weekend. I could use a friendly face who isn't trying to get me to pose for photos to put on my Instagram."

"I'm way ahead of you. I already put in a travel request to work in New York for the rest of the week."

"Really?" A surge of hope rose inside her. "It would be way easier to talk if you were here, but do you think Director Yarrow will sign off on it?"

"I guess you've been too busy working on your social media accounts to look at the news."

"What are you talking about?"

"The conflict in Syria escalated this weekend. Looks like they got a new supply of weapons."

"You think Labyrinth was behind it?"

"They're tied into it somehow."

"Sounds like both of us are going to be busy staring at intel reports today," Kimber said. "Of course, if you come up tonight, you could help me move in tomorrow."

"How much help do you need?" Mark asked. "You took three suitcases with you."

"Yes, but you could pick up a few things from my apartment for me."

"You want me to haul more books up there, don't you?"

"Just a few more."

"I might be persuaded, but only if we can hang out with your sister sometime this weekend."

"You're assuming you'll want to be around Tessa this weekend," Kimber said. "She's made it her mission to get me more followers on social media."

"It looks like the two of you had a great time on Saturday night."

"You're following me on Instagram?"

"I am now, but I saw the photos on Tessa's account."

"Now I really am worried about you."

He laughed. "I'm almost to headquarters. I'll call you tonight to let you know if my travel order got approved."

"Sounds good." Kimber propped her feet on the coffee table. "And I'll text you a list of books I want."

"Five max," Mark warned. "That's the best you'll get out of me."

It was better than nothing. "Fine. I'll send you the list."

• • •

Asadi didn't appreciate interruptions during his weekly golf game, especially when he was playing an unfamiliar course. Yet he couldn't resist answering this call.

"What's the latest?" Asadi asked.

"I may have found a new author for you to use," his key contact said.

Asadi walked a few meters away from the three men currently playing with him. Their game could wait. A new author to help them hide funding would allow Labyrinth to replenish their reserves after their upcoming operations. "Who is he?"

"She. Her name is Kimber Frost."

The name wasn't one Asadi had heard before. "Is she one of ours, or do we plan to turn her?"

"Neither. Her contract is seven figures and already has international interest." The man was clearly excited. "With the potential book shipments and international advance copies, this single author can open the channels that closed down when David Unger had his unfortunate change of heart."

"What about the funding?" Asadi asked. "This Frost woman will certainly notice if she doesn't get paid."

"I can fix the paperwork to double the payments. I'll send half to a new international agent Frost doesn't know about."

Asadi rubbed his lips together. Payments coming into Europe that he could easily access, freight shipments disguised as books, hidden messages sent through advance reader copies. This was exactly what he needed. "Best make sure the contract goes through without a problem."

"It's already under final review."

"What about my man there? He hasn't found the person he's looking for."

"I'll see if we can get him assigned to work the security desk tomorrow. That way he can see everyone coming and going."

"Good. He needs to finish his job and get back here."

"Understood."

CHAPTER 18

THE CONTRACTS WERE done. Brandon had let Amelia know only twenty minutes ago, and he'd already reached out to Patricia to set up a signing meeting on Friday. That would give marketing one final day to prepare for the media frenzy they hoped to create when the deal was signed.

Friday. That was the day when Kimber would have to see him whether she wanted to or not.

He cringed inwardly at what she was about to do. A CIA employee willingly stepping into the spotlight—this was wrong in so many ways.

An alarm went off on Brandon's phone, a reminder to pick up Amelia's dinner order. He suppressed a sigh. Working after hours wouldn't be so bad if it didn't include being treated as an errand boy. He had no idea why Amelia had thus far forbidden him to use DoorDash or Uber Eats. Apparently, she was convinced that her order wouldn't be right if someone she trusted wasn't there to check it for her.

He headed down to the lobby and walked past the two guards at security with barely a backward glance. The walk to Amelia's favorite restaurant took several minutes longer than it should have because of the freezing rain and slick sidewalks, and when he finally returned twenty minutes later, only one guard remained at the desk.

Brandon checked his watch. Four minutes until Amelia's self-appointed dinnertime. He made his way through the handful of people leaving for the day and fought back a wave of envy. He would love to leave at a reasonable hour tonight, not that he had anything exciting to do beyond fixing dinner and checking his phone to see if Kimber had decided to respond to his calls or texts.

He reached the executive elevator as the doors opened. Haseeb, Margaret, and Savannah filed out. Brandon waited for them to pass before he entered. Shifting the takeaway bag into his left hand, he hit the button for his floor. The doors started to close, but someone thrust his hand into the opening at the last second. The doors opened again, and a man entered the small space.

The moment Brandon glanced at the man's face, Brandon's heartbeat quickened. He hadn't ever seen this man before in person, but he'd seen his face repeatedly over the past two weeks. Darragh Byrne was the man believed to have murdered Finlay Addington.

Disbelief morphed into questions. Darragh was wearing a security guard uniform. Was he working at Monroe as part of the Labyrinth organization, or did he have another purpose for being here? And if it was the latter, who had he been sent here to kill?

The moment the elevator doors closed and they started upward, Brandon got the answer to his last question.

Darragh hit the button for an emergency stop and reached for his waistband, undoubtedly to retrieve the weapon he had holstered there. Brandon did a quick assessment of whether he could draw his own pistol before Darragh aimed at him. The answer was no.

Not giving Darragh the chance to complete his intended movement, Brandon dropped the takeaway bag to the floor and rushed forward. He thrust his forearm against the assassin's throat and shoved him against the elevator wall.

Darragh lifted one hand to grip Brandon's arm and used his other hand to retaliate with a jab to Brandon's midsection.

Brandon's eyes watered with pain, and his breath whooshed out of him. He stumbled back, nearly stepping on Amelia's dinner. Ignoring his throbbing abs, Brandon threw a punch of his own. Darragh dodged the right cross, but the following left hook caught the man in the jaw.

Blood pooled at the corner of Darragh's lips. He lifted a finger and wiped at the smear of red. His eyes narrowed. "You'll die for that."

"You plan to kill me anyway," Brandon countered, his fists raised. "I'm surprised you didn't try to in Castle Combe."

"My mistake."

Intel was right. Darragh was indeed Finlay's killer, and the man's role in all this burned through Brandon. Brandon dropped his fists and drew his pistol. He'd barely aimed when Darragh struck out his hand, connecting with Brandon's gun hand.

Brandon managed to maintain possession of his weapon, but Darragh gripped his wrist and twisted. Brandon yelped in pain as his pistol fell to the floor.

A bolt of panic streaked through him when Darragh reached for his own weapon. Brandon's life, his future, depended on the next few moments. Relying on his training and instinct, he kicked out, his foot connecting with Darragh's hand. The Glock went flying, hitting the elevator wall before dropping onto the takeaway bag. Styrofoam crunched beneath the weight of the weapon.

Cringing inwardly, Brandon tried not to think about Amelia's reaction when she received her dinner in a damaged container. Of course, if he didn't survive the next few minutes, he wouldn't have to deal with it anyway.

Darragh surged toward his gun, but Brandon kicked out again, blocking his forward progress, but this time, Darragh was ready for him. He grabbed Brandon's leg and yanked, pulling him off-balance and sending him crashing to the floor right beside where his pistol had landed.

Darragh reached for his gun. Brandon grabbed his own.

Both men aimed, but Brandon was faster, squeezing the trigger twice before Darragh could fire off a shot.

Darragh stared at Brandon, his eyes glazing over as his knees buckled, and he dropped to the floor. Not taking any chances, Brandon stepped on the man's wrist and confiscated his weapon before checking him for a pulse.

Darragh's rapid heartbeat thumped beneath his fingers. Then, over the course of a minute, it slowed and ceased entirely.

Brandon blew out a breath. Darragh Byrne was dead, and Brandon had killed him.

Brandon's stomach churned uncomfortably, and bile rose in his throat.

He fought the sensation and the knowledge that he had taken someone's life. He was still reeling when his phone rang with a call from Amelia.

Fighting for calm, he accepted the call, his hand trembling. He cleared his throat before speaking. "Hey, Amelia. I'll be back in the office in another minute or two."

"Don't bother coming back. I'm leaving for the day."

Brandon glanced at the crushed dinner container, and relief poured through him. He'd survived his encounter with Darragh, and now he would be able to avoid one with Amelia. "Just so you know, the executive elevator isn't working right now."

Amelia huffed out an exasperated breath. "Fine. I'll use the regular one."

Which would buy him a little time. He took a deep breath of his own. "I'll see you tomorrow, then."

"I want you here by seven thirty. We have a lot of work to do," she said. "And make sure maintenance gets that elevator repaired."

"Yes, Amelia." He sagged against the elevator wall. After he ended the call, he pulled up Rafi Ebeid's number and hit the Call button. "Hey, I have a mess I need cleaned up."

"What kind of mess?"

"The kind that needs a body bag and a lot of discretion." Brandon proceeded to share the events of the past few minutes.

When he finished, Rafi said, "Stay in the elevator. I'll call you when my people get there."

"We can't let anyone know I was involved with this."

"No one will even know a death occurred in the building," Rafi said. "Trust me."

The line went dead, and Brandon lowered his phone. Trust Rafi. At the moment, he didn't have a choice.

●　　●　　●

Kimber pulled two suitcases, one with each hand, down the sidewalk, her personal laptop secured inside her backpack. Mark followed behind her, also pulling two suitcases. He'd stopped by Tessa's apartment after dropping his own belongings off at his hotel room.

"Looks like you have some decent restaurants around here." Mark nodded at the Italian place across the street.

A pang of regret rose inside Kimber at the memory of the first time she'd walked through this neighborhood. Seeing Brandon had been such a delightful surprise, and the entire weekend with him had created so many wonderful memories . . . that now served to remind her of what she couldn't have with him.

"This is us." Kimber walked into her building, the implication of what that meant seeping through her. By the end of the week her contract would be signed, and her change of address would become official. New York was now her home, but she'd yet to feel a true sense of permanence despite the likelihood that she would be here for at least the next couple of years.

Mark waited until they'd maneuvered their way into the elevator with all her suitcases before he asked, "How are you feeling about this move?"

"It still doesn't feel real, the move or the reason I'm here." Kimber pressed the button for the eighth floor.

"Maybe it would feel more real if you were the one pulling the suitcases with the books in them."

"No thanks." She glanced down at her bags. "Besides, I take books with me when I go on vacation. That's what this feels like."

"It won't for long," Mark said. "And you did say you wanted to move."

"Yeah." Kimber waited until the doors closed before she continued. "But I didn't expect that a move would include the FBI picking out my apartment for me or that I'd be changing careers." She paused. "Well, sort of changing careers."

"Concentrate on the author part of your life," Mark said. "It will make the rest of it easy."

"Nothing about this assignment sounds easy."

"You can do it," Mark said. "Trust me."

"Last time you told me to trust you, I had to explain to Don why our audit in Reston took all day."

"You have to admit, that barbecue was totally worth stopping for."

"It was an hour out of the way."

"Totally worth it."

Kimber simply shook her head. Sometimes Mark could get a little too excited about food.

They reached their floor, and she exited the elevator into the wide hallway. The wheels of the suitcases caught on the plush gray carpet, and she had to tip both of them onto two wheels to keep them moving forward.

"I can't believe you talked me into bringing all these books." Mark wrestled the suitcases out of the elevator. "It's like carrying an entire library."

"It's not that bad." Kimber checked the apartment numbers until she found hers, the fifth door down from the elevator. She set her luggage beside the door and pulled out her key. "Let's see where I'll be living."

She unlocked the door and reached for the suitcase closest to her.

"You take that one," Mark said. "I'll grab the rest."

Kimber walked into the living room, separated from the kitchen by a counter that ran nearly the entire length of the room. Stainless-steel appliances, white cabinets, four padded stools lining the serving bar. She turned to take in the living space and instantly smiled. A fireplace.

The door clicked closed, and Mark lined her suitcases along the wall beside the door. "I can't believe you have a fireplace." He walked into the room to her left. "Whoa. Look at this."

Kimber found him in a bedroom. Two tall windows were evenly spaced on the long wall, a bed situated beside the far one. Floor-to-ceiling bookshelves framed the other window, and a plush chair occupied the corner beside it to create a cozy reading nook.

She turned in a circle. "This is amazing."

"It's like this apartment was designed for you," Mark said.

"Seriously." Kimber motioned toward an empty space beside the bedroom door. "One more bookshelf there, and I'll be all set."

"If you think you need another bookshelf, I may need to stage an intervention."

"Just one more, and it's getting delivered today."

"Seriously?"

"I didn't know I'd have built-in bookcases in my apartment, and you know I'll be able to fill them."

"You definitely need an intervention."

Ignoring Mark, Kimber returned to the living room and located the instructions on how to turn on the gas for the fireplace. She could already imagine snuggling on the couch with a blanket, a cup of hot chocolate on the end table beside her, her laptop balanced on her legs while she wrote by the fire.

"Before you get distracted with settling in, I need food." Mark motioned toward the door to her left. "Do you want your suitcases in your bedroom?"

"Sure, but if we're going out again, I want to pick up some groceries."

"You're taking advantage of having me here to help you carry them."

"Guilty, but since you brought me more books than I expected, I'll pay for dinner."

"You should pay. You're the one who's about to become a millionaire."

"I'm sure the money will go back to the CIA since they helped set everything up for me."

"That would be the case if the agency had given you the book to put forward as your own, but your writing is your intellectual property. That money is yours." Mark moved the suitcases into the bedroom.

Kimber followed him as far as the doorway. "But what about the money the CIA is fronting?"

"They aren't. Monroe bought the international rights, so the agency didn't have to pay anything there, and a couple other studios are bidding higher than the government's fake offer."

Kimber widened her eyes at the reality he had just set out for her. "The money from Monroe is really going to be mine?"

"It is." Mark headed for the door. "Come on. Let's go. I'm starving."

Kimber opened the door as a woman in her sixties lifted a hand to knock.

Kimber sensed rather than saw Mark move out of view. "Can I help you?" she asked.

"I came by to introduce myself. I'm Trudy." She waved a hand in the direction of the elevator. "I live next door."

"It's nice to meet you. I'm Kimber."

"Welcome to the building." Trudy held out a loaf of bread. "Here's a little something for you. It's banana bread. I thought you might need a snack while you're moving in."

"That's so sweet. Thank you."

"You're welcome." Trudy transferred the banana bread into Kimber's hand and tapped the sticky note affixed to the top. "My phone number is on there in case you need anything."

"I appreciate it." Kimber held up the loaf. "I'd better put this inside."

"Have a good night." Trudy turned and headed back to her apartment, disappearing inside a moment later.

Mark reached for the banana bread. "I can take that."

Kimber held it out of reach. "Oh, no you don't. We'll save this for later."

"But—"

The pitiful look on Mark's face swayed her. "Okay, fine. You can have a piece to take with you."

Mark didn't have to be told twice. With impressive efficiency, he unearthed a knife in one of the drawers and cut off a healthy chunk of the bread. "Do you want a piece?"

"No, thanks."

Mark took a bite. "Mmm. Your loss."

Kimber rolled her eyes. "It'll still be here when we get back."

Mark wrapped the loaf back up. "Okay, I'm ready now."

Kimber took another look around her new apartment before they walked into the hall. An apartment with a reading nook, a fireplace, a large kitchen, and a next-door neighbor who baked. This place was even better than she'd expected.

CHAPTER 19

ONLY FIFTEEN MINUTES passed before Brandon's phone buzzed with an incoming text, but it might as well have been five times that long. Standing in the confined elevator with a dead man was not how he had planned to spend his evening.

His stomach still throbbing from where he'd taken a punch, he read the new message. *Take the elevator to the third floor.*

Eager to get out, he pushed the emergency button to put the elevator back in motion and pressed the three on the control panel. When the doors opened a moment later, two men dressed in custodian uniforms stood on the other side, a custodian cart situated between them.

One of them flashed his badge. "Where's your gun?"

Brandon handed it over.

The first agent took it from him and handed him another pistol. "This is your replacement weapon."

Brandon holstered the Glock. "Now what?"

"Go home. We'll take care of this."

Though curious as to how they were going to remove a dead body without being noticed, Brandon stepped into the third-floor foyer and waited for the two agents to enter the elevator with their cart. As soon as the doors closed, Brandon debated whether to hit the Down button to call another elevator or if he should take the stairs. He took the stairs.

Following standard protocol, he exited the building and took a circuitous route home. When he entered his apartment building thirty minutes later, he was trembling. Whether it was from adrenaline or exhaustion, he couldn't be sure, but he drew a deep breath and fought for calm. What he needed tonight was a hot meal and a good book to distract him from Darragh and how Brandon had killed him.

He held up his trembling hands. Maybe he'd need to trade out the book for a movie.

He crossed the lobby and slowed as he approached the elevators. His stomach clenched. He still wasn't ready to deal with getting into another elevator tonight and opted again for the stairs.

The faint scent of industrial cleaner and stale cigarette smoke hung in the brightly lit stairwell, and his footsteps echoed as he climbed upward. His shadow lengthened as he moved from the first floor to the second, and the cream-colored walls seemed to narrow.

He forced himself to breathe slowly and deeply. Surely his daily workouts had conditioned him enough for the climb to his apartment. He was three steps short of the fifth floor when a door opened somewhere above him and immediately slammed closed.

Brandon stopped, his heart hammering in his chest. Someone else was in the stairwell. Could it be one of Darragh's colleagues? And if so, why would they go to the trouble to kill him?

That thought replayed, and for the first time, the gravity of the situation hit him. Someone had tried to kill him. And whoever had sent Darragh to Monroe might try again.

But why had Brandon become a target? And more importantly, was the other person currently in the stairwell a threat or simply another building resident?

Fresh cigarette smoke wafted toward him from above.

Though the likelihood was low that a second assassin would be waiting for him in his apartment building, Brandon opened the door leading to the fifth floor and crossed the open space to the elevators. He could take the elevator up the last few floors.

Or not. Brandon spotted the sign for another stairwell at the far end of the hall and continued forward. He opened the door, listened for a moment, and then jogged up the remaining stairs to his floor.

Slightly out of breath, he stepped into the hall and glanced at the couple standing two doors down from his apartment, both of them laden with grocery bags.

"I said I'd help you move in," the man said. "That doesn't mean I'm going to rearrange your furniture. And did you have to buy a six-foot bookshelf?"

"I needed the tall one," the woman answered, her dark hair hanging loosely over her shoulders.

Kimber?

She juggled the bags in one hand and dug out her keys. "And I only want to swap the couch and the chair."

"A very heavy-looking couch," the man countered.

Brandon didn't recognize the man—dark-haired, six three, late-twenties—but the familiar voice most definitely belonged to Kimber Seidel. She slid a key into the lock of the door in front of her and pushed it open.

The man turned and sized Brandon up as though evaluating him as a potential threat, stepping protectively between him and Kimber. Though tall and lanky in build, the man looked like he could handle himself if faced with a threat, and his current posture indicated he wasn't sure if Brandon fell into that category.

Kimber disappeared into the apartment, but the man continued to stare at Brandon. He cocked an eyebrow.

It wasn't until that moment that Brandon realized he had stopped walking to stare at Kimber and the man with her. Shaking himself out of his stupor, he pulled his keys out of his pocket and continued forward.

Kimber's friend—Brandon hoped the guy was just a friend—waited until Brandon unlocked his door before following Kimber inside.

Brandon closed his door behind him, his mind racing. It took only a few seconds to put two and two together. Someone in the government had clearly set Kimber up in the same apartment building as him. This wasn't good. He and Kimber were supposed to only know each other professionally, which stung far worse than the injuries he had sustained in the elevator.

A more terrifying prospect emerged, replacing his heartache. If someone wanted him dead, Brandon didn't want Kimber anywhere near him.

He pulled out his phone and dialed Rafi's number.

"I was just about to call you," Rafi said. "Did you make it back to your apartment okay?"

"Yes."

"Good. Do you have time for a quick meeting tonight?"

"Is this a meeting about the man who tried to kill me, or are you going to tell me that Kimber lives two doors down?"

"Both."

"What were you thinking?" Brandon asked, focusing on Kimber's safety rather than his own. "I'm not supposed to know her. If Amelia finds out she lives two doors down, she'll think I arranged for Kimber to get this contract."

"Relax. I have a plan to explain all this," Rafi said. "I told Kimber we'd meet at her place."

"Does she know I live here?"

"I don't think I mentioned it. Why?"

"Just wondering." Brandon should say something about their relationship, but he couldn't quite find a way to put it into words. Technically, they had only gone out on one date.

"I'll be at your apartment in five minutes," Rafi said and ended the call.

Brandon tugged off his tie and debated whether to use those five minutes to change his clothes or find something to eat. The gnawing in his stomach won that battle. He looked down at the drops of blood on his shirt. Okay, so maybe he'd make time for both.

He undid the top two buttons of his pinstriped dress shirt and opened the fridge. What was he thinking? He wasn't going to be able to eat. Someone wanted him dead, which meant either his cover was blown or Darragh remembered him from the night in Castle Combe.

The question was, Did anyone else know Brandon's true identity, or had Darragh taken that secret to his grave?

CHAPTER 20

KIMBER TOOK ANOTHER bite of her lo mein and debated the layout of her furniture. She had hoped to convince Mark to help her shift everything before they ate, but the message from Rafi that he wanted to meet in a few minutes had put a damper on that idea. She only hoped she could take advantage of Mark's presence before he escaped to his hotel after the meeting.

Knuckles rapped against her apartment door in rapid succession.

Mark set aside his chopsticks and stood. "Do you want me to answer it?"

"No. You don't even know what Special Agent Ebeid looks like."

"True," Mark said, but he didn't sit back down.

Kimber crossed to the entrance and peeked through the peephole. As expected, her FBI contact stood in the hall.

She opened the door to find that he wasn't alone. Brandon stood beside him.

Her heart lifted, but then she remembered: Brandon wasn't simply an office worker here in New York. He was agency, and he was an operative.

Without waiting for an invitation, Rafi walked past her and motioned for Brandon to follow. Brandon closed the door behind him.

"You must be Mark." Rafi extended his hand to Mark. "I'm Rafi Ebeid, FBI."

Mark shook his hand. "Good to meet you."

"This is Brandon Hale. Brandon, meet Mark and Kimber."

"Kimber and I have already met," Brandon said, his gaze fixed on her.

Mark's eyebrows lifted, and he cast a curious glance at Kimber.

Kimber gave a slight shake of her head, a subtle signal she hoped Mark would catch, that his interrogation could wait until they were alone. She circled to the couch. "Does everyone want to sit down?"

She wasn't sure how it happened, but instead of Mark claiming the seat on the couch beside her, Brandon ended up in that spot.

"I'm afraid I don't have any updates from Monroe about my contract," Kimber said.

"I do." Brandon shifted on the couch so he was facing her, and his body trembled as though he were having trouble sitting still. "The contracts are done, and I've already talked to Patricia. You're scheduled to sign on Friday."

Two more days of anonymity. Two more days until she would have to become a real author and have to pretend that writing was her only career. She clenched both hands.

As though sensing her raging insecurities, Brandon put his hand on her arm. "It's going to be fine."

"You may be used to pretending to be something you're not, but this is all new to me."

Mark's eyebrows winged up, a sure sign that he was formulating more questions to ask her once they were alone.

Brandon withdrew his hand, taking with it the warmth and comfort his touch had provided. "I may not be as good at pretending as you think."

For the first time since his arrival, Kimber took the time to really focus on him. The tension in his body was obvious, but she'd assumed that had to do with being forced to work with her. Perhaps there was more to it than that.

"Is something going on that I should know about?" she asked.

Rafi tilted his head toward Brandon. "Brandon had an incident at work today."

Mark straightened in his chair. "What kind of incident?"

The muscle in Brandon's jaw jumped. "The kind where an assassin tried to kill me."

"What?" Now Kimber grabbed Brandon's hand. "Are you okay?"

"Yeah." Brandon swallowed hard, his natural reaction contradicting his words.

"Do you have any idea who it was or why he was after you?" she asked.

It was Rafi who answered her question. "We've identified his assailant as Darragh Byrne. He's known to be an enforcer of sorts for Labyrinth."

Kimber looked from Brandon to Rafi. "If Labyrinth is targeting Brandon, he's still in danger."

"Maybe. Maybe not," Rafi said. "We believe Darragh was behind an incident in England. If that's the case, it's highly likely that he recognized Brandon from that night and chose to eliminate him rather than risk being recognized."

"I don't think so," Brandon said. "I never got a good look at the guy that night. He shot from the trees."

"That doesn't mean he didn't see you."

Rafi's phone rang, and he held up a finger as he answered it. "Ebeid." He paused, the faint mumble of a woman's voice carrying into the otherwise quiet room. After a minute, Ebeid thanked the woman and ended the call. "That was one of my colleagues. She's been tracking Darragh's movements through his cell phone."

"And?" Brandon prompted.

"Best we can tell, he was tracking down all the employees at Monroe who started the same week as you did."

"Then, he was here to kill me," Brandon said.

"It looks that way, but this could be good news," Rafi said.

"How is someone trying to kill Brandon good news?" Kimber asked.

"Darragh didn't make any outgoing calls or send any outgoing texts today, so the likelihood is that he didn't share your identity with anyone inside Labyrinth," Rafi said. "And the fact that he was searching through all the new employees means they suspect we have an operative inside, but they don't know who."

Kimber wasn't sure that Rafi's theory made her feel any better. Someone had tried to kill Brandon. And even though the thought of dating him scared her, she couldn't deny that she already cared about him enough to be profoundly affected if something happened to him. She glanced down at where her hand remained on top of Brandon's. Her cheeks flushed, and she pulled her hand away.

"My colleague also cleared the surveillance footage from the elevator where the incident occurred, so no one will know that you were involved," Ebeid continued.

Mark leaned forward and rested his forearms on his knees. "What does all this mean going forward?"

"We'll plant an article about the death of Darragh and an unidentified man," Rafi said. "With any luck, someone from Labyrinth will assume you're the person who was killed."

"That's not going to fly." Brandon shook his head. "If our intel is right, someone at Monroe Publishing is working for Labyrinth. They'll be able to check to see if any of the new employees didn't show up for work."

"Then, I guess I'd better make sure one of them doesn't show up for work tomorrow," Rafi said as though making a person disappear were no big deal.

"Do I even want to know how you plan to do that?" Brandon asked.

"It's not a problem," Rafi insisted. "We'll approach one of the new employees and offer him a better job at another company, one that isn't located too close to where you work, but before he starts, he'll be given a nice, long vacation."

Brandon didn't look convinced.

Rafi continued. "Now that Darragh is dead, the immediate threat is over."

"But we can't be sure someone else won't come after me," Brandon said.

"No, but you bought us time to put more safeguards in place to protect you."

Brandon swallowed hard again. "I'm trusting you on this."

"Always a wise decision." Rafi pulled out his laptop and grabbed the television remote off the end table beside him. He turned on the TV and mirrored his screen to share images of the top-level executives of Monroe Publishing. "We're looking into the top dozen execs at Monroe, but so far, we don't have anything solid on any of them."

"I've been tracking them too," Mark said. "Jamal Gibson recently returned from China. Supposedly, it was to visit printing presses over there. Since he's in charge of new products, the trip could be legit, but it's worth mentioning."

"Any other overseas travel?" Rafi asked.

"Margaret, the art director, traveled to Paris multiple times last year. Ramon went to Europe in October, but we're still trying to figure out where he went after entering through Amsterdam," Mark said. "And then Savannah, the sales director, was in New Zealand, but based on the photos, it looks like it was a vacation with a bunch of girlfriends."

"What about other large purchases that go beyond what would be expected for their salaries?" Kimber asked.

"It's hard to say. All these employees make decent money, but we haven't been granted access to their personal financials yet," Mark said. "I'll keep searching for the typical red flags, but until the warrants come through, I'm limited on how much I can do."

The typical red flags like extensive home renovations, higher-than-normal credit card spending, new-vehicle and real-estate purchases.

"How many of these people have you met?" Rafi asked Brandon.

"All of them except for the CEO and the board of directors."

"If Monroe follows its typical pattern, that will change in a few weeks."

"How so?" Brandon asked.

"Every time they sign a big contract, the CEO hosts a cocktail party." Rafi motioned to Kimber. "Kimber here will be the guest of honor."

The guest of honor. Kimber rolled that concept over in her mind. It would be a dream come true if she'd actually earned this on her own.

"The cocktail party will give Kimber access to those other top execs. Not me," Brandon said.

"I've been thinking about that." Ebeid set his laptop on the table beside him. "Once the contracts have been signed, it may be easier for Brandon to gain access if the two of you appear to be dating."

Brandon stiffened. "I don't think that's—"

"That's not—" Kimber began at the same time.

"A good idea," they finished together.

They looked at each other. After their last conversation, she hadn't expected Brandon to agree with her that they should avoid romantic entanglements. A seed of disappointment planted inside her.

She fought against her growing doubts. She'd set the boundaries between them. It was hardly fair to expect Brandon to want to keep pursuing her after she'd put on the brakes.

Rafi's voice broke into her thoughts. "Whether you think it's a good idea or not, it's the only way we can make sure Kimber has backup and also provide more access for Brandon."

"What about you or Mark?" Brandon asked.

"We can't risk someone identifying me as FBI," Rafi said. "And Mark isn't an operative. Plus, he'll be heading back to DC tomorrow."

"I thought you were staying through the weekend," Kimber said.

"That was my original hope, but Director Yarrow wants me to meet with him on Friday morning. And unfortunately, the resources I need are at Langley, not here." Mark waved toward Kimber. "Besides, Kimber's like my sister. It would be weird to pretend to date her."

A flicker of something showed on Brandon's face. Was that relief?

"I still don't know that this is a good idea," Brandon said. "Someone tried to kill me today. I don't want Kimber anywhere near me if that could put her at risk."

Kimber's doubts about Brandon's feelings for her shifted as understanding dawned. Brandon was worried about her safety, even though he was the one in danger.

She shook her head. "I think you should be more worried about you than me."

Brandon's gaze met hers. "It's easier to worry about you."

"Worrying isn't going to do either of you any good. The cocktail party is our best chance to gain access to the top level of management, and you two are our way in," Rafi said. "Like it or not, becoming a couple is what needs to happen."

"I still think it's a bad idea." Brandon shook his head. "It was bad enough pretending not to know her at work so Amelia wouldn't think I was pushing Kimber's manuscript due to our relationship."

"Technically, you know her now," Rafi said. "Asking her out shouldn't be a big deal."

"Yes, but dating her when Labyrinth could send someone else after me puts her right in the danger zone."

"We already have customs on the lookout for known Labyrinth members at all possible entry points into the US. We won't let anyone get close to you."

"What about the unknown members of Labyrinth?" Kimber asked.

"The evidence indicates no one knows who Brandon is."

Brandon seemed to consider Rafi's directive before he focused on Kimber again. "I guess this means that if I ask if I can take you out to celebrate on Friday night, you should say yes."

Kimber's heartbeat quickened. "I guess so."

• • •

Brandon left Kimber's apartment with Mark and Rafi, but as soon as the other two men stepped onto the elevator, he backtracked to Kimber's door. If he and Kimber were going to pretend to date, they needed to clear the air. He also wasn't quite ready to be alone after what had happened with Darragh.

He lifted an unsteady hand and knocked. The door opened an instant later.

Kimber moved aside and held out her hand to motion him inside. As soon as she closed the door behind him, she asked, "How are you doing? Really?"

How could he answer that question when he didn't know the answer? Rather than try, he said, "I thought we should talk before we have to pretend that we're dating."

"I'm sorry Rafi is putting you in this situation." Kimber clasped her hands together in front of her. "Our work shouldn't have to interfere with our personal lives."

"What I said earlier about us dating being a bad idea—" Brandon tried to push aside the remnants of adrenaline that still lingered. "You know that I'm only concerned for your safety. If you hadn't stepped back from us, we'd likely be dating for real."

"It's not that I don't want to go out with you." She said the words, and instantly, a blush rose in her cheeks.

"What made you step back?" Brandon asked.

Kimber crossed to the sofa and sat, gesturing for him to join her. As soon as he took his seat, she seemed to gather her courage. "I dated a case officer a couple years ago. He was undercover. I wasn't."

"So?"

"So, we went out one night, and he ran into some people he knew from an overseas post. They asked me where I worked, and I stumbled over my answer."

"That can happen to anyone, especially an overt employee who hasn't practiced answering that question."

"Yeah, well, my little mess-up resulted in those guys chasing us when we went to leave. Daniel ended up in the hospital."

Kimber's reaction at the restaurant now made so much more sense. Brandon forced himself to ask, "Did Daniel . . . ?"

"He survived, but that ended our relationship, and I haven't dated anyone since."

"Until me."

Her cheeks colored again. "Well, yeah, but I didn't know you were CIA."

"I almost wasn't."

Kimber's eyebrows drew together in an unspoken question.

"I was going to resign. I had a job lined up in a London publishing house. I was planning to extend the lease on my flat." Brandon lifted a hand in the air. "I never should have been CIA in the first place."

"How did you end up with the agency, then?" Kimber asked.

"My dad died when I was in college. The agency offered to pay my tuition if I agreed to work for them." He was going to leave it at that, but something pushed him to tell Kimber the rest. "I've always wondered if I got the offer because my dad was CIA."

"How long was your dad with the agency?"

"I'm still not 100 percent sure he did work for us, but I've always had my suspicions." He shrugged. "Turns out that gaining access to former employee personnel files isn't exactly an easy prospect."

"Someone must know."

"Yes, but whoever has those answers isn't sharing."

"I'm sorry, Brandon. That has to be so hard having your questions left unanswered." She kept her hands in her lap, but her gaze met his. "What happened to change your mind about resigning?"

"Finlay Addington was one of my assets. He was killed the night before I was going to send in my resignation." Brandon blew out an unsteady breath. "Darragh Byrne is the man who killed him."

CHAPTER 21

ASADI SAT AT his breakfast table and shuffled the handwritten notes he'd made on his two targets. Within the week, the new author would be signed at Monroe, and Finlay's contact would be dead.

His heartbeat quickened in anticipation as he considered what would come next. The headlines would last for months, maybe even years. The pang of loss welled inside him.

The well-placed strike in Europe would interrupt transportation in multiple countries and ripple through the western part of the continent. But the attack in the United States was the one he was most excited about. It would remind Americans that they were far from invincible. It would punish them for creating the environment that had allowed his little sister to be educated and work in her own country before the US troops left, leaving her when she was most vulnerable.

With hatred brewing inside him, Asadi pulled up the latest message from his bombmaker to ensure the shipment was already in progress. The confirmation flashed on his screen, and a new sense of anticipation burned in his chest.

Yes, these attacks were going to happen. Not a single strike but a coordinated effort on the same day, only hours apart. Labyrinth's power would be felt in London, and before the ashes cooled, New York would have her turn.

•   •   •

With his briefcase in one hand and his coat draped over his arm, Brandon peeked into the hall and looked both ways. All night, he had relived the fight with Darragh, but in his dreams, Darragh had shown up here right as Kimber had emerged from her apartment. Those dreams had merged with his talk with Kimber last night after everyone had left.

Two doors down. He still couldn't quite believe the woman he wanted to spend more time with lived so close when her nearness could put her in the crossfire of whoever was trying to kill him. And pretending to date her was going to be pure torture. Even the few minutes together last night had reminded him of the possibilities that hung between them, possibilities that Kimber insisted couldn't be explored.

With a hollowness filling him, he checked the hall a second time before he left the safety of his apartment. He didn't know how he was supposed to act like everything was normal when only twelve hours ago, he had faced a weapon at close range for the first time *and* killed someone for the first time.

Trying to put those memories out of his mind, he walked down the stairs to the ground floor. After he put his coat on, he opened the door and surveyed the lobby. A man exited the elevator and headed for the doors. A woman did the same.

As soon as they disappeared from sight, Brandon hurried to the exit.

Again, he checked for anything or anyone suspicious before he passed through the door. Of course, with the steady stream of pedestrians outside, he couldn't be sure he would spot a potential threat even if one were waiting for him.

He rubbed his hand over his lower back to remind himself that he was still armed before forcing himself into motion. By the time he reached the subway, the waiting passengers were practically shoulder to shoulder. If someone came at him here, he'd have nowhere to run, no way to escape.

He willed his racing heart to steady. Think of something else. Anything else. Like how Mark said he and Kimber were just friends. That tidbit of information had been the one bright spot last night. Well, that and the moment when she had put her hand on his.

How was it that a simple touch could lift his spirits, even after what he'd experienced?

His train pulled up to the platform, and the doors whooshed open. A handful of people exited before the sea of humanity pressed into the already full train.

Brandon gripped his briefcase tighter and scanned the people around him once more. No discernible threats, except for the guy next to him, who was in desperate need of a shower. Brandon turned his head so the body odor wouldn't be quite as strong.

Three stops later, Brandon finally escape the stench and the crowded train.

When he reached his office building, he stopped a few steps from the door. A man was dead because of him. Brandon was still alive only because he had recognized Darragh and managed to use his training to kill him before Darragh had killed Brandon.

Brandon shook his head. He needed to stop dwelling on this. Even as that thought formed, he passed the elevators and opened the stairwell door.

After he climbed the stairs to the eleventh floor, he took a moment to let his heart rate settle before pushing the door open and continuing to his desk.

Mary glanced up as he passed. "Did you hear what happened?"

Brandon shook his head.

"One of the new guys who started working here last week was killed last night."

Brandon stopped walking. "What? Who?"

"I don't know. I thought it might be you, but obviously not." She almost looked disappointed. "I just know someone from the FBI stopped by to see John to ask some questions," she said, referring to the CEO.

"How did you find out someone was killed?"

"Regina overheard them talking. It's all anyone's talking about." Mary tilted her head toward Amelia's office. "Well, that and the big contract for Kimber Frost."

Great. The two topics he'd prefer to put out of his mind.

Maybe he'd get lucky and Amelia would have him running errands all day today. He glanced toward the stairwell door. Or maybe not.

• • •

Kimber made it all the way until noon on Thursday before Mark caught up to her with his questions. He entered her apartment, a pizza box in one hand and his computer bag in the other.

"What are you doing here? I thought you were flying back to DC today."

"I don't have to leave for the airport for a few more hours." Mark set the pizza on her counter. "Are you ready to tell me what the deal is with you and Brandon?"

Playing innocent, she asked, "What are you talking about?"

Mark simply raised both eyebrows. "I'm the one teaching you how to lie, remember? You can't fool me. Something's going on between you two."

Ignoring his assumption, she pulled two plates out of the cabinet, handed one to Mark, and grabbed a slice of pizza for herself.

Mark took two slices and sat on one of the barstools. "Well?" he asked between bites. "How did you meet him?"

She should have known she wouldn't be able to keep her relationship—or almost relationship—with Brandon private, not with Mark in town. "He sat next to me on my flight home from London, and then we ran into each other when I was in New York a couple weeks ago."

"Wait." He set his slice of pizza down. "Is he the reason you were in such a good mood after your weekend in New York?"

"It's no big deal. We just spent that Saturday together." She said the words as though she believed them. Maybe she *could* learn to lie.

"With the way you two were last night, it looked like a lot more than just casual sightseeing happened."

"Nothing happened." Kimber dropped onto the stool beside him. "We talked for a while, but when I came back to New York, I found out he was one of ours."

Mark shook his head in disapproval. "You need to get over this whole phobia you have about dating case officers. What happened with Daniel wasn't your fault."

"If I hadn't been with him, he never would have been stabbed."

"That happened because he didn't trust you to take care of yourself."

Kimber couldn't deny that Daniel had shielded her from the two men who had come after them and that had they faced them together, he might have walked away unscathed. "I'm still the reason those guys suspected Daniel was CIA."

"You stumbled over an answer when asked what you do for a living," Mark said. "Now it's time you put it behind you and move on."

Mark had given her similar advice repeatedly over the past year and a half. Knowing he was right didn't erase the fear that had never quite eased since Daniel's injury. Yet she couldn't deny that she missed talking to Brandon. Somehow, spending time with him while discussing potential suspects wasn't the same as when they talked about their favorite books and movies or wandered the streets of New York together.

She took another bite of her lunch, chewing slowly. Could she possibly open herself up to dating Brandon? And if so, what would that look like once this assignment was over? For all she knew, he would move back to London, and she would be reassigned to another post at headquarters. Assuming she could go back to the CIA after all this exposure on social media. And what would happen with her publishing contract? Would that go forward? She tried to envision life as a published author and a CIA officer. Not the most compatible of careers.

They finished their lunch in silence. Finally, Mark spoke again. "It's time to let the past go."

"I know."

"You do?" Mark stood and moved so he was directly in front of her. He stared for a moment before he spoke. "Wow. Miracles do happen."

"It's going to be a miracle if I survive this assignment." She checked her watch. "Speaking of which, I need to get going. Patricia and I are supposed to meet with the social media and marketing directors at Monroe this afternoon."

"I'll walk with you as far as the subway."

"Actually, Patricia is picking me up."

Mark let out a low whistle. "Fancy."

"I don't think she wants me talking to anyone at Monroe without her until those contracts are signed." Kimber transferred the leftover pizza into a Ziploc bag and put it in the fridge. "Thanks for lunch."

"It's always the easiest way to get you to talk."

"You're using pizza as an interrogation technique?"

Mark shrugged. "I use whatever works."

"I'm not sure it would work on criminals or spies."

"I'll keep that in mind if I ever decide to become a case officer." Mark walked over to the door.

Kimber grabbed her purse and followed. "You'll keep me up-to-date on what you find when you get back to headquarters, right?"

"You know I will." They reached the ground floor and went outside together. "I'll talk to you later."

Kimber gave him a quick hug. After she said goodbye, she crossed the sidewalk to where Patricia was waiting beside a taxi.

"Are you ready?" Patricia asked.

"I think so." Kimber climbed into the cab and clasped her hands together. She had fifteen minutes to mentally prepare for a meeting with the people who hoped to make her a household name. Fifteen minutes to prepare for the possibility of seeing Brandon again. Maybe the cab driver should take the long way to Monroe.

• • •

Brandon didn't know which was worse, avoiding Mary's and Regina's attempts at making him look incompetent or listening to them hash out possible scenarios of who had been killed last night and why.

If it weren't for the three times he'd already gone up and down the stairs to run errands for Amelia, he would search for another task that would take him out of the office. As it was, his quads were already tightening up from the extra exertion. He should have skipped his workout this morning.

He opened a new document on his computer and tried to ignore Mary and Regina's running commentary.

"It has to be Dalton," Regina said. "He's the only new guy who didn't show up for work today."

"Or that security guard." Mary shook her head. "It's too bad. He was cute."

Brandon grimaced. Darragh wasn't so cute when holding a gun.

Brandon stretched his legs out beneath his desk and flexed his feet to relieve the stiffness in his calves.

The art director approached Mary's desk. "I need you to make a reservation for me for tomorrow night at Chef's Table on Fifth."

"What time?" Mary asked.

"Seven thirty," Margaret said. "There will be four of us."

Mary clicked on her mouse, likely to put in Margaret's request.

Brandon texted Rafi. *Margaret Lowell has a reservation for four at Chef's Table on Fifth for tomorrow night. Advise.*

A text message came back a moment later. *Make a reservation for you and your date for fifteen minutes earlier.*

Him and his date. As in him and Kimber.

Rafi seemed determined to put Kimber in the public eye with Brandon, even if being seen together could put her in danger. Fighting back his lingering frustration about the situation, Brandon tapped a reply on his phone. *I'll take care of it.*

He sent the text and promptly made a reservation for two. At least this way he would know where he was taking Kimber to dinner tomorrow even though he had yet to officially ask her out.

The elevator chimed, and Whitney emerged, her usual bubbly exuberance evident in her animated expression. Haseeb followed, his focus on the phone in his hand. Kimber and Patricia emerged next, and Brandon straightened in his seat. What were they doing here? The contract signing wasn't until tomorrow morning.

Amelia walked out of her office in the same moment Kimber's gaze landed on him and held for a long moment. Brandon struggled to turn his attention away from her so he could focus on his boss.

Amelia reached his desk.

"Did the signing for Kimber Frost get moved up?" Brandon asked.

"No. She's here for a strategy session with marketing."

Brandon glanced at the women again. Kimber's attention flickered his way once more before they filed into the conference room down the hall.

Amelia looked from Brandon to Kimber and back again. "Brandon, come with me." Amelia returned to her office.

The abrupt change in her tone, her quick retreat to a private space. He'd seen similar behavior when a marketing assistant had ignored her request to send her an advance reader copy for an upcoming book. It hadn't ended well.

Brandon followed her into her office, not sure what he'd done wrong.

"Close the door." Amelia waited until he complied before she leaned against the front of her desk. "Are you sure you've never met Kimber before?" Amelia asked.

Brandon let his surprise show on his face. "I assure you, I'd never even heard the name Kimber Frost until the day I received her manuscript."

"I think she's a bit taken with you."

His jaw dropped. "Excuse me?" Whatever he had expected Amelia to say, this wasn't it.

"You must have noticed the way she looks at you." Amelia pressed both hands against her desk. "This could work to our advantage."

"What can work to our advantage?"

"You dating Kimber." Amelia's eyes narrowed. "You're single, aren't you?"

"Yes."

"And you find Kimber attractive." Amelia held a hand up before he could respond. "That wasn't a question. It's obvious Kimber isn't the only one who would be willing to explore a personal relationship."

"So, maybe I thought about asking her out." That was beyond true. "But I'm still not following. Why would you want me to date her?"

"If she's dating you, we don't have to worry about her getting distracted from the next manuscript she should be writing. It will also make it more likely that her loyalties will stay with this company." Amelia circled her desk and picked up the lemonade he'd included as part of her lunch order.

He was still trying to follow Amelia's logic.

Clearly sensing his confusion, Amelia said, "You can give her a healthy social life while also helping her stay balanced." She took a sip of her drink. "Trust me. Once that first big check hits, it's too easy for new artists to get sucked into the social scene and lose sight of the hard work it takes to stay on top. That happens far too often with new authors, especially those who hit it big on their first try."

"Do you really think her book will sell that well?"

"If I have my way, Kimber Frost will be a household name by the end of next year."

"That would be an accomplishment."

"Yes, it will be."

CHAPTER 22

KIMBER'S HEAD WAS spinning. She sat at the square, glass conference table, her hands clasped in her lap as Patricia interacted with the two marketing executives from Monroe.

Social media campaigns, preorder sales, endorsements, podcast interviews, talk show appearances. Everything Haseeb and Whitney proposed put Kimber more firmly in the public eye and added to the list of situations she'd been counseled to avoid when she'd first entered the CIA. Her life as a normal agency employee was over. A burning sensation started in the center of her chest and flowed outward. This contract would change everything, and she would have her words out there for the world to see, for the world to criticize.

Inhaling slowly, she fought for calm. She still had time. The contract might be signed tomorrow, but except for the social media campaigns, none of the other efforts would begin until after her manuscript was edited. Assuming that would take a month or more, she could be out of this fake author career before it really began, assuming they could find the mole for Labyrinth and arrest them, resulting in the company either folding or her contract getting canceled.

Mark's comment about her keeping the money circled through her mind, and a new clarity pushed to the forefront. This might have started as a fake career, but once she signed her name, it would be real. She would have a real contract for a real book with her name on it. So unless the government shut down the whole of Monroe Publishing, the word *fake* no longer applied to the career she'd always dreamed of.

Across the table, Haseeb pulled two papers out of the folder in front of him. "I have a list of events here that we would like Kimber to attend." He passed a copy to Patricia and another to Kimber. "The first is a book launch for Elliott Paulson, one of our top nonfiction authors."

Kimber perked up at that. "Isn't he the one who wrote *Top Twenty Habits of a Billionaire*?"

"He is. His new book, *Why Aren't You Rich Too?*, releases on Tuesday," Haseeb said. "The launch party is right here in New York. We want you there."

"It will give us a lot of great photo opportunities," Whitney added. "We'll introduce you two before the event so I have photos to leak to generate extra interest."

Kimber had been around a few famous people before because of Tessa, but she wasn't sure how she felt about being in this position herself because of her writing. She skimmed over the rest of the listed events, all fourteen of them. A movie premiere in Los Angeles, a restaurant opening near Central Park. The rest ranged from attending a show on Broadway to dinner parties spanning over the next several months, including a cocktail party a week from Saturday that John Webb, the CEO of Monroe Publishing, would be hosting.

"We'll add to this as more opportunities arise, but our focus right now is to build your reputation as someone people will want to know."

"Is that even possible?" Kimber asked. "After all, my book doesn't even have an official release date."

"I believe I have that here." Haseeb tapped on the keyboard of his laptop. "You're slated for next October."

Patricia put her hand on Kimber's arm. "I know eighteen months may seem like a long time away, but I suspect Amelia will want to have ARCs available for reviewers anywhere from six to twelve months before your book releases."

"ARCs?" Kimber repeated.

"Advance reader copies," Haseeb explained. "We print a limited number for our top reviewers and influencers. I'll start reaching out in June to give them a heads-up that it's coming. By then, we should be through the copyedit stage."

Editing, socializing, writing, spying. Kimber had no idea how she was supposed to balance it all. And to think, earlier this week, she'd had more time on her hands than she'd known what to do with.

She must have looked like a deer in the headlights because Patricia squeezed her arm. "Don't worry. I'm here to help you every step of the way."

"I'll take all the help I can get."

"We're off to a good start," Whitney said. "I'll make sure we have lots of Instagram-worthy photos. We'll beef up your feed on Facebook and X. By the time those early reviews start coming in, everyone who is anyone in the writing world will know your name."

They would know her pen name anyway.

"Here's my card." Haseeb handed a business card to Kimber. "Call if you have any questions."

"Thanks."

"I'll text you my number," Whitney said. "We'll be spending a lot of time together while we build your social media presence."

"Whitney spends a lot of time checking out the best hot spots in town," Haseeb added. "You're in good hands."

Even though Kimber preferred to avoid crowded social venues, she said, "Thanks for all your help."

"We look forward to working with you." Haseeb stood.

Kimber slipped Haseeb's business card into her purse and stood as well. When she followed Patricia out of the conference room, she couldn't help but glance toward Brandon's desk. It was empty, but a short distance away, he stood beside Amelia's office.

The familiar butterflies fluttered in her stomach. She didn't want to have feelings for him, but she couldn't deny that Mark was right. She couldn't let what had happened with Daniel dictate her future choices.

She forced her attention back to Haseeb and Whitney. "Thanks again for everything."

"We'll see you tomorrow," Haseeb said.

"I'll have my camera ready," Whitney added.

Signing a huge publishing contract and smiling for the camera. This definitely wasn't what she'd expected when she'd joined the CIA.

• • •

Brandon sat at his desk and scrolled through the company directory, mulling over who would have access to funnel money through Monroe's accounts, assuming that Finlay's information had been correct. The CIA's report that there wasn't any unusual activity in Monroe's bank accounts puzzled him, but clearly, Labyrinth was using this company to support its activities somehow. Otherwise, Darragh Byrne wouldn't have been here in New York, and he certainly wouldn't have tried to kill Brandon.

Brandon glanced at Amelia's office. Her door was currently closed, and the indicator light on his desk's phone showed that she was currently on a call. So far, he hadn't witnessed anything about his current boss to raise any red flags, but she clearly wielded a significant amount of influence within the company. When he requested a meeting for her, everyone was quick to accommodate, even Mary and Regina.

Though Brandon had been at the company for three weeks already, he'd yet to meet John Webb, the CEO, but if Rafi was correct, that would be changing within the next few weeks. Obviously, John would have easy access to every aspect of the company and would be a great asset for Labyrinth.

Then there was Ramon Alvarez. So far, no one had managed to trace his travel last fall beyond his flight to Amsterdam. No rental cars. No public transportation. No hotels or vacation rentals. The lack of reservations and credit card charges supported the theory that he'd been picked up by someone locally and resided with him or her during his time in the Netherlands.

Margaret's trips to Paris had been more clear-cut, but unless someone had witnessed her with a member of Labyrinth, there was no way to be certain whether she was working with them or not. Not to mention, she wouldn't necessarily have access to Monroe's bank accounts beyond using her company-issued credit card. The same was true with the other executives.

When following that logic, John and Ramon were the two most likely suspects. Both had easy access to the company's money, and both were high up enough to be able to hide any illegal activity without someone looking over their shoulders.

Haseeb approached his desk, a stack of books in his hands. "Brandon, make sure Amelia gets these."

Brandon stood and took the half dozen paperbacks from him, then set them on his desk and glanced at his office phone to confirm she was still on a call. "I'll take these in to her when she gets off the phone."

Haseeb nodded and headed back toward his office.

Savannah approached next with a thick folder. "Is she available?"

"She's on the phone right now, but I can let you know when she's off."

"That's okay. I have a meeting in a few minutes." Savannah handed the file to him. "Make sure she gets this."

"What is it?" he asked.

"The sales report she asked for."

Before Brandon could respond, Conrad approached, also carrying a file folder. "Is she in?"

As if Conrad couldn't see her at her desk through the glass wall. Brandon checked the phone again. "She's on a call."

"Here." Conrad handed the file over. "Tell her I need to be there during the contract signing tomorrow."

"I'll give her the message."

Conrad and Savannah went their separate ways, and Brandon looked up to see if anyone else had decided three thirty in the afternoon was the exact time they needed to speak to Amelia.

He nearly laughed out loud when Jamal and Margaret rounded the corner together and headed his way. They both glanced at Amelia's closed door before approaching him.

"Any idea when she'll be available?" Jamal asked.

"Sorry, I don't."

Margaret held up an oversized glossy photo of a book cover. "We need her to sign off on this before we can send it to press."

"Do you want to leave it here?" Brandon asked. "I can give it to her as soon as she's off the phone."

Jamal glanced at Amelia's office again as though debating. "Make sure she knows this is a priority. It needs to go to press tomorrow."

Brandon gave his standard response. "I'll let her know."

He took the cover art from Margaret and set it on top of the contract file, the sales report, and the stack of books. He remained standing while Margaret and Jamal continued toward the elevators, then he checked the hall in both directions before he finally lowered back into his seat.

Tilting the cover toward him, he read over the backliner for the upcoming romance novel. He noted a missing comma and wrote his observation on a sticky note. He then focused on the front cover. At first glance, everything looked great until he read the author's name for a second time: Michelle Hart. He had read her before, but he was quite certain she spelled her name with only one L.

He made another note and pressed it to the image.

The light on his phone turned off, and Brandon gathered everything that had been dropped off except for the pile of books. He knocked on Amelia's door and waited for her to call out before he walked in.

"Jamal and Margaret dropped this off for your approval." Brandon set the cover image on Amelia's desk. "I noted a couple of possible typos." He shifted the files in his hands and offered her the first one. "Here's your copy of Kimber Frost's contract. Conrad said he needs to be at the signing tomorrow."

Amelia took it and pointed at the other file in his hand. "And that?"

He held it out. "It's the sales report you asked for from Savannah."

"Tell Savannah I need her to email me this report," Amelia said. "I don't want to lug a physical copy home with me."

Brandon nodded and tucked the file under his arm.

"Is there anything else?" Amelia asked.

"Yes. Haseeb dropped some advance reader copies by for you." Brandon took a step back. "I'll get them." He retreated to his desk and grabbed the books. When he returned to Amelia's office, he asked, "Where would you like them?"

"On the bookshelf over there." Amelia waved at the white shelves that dominated the wall opposite her window.

He complied.

Amelia looked down at the cover art. "Double-check the spelling of Michele's name. I think you're right. I'm pretty sure her name does only have one *L*."

"I'll check her submission forms." Brandon waited for a second longer in case Amelia had any other requests for him. When she remained silent, he retreated to his desk.

He had barely sat down when Ramon emerged from the elevator. This really was turning into Grand Central Station. At least this time, Amelia was available.

Ramon made a beeline for Amelia's office, not bothering to spare Brandon a glance. He knocked on the doorjamb and held up a white envelope.

"I have the check for the Frost contract signing tomorrow."

"Hand delivered by our chief financial officer himself." A touch of sarcasm laced Amelia's voice. "I'm honored."

"Don't be," Ramon said. "I'm not comfortable handing a quarter-million-dollar check over to one of our assistants."

Two hundred fifty thousand dollars for Kimber's first payment. The CIA's plan was working, and Kimber was well on her way to becoming a millionaire.

CHAPTER 23

KIMBER SHIFTED THE canvas bag hanging from her shoulder. She shouldn't have checked out so many books, but once she got started, she couldn't stop.

Patricia had offered to drop her off at her apartment, but Kimber had opted for a diversion to the library instead. If she was going to spend the next several months writing, editing, revising, marketing, and juggling everything else that went with her writing career, the least she could do was take advantage of all the resources available to her.

Thankfully, her search through the stacks had distracted her from the thought that her last visit to the New York Public Library had been with Brandon.

He'd been on her mind since she'd talked to Mark earlier. Who was she kidding? He'd been on her mind since she'd run into him in New York two weeks ago.

She strode down the sidewalk on the way to her building and glanced at the Italian restaurant where they'd gone out together for the first time. It had been only a short distance from here where that unexpected meeting had occurred.

Uncertainty filled her as she forced herself to continue forward. She couldn't deny that she wanted to spend time with Brandon, but the familiar churning inside her served as a reminder of what could happen when she let down the walls she had built around her heart.

A woman with her arms full of groceries headed toward her, and Kimber twisted her body to avoid getting hit by the overly full shopping bags. When she turned back to face forward, she caught sight of

Brandon approaching from the other direction. He walked with purpose toward her building, his eyes scanning as he went. She sensed the moment he caught sight of her, but his hesitation was so brief that for an instant, she thought she had imagined it.

What was he doing here? She hadn't received any messages from Rafi since last night, but she supposed she might have missed one.

He slowed his pace as though making sure she reached the entrance first.

She walked inside, stopping once she was a few yards past the doorway. He entered a moment later.

"What are you doing here?" she asked.

"I live here."

"What?" Kimber shook her head. "You live in this building?"

"Yeah. Two doors down from you." He motioned her forward. "Come on. We can talk upstairs."

Seeing the wisdom of continuing their conversation in private, Kimber automatically walked toward the elevators. She pressed the button and turned back to face Brandon.

He glanced at the elevator doors, his tension evident.

"Are you okay?"

He swallowed hard but didn't answer.

The doors opened, and Kimber stepped inside. Brandon remained rooted to his spot.

"Brandon? Are you coming?" She narrowed her eyes. Then she remembered. Rafi had mentioned his colleague clearing the surveillance footage in the elevator. Logically, that would have been necessary only if Brandon's altercation with Darragh had taken place inside one.

The doors started to close, and Kimber hit the button to keep them open. Gently, she reached out and took Brandon's hand. "Come on. It's just the two of us."

Reluctantly, he crossed the threshold into the elevator. His body trembled, and Kimber gripped his hand tighter.

She pushed the button for the eighth floor. "Have you been on an elevator since yesterday?"

He pressed his lips together and shook his head.

"Then, I'm glad we can ride up together." She couldn't imagine constantly taking the stairs, especially up to the eleventh floor at Monroe.

The doors closed, and Brandon gripped the side rail with his free hand. He drew a deep breath and followed it with another.

"I'm so sorry you had to go through that," she said softly. She wasn't quite sure exactly what had transpired, but whatever it was had clearly rattled him.

The elevator moved upward, finally coming to a stop on their floor.

Brandon exited first, taking refuge in the hall. He took several more deep breaths before he focused on Kimber. His embarrassment evident, he said, "I'm sorry. Taking an elevator shouldn't affect me like that, but—"

"You have nothing to be sorry for."

The door beside hers opened, and Trudy poked her head out. Instantly, she smiled. "Oh, good. I was hoping the two of you had met." She gave a satisfied nod. "These days, people don't take enough time to meet their neighbors."

Kimber's lips quirked up. "You're right."

"Brandon, you look like you're about to fall over. You need to get something to eat," Trudy said.

"I'm going to grab some dinner right now."

"Good." She focused on Kimber. "You make sure he eats something."

"I will."

"Well, I'd best get back to my movie." She lifted a wrinkled hand and waved. "Good night."

"Good night, Trudy," Brandon said. As soon as she disappeared inside, he asked, "How did you meet Trudy?"

"She stopped by with a loaf of banana bread the day I moved in."

"Her banana bread is good," Brandon said. "Of course, I got chocolate chip cookies on my first day here. She must like me better than you."

"Or maybe that's just what she was baking that day." Kimber headed for her apartment. "Did you want to come in? I can fix us something to eat."

"I don't think Trudy meant that you needed to make me dinner."

"You can help me cook." Kimber pulled out her keys and unlocked her door. "Unless you'd rather settle for leftover pizza."

"What are my other options?"

"Tuna casserole or spaghetti. Those are the two things I know I have everything for in my pantry."

"Tuna casserole sounds good." Brandon followed her into her apartment and set his briefcase by the door. "I didn't expect you to be at Monroe today."

"I didn't expect to be there either. Originally, my meeting with marketing was supposed to be for next week." Kimber dropped her purse and book bag down on the couch. "Patricia called me this morning to tell me about the change. I think she didn't want to stress me out, so she waited until the last minute."

"Why would meeting with Haseeb and Whitney stress you out?"

"Because I'm not good at pretending to be something I'm not."

"You aren't pretending to be something you aren't. You're a writer. That's all you have to be."

"I like to write," Kimber corrected. "That's a lot different from being a real writer. And I still have to pretend that I'm only at Monroe because they're offering me a publishing contract. I'm not very good at lying."

He lifted his eyebrows. "You evaded extremely well." Brandon followed her into the kitchen and leaned against the counter beside the stove. "And if you need help in the art of deception, I can teach you to lie."

Kimber suspected he was a little too skilled in that area. She retrieved a box of elbow noodles from the pantry before she turned back to face him. Though she didn't want to notice his features, she couldn't help but appreciate his angular jawline and high cheekbones and the way he looked at her as though she were the most important woman in the world. He was a presence everywhere he went, and she was finding it hard to pretend he didn't matter to her.

Her thoughts turned into words before she could stop them. "Can you also teach me to not notice you when you walk into the room?"

A grin stole across his face. "I'm not sure I can help you with that. I'm having trouble keeping my eyes off you." He straightened and took a step forward. "And it won't matter once everyone sees us dating."

Her cheeks heated. "Maybe we should concentrate on fixing dinner."

His gaze lowered to her lips and held there for a second before he looked back up into her eyes. Regret flashed in his expression, and he nodded. "Maybe so."

. . .

He wanted to kiss her. Brandon fought the urge, his fears for her safety overriding the attraction simmering between them.

He crossed his arms over his chest to prevent himself from drawing her close. Even if he would soon be pretending to date Kimber, it would bode well for both of them to keep their relationship platonic, at least until they were expected to be a couple. "You should probably know that Rafi isn't the only person trying to set us up."

"If you're talking about Trudy, she's harmless." Kimber set a pot of water on the stove and turned the burner on high.

"I was actually talking about Amelia."

"Amelia?" Kimber repeated. "Why would she want us to date?"

"She thinks I can keep you focused on writing your next book."

"Maybe she needs to have a conversation with Haseeb and Whitney. With everything they have planned, I don't know how I'm supposed to write anything new, much less edit the one manuscript they already have."

"Did you have any insights on either of them when you met today?" Brandon asked. The sooner they could identify who was working with Labyrinth, the sooner he could get Kimber away from New York and away from any threat she might face by being close to him.

"I didn't notice anything unusual," Kimber said. "Both of them were wearing designer clothes that were definitely on the pricey side. Once Mark gets access to their financials, he should be able to tell if their incomes would support that."

Brandon hadn't noticed their clothes. "That's a good idea."

"From what Whitney was saying, she and I are going to be spending a lot of time together going to these different events they have me scheduled for."

"Any chance one of them was a dinner party with the board of directors?"

"Yes. It's a week from Saturday." Kimber glanced at the water on the stove that had yet to boil before she looked back up at him. "I don't know how I'll make it through that, much less the contract signing."

"You can do it."

"I'm supposed to go in there and pretend like I deserve to be paid a million dollars for my work even though the only reason I'm getting such a huge paycheck is that the CIA created an illusion that everyone wanted my book." She lifted both hands in a sign of exasperation. "I feel like such a fraud."

"Impostor syndrome is normal, especially in this industry."

"It's not a syndrome. I *am* an impostor. The CIA planted me here."

"No, you're not." The muscles in Brandon's arms twitched as he again fought the urge to pull her close. "I've read your book. It's good. Really good."

"It might be okay, but it isn't seven-figures good." Doubt colored her expression. "At best, I was hoping for an agent to find a publisher who wanted my book as a B-list title. An advance of a few thousand dollars would have exceeded my expectations." Kimber lifted both hands in the air again. "This is all way beyond reality."

Did she not know how talented she was? "You don't strike me as someone who would do something halfway. Why would you settle for the low end of the totem pole in your writing?"

"I just assumed that's what I would have to do."

"Well, you don't. Your book is incredible. You have a gift for characterization and dialogue. Your description is clean and crisp, and your plot never slows down." Unable to resist any longer, he closed the distance between them and placed both his hands on her shoulders. "You have all the makings of a best seller. Tomorrow, you need to walk in there believing that."

"If I can manage that, I really will have mastered the art of deception."

"Believe it," Brandon said, his gaze locking on hers.

Her voice lowered nearly to a whisper. "I'll try."

The water came to a boil, and a drop of scalding water spurted onto his arm. He jerked back and stepped out of the danger zone.

"Sorry. I must have put too much water in," she said.

"It's okay."

Carefully, she poured the noodles into the pot. Then she set a timer.

"While we're waiting for those to cook, you should grab your computer," Brandon said.

"Why?"

"You need to get in the zone to write your next book."

Kimber tucked a lock of hair behind her ear. "I'd love to do that, but I need to work on revising the next one Patricia is sending to Amelia."

"Email it to me. I can do an edit for you while you work on your new one."

Kimber lifted her eyebrows. "You're going to edit for me?"

"Sure. I can save you some time on that process, and you'll feel less overwhelmed if you can work on something else without the pressure of making this book perfect."

"Shouldn't you be researching the possible mole at Monroe?"

"I do that every day," Brandon said. "At this point, I don't think there's much we can do until we have the chance to socialize with them outside the office."

Kimber retrieved her piece of paper from her purse and held it out. "You may want to look at this."

"What is it?" Brandon accepted the offering.

"It's the list of events Haseeb and Whitney have lined up for me."

Brandon read over it. "They're flying you to LA for a movie premiere?"

"Yeah. You'd better start saving your money if you're coming with me."

"You mean, I need to tell the CIA to buy me a ticket."

"Don't do that." Kimber shook her head. "You'll want to buy it yourself and get reimbursed."

"Why would it matter? The agency is pretty well-versed in making sure their transactions look like everyone else's."

"True, but why risk it?" Kimber asked. "With what happened with Darragh Byrne, you don't want anything to look off with your bank accounts or your credit cards."

Brandon's blood chilled. Would Labyrinth believe the fake story and think the person who was supposedly killed was him? Or would someone in the organization keep digging to make sure Brandon had truly been eliminated?

"You don't really think they'd be able to break into my personal info, do you?"

"I do it all the time at work." She must have sensed his sudden spike of anxiety because she reached out and put her hand on his arm. "I'm just saying you can never be too careful. If we're paying for the things a normal New Yorker would pay for, no one will suspect we're anything beyond what we claim to be."

"Which means we need to be paying rent."

Kimber winced. "Yeah. I guess we'd better talk to Rafi about that."

"Like you said, we can never be too careful."

CHAPTER 24

ASADI CHECKED HIS phone for the fifth time in the past ten minutes. Darragh should have called by now, or at least messaged. Not a single word since Wednesday. Two days of silence, two days of waiting. Asadi didn't like waiting.

He crossed the living room to where his laptop lay on his coffee table and opened it to do an internet search for murders in New York City, limiting the results to the past week. He didn't have to look far before reaching an article that included Darragh's name and photo.

Fury rose inside him. Darragh was one of the few people he'd trusted with his day-to-day operations. With him dead, he'd have to find someone new to bring into his circle of trust. He didn't have time for this.

He let out his breath in a huff and kept reading. The details of the double shooting were vague, but it didn't take a genius to figure out the two men had shot each other and neither of them had survived their encounter. The second victim wasn't named, but he was listed as an employee of Monroe Publishing. At least Darragh had completed his task before he'd had the poor sense to get killed.

Asadi dialed his main contact at Monroe. The moment their voice came on the line, he asked, "Why didn't you tell me my man was killed?"

"I only found out yesterday, and with everything going on to prepare for the Kimber Frost contract signing, I didn't have time to contact you." The voice dropped to a whisper. "I don't have any details other than what the police said, but your man wasn't the only one killed."

"You haven't told me anything beyond what's in the newspaper."

"I don't know any more than that."

"Message me when the contract is signed." Asadi stood and paced the room. "We can use some of the advance money to assist your associate there as she prepares for the main event."

. . .

Kimber stood in front of her bathroom mirror while Tessa applied more blush to Kimber's cheeks.

"Okay. That should do it." Tessa stepped back. "You look fabulous."

"Thanks, but I don't feel fabulous." Not only did she have to face this alternate reality she'd landed in, but she'd also learned less than an hour ago that the judge had denied Rafi's request for the warrant that would give Mark access to the financial records of Monroe's upper management. Kimber pressed a hand to her stomach.

"What are you so nervous about? All you have to do is sign your name to the dotted line."

"Sign on the dotted line and produce two books worth the money they're paying."

"You are an amazing author. You deserve this," Tessa insisted. "And Greta is already excited about helping you dress the part."

Kimber glanced at the garment bag that lay across her bed, the bag Tessa had arrived with when she'd come over on her lunch hour. "Don't tell me she sent more clothes over."

"Of course she did." Tessa cocked an eyebrow. "You didn't think I was carrying clothes around the city for nothing, did you?"

"Tessa, you work in the entertainment and fashion industries. You're almost always carrying clothes around with you."

"Okay, you may have a point." Tessa crossed the bedroom and unzipped the white garment bag that had Cherise Moore emblazoned across the top. Cherise had been one of the American designers featured in London's Fashion Week.

Tessa drew out a fitted black dress with a white wool coat. Both pieces were sleek, classic, and exactly something Kimber would have chosen for herself . . . if her funds were unlimited.

Of course, after she signed on that proverbial dotted line, her bank account would be significantly larger. A six-figure advance. It still didn't seem real.

She ran a finger over the coat. "This is gorgeous."

"I knew you'd approve."

"I assume these are on loan."

"Nope. They're gifts from Cherise," Tessa said. "Greta suggested that having you wear her brand will be good publicity for both of you. Cherise agreed."

"This is too much."

"What can I say? Greta likes you, and she has a great head for non-traditional marketing."

"Tell her and Cherise thank you for me."

"You can thank them by tagging them both when you post photos of your contract signing on your social media pages."

Free clothes and all she had to do was mention the donors online. Unbelievable. "I'll make sure that happens."

"Go on. Get dressed." Tessa handed her the dress.

Kimber changed out of her jeans and sweater. Within five minutes, she was dressed and ready to go.

The doorbell rang.

"That's probably Patricia." Kimber walked to the door and opened it, surprised when Brandon stood in the hall instead of her agent. "What are you doing here?"

He stared at her as though he weren't sure he knew the answer to her question. "Sorry. You look amazing."

"Thank you."

He waved in the direction of the elevator. "Amelia asked me to come pick you up. I have a car waiting downstairs."

"That's really sweet of her, but Patricia is supposed to pick me up."

"She's already in the car. I picked her up first."

Nerves bubbled inside her. She pressed a hand to her stomach and drew in a deep breath. "It's time, then."

"It's time."

Tessa grabbed her purse. "Is it okay if I come too?"

"Brandon, this is my sister, Tessa."

"Good to meet you," Brandon said. "I've heard a lot about you."

Tessa's eyebrows lifted, and she cast a glance at Kimber before she responded. "I've heard a lot about you too."

Kimber's cheeks heated. Eager to change the subject, she asked, "Is it okay if Tessa comes?"

"Of course. Are you both ready?"

Kimber drew another deep breath. "I think so." She retrieved her purse from the small table by the door.

"Let's go." Brandon started down the hall.

They made it only a few steps before Trudy opened her door. "Brandon. What are you doing home this time of day?"

"I just came by to give Kimber a ride to midtown." Brandon put his hand on Kimber's back. "She's signing her publishing contract today."

"Well, that is something," Trudy said. "And to celebrate, I'll have a little treat for you tonight. Stop by sometime after four. My next batch of cookies will be ready by then. Snickerdoodles."

"Sounds great." Brandon guided Kimber forward as though he were afraid they'd be caught in a much longer conversation with their neighbor.

"See you later, Trudy," Kimber said.

"Don't forget to stop by," she called after them.

"We won't."

They approached the elevator, and Kimber didn't miss the way Brandon's pace slowed.

Tessa pressed the button and stepped into the elevator without looking back once it arrived.

"Are you okay?" Kimber asked quietly.

Brandon pressed his lips into a hard line, but he nodded, then stepped in as well.

When they reached the lobby, they walked across the open space and outside to a waiting Lincoln Town Car, where Patricia was already seated in the back.

Brandon opened the back door for Kimber and Tessa. Kimber took the middle seat between Patricia and her sister.

"Did you look over the contract details I sent you?" Patricia asked the moment Kimber was settled.

"Yes." Her class in business law helped her decipher the legalese, but she was grateful Patricia's attorneys had also reviewed it. She also now knew that once she signed the contract, it was binding. The only way it would fall through would be if Monroe went out of business.

Brandon closed the car door and took the spot in the front seat beside the driver.

"I like the outfit. I assume Greta or Cherise sent it over," Patricia said.

"How did you know that?" Kimber asked.

"They both reached out about endorsements yesterday."

"I hope that's okay if we mention them on my social media pages," Kimber said. "Greta's been really good to me, and Cherise was so sweet to give me this outfit to wear."

"It's not a problem. With Tessa working in the fashion industry, it's a natural match," Patricia said.

Technically, Tessa did more work in the entertainment industry, but Kimber didn't bother to share that detail. Nor did Tessa.

The driver pulled into traffic, and within moments, they arrived at Monroe Publishing.

Brandon ushered them inside, again tensing when they reached the elevator.

Kimber resisted the urge to reach for his hand, barely. It wouldn't do for them to appear to be a couple prematurely. The current plan was for him to ask her out after her contract signing was complete.

Brandon drew one long, slow breath after another until they reached the eleventh floor.

Then Amelia whisked Kimber into the conference room, where Conrad, Haseeb, and Whitney were waiting. A photographer also stood in the room, his camera at the ready.

"Kimber, Patricia, come sit over here," Haseeb said.

Kimber took her appointed seat.

"Who's this?" Amelia motioned to Tessa.

"This is my sister, Tessa," Kimber said. "She's the one who works for Greta Meyer."

"Oh, yes." Amelia offered her hand. "It's good to meet you."

"You too," Tessa said as though she already knew who Amelia was. No doubt Tessa would quiz Kimber later on who was in the room and whom she should know.

Haseeb offered Tessa a chair on the side of the room while everyone from Monroe remained standing.

As everyone got situated, Patricia skimmed over the contract on the table, then finally looked up. "Everything appears to be in order."

"In that case, it's time." Amelia glanced at the photographer to make sure he was ready. Then Amelia handed Kimber a fountain pen. "May this be the first of many."

Kimber looked up at the open doorway, where Brandon stood. He gave her an encouraging nod.

Kimber's hand trembled as she pressed the pen to the page where *Kimber Frost* was typed beneath the signature line.

Across from her, Whitney lifted her cell phone as though preparing to take a photo. Or perhaps it was a video. Kimber hoped it was the former so no one would see the way her hand was shaking.

This is real. My first publishing contract. Kimber's throat closed as the gravity of the moment crashed over her. She glanced up at Brandon again. Then she signed the name Kimber Frost in the indicated spot.

The moment she set the pen down, a flurry of congratulations followed.

CHAPTER 25

BRANDON STOOD BY while the various top executives and a few key staff members had their photos taken with Kimber. Even though he could see the occasional tremor in her body, a sure sign of nerves, somehow, she managed to keep smiling for the camera and conversing with one Monroe employee after another.

Jamal stepped into the hall and stopped beside Brandon. "You're going to have your work cut out for you over the next few months."

"How so?" Brandon asked.

"With Amelia's workload, it will fall to you to coordinate the edits and marketing efforts." Jamal pushed his glasses more firmly onto the bridge of his nose. "Inevitably, that means you're in for some long hours."

"I'm sure Amelia and I will manage." And if he were lucky, those long hours would include additional access to information that otherwise wouldn't be granted to him.

Jamal gave a slight nod and headed toward his office.

He'd barely left when Tessa walked out of the conference room. "I need to get back to work. Thanks for letting me tag along today."

"I'm sure it meant a lot to Kimber that you could be here," Brandon said. "It was a big moment."

"Definitely." She gave a quick goodbye and headed down the hall.

Over the next few minutes, one person after another filed out of the conference room until only Kimber, Patricia, Amelia, and Whitney remained.

"We'll touch base on Monday about your upcoming appearances," Whitney said. "I want to see how your following is after we leak the contract details to the public before we lock in any more events beyond what we've already discussed."

"And we'll all see you at the celebration party with the board of directors," Amelia said. "Everyone is anxious to meet our new rising star."

Kimber gripped her hands in front of her, the red polish on her fingernails contrasting against her black dress. She really did look stunning.

Suspecting she was ready to escape the spotlight, Brandon asked, "Are you all done?"

"I think so."

Patricia handed a copy of the contract to Kimber and collected another copy for herself. "I need to deposit this check." Patricia held up the white envelope Ramon had given Amelia yesterday. "Kimber, are you okay getting back to your apartment on your own?"

"I'll be fine."

Patricia slipped the check and her copy of Kimber's contract into her oversized purse. "Enjoy your weekend. We'll talk first thing on Monday."

Amelia stepped forward. "Brandon, can you walk Kimber downstairs and have my driver take her home?"

"No problem." Brandon pulled out his cell phone and texted Amelia's driver. Then he looked up at Kimber. "Are you ready?"

"Yes, thank you."

Even though the thought of stepping into the elevator brought with it a fear he had yet to conquer, he forced himself to walk with Kimber. He glanced at Mary as he moved past her cubicle before turning his attention back to Kimber.

"Any chance you're free tonight?" Brandon asked. "I thought maybe I could take you out to celebrate."

"I'd love that." Kimber offered him a smile that would convince anyone watching that she meant what she was saying. Maybe she did mean it.

They continued to the elevator, and Kimber lowered her voice. "Do you want to take the stairs?"

"I'm not going to make you walk down eleven flights." He glanced down at the high heels on her feet. "Especially wearing those shoes."

She looked down as though she'd forgotten she had dressed for the special occasion. "I hadn't thought of that."

When the elevator arrived on their floor, the two people inside exited, leaving the car empty. Brandon's shoulders tensed as he followed Kimber inside.

"I wish taking the elevator didn't bring up such bad memories," she said.

"Me too." He pressed the button for the lobby. What he needed was a distraction, something to think about besides his meeting with Darragh.

The moment the doors closed, Kimber took his hand and gave it a squeeze. The gesture was likely meant to comfort, but all it did was rekindle the attraction that had been humming between them since their first meeting.

He stared down at her, and his heartbeat quickened, not from fear and stress but from anticipation. "Maybe I need to replace the bad memory with a good one."

Kimber tilted her chin up to look at him, and Brandon couldn't resist slipping his hand around her waist.

His gaze dropped to her lips, only this time, he didn't resist the urge to close the distance between them. He leaned down until he heard Kimber's quick intake of breath. Then, as though he had done so a thousand times, he kissed her.

The softness of her lips, the way she leaned into him, the swirl of attraction pumping through him. Each sensation was familiar and unexpected at the same time.

His heart bounced to the bottom of his stomach, and his breath backed up in his lungs.

The sensation of his lips on hers flowed through him, bringing the comfort he'd longed for while also stirring the sense of belonging he experienced every time he was with Kimber.

The elevator lowered, and for the first time in days, Brandon wished his time in this metal box wouldn't end.

Kimber slipped her free hand around his neck, and Brandon drew her closer still. He changed the angle of the kiss until they were interrupted by the chime announcing their arrival at their destination.

They broke apart, but Brandon kept his hand on her waist. He faced the handful of people waiting for the elevator, and it took him a moment to gather his composure before he stepped into the lobby.

Neither of them spoke until they reached the door.

"I'm serious about taking you to dinner tonight," he said.

Kimber smiled. She pushed onto her toes and brushed a kiss across his cheek. "I was serious when I said yes."

Another wave of anticipation washed over him. "I'll pick you up at quarter to seven, if that works for you."

"Sounds great." She took another step toward the exit.

"Hey, Kimber?"

"Yeah?"

"You should wear that dress tonight."

Her smile widened. "I think that can be arranged."

●　　●　　●

She wore the dress. And she couldn't stop thinking about the kiss.

Kimber was crazy to let herself fall for another case officer, but she was having a hard time regretting her time with Brandon. Quite the opposite. She couldn't wait to see him again.

She checked her purse one last time to make sure she had the essentials: wallet, keys, phone, lipstick. She sat on the barstool where she'd left her coat and slipped the strap of her purse over her head so it hung over her shoulder crossbody style.

She'd barely sat down again when a knock sounded at her door.

Slipping on her coat, she crossed the room and pulled the door open. As expected, Brandon stood in the hall, but he'd changed out of his typical work clothes and now wore a charcoal gray suit, his tie a shade darker than the single red rose he held in his hand.

He stared at her for a moment. Then he leaned forward and kissed her cheek. "You look just as stunning now as when I picked you up earlier."

Butterflies took flight in her stomach. "Thank you. You look rather handsome yourself."

He held out the rose. "This is for you."

"Thank you." She stepped back at the same time the door next to hers opened. "Let me put this in some water."

Trudy's voice carried to her. "My, don't you look dapper tonight. Who's the lucky lady?"

"Kimber and I are going out to dinner," Brandon said.

"Oh, how nice. Before you go, let me give you those snickerdoodles."

"Thanks."

Kimber retrieved a tall glass from her cabinet, quickly filled it with water, and slipped the rose into it. Hoping to save Brandon from an interrogation at the hand of their inquisitive neighbor, she hurried back into the hall.

"You really do look fabulous in that dress." Trudy held up a second plate of cookies identical to the one Brandon now held.

"Thank you." Kimber smiled at Trudy and accepted the offering. "Let me put these away really quick."

"Can you leave mine in your apartment too?" Brandon asked. "I can pick them up when we get back."

"Sure." She returned to her apartment, set the cookies on the counter, and walked back into the hall. She turned to Brandon. "Are you ready?"

"I am." Brandon offered her his arm. "Good night, Trudy."

"Good night. You two have a nice time."

"We will." Brandon led Kimber to the elevator, and for the first time since his run-in with Darragh, he seemed completely relaxed.

When the door closed, he looked down at her. "You really do look amazing."

"Thank you." She tightened her hold on his arm. "Where are we going tonight that we need to be all dressed up?"

"The Chef's Table on Fifth." Brandon cast her an apologetic look. "I'm sorry, but it's as much for work as for pleasure."

"How so?"

"Margaret, the art director from Monroe, is having dinner there tonight," Brandon said. "Rafi wants us to see who she's with and try to create a connection between you and me outside of work."

A touch of disappointment tainted her mood. "I liked it better when I thought it was just the two of us going out to dinner."

"Me too." He stared down at her. "Does this mean you've had a change of heart about dating me?"

She had. Or at least, she was attempting to. "I'm trying to keep an open mind."

"That's good."

His earlier reservations seemed to have faded, but Kimber had no idea if he had accepted Rafi's directive that they create the appearance that they were dating or if he wanted to pursue a real relationship with her. With the way he had kissed her in the elevator, she hoped it was the latter.

Needing clarification, Kimber asked, "So, are we dating for real now? Or is this just for show?"

His gaze met hers. "I want it to be real."

A grin stole over her face. "Me too."

They reached the lobby, and Brandon took her hand in his as they headed outside. A light snow fell, fat snowflakes drifting down from the night sky. Brandon guided her to a waiting car.

"Please tell me you didn't hire a car service for tonight."

"Amelia lent me hers." Brandon stopped beside the driver, who stood by the open back door. "Thanks, Eric."

"Of course, sir."

Kimber also offered her thanks and slid into the heated vehicle. Brandon claimed the seat beside her and leaned close. "I'm not sure if Amelia is trying to help me impress you or if she wants her driver to spy on us."

"I guess we'd better make it look like we're just getting to know each other," Kimber whispered back. She waited for the driver to take his place behind the wheel and, in a normal voice, asked, "What do you know about this restaurant?"

"I heard about it from one of my coworkers. She said her boss had her make a reservation there for some time this weekend, so hopefully it's good."

They chatted on the short drive to the restaurant. By the time they reached their destination, the snow had thickened.

"I can get the door," Brandon told the driver.

Eric swiveled in his seat to face them. "I'll park back at Monroe. Call me when you're ready for me to pick you up. It'll take me ten to fifteen minutes to get here."

"That sounds great. Thank you." Brandon opened the door and offered Kimber his hand.

Kimber took it and stepped onto the curb. She waited until Brandon closed the door before she leaned closer and whispered, "You know this undercover world is all new to me, right?"

"Just remember you're a writer."

"That's what Mark always tells me."

Brandon cocked an eyebrow. "Maybe don't mention Mark while we're inside. We don't want anyone to think you're talking about an old boyfriend."

"Mark has never been my boyfriend."

Brandon pulled open the restaurant door. "Has he ever wanted to be?"

"No, but he wouldn't mind dating my sister." She walked inside.

Brandon entered as well. "That's good to know."

Kimber took a moment to take in her surroundings. Classical music playing overhead, muted lighting, candles on every table, and the aroma of fresh bread, cream sauce, and grilled meat wafting on the air.

Brandon approached the maître d'. "Reservation for Hale."

The middle-aged man checked the paper on his podium. "Yes, sir." He retrieved two menus from a lower shelf. "Right this way."

Brandon put his hand on Kimber's back as they followed the maître d'. When they reached the square table a short distance away, Brandon guided Kimber toward the seat where she would have her back to the door.

The maître d' pulled out her chair for her, and she sat. "Thank you."

He simply nodded and handed her a menu as Brandon took the seat opposite her. After handing Brandon a menu as well, he said, "Your waiter will be with you shortly."

"Thank you." Brandon held his menu without opening it. As soon as the maître d' left, he leaned forward. "Take your time deciding. Margaret isn't supposed to get here for another fifteen minutes."

"Sounds like we should start with an appetizer." Kimber opened her menu—her menu that didn't list any prices. "Brandon." She pointed at where she would have expected the prices to be.

"Don't worry about it."

"But—"

"You just signed a huge publishing contract. I think for tonight, we can enjoy a meal without worrying about what my credit card bill will look like." He winked at her, and his underlying meaning sank in. Brandon might be the one who would sign the credit card slip for tonight's meal, but whether they looked like a real couple or not, ultimately, the government would be paying the bill.

CHAPTER 26

BRANDON CAUGHT A glimpse of Margaret when she walked into the restaurant, and he deliberately focused on the calamari he and Kimber were currently sharing so he wouldn't look like he was anticipating her arrival.

Kimber must have sensed the shift in his attention because she lifted her eyebrows as though asking a silent question.

He gave a subtle nod before he let his gaze wander to the entrance again. When the maître d' approached with Margaret and three men, one her age and two much younger, Brandon stood. "Hi, Margaret."

"Brandon." Margaret lifted her eyebrows. "What are you doing here?"

"I brought Kimber out to celebrate her signing her contract." Brandon turned to Kimber. "Kimber, have you met Margaret? She's the art director at Monroe. She'll be the one overseeing the design of your book covers."

"I haven't." Kimber stood and offered her hand. "It's nice to meet you."

"You're Kimber Frost?"

"Yes, ma'am."

"Well, it is a pleasure. I've been hearing quite a lot about you." She turned to the older gentleman beside her. "Honey, this is the author I was telling you about."

"Forrest Lowell. It's good to meet you." He shook Kimber's hand. "These are our sons, Zander and Porter."

"Are you here for a celebration as well?" Kimber asked.

"We are." Margaret beamed. "Porter just found out he made it into Princeton."

"Congratulations," Kimber said.

"Thanks," one of the younger men, presumably Porter, said.

Forrest put his hand on Margaret's back. "We should find our table."

Margaret nodded. "It was nice to finally meet you, Kimber."

"You too." Kimber took her seat.

Brandon found his seat as well. "Princeton. That's something."

"I can't imagine attending an Ivy League school."

"It's not easy." Brandon could still remember his shock when he'd been accepted to Brown, just as he could easily remember his disappointment when he hadn't made it into his first-choice school, Columbia. Yet now, here he was, finally living in New York, working for a publishing company.

"Where did you go to school?" Kimber asked.

"Brown."

"So, you went to an Ivy League school. That's impressive." She leaned closer and whispered, "And it sounds expensive."

Brandon cast a quick glance at Margaret and her family. "With what Margaret makes, I can guarantee they'll be paying full tuition. The Ivies only give need-based scholarships."

"They must be doing quite well. They probably wouldn't have come to a restaurant this expensive if they were worried about how to pay for college."

Brandon suspected Rafi would let them know once Mark was granted access to her finances.

"Tell me more about you," Kimber said at normal volume, her words breaking into his thoughts. "How long have you worked for Amelia?"

"A few weeks."

"Really? It seems like she already relies on you a lot."

"I think she was just relieved that I could figure out her coffee and lunch orders without needing a road map." And survive his coworkers' efforts at sabotage.

"I suspect working for Amelia entails a lot more than picking up food."

"It does. I schedule a lot of meetings too."

Kimber took another bite of calamari. "How do you like your job so far?"

The sincerity in her voice caught him off guard. She no longer sounded like she was carrying on a conversation for the benefit of those around her. Rather, she seemed genuinely interested. Maybe she was, or maybe she was a much better actress than he gave her credit for. She certainly was playing well the part of someone on a first date.

"I think a few people were a bit disappointed that the company didn't promote someone from within for my position, but I think things will get better."

"Someone's giving you a hard time?"

"Things will get better," Brandon repeated. If for no other reason than to remind himself that this job was only temporary. "Enough about me. How's your writing going? Are you working on something new?"

"I've been trying to. Patricia's been going over the two manuscripts I've already completed. She'd like to submit one of them to Amelia by the end of the summer."

"Why wait so long if the manuscripts are already finished?" he asked.

"I think she wants to see what kind of editorial comments I receive on the first book before we submit the second."

"That makes sense." Brandon glanced over at where Margaret and her family were currently seated several tables away. They were all still looking at their menus as though reading them for the first time.

A waiter approached Margaret's table, and Margaret's husband asked him several questions before giving his order.

Kimber reached for Brandon's hand and leaned forward. "They don't come here often."

"If ever," Brandon agreed. "Although with the way Margaret asked Mary to make the reservation, it seemed like this was a usual spot for her."

"Maybe the restaurant is just new to Margaret's family," Kimber suggested. "It's possible she comes here for work without them. Either way, it doesn't prove anything."

"No, but maybe I can gain access to her credit card account," Brandon said. "Finance usually has the executives note who their meals were with on their expense reports."

"That makes sense. It makes it far easier when they do their taxes, and it protects them in case of an audit." Kimber's eyes lit up. "And we shouldn't limit ourselves to Margaret's expense account. It's amazing how much you can learn from someone's credit card statements."

Brandon couldn't help but smile. "Your financial side is showing again."

"I can't help it." Kimber shrugged. "It's what I'm good at."

"You're good at writing too."

"That's debatable."

"Trust me." Brandon squeezed her hand. "I know what I'm talking about."

$$\bullet \quad \bullet \quad \bullet$$

Kimber stood outside the restaurant entrance while she and Brandon waited for their driver to arrive. They'd timed their exit to correspond with Margaret's, but other than a short chat with her as they left and their brief meeting when they arrived, the evening had been uneventful.

The temperature had dropped while they'd been inside, and Kimber rubbed her arms in an effort to keep warm.

"We shouldn't have to wait much longer for the driver," Brandon said.

Kimber tilted her chin upward. "Should I be worried that Amelia's driver knows where I live?"

"With as many security cameras as they have in our apartment building, I doubt anyone is getting in there without the FBI knowing it."

"I guess it's best not to kiss you good night in the elevator, then, huh?"

Brandon leaned closer. "I wouldn't complain."

Kimber laughed at the hopeful expression on his face. "Sorry, but I'd rather not have my personal life turn into a topic of conversation for our FBI support team."

"Rafi *is* the one who wanted us to date."

Kimber lifted an eyebrow. "Just Rafi?"

"Okay, so maybe I'm benefiting from this arrangement more than he realizes." Brandon slid his hand around her waist and lowered his lips to hers. Slush splashed beneath car tires, and someone whistled for a cab. The sounds faded in that moment as Kimber let herself get lost in the kiss.

The sense of someone passing by caught her attention, and she pulled away. "I don't think this is any different from being in front of surveillance cameras."

"Probably not." Brandon gave her another quick kiss and kept his arm firmly around her waist as he shifted to look out at the road.

Kimber leaned into him, her gaze scanning for their ride. A woman approached a car across the street, the movement catching Kimber's attention. She started to look past the tall woman in the black overcoat, but when the headlights of an approaching car illuminated her face, Kimber did a double take. She'd seen her before. Evangeline, the woman she'd met on the subway last week, was standing across the street.

Kimber slid her arm around Brandon's waist and leaned closer. "I think we're being watched."

"What?" Brandon's gaze dropped to hers.

"The woman across the street. Black coat by the white car over there. I talked to her on the subway last week."

Brandon pulled his phone out of his pocket and discreetly aimed the camera in Evangeline's direction. As soon as he clicked several photos, he shifted so he was between Kimber and the street. "Let's walk." He hit a button on his phone, and Kimber heard ringing and then a muffled male voice.

"How close are you?" Brandon asked. He paused and waited for an answer. "We had a little change of plans. Can you pick us up on the corner of Broadway and Thirty-First? We're walking there now." Another pause. "Okay, thanks. We'll see you in two minutes."

"Eric is close?"

"Yeah." Brandon picked up his pace, and Kimber matched his stride.

She glanced over her shoulder. Evangeline was now walking down the street opposite them, mirroring their movements. "She's following us."

"What happened on the subway?" Brandon asked. "How did you meet her?"

"A guy tried to steal my wallet. I stopped him, and she started talking to me before we got on the train."

"And?" Brandon looked across the street.

"And she seemed a little too friendly, so I got off a stop early. That's the last I saw of her."

"Until tonight," Brandon said.

"Yes, until tonight."

"Where were you when you saw her on the subway?" Brandon kept his pace steady.

"It was the station closest to the restaurant where we were supposed to have dinner together."

"I don't like this." He looked across the street again. "She's still shadowing us, and the car that was beside her is idling. It looks like she may have a driver."

"Which is odd, considering she was taking the subway last week."

"Agreed."

"So, what do we do now?" Kimber asked. They were quickly approaching the intersection where they were supposed to meet their driver.

"We'll go on a little sightseeing adventure," Brandon said.

The Town Car pulled up beside them, and Brandon opened the back door.

Kimber did a quick check to make sure the driver was indeed Eric before she climbed in.

Brandon took the spot beside her and snapped his seat belt in place while staring through the driver's side window. "We're all set."

Eric signaled to pull back into traffic, but the light turned, trapping them where they were.

Kimber scanned the sidewalk across the street until she spotted Evangeline climbing into the white car she'd been approaching a few moments ago. Kimber gripped Brandon's hand and whispered, "She's still there."

"I see her," Brandon whispered back.

Kimber spoke again at normal volume and asked Brandon, "Would you mind if we drove by the Empire State Building?"

"That's a great idea." Brandon leaned forward. "Eric, can we make a detour?"

"No problem."

The light turned, and Eric pulled out into traffic. He didn't make it half a block before Evangeline's driver took position three cars back.

"Now what?" Kimber whispered.

Brandon leaned down and kissed her cheek before whispering, "Now we see if we can lose them in the traffic."

"And if we can't?"

"We come up with a plan B."

CHAPTER 27

THE CAR WAS still back there. Eric had already reached the Empire State Building and circled around it, but now Brandon had a decision to make. Did they call Rafi for reinforcements and possibly tip their hand as to their connection with the US government, or did they try to handle the situation on their own?

"Back to Miss Frost's apartment?" Eric asked as he circled back toward their building.

Brandon's mind raced. They needed a new destination. Fast. He was still grasping for options when Kimber spoke.

"Actually, I'd love to stop at Barnes & Noble." Kimber checked the time on her phone. "It's still open, isn't it?"

A bookstore, one with a single entrance. That was risky. "I think the one on this side of town closes at eight or nine."

"Then, that won't work. It's already after nine."

Brandon pulled up the maps app on his phone and zoomed out. "How about a walk in Central Park?" Brandon asked. "And afterward, we can stop for some hot chocolate."

"Good idea."

Remembering his walk in Central Park the day of their first official date, Brandon debated where to have their driver drop them off.

Kimber beat him to it. "Can you drop us off by Columbus Circle?"

Brandon didn't remember being in that part of the park, but he trusted Kimber to know where they would have the best shot at losing their tail. "And after you drop us off, you can go on home," Brandon added. "I don't want you to have to wait on us."

"I don't mind," Eric said.

"I appreciate that, but since we plan to stop for hot chocolate afterward, there's no need for you to wait around for us." Brandon stretched his arm across the back of the seat and peeked through the rear window. In the dark, he couldn't easily identify where their pursuer was now. An SUV pulled into the spot behind them, further blocking his view.

Kimber tilted her chin up and whispered in his ear. "Is she still back there?"

"I can't tell," he whispered back. "Probably."

Eric pulled into what appeared to be a large roundabout, a statue in the center of it. He circled past several skyscrapers before he pulled beside the curb at the entrance to Central Park. "Are you sure you don't want me to wait?" he asked.

"I'm sure." Brandon pushed the door open, climbed out, and reached for Kimber's hand.

She stepped beside him as a white sedan approached. "That's her!" Kimber whispered.

"Come on." Brandon closed the car door and moved past the concrete barriers that separated the road from the sidewalk and headed for the main entrance, Kimber right beside him.

They'd barely made it past the large monument on their left before Kimber slipped on a patch of ice.

Brandon grabbed her with his free hand to keep her upright, turning as he did so to look over her shoulder. The blonde woman was walking steadily toward them.

He did a quick analysis. No sign of a weapon, but with her long coat, he couldn't be sure what she might be hiding beneath it.

Kimber took a step and slipped again. "I can't run in these shoes."

"Do the best you can." Brandon released her hand and slid his arm around her waist to steady her. "Which way?"

"Over here." She pointed around the back of the monument, and they moved as quickly as her high heels would allow. Her feet had to be freezing.

"I'm sorry. We should have tried the bookstore," Brandon said, "but I was afraid she would wait for us to come back out."

"No, Central Park was a good idea." She glanced at her watch. "If we time things right, we'll be able to lose her."

They continued down the sidewalk for several more yards. Then Kimber squeezed his waist and stepped onto the snow-covered lawn.

"If we go through there, we'll leave tracks."

"I know, but it's not going to matter." Kimber continued on her intended path, the snow coming up past her ankles.

With no choice but to trust her, Brandon stayed at her side.

They moved past several trees, and then Kimber changed direction, going on a parallel path to where they had been originally headed.

Footsteps crunched on the frozen snow, theirs and someone else's, but Brandon couldn't identify the source through the trees.

"Where are we going?" he asked, his voice low.

"It depends on if we see a bus when we get to the bus stop." Kimber pulled her phone from her coat pocket and tapped the screen without slowing. "If there isn't one, we'll keep going to the closest subway station. There are two pretty close to the bus stop."

The likelihood of the bus arriving at the exact moment they hoped for was slim, at best.

They reached an open space where a mix of other footprints marked the snow.

Kimber leaned down and took off her shoes.

"What are you doing?" Brandon asked.

"We need to get across the lawn before she gets here." She released him and motioned toward the trees on the far side of the snow-covered clearing. "Hurry."

Brandon stared for a full second as Kimber sprinted forward, her feet bare. Then he raced after her.

They crossed the fifty yards of open space, Brandon reaching her side before they passed into the wooded area. He grabbed her hand to stop her from continuing forward and pulled her behind a tree.

"We need to keep going," Kimber said, her breathing coming heavily.

"We need to see if we're still being followed," Brandon countered. With their bodies close to keep them both out of sight, he peeked around the side of the tree. Sure enough, less than a minute passed before the woman emerged, but this time, she had a man by her side.

In the dim light, Brandon couldn't make out much about the new arrivals except that the man appeared to have some sort of strap across his torso. Whether it was a messenger-bag strap or a gear strap for a rifle, Brandon couldn't tell. He needed a photo, but he couldn't easily retrieve his phone without drawing attention to them.

His gaze landed on Kimber's hand, her phone still clenched in her fingers. "Let me borrow your phone."

With a trembling hand, she unlocked the screen and handed it over. He turned it toward him to make sure the couple following them wouldn't see the illuminated screen. Then he minimized the app—it appeared to be a city transit map—and opened Kimber's camera.

Not risking a flash going off, he switched the camera app to video and zoomed in as far as he was able. He then took some clips of the couple talking and pointing.

Once he was done, he darkened Kimber's screen and handed the phone back to her. He jerked his chin in the direction of the next tree over. "Work your way through the trees. We need to move slowly so they don't hear us."

"I'm more concerned about being seen." She nodded down at her white coat. "This isn't exactly great for blending into the dark."

"You definitely need a new coat." Opting for the most logical solution, he motioned her forward. "You go first. I'll stay behind you."

Kimber nodded. Then, with her feet still bare, she rushed deeper into the trees.

•   •   •

Kimber was going to freeze to death if she didn't get her bare feet out of the snow soon. Her shoes still in one hand and her cell phone in the other, she emerged onto the sidewalk near the park exit by the bus stop. She glanced at the transit app on her phone. Three minutes until the bus was supposed to arrive.

"Come on." She raced toward the exit and called over her shoulder, "We're almost there."

"Don't you want to put your shoes on?" Brandon asked, jogging by her side.

"There's no time." They reached the sidewalk as a hiss carried toward them, likely the brakes from the bus. Though her feet were numb and the muscles in her thighs were burning, she turned toward the bus stop where she had often caught a ride to Tessa's apartment when she'd first visited New York.

"The bus is there!" Brandon grabbed her arm as though dragging her forward would help her go faster.

She raised her other hand, shoes and all, to signal the driver to wait.

The doors closed, and panic welled up inside her. The bus didn't move despite someone honking behind it.

They raced the last few yards, and the doors whooshed back open.

"Thank you so much," Brandon said, gripping the side of the door and motioning Kimber forward.

"Yes, thank you," Kimber said breathlessly. She dug her MetroCard out of her purse and swiped it as she passed. She glanced back at Brandon, quickly realizing he might not have a card. She swiped hers a second time to pay for him too.

"Thanks." Brandon walked behind her down the aisle.

She spotted two seats together near the rear doors and collapsed into the one closest to her. Brandon stood beside her until she moved to the seat by the window to make room for him.

As an afterthought, she looked out the window toward the park entrance. No sign of the woman following them.

"Who do you think she is?" Kimber asked.

"I don't know." Brandon leaned forward, also looking out the window. "But when we get back to your apartment, we'll see if we can find out."

She didn't need him to expand on his comment. Clearly, he'd used her phone to take photos so the FBI could run the woman's image through facial recognition.

Kimber debated whether to put her shoes on, but with the moisture still dripping off her feet, she kept her shoes in her lap and pulled her coat more tightly around her. A shiver rippled through her.

"You have to be freezing." Brandon took her hands in his and rubbed them to help her warm up. "Do you want to stop and get a hot chocolate?"

She clenched her teeth together to keep them from chattering and nodded.

"There's a place down the street from our building. It shouldn't be busy this time of night." He looked up at the route map on the side of the bus. "Do we need to make a transfer to go home?"

She nodded again.

"I'll call a taxi." He pulled his phone out. "I don't want you to have to wait out in the cold for another bus."

She nodded again, snuggling closer to Brandon. Maybe by the time they got back to their apartments, she'd be able to feel her feet again.

• • •

They got their hot chocolate to go.

With his paper cup in one hand and his other arm wrapped around Kimber, Brandon walked toward her apartment. Even though Kimber's shoes were back on her feet, Brandon suspected she needed a blanket and a fire to go with her hot chocolate. And maybe some snickerdoodles.

Trudy must have read his mind. The door between his and Kimber's opened, and Trudy stepped into the hall, a thick terry-cloth robe wrapped around her. "I had just about given up hope on seeing you again tonight." She held out a plate of cookies. "I have too many cookies left over, so I wanted to give you more."

Brandon released Kimber so he could take them. "Thanks, Trudy."

"Did you have a nice time?"

"We did," Brandon said. At least for the first half of the evening.

"I'm going to sit by the fire," Kimber said. "Brandon, do you want to join me? We can have some of those cookies for dessert."

"I'd love to." Brandon held up the plate. "Thanks again."

"Enjoy." Trudy gave a quick wave and disappeared back inside.

"Come on." Brandon continued to Kimber's door. "Let's get that fire started."

Kimber pulled her keys out of her purse, but her fingers were shaking so badly, she struggled to slide the key into the lock.

"Here. Let me." Brandon tucked his hot chocolate into the crook of his arm so he could unlock the door. Once he opened it, he moved aside to let her enter first.

He set the cookies and keys on the kitchen counter before crossing to the fireplace. After he located the tool to turn on the gas, he flipped the switch to bring the flames to life.

Kimber headed for the hall. "I'm going to change into something warmer."

She closed her bedroom door, and Brandon returned to the kitchen. He grabbed some napkins from the napkin holder on her counter along with the cookies and carried them to the couch. He set them on the coffee table and sampled one of the snickerdoodles. The sweetness of cinnamon and sugar melted in his mouth.

The bedroom door opened a minute later, and Kimber emerged wearing a pair of flannel pajama pants, a long-sleeved shirt, and fuzzy purple socks. "How are the cookies?"

"They're even better than her chocolate chip."

"Then, I have to try one." She grabbed the afghan off the back of her couch as she sat down and spread the blanket over her legs.

"How are you feeling?"

"I'm starting to feel my toes again."

"I can't believe you ran through the snow barefoot."

"I didn't have much choice." She held up her cup of hot chocolate. "Thanks for this though. It definitely helped thaw me out."

"Now that we're alone, tell me more about the woman who was following us."

"She said her name was Evangeline." Kimber tucked her leg up beneath her and turned so she was facing him on the couch. "A guy tried to steal my wallet out of my purse. Right afterward, she started talking to me."

"What did she say exactly?" Brandon asked.

"Just that she was impressed that I stopped the guy, and she suggested I buy a new purse that didn't have a zipper on top."

"That doesn't sound weird."

"The weird part was afterward. She was asking me if I lived in New York, what I was doing for the weekend . . ." Kimber's brow furrowed. "Even the way she ended up standing next to me on the train felt a bit off."

"Did you give her your name?" Brandon asked.

"My first name, but that's it. And I didn't give her any specifics about where I was staying or what I do for a living," Kimber said. "There's no reason she should have been able to find me tonight."

"Unless she already knows who you are and was following you."

"Why would she care to know who I am?" Kimber asked. "I ran into her right after I left you at the restaurant."

"The day you found out I worked for Monroe."

"Yeah." Kimber tucked the blanket more firmly around her legs. "The day we realized we're both CIA."

Brandon struggled for a motivation for the woman to target Kimber then or now. "I have no idea why someone would have tried following you that day," he finally said. "Maybe if she'd followed you after your meeting at Monroe, it would make sense, especially if she knew you were about to sign a big deal, but what you're describing sounds totally random."

"It didn't feel random tonight."

"I agree. If she didn't care about you, she wouldn't have followed us into the park." Brandon pulled up his phone and retrieved the few photos he'd snapped of the woman when she'd been on the street across from Chef's Table on Fifth. "Can you text me those videos I took on your phone?"

"Sure." Kimber picked it up off the coffee table and AirDropped the videos to him. As soon as she set it back down, she grabbed another cookie off the plate. "Are you sending the images to Rafi?"

"Yeah. He should be able to run screenshots of her and the guy with her through facial recognition." Brandon selected the best videos and forwarded them to Rafi.

Kimber picked up her phone and looked at one of the videos. Then she paused it and lifted her gaze to his. "You aren't going to believe this."

"What?"

"The guy with her"—Kimber held up her cell—"he's the one who tried to steal my wallet."

"What?" Brandon straightened. "Are you sure?"

"Yes. I got a good look at him while I was deciding whether to break his thumb or not." Kimber held her phone out so the screen was facing Brandon. "That's definitely the same guy."

"They were working together." Brandon leaned back on the couch again.

"Yes, but why?"

"I don't know, but we need to find out."

CHAPTER 28

KIMBER HATED WAITING. She'd already showered and dressed for the day, started her laundry, and eaten five snickerdoodles. Maybe she should have added making breakfast to her list for the morning, but the easy sugar rush was way quicker and less stressful.

Now here it was, already ten o'clock, and she hadn't heard a word from Rafi about the images Brandon had sent him last night. She suspected the weekend would interfere with them receiving any updates before Monday, but that didn't make the situation any less frustrating.

At least she'd finally thawed out after her barefoot tromp through Central Park last night. She opened the blinds to a swirl of fresh snow falling. Maybe another fire was in order.

She turned on the fireplace and sat on the couch. Who was Evangeline really? And why had she been following them? Them. That word gave Kimber reason to pause.

Not bothering to put on her shoes, she turned the fireplace back off, grabbed her cell phone and the key to her apartment, and headed into the hall. She passed Trudy's apartment and knocked on Brandon's door.

Brandon opened it wearing jeans and a T-shirt, definitely not the clothes she was used to seeing him in. She rather liked the casual version of him.

A line formed on his brow. "Is everything okay?"

"I'm not sure." Kimber glanced toward Trudy's apartment. "May I come in?"

"Sure." Brandon stepped aside and waited for her to pass through before he closed the door.

She scanned his apartment, which was a mirror image to her own, before turning to face him. "What if Evangeline was following me because of you?"

"Why would she follow me? I've never met her."

"Neither had I, but I came from the restaurant with you," Kimber said. "Is it possible she and her partner were trying to find out who I was because they wanted to learn more about you? After all, you're the one who made reservations at both the restaurants we were at together when she showed up."

"That's a stretch." Brandon led her to the couch, where his laptop lay on the center cushion. He shifted it to the coffee table. "We know Darragh didn't know my name, or he wouldn't have been tracking down all the new employees at Monroe."

She'd forgotten about that.

A new thought arose, bringing with it a wave of panic. "Do you think it's possible she knows where my sister lives?" Kimber grabbed his hand. "That's where I came from when I went to meet you at the restaurant."

"I doubt it," Brandon said. "Otherwise, you probably would have seen her before tonight."

Kimber released his hand and dropped onto the couch. "I am so not cut out for this kind of work."

"You helped us get away last night without being followed home." Brandon lowered to the spot beside her.

"Yeah, but that was only because I know my way around Central Park and use public transportation so much when I visit my sister." She shook her head. "I can't let my job endanger Tessa. We have to figure out who is involved with Labyrinth."

"We're trying."

"We need to try harder." She stood again and paced the length of the room before turning back to face him. "Margaret's corporate credit card. We should see if we can hack into her account and the others for the top executives."

"I already emailed the request to Rafi, but he hasn't been able to get a judge to sign off on it. Not enough evidence. Or so the judge said. Apparently, he doesn't believe there's an imminent threat."

"That's understandable. We don't know for sure that Labyrinth is planning another terrorist attack. Everything is still speculation."

"They're planning something," Brandon said. "Otherwise, they wouldn't have bothered trying to kill me."

Kimber stopped pacing the room and stared at him. "They think you're a threat. Why?"

"Because I'm the person who met with the man we had working inside their organization," Brandon said. "Asadi Mir must think Finlay gave me more information than he did."

"Let's see if we can figure out what they think you already know." Kimber debated how best to approach hacking into the corporate credit card accounts. "I don't suppose you know which bank Monroe uses for their credit cards, do you?"

"Actually, I do." Brandon crossed into his bedroom and returned a moment later holding a credit card. "Here's mine."

"You have a corporate credit card?"

He nodded. "I imagine most of the administrative assistants have one."

"This is great. I should be able to hack my way into their account without them knowing we were there."

"You realize that credit card companies have a ridiculous number of safeguards set up to prevent people from hacking their system."

Kimber simply nodded. "Did you know the US government helped develop many of those safeguards to prevent fraud?"

"You really think you can do this?" Brandon asked skeptically.

"The whole case officer thing may be new to me, but when it comes to tracking financial data, I'm a pro."

"Just don't get caught."

Kimber smiled. "I never do."

• • •

Brandon lugged a new printer and a bag filled with various office supplies back to Kimber's apartment. A run to the local office supply store hadn't been on his list of things to do today, but Kimber insisted they would need a way to print out Monroe's corporate credit card statements.

As much as Brandon admired Kimber's confidence, he couldn't help wondering if his efforts were a waste of time. It was entirely possible she would spend her entire weekend trying to hack into the financial system that the FBI might be able to access within the next week anyway. Assuming the judge could be persuaded that the attack on Brandon was a sign of a direct threat against the United States.

Brandon reached Kimber's apartment and used his elbow to knock.

She opened the door a moment later and waved him inside. "Let's set the printer up in the office."

"I'll set it up so you can keep working on accessing the accounts."

"I already did."

Brandon balanced the printer box on the edge of the couch so he could turn to look at her more easily. "You what?" He couldn't have heard her right. "I was only gone for forty-five minutes."

"I know." Kimber relieved him of the bag he carried and took it into the second bedroom, which she had converted into an office. "Getting in is the good news. I'm afraid there's bad news too."

"What?" Brandon set the printer on the lateral filing cabinet in the corner. If his suspicions were right, it housed a government-grade safe inside. "What's the bad news?"

"I can see all the credit cards, but there aren't names attached to them." Kimber set the bag of supplies on the table and started pulling them out. "The only way to identify who they belong to is to match them up with their purchases."

"How many corporate credit cards are there?"

"Fourteen."

"I'm starting to understand why you wanted me to buy highlighters." Brandon pulled his keys from his pocket and used the sharp edge of his house key to open the box. As soon as he had the printer in place, he asked, "Do you have the files ready to print?"

"Most of them. I'll go prep the rest."

"Sounds good." Brandon finished setting up the printer and established the security protocols to ensure no one could access it besides him and Kimber.

He returned to Kimber's living room. "Okay, you're all set."

"Great." She clicked on her mouse and then held her computer out to him. "Can you set up the connection between my laptop and the printer? I can never figure out how to do that on my own."

Brandon took her laptop and stared at her. "You hacked into secure financial systems in less than an hour, but you don't know how to connect your laptop to a printer?"

"Hacking financial systems is easy."

"Trust me." Brandon sat on the couch beside her and opened her settings tab. "Connecting your printer is way easier."

"I hear what you're saying, and I don't believe you."

Brandon chuckled. "If this is all we disagree about, we're off to a good start."

Kimber leaned back on the couch. "How fast do we want to take this fake relationship?"

"Fake relationship?" Brandon asked.

She furrowed her brow. "This is weird, juggling a real relationship with a fake one."

Brandon turned to her and leaned in for a kiss. The sensation of his lips on hers brought with it hopes and dreams for a future he'd never before let himself explore. Clinging to that hope, he pulled back, and his gaze met hers. "I say we have our fake relationship catch up to our real one as soon as possible."

She smiled. "I can ask Whitney if you can come with me to the book launch on Tuesday."

"What book launch?"

"It's the new nonfiction book for Elliott Paulson."

Kimber going out in public, where Whitney would undoubtedly try to shine the spotlight on both Elliott and Kimber. Even though Brandon preferred to steer clear of cameras, he wasn't about to send Kimber into that situation alone.

"Text Whitney on Monday to see if she's okay with you bringing a date," Brandon said.

"Or maybe I should just bring you so she doesn't have the chance to say no," Kimber said.

"That could work too." Brandon finished connecting Kimber's laptop to the printer and handed it back to her. "Here you go."

"Thanks." Kimber hit a few keys, and the printer in the next room whirred to life. "Are you ready to stare at numbers for a while?"

"Not really, but if it will help us find answers, I'm willing to try."

"Good, because you're our best bet at figuring out which credit cards belong to whom."

"I have a feeling I'm going to be paying a lot more attention to people's spending habits when I'm at work this week," Brandon said.

"Yes, you are." Kimber sent the next file to print.

"How did you get into those credit card statements so quickly anyway?"

She tilted her head to one side and lifted an eyebrow. "This is what I do for a living."

"Is there some sort of back door I don't know about?"

Her eyes gleamed with mischief. "There's always a back door."

CHAPTER 29

STACKS OF CREDIT card statements lined the entire length of Kimber's serving bar. Their dinner dishes sat in the sink, the lingering scent of egg rolls and Szechuan beef hanging in the air.

The shared meal had been a nice reprieve from their research, but at this point, Kimber wanted answers, and she really wanted Rafi to call them back with news on Evangeline's true identity.

"This one has to be Margaret's," Brandon said, interrupting Kimber's thoughts. "It has so many charges at the print shop, it could only be hers."

"How do you know it isn't her assistant's?"

"Because there aren't any lunch charges on it. Mary sits at the desk next to mine. I've seen her put the orders in for Margaret, so it's unlikely she'd use Margaret's card instead of hers."

"Put Margaret's name at the top then and pencil in Mary as another possibility," Kimber said.

So far, they'd only managed to speculate on who the signatories were on the various accounts, with the exception of Brandon's and Amelia's.

"As much as I hate to say it, we may have to wait until you're back at work on Monday to narrow this down further," Kimber said.

"I agree. We've been at this most of the day, and we still have more questions than answers." Brandon swiveled on his barstool to face her. "And we can't be sure if knowing which credit card belongs to whom will even make a difference. So far, I haven't seen anything suspicious."

"I'm not even sure what to look for," Kimber admitted.

Someone knocked on her door.

Kimber looked down at the papers scattered everywhere, papers that could arguably be considered classified.

Brandon started stacking the pages in front of him. "Go see who it is."

Kimber nodded and crossed to the door. She looked through the peephole, expecting to see Trudy on the other side, but instead, it was Tessa.

Kimber turned to Brandon and mouthed the words, "It's my sister."

He held up one hand to signal her to wait. He finished stacking the bank statements and carried them into Kimber's office.

As soon as he disappeared from sight, Kimber opened the door. "Tessa. What are you doing here?"

"I'm here to pick you up."

"Pick me up for what?" Kimber's gaze lowered to the garment bag draped over her sister's arm. "We didn't make plans."

Tessa breezed past her. "We have plans now."

Brandon emerged from the office. "Okay, your printer's all set up." He looked at Tessa as though he were surprised to see her. "Hey, Tessa. How's everything going?"

"Good." Tessa looked around the room, pausing when her gaze landed on the dirty dishes. "So, what's the deal with you two?"

"We just had some dinner together," Kimber said.

"Then, you're getting along again?" Tessa said, clearly fishing for more details.

"I can head home if the two of you want to hang out," Brandon offered. Of course, Tessa had no idea that going home only required his walking down the hall.

"Actually, I think you should come with us."

"Come with you where?" he asked.

"We're going to a private event at the Met."

Kimber narrowed her eyes. "What private event? The Met Gala isn't until May."

"I know. This is a private, unannounced party, but coming to it will totally put you in the inner circle here in New York." Tessa cocked a hip and wiggled her eyebrows. "Are you in?"

"I don't know." After having Evangeline follow them last night, Kimber would be happy to stay in her apartment building for the next week if she could get away with it.

"Trust me," Tessa pressed. "Your publisher will love the exposure."

Still uneasy, Kimber turned to Brandon. "What do you think?"

"I'm sure Whitney will love it if you're rubbing elbows with the who's who here in the city," Brandon said. "And Tessa did say it's a private party."

Private, as in no unwanted visitors allowed. That gave Kimber some comfort. Abandoning her hope for a quiet evening at home, she said, "Fine. I'll go if Brandon comes too."

"Great." Tessa held up the garment bag in her hand. "Brandon, I hope you live close and already have a tux because it's a black-tie event, and we're leaving in an hour."

"I'd better go iron my tux, then." Brandon moved toward the door. "I'll meet you back here in forty-five minutes."

"Perfect." Tessa carried the garment bag into Kimber's bedroom.

Kimber followed Brandon to the door. "Are you sure about this? My sister is being pretty vague."

"I'm sure. It'll be good for us to be seen as a couple sooner rather than later, and if we can get some good photos for Whitney to use in her social media campaign, so much the better." Brandon leaned close. "As long as I'm not in the photos with you."

"And if someone tries to follow us again?"

"If this is a private event with celebrities attending, I'm sure security will be far tighter there than it is here."

"Good point."

"And I promise to stay right by your side the whole time." He paused. "Except when people have their cameras out."

The prospect of dressing up for an evening out with Brandon gave her the last nudge she needed. "Okay. I'll see you in a little while." She started to close the door but stopped. "Do you really have a tux?"

"Yes. Having one is a necessity when working at the embassy." Brandon grimaced. "And I'm afraid it really does need ironing."

Kimber laughed. "Good luck."

"Thanks." Brandon disappeared down the hall, and Kimber joined her sister in the bedroom.

Two gowns lay on her bed, one in gold, the other in red.

"Oh, wow." Kimber ran a finger along the gold silk. "This is stunning."

"Yes, but tonight, you're wearing the red." Tessa opened her purse and started pulling out an assortment of makeup supplies.

"Where did these gowns come from?"

"Cherise Moore. They're sneak peeks from her fall collection." Tessa grinned. "I'm rather liking this arrangement you have with her."

"I bet."

"Come on." Tessa grabbed Kimber's arm and pulled. "Makeup first."

Kimber followed her into the bathroom. "Are you going to tell me what we're doing tonight?"

"We're going to a birthday party."

"A birthday party for whom?" Kimber asked.

Tessa grinned again. "That's the surprise."

• • •

They were at a birthday party for Madison Peters, one of the most well-known actresses of their generation. Everywhere Brandon looked, he spotted another familiar face, familiar to him only from their images on the screen.

"How in the world did we end up with invitations to this?" Brandon asked.

"Madison is one of Greta's clients," Tessa said. "When she found out my sister had just signed a big publishing contract, she insisted I bring you along."

"Did you tell her about the contract, or did Greta?" Kimber asked.

"Greta." Tessa shrugged. "Like I said, she's a genius at nontraditional promotion. And she offered to help put you in the spotlight."

"There's plenty of spotlight here tonight." Far more than Brandon had anticipated.

"Yes, but there's no reason for any of it to shine on me," Kimber said.

"Not yet, but if we can get some photos with you and some of the celebrities here, we'll have some great material to increase your exposure," Tessa said.

"I hate the idea of using famous people to inflate my own importance." Kimber sighed. "I'd rather get to know people for who they are, not for what movie they starred in."

Brandon sensed someone behind him right before a man's voice interrupted their conversation.

"That's a refreshing attitude," a man said.

Brandon turned, and identified the owner of the voice: Ian Sawyer, the winner of several Oscars, at least three of which were for Best Actor. Brandon fought to keep his jaw from dropping. Judging from the stunned expression on Kimber's face, she was having the same struggle.

"I'm Ian Sawyer." Ian extended his hand toward Kimber.

"Kimber Frost." She put her hand in his. "It's an honor to meet you."

Tessa offered her hand. "I'm Tessa Seidel. I work for Greta Meyer."

"Oh, yes. Greta's right-hand gal."

"More or less." Tessa nodded.

Ian turned to Brandon. "And you are?"

"Brandon Hale." Brandon shook the older man's hand. "It's nice to meet you."

"You too." Ian turned his attention back to Kimber. "Forgive me for eavesdropping, but your conversation piqued my curiosity." A smile tugged at his lips. "Tell me. What are you about to be famous for?"

"I don't know that I'll ever be famous, but my publisher is hoping I will be," Kimber said. "I signed a two-book deal with Monroe Publishing yesterday."

Ian's face lit up. "Congratulations. That's worth celebrating."

"We've been telling her the same thing," Tessa said.

Ian pulled his cell phone from his pocket and held it up. "Who's going to be our photographer?"

Kimber's eyebrows lifted. "Excuse me?"

"We can't very well help you get famous if we don't document this moment."

Was this guy for real? Brandon studied Ian, not quite sure what to think about his easy offer. Seeing no sign of false pretenses, Brandon held out his hand. "I can take the photos."

Ian handed his phone over. "Kimber, you'll want some on your phone too."

"Are you sure about this?" Kimber asked. "You just met me."

"Yes, but I remember what it was like the first time I signed a movie deal. I would have loved to have someone more established give me a boost." Ian tilted his head toward her. "Besides, it's not often I rub shoulders with a soon-to-be famous author."

"It won't be too soon," Kimber said. "My first book won't come out for another eighteen months."

"That time will fly by faster than you think." Ian motioned for her to join him.

With gratitude and acceptance in her expression, Kimber pulled her phone out of her purse and handed it to Tessa.

Ian slid his hand around Kimber's shoulders and angled himself in front of a statue. Brandon lifted Ian's phone and snapped several photos while Tessa took pictures with Kimber's.

Ian moved several feet to the side so they could do a few more with a different background.

As soon as they finished, Ian said, "Tag me on your social media, so I can tag you back."

"Thanks so much. I really appreciate it."

"Now that we have photos, let's introduce you around."

Now Kimber's jaw did drop. "What?"

Ian cocked an eyebrow, an expression that had been captured on film repeatedly over the years. "You didn't think I was just going to pose for the camera and abandon you, did you?"

"That's what most people would do," Kimber said.

"I'm not most people." Ian put his hand on Kimber's back for a moment before he pointed to his right. "Let's start over here."

Brandon leaned close to Tessa and whispered, "Should I be worried about Kimber with this guy?"

Tessa rolled her eyes. "Ian is old enough to be our father."

"I know." Brandon watched Ian guide Kimber to a table filled with other actors and actresses. "Should I be worried?"

"No." Tessa laughed. "Not at all."

CHAPTER 30

KIMBER HAD STEPPED into an alternate reality. Again.

True to his word, Ian had introduced her to dozens of people—more than half of them celebrities—and the majority of them had taken the time to chat with her and even congratulate her on her book deal.

Ian made a point of bringing up her book deal in every conversation, and Kimber was starting to think he enjoyed diverting the attention away from himself. She tried to believe she'd earned the contract everyone was congratulating her on, that she really was on her way to becoming a best-selling author, but it still felt too good to be true.

Brandon had designated himself as her photographer, undoubtedly to keep from being in the pictures. He took a photo of her with yet another one of Hollywood's famous couples before they all parted ways.

Tessa took Kimber's phone from Brandon and scrolled through the photos. "We have some great shots here." She tapped on the screen several times before handing it back to Brandon.

Almost immediately, the phone chimed with an incoming notification. Within seconds, it chimed several more times, the notifications coming in rapid succession.

"Sorry. I don't know why my phone keeps going off," Kimber said.

"Get used to it," Ian warned. "These photos from tonight all have the potential of going viral."

"I don't have that many followers," Kimber said.

"That's about to change."

Another chime from her phone. Kimber grabbed her phone and pressed the button to silence her notifications, then looked up and caught sight of a woman in her late forties approaching them. The woman cast a curious glance at Kimber and Tessa before stepping past them to reach Ian's side.

Ian's face brightened the moment he saw her. "There you are." He leaned down and kissed the newcomer's cheek.

The woman nodded at Kimber. "I see you found someone to keep you company while you waited."

"Everyone, this is my wife, Phoebe," Ian said. He then gestured to Kimber. "Phoebe, this is Kimber Frost. She's an up-and-coming novelist who just signed her first contract with Monroe Publishing."

Phoebe's face lit with genuine delight. "Congratulations."

"Thank you."

"And this is Tessa Seidel and Brandon Hale," Ian said.

Brandon and Tessa both exchanged greetings with Ian's wife.

"How long have you been writing, Kimber?" Phoebe asked.

"Since high school, but this is the first time I've forayed into the publishing world."

"It's an exciting time, to be sure."

"And overwhelming." Kimber said the words and instantly regretted them. She was supposed to be establishing herself as a confident artist, not someone who needed her hand held.

To her surprise, Phoebe's polished smile softened. "The entertainment world isn't easy."

"My wife should know," Ian said. "She's been keeping me grounded for nearly thirty years."

"And believe me, that's no easy task." Phoebe's eyes brightened, and she turned to Ian. "We should have Kimber out to the Hamptons this summer." She put her hand on Kimber's arm. "We have some lovely views, and it's a peaceful place to write."

"That's a wonderful idea." Ian nodded. "Feel free to bring your friends too."

Nearly stunned speechless, it took a second before Kimber managed to form words. "Thank you."

"Here." Phoebe grabbed her cell phone from her purse and handed it, unlocked, to Kimber. "Put your phone number in, and we'll be sure to stay in touch."

"Thank you," Kimber said again, not quite sure if this night could get any more surreal. Ian Sawyer's wife, whom she had just met, wanted her number. She entered her name and phone number and handed it back to Phoebe. Then again, maybe nothing would come of it.

Phoebe tapped on her phone screen before putting it back in her purse. "Who haven't you met yet?"

Kimber scanned the vast room, not sure how to answer the question.

Thankfully, Brandon answered for her. "It feels like we've met everyone here."

"Not quite. You need to meet Tyrone Brooks next," Ian said, referring to the star of a Broadway musical set to open in a couple of weeks. "He's a good person to associate yourself with."

"I'm surprised he's here tonight," Tessa said.

"Why?" Kimber asked.

"Broadway actors tend to avoid larger gatherings," Tessa told her. "It's hard on their voices to try to be heard over the din."

"You've clearly learned the business well," Ian said.

"Greta is very protective of her talent." Tessa shrugged. "It isn't hard to pick up on those nuances."

Surprise illuminated Phoebe's face. "Tessa, what do you do?"

"I work for Greta Meyer," Tessa said.

"Maybe Tessa can arrange an introduction for us." Phoebe focused on her husband, and a silent message passed between them.

After a moment, he nodded. "That's not a bad idea." He turned to Tessa. "Would you mind introducing us?"

"I'd be happy to," Tessa said. "I'll go find her while you chat with Tyrone." Tessa gave Kimber's arm a squeeze and moved past her.

"Thanks." Ian weaved through the tables to where Tyrone currently sat with another famous couple and the birthday girl.

This time, when introductions were made, Ian's obvious friendship with Tyrone allowed Kimber to remain safely in the background. She hadn't realized how exhausting making conversation could be.

Only a few minutes passed before Tessa returned with Greta by her side.

"Kimber, you look stunning." Greta kissed Kimber's cheek. "I knew Cherise Moore's line would be the perfect match for you."

"Thank you for everything, Greta," Kimber said, her words falling short of fully expressing her gratitude.

"I'm happy to help." Greta looked past her and introduced herself to Ian and his wife. "Tessa said we needed to meet."

"Yes. Do you have a moment to spare?" Ian asked.

"I do." Greta put her hand on Kimber's arm. "Please excuse us for a minute."

As soon as Greta, Ian, and Phoebe left, Madison, the birthday girl, asked, "Kimber and Brandon, what do you do?"

"I work for Monroe Publishing," Brandon said. "And Kimber just signed on to be one of our lead authors."

"Really?" Madison asked.

Kimber nodded.

"A debut novelist, huh?" Madison waved at the others at the table. "Come on, everyone. We need to take a photo with Kimber. She's going to be famous someday."

Kimber let out a nervous laugh. "I'll never be as famous as any of you."

"You never know." Madison took Tyrone's arm and circled the table to stand beside Kimber.

"I can take the photos," Brandon offered, holding up Kimber's phone.

"I can as well," Tessa said.

Madison handed her phone to Tessa.

Tessa and Brandon took the photos, and Kimber was given the now-common request to tag them in her posts.

After they finished, Madison settled back in her seat. "All of you sit down." She waved at the empty seats beside her. "If it looks like we're visiting, maybe I can put off making my rounds. My face hurts from smiling so much."

"I don't know how you all do it," Kimber said. "It must be exhausting to know that everywhere you go, someone is probably watching."

"You may be joining our ranks soon enough," Tyrone said.

"He's right." Madison nodded. "If Greta is pairing you up with her favorite designers, she's expecting you to make a splash in the entertainment world."

Kimber couldn't imagine it, but she did her best to step into her role and believe the four little words *I am a writer.* "You know what the best part about being a writer is?"

They all shook their heads.

"No one cares what I look like," Kimber said. "Everyone will only recognize my name and the book cover."

Tessa put her hand on Kimber's arm and squeezed. "You keep believing that."

"And enjoy anonymity for as long as it lasts," Tyrone added.

Kimber took a deep breath and nodded. "That sounds like great advice." Too bad the FBI and CIA didn't want her to take it.

• • •

Brandon scanned the area outside the Met before he crossed to Greta's waiting car. The driver stood beside it, both the front and rear passenger doors open and waiting for them.

Kimber climbed in first, then Tessa and Greta. Brandon waited until they were all safely inside before he climbed into the front seat.

The driver closed the rear passenger door and circled to take his spot behind the wheel.

"Thanks again for the ride," Tessa said.

"Trust me. You don't want to try to call a cab when a party is breaking up. It's way too hard to find your ride," Greta said. "And this is an easy way to thank you for introducing me to Ian and Phoebe."

"I think providing us with our wardrobe tonight is plenty thanks enough," Kimber said.

"Is Ian going to sign with you?" Tessa asked.

"It's looking promising," Greta said. "We'll meet for lunch on Tuesday."

A phone vibrated in Brandon's pocket, a reminder that he still had Kimber's cell from their last round of photos. He pulled it free, and a slew of Instagram notifications lit up her screen.

Brandon swiveled in his seat so he could pass Kimber's phone to her. "Here. With the way your phone keeps vibrating, I have a feeling someone may have tagged you in a photo tonight."

"Oh, that was me," Tessa said.

"What? When?" Kimber asked.

"I put a post up from one of the first pictures I took of you and Ian." Tessa took Kimber's phone and swiped at her screen. "Here it is."

Kimber's eyes widened. "There are over four hundred likes on this photo."

"You have almost a thousand on the one I posted with Tyrone and Madison." Tessa grinned.

Kimber's face paled, and she lifted her gaze to Brandon's before she held her phone out for him to see. "She tagged that we were at the Met."

The simple statement likely sounded innocent enough to Tessa and Greta, but Brandon understood her concern completely.

He took the phone from her and clicked on the first of the two posts Tessa had made on Kimber's behalf. The first was from shortly before eight o'clock, over five hours ago. If Evangeline and her friend knew who Kimber was, they would have had plenty of time to get to the Met and wait for them.

"It's going to be fine," Brandon assured her. For Greta's and Tessa's benefit, he added, "Fame is a by-product of being a big-name author. Having these photos out there now will give you the chance to adjust to the attention before your book hits the stands."

"I'd rather find out if people like my book before getting all this attention."

"They'll like your book," Brandon assured her. He scanned the cars behind them for any possible tails, unable to determine whether the other vehicles were following them or simply traveling in the same direction.

Kimber's phone chimed again with an incoming text message. A second one immediately followed.

Brandon read the pop-ups on the screen, and his jaw dropped. "Um, Kimber?"

"Yes?"

"Ian and Phoebe just texted you their phone numbers."

"What?" Kimber took her phone back and stared at the screen. "Oh my gosh. Ian just invited us to go to opening night for Tyrone Brooks's new musical."

"All of us?" Brandon asked.

"All four of us." Kimber sent a quick text in response and passed her phone back to Brandon so he could read the full message. Then she leaned forward so she could see Greta more easily. "You're included, too, Greta."

"That was nice of him." Greta's tone was such that she didn't seem the least surprised by the offer. "Tessa, see if you can make that work in my schedule."

Another night spent with the rich and famous. Not exactly the ideal situation for an undercover CIA operative. Brandon had to remind himself that this was part of Kimber's undercover assignment. Still, the concept of keeping her safe while her location and identity were being thrown out for all the world to see would be more of a challenge than he'd first anticipated, especially while they were dating publicly.

The driver made the turn toward their apartment building, and Brandon's stomach churned uncomfortably. He'd rather hoped they would drop Greta or Tessa off first so he could verify whether any cars matched their movements. As it was, three cars made the same turn, and he couldn't tell in the dark if they were the same ones that had been behind them when they'd left the Met.

The driver pulled up at the curb, and Brandon quickly climbed out. "I can get the door."

"Thanks again for the ride." Kimber waited for Brandon, then climbed out.

Brandon gave a quick wave before closing the door and stepping back. He scanned behind them, but the only approaching traffic was the cars turning onto the street at the intersection a short distance away.

By the time he turned his attention back to Kimber, she was already halfway to the door.

As soon as they both passed through the entrance, she asked, "Anything?"

"I can't tell. The red light stopped the traffic behind us, so there's no way of telling if anyone was following us."

"Maybe we should take the stairs up to make sure no one will see what floor the elevator stops at."

"That's a good idea." Brandon pressed the Up button.

"What are you doing?" Kimber asked.

"Sending the elevator to the nineteenth floor." He crossed to the stairwell.

As soon as the door closed behind them, Kimber took off her shoes and started up the stairs.

"Sorry for the unexpected workout," Brandon said.

"It's okay. If it helps us make sure no one can find us, it's worth it." Kimber's expression clouded. "Of course, that's assuming no one will be waiting for you when you go to work on Monday."

"As soon as we get upstairs, I'll tap into the building's surveillance cameras. If someone follows, I'll know it."

"Good." Kimber continued up the stairs. "I could use a decent night's sleep."

CHAPTER 31

KIMBER CROSSED HER arm over her eyes to block out the sunlight streaming through the window. After arriving home last night, she'd bolted her door, changed into pajamas, and collapsed onto her bed. Even the prospect of Evangeline following her and Brandon to their building hadn't been enough to override her exhaustion.

She let herself drift in the dreamlike state of semiconsciousness as memories of the party flooded her mind. She'd met so many people, so many of them showing her such kindness, particularly Ian and Phoebe. She now had their numbers in her phone, which still blew her away. Or at least she would have their numbers in her phone once she added them to her contacts.

She rolled over in bed and reached for her phone. Her fingers brushed against her charging cord, which wasn't attached to anything.

Forcing her eyes open, she propped herself up on her elbow and peeked at her empty bedside table.

"Must have left it in my purse," she muttered to herself.

She lay in bed for another minute before she gathered the energy to stand. She crossed to her purse and opened it to find lipstick, keys, tissues, and her wallet but no phone. She checked her coat pockets. Empty.

Her dress from last night didn't have pockets, and surely she hadn't left it in Greta's car. She did a quick search of the kitchen and bathroom counters without success.

She'd had it in the cab last night when she'd received the text messages from Ian and Phoebe, but she couldn't remember using it since arriving home with Brandon.

Brandon. She'd handed her phone to him when she'd shown him the text from Ian. Had he ever given it back?

If she had her cell phone, she could call and ask. With a frustrated huff, she headed for the shower. As soon as she was dressed for the day, she checked the time. Ten thirty-two. Brandon should be up by now. She hoped.

Maybe if she were lucky, Trudy would hear her walk by and offer her baked goods. She really did like her new neighbor.

With a half smile, Kimber opened her door, then immediately gasped when she found herself face-to-face with Evangeline.

Acting instinctively, Kimber tried to slam the door closed, but Evangeline slapped her hand against it and used her foot to block it open.

"No!" Kimber shouted the word. Her heart pounding, she tried to use her weight to close the door. No luck.

"I'm not here to hurt you," Evangeline said, her voice low and calm and decidedly British. "I'm here to help you."

"Who are you?" Kimber eased the pressure off the door.

"Evangeline Moore." She slipped a small black ID case from her purse and held it out. "MI6."

"You're with MI6?" Kimber leaned closer so she could inspect the ID more closely.

The door beside hers opened, and Trudy peeked her head out. "Is everything all right?"

Evangeline instantly dropped her hand so her ID was no longer visible.

"Yes," Kimber said. At least, the ID looked real enough. "But could you do me a favor?"

"What is it?" Trudy asked.

"Would you mind calling Brandon and asking if he can bring me my phone? I think I left it with him last night."

"I'd be happy to." Trudy eyed Evangeline warily. "You sure you're okay?"

"Yes, I'm fine."

Trudy cast another suspicious look at Evangeline before she disappeared back inside her apartment.

"Can we take this inside?" Evangeline asked.

"Let me see your ID again."

She held it out. After another quick inspection, Kimber let Evangeline enter.

The moment Evangeline closed the door, Kimber asked, "Why were you following me?"

"I needed to see if you were intel or just someone who was getting in my way."

"Getting in your way for what?"

Footsteps pounded in the hall, followed by a quick knock on Kimber's door. It opened before Kimber had the chance to answer it, and Brandon rushed in, gun in hand.

He lifted his pistol. "Who are you?"

"She says she's with MI6."

Evangeline held up her ID again.

Brandon lowered his weapon. "Then, why were you following us?"

"That's what I asked," Kimber said.

"And?"

"I followed pretty boy here from Monroe Publishing last week." Evangeline jerked her thumb at Brandon. "When I saw you meet him for dinner without staying to eat, I thought I might be able to learn more about him from you."

"Your partner tried to steal my wallet to find out who I am?" Kimber asked, the pieces of the puzzle starting to take shape.

"Yes. When you stopped him, I realized you were either intel or a member of Labyrinth. I just didn't know which one."

"Wait." Brandon holstered his gun at his belt and held up his hand. "You thought I was with Labyrinth?"

"Your mobile was in the same place as Finlay Addington's when he died. The chances of you being the person who killed him were high."

"If you're here, I assume you know that I was the one he was meeting, not the person who shot him."

Evangeline nodded. "The CIA confirmed your identity on Friday."

"Then, why were you following us on Friday night?"

"We know one of Labyrinth's hit men arrived in New York with orders to kill the man who met with Addington," Evangeline said. "We were following you, hoping to find him."

"For the record, all you did was freak us out," Kimber said.

Brandon moved to her side. "Did you ever think about telling us who you were and why you were there?"

"We weren't sure if your girlfriend here was with Labyrinth or not."

"Why would you think that?" Kimber asked. "You just said you saw me meet him at the restaurant."

"Yes, but we couldn't be sure you weren't trying to worm your way into his life to interrogate him on what Addington told him."

"How did you figure out that I'm not with Labyrinth?"

"For one thing, Mr. Hale is still alive," Evangeline said. "And it was clear that you were working together to evade us. If you were Labyrinth, you would have killed Brandon and disappeared on your own."

"Did you find out where we live by following us home from the Met?" Kimber asked.

"Yes. It took my partner a little time to hack the security cameras in the building, but once he did, we were able to find your apartment."

"Now that you're here, what do you want?" Brandon asked.

"We want the same thing you do," Evangeline said evenly. "To stop Labyrinth."

•　•　•

It took less than twenty minutes for Brandon to confirm Evangeline's story and her identity.

Evangeline sat in Kimber's living room, completely relaxed, while Kimber sat across from her, her fingers laced together, waiting impatiently for Brandon to check in with CIA headquarters.

Brandon hung up the phone with Director Yarrow and sat beside Kimber on the couch. "Now that we have that out of the way, tell us what you know."

"Do you know who Asadi Mir is?" Evangeline asked.

"I'm pretty sure he's the one who had Finlay killed."

"We think so too. He's also planning a major attack in the UK."
Evangeline rested her elbow on the arm of the love seat. "We believe he's
targeting the US at the same time."

"Where are you getting your intel?" Brandon asked.

"We picked up a phone call between Asadi and someone at Monroe
Publishing."

The person he and Kimber were actively trying to identify. "Do you
know who he was talking to?"

"No. We think it was a man, but the call was made through an en-
cryption program so the sound quality isn't the greatest."

Having a clue about the gender of the Labyrinth mole in Monroe
would narrow their suspect field significantly.

"What did they say?" Kimber asked.

"They were vague, but Asadi mentioned two upcoming events, one
in London and one in New York."

"Here?" Kimber asked.

"Labyrinth usually targets Americans overseas, not here," Brandon
said.

"Based on the conversation, that's about to change," Evangeline said.
"Our intel suggests he blames the British government for the death of
his brother, who was killed during the early days of our involvement in
Afghanistan. The Americans are the ones he blames for his sister's death."

"What happened to his sister?" Kimber asked.

"She was an actress. She had success in some Indian films before she
made the transition to theater. Unfortunately for her, she was visiting
her brother in Kabul when the US pulled out. She wasn't allowed to
leave, so she tried to use her fame to demonstrate the lack of women's
rights under the Taliban. She was killed less than a week later."

"That's terrible," Kimber said.

It was terrible, but they needed to focus on the future now, not the
past. "Do you have any idea when this attack is supposed to happen?"
Brandon asked.

"No, but based on the fact that they appear to be using a new publishing contract to hide their flow of money, my guess is that it's soon."

"That's scary," Brandon said. "I've been there for three weeks, and all I've been able to do is identify more suspects."

"We know Asadi Mir met with his funding source in October somewhere in the EU. We hope you can access passport records that will lead back to an employee at Monroe."

"Assuming whoever it was used his or her real passport," Brandon said. "We've seen an uptick in forgeries over the past few years."

"Do you know exactly when this meeting would have happened?" Kimber asked.

"We have a pretty good guess." Evangeline pulled out her cell phone and scrolled through several screens. "It would have been sometime around October 14 or 15."

"That may help us narrow our suspect list down," Kimber said.

Brandon straightened. "I think both Ramon and Margaret were in Europe around that time."

Kimber pushed off the couch and disappeared into her office. She returned a moment later with the stack of bank statements and a handful of highlighters that she carried to the serving bar. "Come on. You can help."

Curious, Brandon followed her.

"Help with what?" Evangeline asked, also abandoning her seat in the living room to join Kimber in the kitchen.

"These are the last six months of credit card statements for Monroe Publishing," Kimber divided the stack into three piles. "We need to highlight every charge that occurred on October 14 and 15."

"If you're hoping to find charges made in Europe, I think you're out of luck," Brandon said. "We already looked through these."

"Yes, but we were searching for what was on the statements, not for what was missing."

Understanding dawned. "Whoever was at that meeting couldn't have been here in New York using his or her credit card."

"Exactly." Kimber nodded.

"We already know Margaret and Ramon traveled to Europe around that time," Evangeline said. "We should focus on the two of them."

"Agreed, but like Brandon said, whoever is working with Labyrinth could have used a fake passport. The organization certainly has the resources to pull that off."

Evangeline sat on a stool. "Hand me a highlighter."

Kimber passed one to her along with a stack of credit card statements. She then handed another stack and a highlighter to Brandon, keeping the final set for herself.

Brandon grabbed the seat two spots over from Evangeline, leaving the spot between them for Kimber. "You realize that we still don't know who these accounts belong to."

"I know, but you'll figure it out." Kimber took her seat and started flipping through pages.

"I wish I had your confidence," Brandon muttered.

Evangeline highlighted a charge. "My partner had to leave for Paris last night, but I'm here for at least a few more weeks. I can help you."

"How?" Brandon asked. "The only way to figure out who's using which credit card is to monitor their purchases."

"Yes, but some of these charges happen regularly." Evangeline held up a page. "The same coffee shop five days a week. It won't take long for me to set up surveillance and figure out which one of your coworkers is making those purchases."

"She's right," Kimber said. "Especially if you can give her photos of the employees on our suspect list."

Brandon considered how much faster Evangeline's method would be over his trying to overhear other people's orders and watch for deliveries coming into the office. "Kimber, we might want to have you do the same thing," he suggested.

"Me?" She looked up at him.

"Yeah. A coffee shop would be a great place for you to write, and it would give you the chance to 'accidentally' run into someone from Monroe."

"That's not a bad idea." Kimber nodded thoughtfully.

Evangeline held up a credit card statement. "I may have found the one we're looking for." She passed it to Kimber. "No charges on this one from October 12 through October 18."

Kimber skimmed the page before passing it to Brandon. She then motioned to the pages still in front of Evangeline. "Let me see the recent month for that card." She leaned close to Brandon to look again at the paper she'd given him. "It ends in 0794."

"Here you go." Evangeline passed her two more pages.

Kimber let out a sigh. "I'm afraid this one doesn't have any daily charges that we'll be able to scout out."

"Then, we start identifying the ones we can and work through process of elimination," Brandon said.

Evangeline picked up her highlighter again. "If my colleagues in Europe are correct, we need to work fast."

CHAPTER 32

THE PLAN OF attack was complete. And it was brilliant. Though it wouldn't have the death toll of 9/11, the impact would be just as immediate. A strike that would begin with an assault against the heart of London's Society, from the well-to-do all the way up to the lesser royals. Hours later, he would strike again, but this time in America's city that never sleeps. Asadi would make sure they didn't sleep—at least not easy—for a very long time.

He walked down the stairs to his private beach and dialed his supplier.

"Yes?" his supplier asked.

"I have the details for you." Those details would be coded and sent via messenger rather than spoken on the phone.

"How long will it take you to get everything in place?"

"The messages are already inserted, and the date is set."

"Estimated numbers?" his supplier asked as though he were speaking about only the dollars and cents his plan would cost to implement. Asadi suspected he was more interested in the casualty count. He knew he was. Bombmakers tended to enjoy seeing the results of their work in the headlines.

Asadi gave him both sets of data. "Two hundred thousand," he began, not giving the currency. They dealt in British pounds. Always in British pounds. "Between two and three thousand at 10 percent."

"That's an acceptable rate," his supplier said. "You're certain this event will draw attention?"

"It will make headlines around the world."

"I'll send a messenger tomorrow to pick up the specifics."

Finally, after all this planning, after waiting for his chance to get the world's attention, the game was about to begin. Sweet adrenaline rushed through him, and Asadi couldn't help but grin. "I'll have them ready."

• • •

Kimber set the three credit card statements aside, all of them lacking activity during the window Evangeline had given them. Two unidentified credit card holders and one whose name they knew: Amelia.

"Is it possible Amelia could be involved?" Kimber asked. "I mean, I know she's all business, but it's hard to imagine her working with a foreign terrorist group."

"It's hard to imagine anyone working with terrorists," Brandon said.

"Three possibilities." Evangeline swiveled in her barstool and stood. "That's not bad."

"It would be great if we knew who the other two cards belonged to," Brandon said. "I'm afraid we're going to have our work cut out for us this week."

"You need to stay close to Amelia," Evangeline said. "Kimber and I can try to locate the other two card users."

Brandon shook his head and spoke to Evangeline. "You can look for the other two card users." Brandon motioned to Kimber. "Kimber can work on eliminating our other potential suspects."

Evangeline looked at him. "It would make more sense to focus on identifying the two—"

Brandon held up a hand to stop her. "Kimber isn't a field operative. Eliminating people who we know aren't involved is one thing. Looking for Labyrinth's inside contact is another."

The sentiment was sweet, and Kimber could admit that she didn't have any interest in setting herself up to be alone with a potential terrorist, but she could also sympathize with Evangeline's position. Focusing on another option, she said, "We could have Rafi help Evangeline." She held up the questionable statements again. "Plus, if Rafi can get a warrant and the credit card company will pull the signature slips, we might not need to go to any of this trouble in the first place."

"That's true," Brandon conceded.

"Give me one of those, and I'll start my search tomorrow." Evangeline held out her hand.

Kimber took a photo of the top of the statement with her phone so she could print out a new set for herself. Then she handed it over.

"While you have your mobile out, we'd best exchange numbers." Evangeline pulled her own out of her pocket.

After the three of them added each other's numbers to their phones, Evangeline moved to the door. "I'll be in touch." She left the apartment and closed the door behind her.

"Well, that was unexpected." Kimber leaned back in her chair.

"Yes, it was."

Kimber held up her cell. "Thanks for bringing me my phone though."

"I didn't even realize I had it until Trudy called me."

"Yeah, that was a little terrifying, having Evangeline at my door and no way to contact you."

"I'll bet, but you handled it well." Brandon put his hand on her knee and leaned closer. "Rushing into your apartment and pointing a gun at someone wasn't how I planned to greet you this morning."

"Oh, really?" The warmth of his touch radiated outward, filling her with anticipation.

"Yes, really." He leaned in, using his free hand to cup the back of her neck. His lips were a whisper away from hers when a knock sounded at the door.

They both startled and pulled back.

Brandon groaned. "Whoever that is has terrible timing." He pushed out of his seat and peered through the peephole. "It's Trudy." He pulled the door open.

Trudy glanced at Brandon and then peered around him to where Kimber sat. "Are you both okay?"

"Yes." Brandon stepped aside to let their neighbor in. "Why wouldn't we be?"

"That woman who was here earlier." Trudy motioned in the general direction of the elevator. "She had a suspicious look about her."

"She's fine," Kimber assured Trudy. "She's someone Brandon used to work with."

"Then, why was she at *your* apartment?"

Whoops.

"I told her to meet me at Kimber's," Brandon said before Kimber could fumble for a response. "My friend was running early, and I was running late. It caused a bit of confusion."

"Especially since I forgot to get my phone back from Brandon last night," Kimber added.

"I guess that makes sense, but the whole scene had me worried," Trudy said. "I think we need a code word."

"A code word?" Kimber repeated.

"Yes, you know, a word you can say when you're in trouble," Trudy explained. "A word that signals if one of us should call the police."

Though amused by Trudy's suggestion, Kimber shrugged. "That's not a bad idea."

"*Popcorn*." Trudy gave a definitive nod. "That should be our word."

"Why *popcorn*?" Brandon asked.

"Because I never eat it, and if you ask if you can borrow some, I'll know you need help."

"Or if you ask us to borrow some, we'll know you need help," Brandon said.

"Precisely."

"Okay." Kimber couldn't fault that logic. "*Popcorn* it is."

"Good. Now that that's settled, both of you come on over. Dinner should be ready by now."

"Dinner?"

"It's Sunday," Trudy said as though that explained everything.

Kimber was still processing possible explanations when Brandon asked, "Are you inviting us over for Sunday dinner?"

"Of course." Trudy hooked her arm through Brandon's. "That's what neighbors do."

Kimber grabbed her keys. "You may be the best neighbor ever."

"Of course I am." Trudy grinned. "I even made apple pie."

CHAPTER 33

BRANDON STIFLED A yawn as he entered his office Monday morning. Between his and Kimber's adventurous route home on Friday night, getting home late after Madison's birthday party on Saturday, and the full day of work with Kimber and Evangeline yesterday, he was exhausted. At least the meal at Trudy's had been relaxing. She'd even sent him home with a slice of apple pie to save for later. Later had lasted only until this morning when he'd eaten the pie for breakfast.

He glanced at Mary's empty workstation, relieved that he didn't have to deal with her yet. Regina, however, was already seated at her desk, her laptop open in front of her. She looked up at Brandon as he lowered into his chair.

With a look of disdain and a hint of sarcasm in her voice, she asked, "How did things go with our new author?"

Opting for a neutral response, Brandon said, "It was nice getting to know her better."

"With that fat check in her bank account, I'll bet you'd like to get to know her a lot better."

"Don't be rude." Brandon turned on his computer. "I would have been interested in her whether she'd signed with Monroe or not."

Regina shot him a look of disbelief. "You're telling me you don't care that she just received a six-figure check or that it's one of many to come?"

"Honestly, it would be way easier on me if everyone weren't trying to shove her into the spotlight," Brandon said. "And I don't care about her bank account."

"Right." Regina shook her head.

The elevator doors chimed, and Amelia emerged. She strode with purpose toward her office and pointed at Brandon. "My office."

The curt tone wasn't what he'd expected from her first thing on a Monday morning. He stood, hoping Amelia's foul mood didn't have anything to do with him.

He walked into her office, and she closed the door herself with more force than necessary.

"What were you thinking?" she asked.

So much for him not being the source of her anger. "I'm not sure what you're talking about."

"I asked you to take Kimber out so you could help keep her focused." Amelia stormed around the far side of her desk and dropped her purse on top of it. "Instead, you take her out on both Friday and Saturday. I can almost guarantee she didn't write a single word all weekend."

"It was the weekend," Brandon reminded her. "And she's at this very moment sitting at a coffee shop, working on her next novel."

"You kept her out all weekend, and you really think she's up at"—Amelia checked her watch—"seven thirty on a Monday morning, working?"

"I'm positive she is. I walked her there myself," Brandon said. "And she did get some work done on Saturday before we went to the party."

He wasn't going to elaborate on what kind of work Kimber had been doing or that the result of that work had landed Amelia at the top of their suspect list.

Amelia pulled her phone out of her purse. "How did you two end up at this party in the first place?"

"Greta Meyer invited us." Sort of. "We got some great photos of Kimber with different celebrities."

"I've already seen them." Amelia set her phone down with a thud. "And while I'm sure that Whitney and Haseeb will be thrilled, I need Kimber focused on writing. Once we get close to her release date, marketing is going to take over her life."

"She is focused," Brandon assured her. "She's already done some initial revisions with Patricia on the manuscript they plan to submit next, and she's got a start on another one."

"You'd better not be lying to me."

"I'm not."

Someone knocked on Amelia's door.

Amelia nodded at Brandon to signal him to open it. He did, and Whitney rushed in.

"Have you seen Kimber Frost's social media pages?" Whitney held up her phone. "She has over five thousand followers on Instagram, and her interaction is fantastic."

"I saw." Amelia sat and nodded toward Brandon. "We were just discussing it."

"I don't know how she managed to meet Madison Peters, Tyrone Brooks, or Ian Sawyer, but those images she posted are getting a lot of attention."

"She has a lot more she can share," Brandon said. "She thought it would be best to spread them out over a few days."

"Who else does she have photos with?"

"I'll make you a list." Brandon shrugged. "There were probably another fifteen or so from the party on Saturday night."

"I need to call her."

"No." Amelia shook her head. "She's off-limits today."

"But I need those photos," Whitney said.

"Monday isn't a great social media day anyway," Amelia insisted. "And if you need to get a message to her, give it to Brandon. He'll take care of it."

"I'll have Kimber forward you the photos," Brandon said.

"Good. We want to keep her relevant on social media for as long as possible."

Brandon bit back a sigh. "I'm sure you do."

• • •

Kimber didn't know how she was going to get any writing done when she was spending more time staring at the people walking through the door than looking at her screen. She'd arrived at the coffee shop at six thirty, and it had taken her nearly fifteen minutes to secure the table she wanted. But now she was perfectly situated, where anyone entering would see her, and she could see everyone entering.

Based on the credit card receipts, the person from Monroe typically arrived between seven and eight. That window had already come and gone. Either they had decided to skip the coffee today, or Kimber hadn't recognized them. She'd have to spend more time studying the employee photos Rafi had provided them.

Kimber's phone chimed.

A text from Brandon. *Any luck?*

She texted back. *Not yet. Looks like a no-show.*

A frowny face emoji replaced the jumping dots.

The bell at the front door jingled, and Kimber looked up. Another person she didn't know.

She focused on her laptop screen, rubbing her thumb over the mouse pad to bring the laptop back to life.

The bell over the door jingled again. A woman around her age walked in, and Kimber identified her as the woman who sat in the cubicle beside Brandon. Kimber dug into her memory for a name but couldn't recall it.

The woman was so focused on her phone as she waited in line, she didn't look in Kimber's direction.

Kimber waited until the woman reached the front of the line and gave her order before she spoke. "Excuse me. Don't you work at Monroe Publishing?"

"Yes." The woman finally lowered her phone. "You're Kimber Frost."

"I'm sorry. I don't remember your name."

"It's Mary."

"Good to officially meet you." Kimber leaned back in her seat and waved at the spot across from her. "Do you want to join me while you wait for your order?"

"That's okay. It won't take them long." Mary remained standing. "What are you doing here?"

"Trying to write."

Mary leaned an elbow on the high table. "How's it going?"

"Slowly, but sitting in places like this always helps." She lifted her chin toward the people at the tables opposite her. "Seeing lots of people, hearing different conversations, it all tends to trigger the imagination."

"I know what you mean."

The way she said it caught Kimber's attention. "Are you a writer too?"

"Not really. Not like you."

"In case you missed it, until last Friday, I was an aspiring author too," Kimber said. "What do you write?"

Clearly surprised by her question, Mary blinked twice. "Fantasy."

"Wow. That's a genre I've never dared enter. The world-building alone is so daunting."

Mary's eyes lit up. "That's the fun part."

The barista called out Mary's name.

"That's me." Mary gathered her order. As she started toward the exit, she paused. "Good luck with your writing."

Kimber smiled. "You too."

As soon as Mary left, Kimber made a note on the spreadsheet she'd created to track their suspects and the credit cards matched to them.

One more credit card down. Another ten to go.

• • •

Brandon knocked on Kimber's door, eager for the latest update on her efforts to match credit cards to the people using them.

She opened the door, a pen in her hand and her hair tousled like she'd just run her fingers through it. "I was wondering when you were going to get here."

"It was a crazy day at work." He started to lean in for a kiss, surprised when Kimber stepped back rather than moving toward him. She waved him inside, and he spotted the reason she'd avoided the display of affection. Evangeline sat on the couch, her gaze on them.

"Any luck at the office?" Evangeline asked.

"I took notes on all the deliveries today and who signed for them. I can't be 100 percent sure the recipients are the same as the people who placed the orders, but it should help us narrow it down."

"Send me your notes, and I'll match them to today's charges," Kimber said.

"I'll text them to you." Brandon pulled up his notes app and shared his list of observations with Kimber.

She grabbed a pad of paper and moved to the counter, where her computer sat open.

"Did Rafi have any luck pulling signatures from the credit card company?"

"Yes, but most of them aren't going to do us much good," Kimber said.

"Why's that?"

"Take a look." She pushed her laptop toward him. Several scanned receipts filled her screen, but all of them were little more than a line scribbled across the signature block.

"You can't even make out any letters," Brandon said.

From her spot in the living room, Evangeline twisted her body to look at him. "We did manage to find a few that were legible."

"How many credit cards do we still have that don't have a name attached?" Brandon asked.

"Seven."

Almost half as many as when they'd started this morning. Not bad for only one day of searching. "We're getting closer."

"Let's see if your notes can help us narrow it down further," Kimber said.

Evangeline's phone rang, and she answered it. "What do you have for me?" She listened for a few seconds, then she bolted to her feet. "Are you sure?" Her fingers tightened on her phone, and she looked up at Brandon and Kimber. Alarm lit her eyes, and her face paled as she continued to listen to whoever was on the other end of the call. "There has to be some way to trace them."

She fell silent again, this time only for a few seconds. "Okay. Let me know as soon as you find anything."

Brandon sat on a barstool. "That didn't sound like good news."

"No, it wasn't." Evangeline blew out a breath as though trying to mentally prepare for what she was about to share. "One of my colleagues just finished a search of Asadi Mir's last known residence in Wales. They found a calendar. The page with March was ripped out of it."

Kimber's eyes widened. "It's already March 14," she said, stating the obvious.

"Yes. If we're right, the attack will happen within the next two weeks."

"The CIA did a complete sweep of Mir's residence," Brandon said. "There's no way they missed that." He shook his head. "This has to be fake intel someone planted for your people to find."

"I wish it were," Evangeline said. "The CIA searched his house on Anglesey, not his flat in Rhos-on-Sea." Evangeline held up her phone. "My colleague tracked him there and finally figured out where he was staying."

Brandon's blood turned to ice. "That must have been where he went after Finlay was killed."

"We have to find the operative at Monroe," Kimber said. "That may be the only way to stop whatever Labyrinth has planned."

Evangeline leaned down and picked up the stack of credit card statements that lay on the coffee table. "We don't have time to eliminate these one at a time. We've narrowed our suspects down to three. Now it's time to find out for sure who these other two credit cards belong to."

Evangeline was right, but he didn't care for the reckless light shining in her eyes.

"What do you propose?" he asked.

"I need the two of you to create a distraction," Evangeline said.

"For what?" Kimber asked.

Evangeline crossed her legs and leaned back on the couch. "For me to break into Monroe and search the finance person's office."

Kimber's eyes widened. "You can't be serious."

"If we don't do this, people will die." Evangeline waved the statements in the air. "We need answers, and we don't have time to wait."

Though Brandon didn't look forward to whatever his part was in Evangeline's plan, he said, "She's right. We need answers now."

"What about the FBI?" Kimber asked. "Maybe they have a way to access those records."

"They already got us the scans of the receipts, but that's as far as the FBI can go without us tipping our hand that we're closing in on them," Brandon said.

"I say we go in tonight." Evangeline glanced at her mobile phone. "Everyone should clear out of there within the next hour or two."

Brandon tried to visualize the most direct way to infiltrate Sheila's office. "Going in at night is too risky."

"Surely, you don't think going in during the day would be better," Evangeline said.

"Actually, I think it would." A plan began to form, and he looked from Evangeline to Kimber. "Kimber, meet your new accountant."

"Excuse me?" Kimber said.

Brandon winked at her. "Trust me. I have a plan."

CHAPTER 34

COOKIES. KIMBER WAS using cookies as a distraction technique while her sort-of boyfriend and her almost stalker broke into Sheila's office. Kimber didn't even know who Sheila was beyond the outdated photo on her driver's license.

Kimber used a spatula to transfer the last batch of freshly baked chocolate chip cookies into the decorative basket that had previously housed her to-be-read pile of books.

A knock sounded, and Kimber called out, "Come in!"

Trudy opened the door, balancing a plastic container in each hand. "I made soft ginger cookies and snickerdoodles. I know Brandon likes those."

"They're perfect. Thank you so much for your help."

"It's a nice thing you're doing, making sure your publisher knows you appreciate them." She handed one of the containers to Kimber. Together they loaded the cookies into the basket. When they finished, Kimber draped a tea towel over the top and grabbed her purse. "Thanks again."

"Happy to help." Trudy opened the door, and they started down the hall together until they got to Trudy's apartment, then she stopped. "Let me know how it goes."

"I will." Kimber lifted the basket. "And thank you again."

Twenty minutes later, Kimber stepped out of the cab in front of Monroe Publishing. The scent of exhaust mingled with hotdogs, no doubt from the hotdog stand down the street. Her stomach churned uncomfortably. Had she forgotten to eat breakfast? Probably, unless cookie dough counted as a meal.

Nerves rushed through her at the prospect of what she, Evangeline, and Brandon were attempting to do. Corporate espionage in broad daylight.

A distraction—that's all she was. Evangeline would be the one most at risk.

The cab pulled away, reminding her that she needed to move forward.

She glanced around in search of Evangeline but didn't see her anywhere. Not willing to stand outside in the cold, Kimber continued into the building.

Evangeline was already waiting by the security desk, a visitor badge in hand. "There she is." Evangeline waved at her. As soon as Kimber reached her side, Evangeline said, "I've already signed us in."

"Thanks." Together they went to the elevators and rode up to the correct floor, the crowd of others riding with them preventing any conversation. Not that they could safely discuss their plans in this building anyway.

As soon as they stepped off the elevator, Kimber nodded to her right. "It's this way."

Evangeline grabbed Kimber's arm before she could turn down the hall and lowered her voice to a whisper. "We aren't supposed to know that."

"Right." And if Kimber were a real operative, she would have thought of that. At least they hadn't been close enough to anyone for her mistake to be overheard.

Evangeline moved to the closest cubicle, where a man in his twenties sat, his fingers on his keyboard. "Excuse me. Can you tell us where your finance office is?"

"Down that hall to the left." Without looking up, he tilted his head to reinforce the direction he intended.

"Thanks," she said, and they both turned that way.

As they drew closer, Kimber's steps slowed. Could she really do this?

Evangeline put her hand on Kimber's arm, a subtle reminder that she couldn't show her hesitation or make it appear that they were anything beyond author and accountant.

"Just like we rehearsed," Evangeline whispered.

Like they'd rehearsed. Kimber took a deep breath, trying to pretend she was about to step on a stage instead of into a real-life scenario that could get someone arrested or worse.

They reached Sheila's office, and Evangeline knocked on the open door. "Are you Sheila?"

"Yes. Can I help you?"

"I'm Evangeline Moore, and this is Kimber Frost."

"Oh, yes." Sheila stood and focused on Kimber. "Patricia mentioned you might be stopping by."

"Do you have a minute to chat?" Kimber asked.

"Of course." Sheila motioned toward the two chairs opposite her desk. "Please, sit down."

"Thanks." Kimber deliberately waited for Evangeline to take the seat beside the wall so she wouldn't have to move when Kimber left.

"What can I do for you?" Sheila asked.

"I was hoping you could give me the background of how my advances and royalties will work." Kimber sat and balanced the basket of cookies on her lap. "This is all new to me."

"It's a lot simpler than people make it out to be." Sheila reclaimed her seat, then proceeded to explain the nuances of how Kimber's payments would be made, when each installment of her advance would come due, and how royalties would work if she earned out on her advance.

When Sheila finished, Kimber said, "This was so helpful. I appreciate your time."

"It was my pleasure."

Kimber stood and held up the basket of cookies. "By any chance, would you mind showing me where the main conference room is? I brought some cookies to share with everyone, and Brandon thought that would be the best place to take them."

"I'd be happy to." Sheila stood and followed Kimber to the door.

Evangeline held up her phone. "Do you mind if I wait here? I need to make a call."

"I'm sorry." Sheila shook her head. "I can't leave anyone in my office unattended."

"I understand," Evangeline said as though it were no big deal that Sheila's response had unraveled their plan to gain access to the records they needed.

The three of them left Sheila's office, and Evangeline closed the door behind her.

Sheila waited for Evangeline to move past her before she turned back and used a key to lock her office. Brandon was going to have his work cut out for him.

•   •   •

Brandon spotted Sheila and Kimber down the hall near the conference room. The subtle shake of Kimber's head was not the signal Brandon had been hoping for. Evangeline came into view, proving that their plan to pull Sheila away from her office while leaving Evangeline behind hadn't worked.

Time for plan B.

He headed for the far stairwell that would put him on the finance side of the ninth floor and raced down the two flights of stairs, then opened the door slowly. The hall was empty, and the handful of employees sitting in cubicles in the open area at the end of the hall appeared to have their attention on their work. He continued to Sheila's office.

He put his hand on the doorknob and tried to turn it only to find it locked. "Great," he muttered under his breath. He hadn't needed to pick a lock since he'd taken the class at the farm during his initial training.

His phone chimed. He silenced it before he pulled his phone free and glanced at the screen. The message was from Evangeline.

I blocked the door open. Just push.

He looked up to see if she was anywhere nearby, but she wasn't visible.

Following her simple instructions, he pushed on the door. Sure enough, it gave way. He had to open it only a fraction to see why. Evangeline had taped the latching mechanism so it wouldn't click closed despite Sheila's locking it.

Brandon ripped the tape off to hide the evidence that the door had been tampered with and quickly crossed to the filing cabinet, where

Sheila kept her credit card log. Again, it was locked. Apparently, he was going to have to rely on his lockpicking skills after all.

• • •

Kimber chatted with the various staff members at Monroe. As she'd hoped, the news that she'd arrived bearing home-baked goods had resulted in an impromptu break for everyone, and so far, Sheila appeared to be enjoying Trudy's soft ginger cookies.

Evangeline moved to Kimber's side and lowered her voice. "I just got a message from a colleague. I really do need to make a call."

Which would leave her on her own with Sheila and the rest of the staff. "Can't it wait?"

"Sorry. It can't." Evangeline patted her shoulder. "I'll be right back. Promise."

Kimber heard the unspoken words. *Don't panic.* But she was panicking. What if Sheila decided to go back to her office before they heard from Brandon?

Almost as though she'd heard Kimber's thoughts, Sheila took one more cookie out of the basket and said, "I'd better get back to my office. I have a meeting this afternoon that I need to prep for." She stopped beside Kimber. "Thanks for the cookies."

"You're welcome." Desperate to give Brandon every second possible, Kimber said, "Do you want to a take a few with you? I brought plenty."

"I'd better not." She patted her stomach. "I'm already going to need to add in an extra workout with what I've eaten."

"You don't look like you need to worry about that."

"Thank you. That's sweet, but at my age, every calorie comes back to haunt you if you aren't careful."

"You also don't look old enough to be using the phrase 'at my age,'" Kimber said.

Sheila laughed. "Flattery will get you everywhere." She sidestepped Kimber. "I'll see you later. Thanks again for the treat."

Not sure what else she could say, Kimber let her pass. She took a step back so she could peer into the hallway. Unfortunately, Evangeline was nowhere in sight.

Kimber quickly pulled her cell phone from her pocket and texted Brandon and Evangeline.

Sheila just left the conference room. Brandon, hurry!

She tucked her phone back into her purse and looked around the room. Over a dozen Monroe Publishing employees still lingered around the conference table, enjoying both the cookies and the relaxed conversation.

Anxiety rising inside her, Kimber started to follow Sheila, but Amelia approached her.

"This was very thoughtful of you to bring something in for the staff," Amelia said. "This isn't typical for our top authors."

"You're putting a lot of faith in me. I want you to know how much I appreciate it." Kimber glanced down the hall again. "Would you excuse me for a minute? I need to find the restroom."

"Of course." Amelia pointed in the general direction of the elevators. "It's down that hall."

"Thanks." Kimber headed in the direction Amelia indicated. Now she just needed to find a way to get downstairs without being noticed. Her heart pounded. She really wasn't cut out to be a spy.

CHAPTER 35

BRANDON ROLLED HIS shoulders to alleviate the tension that had settled there as he prepared for another attempt to pick the lock. He put pressure on the two straightened paperclips and turned them simultaneously. The lock clicked open. Finally. He'd spent far too much time on this.

He opened the drawer and identified the file with the credit card users in it. He lay it open on the desk and pulled out his phone to photograph the contents.

Before he could unlock his screen, a man's voice, then a woman's voice carried to him in conversation. Was that Sheila? Their discussion continued, and Brandon quickly photographed the first several pages. When the voices went silent and a key fit into the lock, Brandon quickly closed the file drawer, grabbed the file, and ducked behind the desk.

The door opened, and Brandon froze. Sheila coming back to her office before he finished wasn't part of his plan. If she caught him in here—She couldn't catch him, but he was trapped with no way out.

Another woman's voice interrupted his panicked thoughts. "Excuse me, Sheila. I'm so sorry to bother you again, but I think I'm lost."

"Kimber? What are you doing back down here?"

"I need to check in with Haseeb about an event I'm going to tonight. Could you possibly show me where his office is?"

"Just take a left at the elevators and then follow that hall. It's the second to last one."

"I walked down there and, for the life of me, couldn't find it," Kimber said. "Would you mind showing me?"

"I guess I can do that." The door closed again.

Brandon waited two seconds before he put the file back onto the desk. His adrenaline pumping, he photographed the last six pages and returned the file to its proper place.

With no time to relock the filing cabinet, he grabbed the two mangled paper clips and rushed out the door.

. . .

Kimber greeted Haseeb and thanked Sheila one last time, unable to think of anything else she could do to delay the woman's return to her office.

"What can I do for you?" Haseeb asked.

Kimber glanced at Sheila's retreating back. The woman was walking far too quickly back toward her office.

Kimber focused on Haseeb. "I wanted to ask you about the book signing tonight."

Haseeb motioned for Kimber to take a seat. "Ideally, I'd like you to be there early. That way, you can meet Elliott before everything gets too crazy."

Kimber sat, her ears tuned for any unexpected shouts from down the hall. "How early?"

"Just a few minutes. By then, the store will be ready, and Elliott will be prepared to meet people."

Kimber's phone buzzed, and she glanced at the screen.

Clear. Brandon's single word settled her pulse and brought a wave of relief.

With the knowledge that Brandon was safe, Kimber tried to relax as she took in Haseeb's office.

A tall, white bookshelf occupied the far corner, each of the shelves filled with multiple copies of the same books. Framed photos lined the credenza behind him, most of them taken at the beach. Haseeb and his family were featured in many of them. His desk held his laptop and two shipping boxes, which had been pushed as far to the side as possible.

Haseeb continued, breaking into Kimber's thoughts. "The signing is just a chance for you to be seen."

"Will you be there?" Kimber asked.

"No. I have some other obligations," Haseeb said, "but Whitney will make sure we have lots of photos to tease on social media."

"Sounds good." Kimber's gaze strayed to the books on the shelf beside Haseeb. "Is that an advance copy of Rebecca Hamilton's new book?"

"It is. It just arrived from the press yesterday."

"I hear it's going to be amazing."

Haseeb reached for a box on his desk and tugged it closer. He pulled out another copy of the book. "Here. You can have this one."

"Really?" Kimber leaned forward to take it.

"Absolutely." Haseeb pushed the box back into place. "In fact, if you have time to read it in the next two weeks, I'd love an endorsement for the book. It would be good to tie your name to Rebecca's."

"I'm sure I could read it by then," Kimber said.

"We've already revealed the cover, so feel free to post a photo of the book on your social media too," Haseeb said. "Just make sure you tag Rebecca to get the crossover attention."

"I can do that."

"Great," Haseeb said. "If you need help crafting a blurb, let me know. I'm happy to assist with that."

"Thank you." Kimber stood and held up the book. "I look forward to reading this."

"I hope you enjoy it," Haseeb said. "And have fun tonight."

"I'll certainly try."

•　•　•

Amelia Franklin, Haseeb Malouf, and Ramon Alvarez. Brandon wouldn't have put either the managing editor or the marketing director at the top of his suspect list, but as chief financial officer, Ramon had been a leading possibility from the beginning because the royalty department being housed at the main offices alone was suspicious. From what Brandon had learned from his friends in the business, most auxiliary departments were usually kept in lower rent zones.

"It has to be Ramon Alvarez." Evangeline paced Kimber's apartment. "He has access to the funding, and he could easily doctor the books."

"I agree," Kimber said. "He has access; he has the knowledge base to pull it off and possibly create a paper trail that would pass a cursory audit. Not to mention, he was in Europe last October."

"So, how do we prove it?" Brandon asked. "Narrowing this down to one suspect is great, but we need something that ties him back to Labyrinth, or we won't have anything to hold over him in an interrogation."

"We pool our resources," Evangeline said. "I'll have my office search for any overseas travel. You can have your FBI and CIA do a deep dive into his background and financial history. There has to be something that ties him to Labyrinth."

"We haven't found anything so far, but maybe having only one person to focus on will help." Brandon pulled out his phone. "I'll call Rafi and fill him in." He motioned to Kimber. "You call Director Yarrow."

"It's after hours, and we only have suspicions right now," Kimber said. "I'm better off calling Mark."

"He won't be in the office either this time of day," Brandon said.

"I know, but I can let him know that we have a specific person we want him to do a search on," Kimber said. "That way he knows I need him to go in early tomorrow."

"Sounds like we're at a standstill until morning." Evangeline let out a sigh. "I hate waiting."

"That makes two of us," Brandon said.

"Three of us," Kimber corrected. "But for now, all we can do is line up our resources and focus on the data we do have." Kimber moved to the hall. "I'll give Mark a call now."

Brandon dialed Rafi's number while Evangeline also made a call.

"What's the latest?" Rafi asked.

Brandon filled him in on their shortened suspect list.

"I agree. It sounds like Ramon Alvarez is our guy," Rafi said. "I'll put a tail on him and get a warrant to tap his phones."

"Kimber is pulling Mark in to dig into his financials, so you'll need a warrant for that too."

"I'll see what I can do," Rafi said. "In the meantime, do what you can to keep an eye on Ramon at work."

Ramon, who worked on a different floor and had little interaction with the editorial department. "I'll do what I can."

Kimber returned to the living room as Brandon ended his call.

"Mark will take a look at Ramon's financials tomorrow, assuming Rafi can get him access." She moved to her computer. "For now, I'll start on the detailed transactions on his credit card."

Brandon glanced at his watch. "Sorry, Kimber. That will have to wait. We need to leave for the book signing in a few minutes."

"I totally forgot about that." She closed her laptop. "I'd better go change." She headed to her bedroom.

"While you two are at the book signing, I'll look through the detailed reports," Evangeline said. "Maybe with the information my contacts in London gave me, I'll be able to trace Ramon to north Wales. That's the likely meeting place if Ramon is working with Asadi Mir."

"We couldn't track his movements beyond Amsterdam," Brandon said. "If you can figure out where he went, more power to you."

• • •

A line of people stretched out of the bookstore and onto the sidewalk. It was every author's dream . . . or maybe not. Kimber wasn't sure the introverted sort would particularly care to sit and talk to this many people in a short period of time.

"Is it bad that I wish we were at my apartment helping Evangeline instead of here?" Kimber asked.

"No. I feel the same way." Brandon pressed his hand against her back and guided her past the line. "Come on. We can go in the other door."

"Thank goodness." Kimber took another look at the line. Those people were going to be standing there for at least an hour before they reached the front.

A rather tall and stocky store employee waited by the second set of doors and stepped forward when they approached. As soon as Brandon went to open the door, the employee said, "I'm sorry. Everyone has to go through the other entrance."

"We're with Monroe Publishing," Brandon said. "I'm Brandon Hale, and this is Kimber Frost."

The man glanced at the clipboard he held and checked off their names. He stepped aside. "Go ahead."

"Thanks." Brandon guided Kimber forward, taking a path parallel to the line.

Kimber spotted Whitney near the signing table. Books were stacked on one side of the table, and several pens and a water bottle were arranged in front of an empty chair.

Whitney waved at them to join her. As soon as Kimber and Brandon reached the signing table, Whitney said, "I'm so glad you're here early. I want you to meet Elliott."

"Where is he?" Brandon asked.

"Go straight back. There's an office on the left." Whitney pointed in the direction of the cookbook section.

Brandon took Kimber's hand and led her past several displays. They made it as far as the gardening section before a man's voice carried to them.

"This is unacceptable," he said. "There should be at least two employees working the line and another sitting next to me to make sure no one lingers too long."

"I've called another employee in," another man said in a placating voice. "She should be here in a few minutes, but until she arrives, I don't have three staff members to spare without leaving the checkout registers severely understaffed."

"You should have thought of that before I arrived," the man, presumably Elliott, said. "And the music. Why are you playing that? You should have the audiobook coming over the speakers to tease readers into buying my book."

Kimber glanced at Brandon and lifted her eyebrows. This was the man Whitney and Haseeb wanted her to meet?

"I'll take care of it," the other man said.

"See that you do."

Brandon stepped into the doorway, pulling Kimber with him.

Elliott stood beside the manager's desk, his arms folded across his chest, a look of indignation on his face.

"Mr. Paulson?" Brandon released Kimber's hand and extended his to the author. "I'm—"

"I don't talk to fans before the signing. You'll have to wait in line like everyone else."

Brandon lowered his hand to his side. "Actually, Amelia Franklin sent me—"

"You can tell Amelia that this bookstore is understaffed for a book signing of this caliber."

"I'll let her know." Brandon shot an apologetic look at Kimber. "Perhaps I can help work the line to alleviate that problem."

The store manager looked at Brandon like he had just thrown him a life preserver in the middle of a stormy sea. "Could you do that? At least for the first few minutes?"

"I'm happy to."

The manager grabbed two pens and two pads of sticky notes off his desk and handed them to Brandon. "We need everyone in the line to write down how to spell their name if they want their book personalized."

"Make sure it's legible," Elliott added. "And make sure the book is opened to the title page for me."

"I'll take care of it." Brandon stepped back, and Kimber followed him to the signing table. "I'm so sorry about that. I thought he would have been expecting you."

"It's okay." Kimber glanced over her shoulder. "I'm not sure I want to know him anyway."

"It looks like I'm going to be stuck helping out. Do you want me to call you a cab, or do you want to hang out here?"

"I'll help you," Kimber said.

"You're going to help me deal with an egotistical author?"

"We're both going to help that poor manager survive the night." Kimber jutted her chin toward Whitney. "We'll let Whitney decide if she can salvage any photos worth posting."

"Thank you."

"You're welcome." Kimber looked back at the manager's office again. "Just promise that if I ever start acting like that, you'll knock some sense into me."

"Trust me. You will never be like that."

"I certainly hope not."

CHAPTER 36

BRANDON WENT TO work early. With a potential terrorist attack looming, he didn't have time to simply absorb information while performing his regular duties. He needed to expand his contact base and his access to their leading suspect. The only way he could think of to do that was to arrive well before Amelia.

At barely seven o'clock, he walked down the hall past the dark offices on the ninth floor. Light emanated from under Conrad's door, and more light spilled out from Sheila's office.

Brandon paused when he reached Sheila's. "You're in early today."

She looked up from her desk. "I'm always in early."

"I didn't realize that. I'm never up here this time of morning."

Sheila motioned toward Ramon's office. "Ramon lets me work an early shift so I can pick up my kids after school."

"That's nice of him." Nice for a terrorist. Assuming he really was their man. "Does he work early hours too?"

"Depends on the day and which meetings he has." Sheila opened a file folder that topped the stack on her desk. "McKenzie would know what time he's coming in."

"I'll check with her. Thanks."

"No problem."

Brandon continued down the hall, where Ramon's personal secretary already sat at her desk. "Good morning, McKenzie."

She looked up from her computer. "Morning." Her brow furrowed slightly. "What are you doing down here?"

"I'm about to make a coffee run to get Amelia's latte before she comes in. Do you or Ramon need anything?"

"It depends on where you're going."

"Starbucks."

"In that case, it would be great if you could grab our order too," McKenzie said.

"Can you text me what you want?"

"Sure. What's your number?"

Brandon gave it to her.

"I'll send it to you now."

"Sounds good. I'll be back in twenty minutes."

Brandon headed back down the hall and was nearly to Conrad's office when his door opened.

"Brandon. What are you doing down here?"

"Just making a coffee run. Do you need anything?"

"No, thanks. I don't drink coffee, but you can take some documents to Amelia." He returned to his office and retrieved a file off his desk. "She'll want to see these."

"I'll give them to her as soon as she gets in." Brandon continued down the hall, opting to take the stairs rather than wait for the elevator this time of day. At least now he could face the possibility of stepping into an elevator without breaking into a cold sweat.

He stopped at his office and secured the legal documents in his desk drawer, then made his way back to the stairwell. He could use the elevator on his way back up.

Fifteen minutes later, he approached McKenzie's desk carrying a drink carrier filled with coffee. "Here you go." He set it down on McKenzie's desk and removed the one for Amelia.

"Thanks so much."

"No problem." He glanced at Ramon's closed door. "Is he even in yet?"

"No, but he should be within the next five minutes. He has a conference call with someone in London at eight thirty."

London. If Rafi could trace the call, maybe they'd find the missing link to tie Ramon to Labyrinth.

Keeping his expression neutral, Brandon stepped back. "Have a good one."

"You too."

Brandon retreated down the hall and went up the two flights of stairs to the eleventh floor. He emerged from the stairwell at the same time Amelia stepped out of the elevator.

Brandon stopped at his desk long enough to retrieve the file from Conrad and crossed to her office. "Good morning." He handed Amelia her morning latte and the file.

She set both down without so much as an acknowledgment. "I need to prep for the new products committee meeting this afternoon, so hold my calls."

"Will do."

If Amelia followed her normal pattern, she'd be occupied most of the day, and Brandon would have time to do some more snooping into Ramon's activities.

Brandon took a step back and asked his standard departing question. "Is there anything else you need?"

"Yes." She took a sip of her latte. "The first proofreader just returned her comments on *Countdown*. I want you to go through it and note which ones you agree with and which you think I should reject. Then forward it to me."

So much for having free time today. "I'll do that this morning."

Brandon returned to his desk. After sending a quick text to Rafi to inform him of Ramon's impending call to someone in London, Brandon downloaded the PDF of the typeset novel. Then he leaned back in his chair and began to read.

•　•　•

Kimber leaned back in her office chair and rubbed her eyes. All day, she'd been staring at financial reports, credit card statements, and the FBI's surveillance reports on Ramon Alvarez. She'd even browsed through the FBI's transcripts from the listening device Brandon had planted in his own office. So far, no one had uncovered anything that remotely tied Ramon to Labyrinth or any kind of illegal activity.

She'd had a brief hope that a phone call between Ramon and a London publishing house this morning would give them a lead, but according to Rafi, it had been a typical business call about distribution in the UK for an upcoming book.

Needing a break from staring at screens, she walked into her living room and turned on the fireplace. She would make a cup of hot chocolate, curl up in front of the fire, and read a good book. Or what she hoped would be a good book.

She retrieved the advance reader copy Haseeb had given her and sat on the couch. The hot chocolate could wait.

Within minutes, she lost herself in the story, letting the cares of her current life fade away. A little inaccuracy about a CIA procedure pulled her out, but she managed to suspend her disbelief and continue reading.

She was twenty-three pages in when she spotted a typo, a period where a comma should have been. Rather than mark it the way she normally would have, she took a photo of it, making sure the page number was visible, so she could pass the information along to Brandon. He could let Amelia know she'd found a mistake.

She kept reading. Another twenty-three pages in, she discovered another error, this one the same problem as the first. She made another note.

When she reached page 69 and a third error popped up, she stopped. Three mistakes, all twenty-three pages apart. What were the chances?

She flipped forward another twenty-three pages and skimmed over the page. This time, however, there were no typos to be found.

Her cell rang, and she grabbed it, surprised to see Ian's name light up her phone. She answered with a tentative, "Hello?"

"Kimber, it's Ian Sawyer."

"How are you?" That seemed like a logical question to ask someone she'd met only once, even if that someone was ultra famous.

"Good, but we need to do some damage repair to your image."

"Excuse me?"

"The photos of you at Elliott Paulson's book signing last night. What in the world were you thinking?"

"I was just helping Brandon out." Kimber hadn't checked her social media yet today, but she knew Whitney had taken several photos of her at the signing.

"Elliott had no idea who you are, did he?"

"I'm not anyone worth his notice," Kimber said. "And how did you know that?"

"I've met the man before. He came to one of my movie premieres a couple years ago. He was very flattering to me, but the way he treated my assistant was atrocious."

"I wish I could say I'm surprised."

"Tomorrow, we're going to make him wish he'd paid more attention to how he was treating people."

"What's tomorrow?"

"You're going to join me for lunch with Tyrone. He needs a little extra attention as they ramp up the publicity for his new show, and you need to be there."

"Don't take this the wrong way, but why are you being so nice to me?" Kimber asked. "Before Saturday night, you'd never even heard of me."

"That's true, but I appreciated that you aren't the sort to judge people on their level of fame," Ian said. "And I have to confess, I do have an ulterior motive."

"What's that?"

"My wife has written a book."

Now his kindness was starting to make sense. "You want me to help her with it."

"Or help her find someone who will give her honest feedback," Ian said. "She's had it professionally edited twice, but so far, no one has come back with any advice beyond where to put the commas."

"You're afraid they're not fully editing her work because of who she is?"

"That's exactly what I think," Ian said. "I've seen more edits on my dailies than she's getting on her entire novel."

Kimber wasn't entirely sure what a daily was, but she guessed it had to do with his scripts. "I do have a couple of friends who are great at editing. One of them is Brandon."

"Would you be willing to have him look at it without telling him who the author is? I'm happy to pay him for his time."

"I don't think it would matter if he knew your wife wrote it, but I'd be happy to ask him."

"Great. Now, about lunch. We're meeting at the Gershwin Theatre at noon. Tyrone will leave your name with security."

Even though Kimber would love the chance to hang out with two prominent actors, she said, "You don't have to take me out to lunch. Doing a favor for your wife is the least I can do after all you did for me last weekend."

"Nonsense. You're becoming the celebrity you're destined to be, and I don't want the lack of attention from Elliott to derail our efforts," he said. "Besides, this will give you the chance to meet a few of the cast members for *Freedom* before opening night."

"Well, how can I refuse?"

"You can't." His grin was evident in his voice. "I'll see you tomorrow at noon."

"Okay, I'll see you then."

• • •

Brandon knocked on Kimber's door, his laptop bag still hanging from his shoulder. He probably should have stopped at his apartment to drop off his things and change clothes, but he was too tired to even do that. It had taken every ounce of willpower today to not point out the inaccuracies in the book he had checked the proofread on today. The author had done her research, but her handle on CIA protocols was severely lacking.

All he wanted now was to clear his mind and spend time with Kimber, preferably talking about anything but work.

She opened the door, smiled, and leaned in to kiss him.

He put his hand around her waist to hold her in place, drawing out the kiss. "If you're greeting me like that, I assume Evangeline isn't here."

"No, she's traveling today, and I haven't heard from her yet." Kimber ushered him in and closed the door. "I do have some news for you though."

"What's that?"

"Two things actually: First, Ian called me today."

Brandon replayed her words. "Do you know how crazy it is to hear you say that?"

"Yes, I do." Kimber moved to her couch and sat down. "I could hardly believe it myself."

"What did he want?"

"A couple of things, one of which involves you."

"How?"

"I'm not supposed to tell you this, but I doubt I'd be able to lie to you anyway." Kimber waited for him to sit beside her. "His wife has written a book and needs some honest feedback. Apparently, the editors they hired previously were too starstruck with Ian to do a decent job."

"That's easy enough."

"He also invited me to go to lunch at the theater with him and Tyrone tomorrow."

"Seriously?"

"Yeah. He saw the posts Whitney tagged me in on social media, and he wasn't happy about how Elliott treated me at his signing."

"You told him about that?"

"He guessed." Kimber shrugged. "Ian has had dealings with Elliott before and was less than impressed."

"Let me know if you need someone there to take photos," Brandon said.

"Thanks, but I don't think my social media accounts are more important than you being at work to keep an eye on our suspects."

"Probably not, but I don't love the idea of you being out there without me close by."

"I'll keep you and Rafi on speed dial."

"Good."

"There is one more thing I want to show you." Kimber grabbed a book from the end table.

Brandon spotted the familiar cover. "How did you get a copy of that?"

"Haseeb gave it to me." Kimber flipped a few pages in.

"If you're going to point out the errors in CIA protocols, don't bother. There's no way I can suggest corrections without blowing my cover."

"Those were frustrating, but I've got something else." She pointed at a typo on the page. "Look at this."

"This is an uncorrected proof. Sometimes a typo gets through and isn't caught until the proofread." But he hadn't noticed that particular typo, and he should have.

"And this one." Kimber flipped to the next bookmarked page.

Brandon leaned forward. The same typo, this one twenty or so pages later. He hadn't noticed that one either.

"There are three with the exact same problem, all of them twenty-three pages apart."

"I was just doing proof corrections on this file, and I didn't see any of these." Brandon pulled his laptop from his bag and opened the file. He scrolled to page twenty-three. He compared Kimber's copy to the page on his screen. "It's not wrong in this file, and this should have been the same one that went to the printer."

"Why would there be a new error, then?" Kimber asked.

"Can I see that?" Brandon reached for the book.

Kimber handed it over.

He rubbed his hand over the spot where a period had been inserted instead of a comma. "I don't suppose you have a magnifying glass, do you?" Brandon asked.

Kimber's eyes widened. "You think these are microdots?"

"Only one way to be sure."

"I'll be right back." Kimber hurried into the hall and returned a moment later holding a rectangular magnifying glass. She handed it to him and turned on the lamp beside him.

Brandon held the magnifying glass over the book and shifted so the page was more fully in the light. He focused on what appeared to be a small black dot on the page, but now, under high magnification, words formed.

"Kimber, there's a message in here."

She grabbed her laptop. "What does it say?"

"The London Coliseum," Brandon said. "That's the largest theater in London."

Kimber jotted it down on her notepad. When he didn't continue, she looked up. "That's it?"

"That's all on this one." Brandon flipped to page forty-six and repeated the process of reading the information coded within the tiny black dot. "This one has an address." He read it off to her.

"Is it the address of the theater?"

"No, it's not in the same part of town."

"What about the last one?" Kimber asked.

"It's a string of numbers." Brandon passed the book and magnifying glass to her. "See if you can make out what they mean."

Kimber looked down at the number string and wrote them on her paper. She handed the book back to him and said, "Read the numbers out to me so I can double-check that I wrote them down right."

Brandon read them out loud. After he finished, he asked, "Well? Do you know what they mean?"

"It looks like a bank account number." Kimber grabbed her laptop. "I'll email it to Mark and see if he can trace it."

"Send it to Rafi too."

"I will, but this isn't a domestic bank. Mark will have a better chance of tracking it down."

"While you do that, I'll let Evangeline know that we have another lead." Brandon picked up his phone.

Kimber put her hand on his arm. "Brandon, who could have made the changes on the advance reader copy in time for it to be printed and then change it back before you received the file to review?"

"I can think of a few people," Brandon said.

"Such as?" Kimber asked.

"Margaret, Haseeb"—Brandon hesitated—"and Amelia."

CHAPTER 37

KIMBER COULDN'T BELIEVE intelligence agencies around the world were working overtime to trace the clues she and Brandon had uncovered last night, while she was getting ready to go out and socialize with celebrities. She had wanted to cancel, but Rafi had insisted she needed to go. After all, who in their right mind would turn down the chance to hang out with the cast of one of the most anticipated musicals of the season?

With only a half hour before she needed to leave, she typed in the security code that would allow her to make a secure call and dialed Mark's office number. He answered on the second ring. "This is Mark."

"It's me. Anything new?"

"Yeah. I was about to call you," Mark said, his words coming more quickly than usual. "The bank account is one out of Singapore, and it belongs to a company called Knight Enterprises."

"What do you know about it?"

"I'm still researching it, but at first glance, it looks like a shell company. Lots of money coming in and going out, but there isn't any evidence of real goods or services being provided."

"Let me guess: It's a consulting firm."

"Got it on the first try," Mark said. "We're working on getting access to the account activity. I'll let you know when we have more intel."

"Thanks."

"Any updates from the FBI or MI6?" Mark asked.

"Nothing yet. Our MI6 contact left for London last night, but I haven't heard anything from her yet."

"Let me know if you do," Mark said. "You and Brandon are the hub of communication for everyone right now."

"That's a scary thought."

"You've got this," Mark said. "It was huge that you found the microdots."

"That was mostly Brandon."

"That was the two of you being a good team."

Kimber couldn't deny that. She checked the time on the clock on the microwave. "I'd better get going. I have a lunch to get ready for."

"That's right. Eating with Hollywood royalty."

"Ian's a great guy," Kimber said. "You'd like him."

"I'm not the type of person who will ever be in his social circle."

"I never expected to be either," Kimber said. "And with me being friends with both of you, it's always possible that those social circles could collide."

"Yeah, I don't see that happening," Mark said. "I'll talk to you later. Have fun."

"Thanks." Kimber hung up and made another call, this time to Evangeline.

Her call went unanswered.

Surely Evangeline and MI6 must know something by now. After a quick check of the time, Kimber secured her laptop in her safe and headed out the door.

A short taxi ride later, she reached the theater and made her way inside.

A security guard stood near the main entrance and stepped forward. "May I help you?"

"I'm Kimber Frost. I'm here to see Tyrone Brooks."

The guard picked up a clipboard from a nearby chair and scanned through it. "Yes, it says here he'll meet you in his dressing room."

His dressing room. That wasn't what she'd expected, nor did she particularly care to go into a man's dressing room alone.

The door opened behind her, and Ian walked in.

"Kimber, have you been waiting long?" He approached her and kissed her cheek as though they were old friends rather than acquaintances of only a week.

"No, I just arrived."

"Good." Ian turned to the guard. "We have a delivery coming in the next few minutes. Can you have it brought back to Tyrone's dressing room?"

"Yes, Mr. Sawyer."

"Thanks, Steve." Ian moved past the guard. "Come on. I'll show you where we're going."

"Thanks again for inviting me today."

"I'm glad you were available on such short notice." Ian led her into the main theater, where Tyrone stood on stage with several other people. "Let's sit back here until they break for lunch."

"What's up next for you?" Kimber asked. "Are you staying in New York for a while?"

"I am. It hasn't been announced yet, but I signed on to do a new television series set here in New York City." Ian sat in one of the seats near the back. "We start rehearsals in a few weeks."

"If you're already starting rehearsals, why hasn't the project been announced?" Kimber asked.

"It's all about timing and playing the publicity game," Ian said. "Right now, everyone is spinning all sorts of stories about why I'm still in New York when rumors have been flying about me getting back into TV."

"I'm sure having you pop up on so many posts at Madison Peters's birthday party fueled that fire."

"Most certainly."

On stage, the director called for everyone to take their places. Music started, an upbeat tune with an African flair. Then Tyrone's voice carried over the instrumentals.

The song grew in volume and energy, the talented actors bringing the words to life.

"They're incredible."

"Wait until opening night when they're all in costume," Ian said. "It will be quite a sight."

"I'm sure it will."

• • •

Brandon wasn't getting anywhere. He'd come in early and checked the advance reader copy of *Countdown* in Amelia's office. As he'd suspected, it had contained microdots too. Assuming the ARCs were printed only once, someone would have had to place the codes in the ARC file to have them printed in every book, likely because whoever was sending the messages didn't have control over which copy would be sent to which person. That dropped Haseeb into the unlikely category as a suspect since he oversaw the shipment of the review copies. If only Brandon had access to the list of ARC recipients.

Brandon did his rounds, swinging by Ramon's office for the third time today. His current excuse was to drop off his latest credit card receipts to Sheila. As usual, Sheila's door was open. Ramon's was closed.

Without any access to Ramon, Brandon returned to his floor with the intent of searching through the file history for *Countdown*. Surely there was evidence somewhere showing who had made the changes in the file before the ARCs had gone to print. From what he'd gathered during his time at Monroe, that person would have to be one of the typesetters, but how would a typesetter access the firm's funds? Unless perhaps someone had access to the typesetter's password. More questions with no answers.

He approached his cubicle, not surprised to find Mary standing beside Regina's desk.

Mary gave her customary sneer. "So, are you going to use Kimber to get invited to the party at John's house?"

Even though Brandon was certain Kimber wouldn't want to go alone, he said, "I'm not sure yet if I'll be going with her."

Regina gestured to his cubicle. "There's another invitation that needs to be sent to her for some movie premiere in LA."

Brandon continued to his desk, where an embossed envelope lay with Kimber's name written on the front in calligraphy. He slipped the invitation into his bag.

"Planning to hand deliver it, huh?" Regina asked.

"No point in putting it in the mail since I'm going to see Kimber tonight anyway." Not that it was any of their business.

"So, what are you two doing tonight?" Mary asked.

Brandon's phone chimed with an incoming text, and he used that distraction as a way to ignore Mary's question. He expected the text to be from Kimber, but instead, it was from Evangeline.

He deciphered the coded message. *Tonight. Page 46.* An encrypted link was attached.

"Well?" Mary pressed. "What are you doing tonight?"

"After dealing with Elliott's signing last night, I think we'll probably just hang out and watch a movie." Most likely, that movie would be security feed to help in the search for Asadi Mir.

Regina gave him a disapproving look. "A movie at home? Sounds boring."

Brandon pocketed his phone. "I certainly hope not."

• • •

Kimber wrapped her fingers around her cup of hot chocolate and leaned forward on the couch. Evangeline had arranged for Kimber and Brandon to have access to the live feed from the MI6 raid at the address in London, which was now streaming onto Kimber's television, but so far, all they could see was the faint silhouette of a row of townhouses in the darkness. Even though it was only nine o'clock at night here in New York, in London, it was already tomorrow morning. One o'clock in the morning, to be exact.

"Do you think Asadi Mir is really there?" Kimber asked.

"I hope so. Capturing him could shut down Labyrinth's efforts entirely."

Kimber didn't need Brandon to tell her that. Everyone who had ever dealt with Labyrinth believed Asadi Mir was the man running the terrorist group. If he were neutralized, the whole organization would implode. Tonight was a great night for an implosion.

Two figures appeared at the edge of the screen, both clad in body armor and carrying assault rifles. They crept steadily forward, and whoever was wearing the body camera moved with them.

They closed in on the front door. The man on the far right held up his hand and counted down using his fingers.

Kimber instinctively grabbed Brandon's hand. Her heart pounded as though she were right there with the men, preparing to invade a potentially hostile space.

When the team leader's hand fisted, the door burst open, and three—make that four—men rushed through the door.

Shouts ensued, providing proof that the audio was working.

A gunshot echoed, then several more.

"Kitchen's clear," a man said, his voice low.

Another man responded. "Living room's clear."

"Check upstairs." Those words came from a woman. Was that Evangeline?

The camera angle shifted to two men climbing the stairs ahead, more footsteps following them. Rifles at the ready, the men cleared the room on the right. When one of them opened the door on the left, another gunshot fired.

This time, Kimber could see the man inside the room, who had a pistol raised. His shot must have gone wide because the only response from the Brits was to return fire.

The man dropped to the ground, and someone shouted, "Got something."

Evangeline came into view as the body camera focused on a long table. One side of the table was empty, but on the other side lay a bomb.

"Call the bomb squad," Evangeline ordered. She took a step closer, and suddenly, the panel on the front of the explosive device lit up, and thirty seconds flashed on the screen.

"Oh no," Kimber whispered.

The numbers ticked down—twenty-nine, twenty-eight . . .

"It's active!" Evangeline headed for the door. "Get out now!"

The camera spun, the owner of it following at a full sprint behind his teammates.

The seconds ticked off in Kimber's head. Ten, nine, eight . . .

The assault team rushed outside and continued running until the bomb detonated and the force of the explosion knocked them to the ground.

The image froze for a moment, and then the screen went blank.

• • •

Three hours and still no word. Brandon should be in bed by now, but he wasn't going to be able to sleep until he received the status update from the London office. Plus, he didn't want to leave Kimber alone while she was still so shaken up.

She hadn't cried, despite the tears that had formed upon witnessing such an awful scene. She'd also barely moved from her spot on the couch since they'd lost their audio and visual feed. Sitting on the corner cushion, she had her legs up and her arms wrapped around her knees as though curling into herself would somehow protect her from the shock of watching a bomb explode and British operatives flying through the air before crashing hard against the ground.

Brandon, on the other hand, had worn a path in the carpet as he had alternated between sitting at her side, checking his laptop for cable traffic, and retreating to Kimber's office to take calls from Rafi. So far, all those calls had simply been reaffirmations that no one had received word from the British authorities.

Brandon sat on the couch beside Kimber again and put his hand on her arm. "It's going to be okay."

"We gave them that address." She looked up at him, her eyes dampening. "If it weren't for us, this wouldn't have happened."

Guilt. He knew the feeling all too well. He'd experienced it when Finlay was killed. He'd felt it when he'd killed Darragh. And he suffered from it now.

In an attempt to make both of them feel better, he drew her close. "If it weren't for us, that bomb would have gone off where a lot more people would have been injured or killed."

She blinked several times, and for the first time since the bomb had exploded, tears spilled over.

"Hey, we're going to get through this." Maybe if he kept saying the words, they would be true.

She shifted her legs and leaned against his side, her head resting on his shoulder. An unexpected tenderness welled up inside him. He felt her pain, but the worry and frustration he was currently experiencing faded as he focused on the woman beside him. He kissed the top of her head, keeping his arm firmly around her.

"Do you think Evangeline and the others survived?" she asked.

"They cleared the house before the bomb went off. There's a good chance," Brandon said. "And no matter what, those agents knew the risks going in. Their actions saved lives."

"You're right, but what happens next?" Kimber straightened and swiped away the moisture on her cheeks. "Whoever planted those microdots is still at Monroe." She gestured helplessly with one hand. "We stopped one attack, but we didn't stop Labyrinth."

"You're right." Brandon took a deep breath, and a new resolve swept through him. "But we can tie tonight's incident to Monroe. That should be enough for Rafi to obtain the rest of the warrants we need. Tomorrow, we'll scour through everything we have and everything Rafi can get us. We'll find the answers."

"Tomorrow's Friday. You have to work."

"Tomorrow night, then," Brandon said. "And whether Rafi likes it or not, he's going to put in some overtime. We need reinforcements."

Brandon's phone rang, and he answered. "Yes?"

"We have the initial incident report from the Brits," Rafi said.

"And?"

"Three dead, two of Labyrinth's men and one of ours," Rafi said gravely. "Five more are in the hospital."

"Any word on Evangeline?" Brandon asked.

"She's in serious condition. That's all I know."

"Thanks, Rafi." Though Brandon could feel Kimber's questioning gaze on him, he said, "We need the rest of the financial information on the execs from Monroe. Tomorrow."

"I'm way ahead of you. I already put in an urgent request for their financials, cell phone records, and everything else I can think of," Rafi said. "After tonight, I suspect the judge will give us a blanket authorization to make up for putting up unnecessary roadblocks earlier."

"Good. We'll meet at Kimber's apartment at six tomorrow night."

Brandon expected some resistance, but Rafi simply said, "I'll bring dinner."

"Thanks, Rafi. See you tomorrow." Brandon hung up.

"Well?" Kimber asked.

"One of ours didn't make it." Brandon paused, swallowing hard to make sure his voice was steady before he continued. "Five more were hospitalized, including Evangeline."

"Do we know her condition?"

"Serious. That's all Rafi could tell me."

Kimber pressed her lips together for a long moment. Then she took a deep breath and lifted her teary gaze to meet his. "We have to stop them."

Brandon took her hand and squeezed. "We will."

CHAPTER 38

PHONE CALLS RECEIVED in the middle of the night were supposed to give good news. An attack gone right, reports of high casualty rates, even a successful weapons transaction. What Asadi didn't care for was news that the main attention-getter he had planned for London had gone up in smoke. Literally.

Two men lost. At least he had consolation that the bomb designed for the American theater had already been transported to the United States.

He had the bomb; he had a staff member planted. Now all he needed was for his men to execute their plan as intended. As for the London theater, its turn would come—just as soon as he could get another bomb constructed. Perhaps that particular incident could occur on the anniversary of the Americans' event. How fitting that would be. The capitalists who had soaked in his sister's talents when she'd been alive and then had abandoned her in her time of need would finally get a glimpse of how deeply painful such a loss could be.

His phone rang, likely another update from his London contact. He looked at the screen and grimaced. Not his London contact, but his bombmaker.

"I assume you heard about London," his supplier said in lieu of a greeting.

"How did MI6 find out about that location? We've only been using it for three months."

"I don't know." Apparently willing to throw a dead man under the bus, he said, "It must have been Finlay. We know he was talking to the CIA, and the CIA and MI6 have been known to share information."

"Finlay didn't have any knowledge of my plans for New York," Asadi said, speaking to himself as much as to the man on the other end of the call. "We finalized that scenario after he was eliminated."

"Then, those plans will go forward as they should."

"Yes." Asadi crossed to the balcony doors and looked out into the darkness. He'd gotten rather used to commanding his empire from a peaceful location, where the water washed upon the shores and the danger belonged to others, but Asadi wasn't willing to take any chances. "I need to be there in person to make sure nothing goes wrong."

"Are you sure?" his supplier asked.

"Quite," Asadi said. "This is a time when I need to lead by example."

• • •

Three people were dead because Kimber had found three typos in a book she shouldn't have even been reading. One life lost for each period that should have been a comma.

She could come to terms with knowing that eliminating the two operatives from Labyrinth had ultimately saved lives in the long run, but she was still struggling with the knowledge that some family in London had lost a family member while he was doing his job. Kimber didn't even know the man's name.

Logically, she knew things like this happened in the field, but before, she had always learned of such news as a bulletin in some daily report or in the form of a rumor circulating around the office. Never before had she experienced a personal connection with an event or a loss.

With a sense of determination, she dressed for the day and headed for the closest office supply store. Thirty minutes later, she returned carrying plastic bags with ten whiteboards and two packs of dry-erase markers.

Kimber strode with purpose down the hall and made it into her apartment without Trudy catching her in the hall. The woman was wonderful, but today, Kimber couldn't deal with anyone who couldn't know the truth—she was CIA, and she was hurting because of the ramifications of intelligence she had helped produce.

Kimber set the whiteboards down and pulled the protective plastic wrap off all of them. She wrote the name of a suspect across the top of each one and set them along the wall on either side of the fireplace. Time to create a more accurate picture of the people working with Brandon.

She grabbed her phone and called Mark.

"Hey, I heard about an incident in London last night. Did that have to do with you?"

"Yeah." Kimber drew a deep breath, trying to gather the strength to share her inner turmoil, but she couldn't get the words out. "I'll tell you all about it later, but for now, the two of us are digging into the employees at Monroe."

"Did Rafi ever get those warrants?"

"They should be coming through any minute, but I thought we could review what we do know while we're waiting on the rest of the financials."

"You tell me where you want to start."

With a dry-erase marker in hand, she moved to the spot in front of the whiteboard with Amelia's name on it. "Let's start with Amelia Franklin. I want to know everything there is to know about her."

• • •

Brandon was halfway between Amelia's favorite Italian restaurant and his office when the text from Rafi came through. It was simple and to the point. *Got them.*

Them, meaning the authorizations to access the financial accounts of Monroe's top management. This should be interesting. He would spend tonight searching through their personal information, and then tomorrow night, he and Kimber would be at the CEO's home, socializing with the lot of them. He hoped Kimber would be okay with transitioning from CIA research mode to author mode that quickly.

He'd stayed at her apartment until shortly after midnight when she'd finally insisted he go home and get some sleep. Since her norm was to think of others before herself, he took her awareness that he needed rest as a good sign.

Remembering all too well the turmoil he'd experienced after Finlay's death, he suspected she could use all the emotional support he could give her, so he pulled up Mark's office number and dialed.

Mark answered on the second ring. "This is Mark."

"Hey, it's Brandon."

"I figured you were Kimber," Mark said. "Did you hear? The search authorizations came through."

"Yeah, I heard." Brandon slowed his steps as he approached his office building. "I actually wanted to see if you've talked to Kimber. She may need an extra shoulder to cry on."

"I've already talked to her a dozen times today. I'm worried about her."

"Me too." Brandon sidestepped a couple holding hands as they strolled down the busy sidewalk clueless as to how much precious space they were taking up. "How much did she tell you?"

"Nothing, but it's obvious that she feels responsible for whatever went down last night."

"Yeah, she does, and we have a big party to go to tomorrow night," Brandon said. "The transition might be rough on her."

"I'll talk to her again," Mark said. "She may not realize it yet, but she's getting good at the art of deception."

"Yes, she is." Brandon ended the call and made his way into the office building. He delivered Amelia's lunch to her, her attention on whoever she was talking to on the phone.

Amelia picked up her lemonade as though it had been there the whole time, never lifting her gaze to Brandon.

Brandon passed Regina, who was also on the phone, but rather than the bored expression she typically wore, her eyes were alight with excitement.

"Thanks for letting me know." Regina hung up and stood. "Mary, the new job postings go up on Monday."

Mary stood as well. "And?"

"A spot for an associate editor in the London office and two editorial assistants here in New York," Regina said. "I'm applying for the ones here, but you have to try for the one in London."

"Is that what you'd like to do next?" Brandon asked Regina. "Work as an editorial assistant?"

"It's a good place to get my foot in the door for something better," Regina said, the edge in her voice not quite as sharp as usual. "Look at what it did for Whitney."

"I didn't realize that's where Whitney started," Brandon said.

"She wasn't always designer clothes with an apartment in Manhattan," Regina said.

"Where did Amelia start out?" Brandon asked.

"She worked her way up the editorial ranks at Henderson Publishing before she got the job as managing editor here."

"But the managing editor before her started here at Monroe and worked his way up," Mary said, almost as though she needed to speak the possibilities to believe they were possible.

"Are you applying for the editorial position in London?" Brandon asked her.

"Why? Are you planning to snag that from me too?"

"I think I'll stick with living in New York for a while longer."

"Brandon?" Amelia called out from her office.

Brandon retraced his steps.

Amelia held out her food. "This pasta is cold. Go heat it up."

"Sorry about that." Brandon took the plate. "I'll be right back."

He passed Mary's desk, and she shook her head. She lowered her voice enough to make sure she wouldn't be overheard. "Maybe it's a good thing you got that job instead of me. Amelia won't be there if I get the job in London."

Brandon nodded. "I know what you mean."

• • •

Asadi climbed out of the taxi and looked up. Skyscrapers towered above him at dizzying heights, the tops of the buildings not visible from the ground.

A man bumped into him and kept going as though Asadi didn't exist. Asadi clenched his jaw. He did exist, and everyone in this city would know of his presence soon enough.

He sidestepped a woman and her schnauzer, bumping into another woman in the process.

A curse that was anything but ladylike spewed at him like venom. Yes, this city was the perfect spot to remind Americans that Labyrinth's reach wasn't confined to across the ocean.

Turning his back on the woman who had finished her one-way scolding, he crossed the sidewalk to the apartment building where he would spend the next few days. He pushed through the revolving door and looked back through the glass at the rush of Friday-night pedestrian traffic.

No sign of the ocean in sight, the noise of cars and a distant siren carrying in the air, the smell of exhaust and humanity permeating every space. How could people live like this?

He took the lift to the twentieth floor, located his contact's flat, and knocked.

Hurried footsteps carried from the other side of the door. They would do well to invest in some soundproofing.

The man opened the door, his button-up shirt open at the collar, his sleeves rolled up as though he'd been relaxing after a long day.

Asadi didn't wait for an invitation to enter. He pushed past the man and continued through the entryway to the large living space beyond.

Through the wall of windows facing him, the lights of the city spread out before him. Maybe New York did have some redeeming qualities.

His host followed him. "The first shipment arrived this morning."

"Let me see it."

"This way." He walked into the hall on the far side of the room. When he reached the last door on the right, he opened it and flipped on the light. He then slid the closet doors open to reveal a large trunk trimmed in silver.

Asadi inspected the interior of the prop, the bomb already intact except for the explosive material that would turn the tangle of wires deadly. "When will the C-4 arrive?"

"It's already cleared customs and will arrive on Monday."

"Excellent. And your associate will be able to put the bomb in place?"

"Once this is intact, she'll arrange for a moving company to have the prop delivered to the theater."

"How do we keep it from exploding en route?" Asadi asked. A bomb going off on the streets of New York would garner attention but not enough for his purposes.

"The designer created an activation switch." He pointed at the bottom corner of the trunk. "A metal pin will be inserted through each side. Once those are in place, any movement will trigger the timer."

"And you know how much time to set it for to ensure maximum damage?"

"Our friend at the theater is working on that as we speak."

Asadi nodded his approval. "Excellent."

• • •

Kimber made another note on the whiteboard with Ramon's name at the top. Of the details she and Mark had compiled today, not one eliminated him as a suspect. The same was true of Amelia. Though neither had easy access to the advance reader copies, they both could have managed placing the microdots after hours without being noticed.

Her efforts with Mark had unearthed an obscure receipt with Haseeb's signature on it from a personal credit card in the date range Evangeline had noted, confirming that he'd been in the United States at the time. With him off the suspect list, they really were down to only two possibilities. If only they'd narrowed this list down sooner.

The thought of Evangeline lying in a hospital right now caused Kimber's stomach to churn uncomfortably. She'd received an update on the injured agents midday. Three were still in serious condition, including Evangeline, who had been put in a medically-induced coma to combat swelling on her brain.

Kimber tightened her grip on the marker in her hand as Brandon's signature knock sounded at the door. She answered it, the mere sight of him calming her frazzled emotions.

"Hey." He walked in, closed the door, and placed his hand on her waist as he leaned in for a kiss.

The brief meeting of their lips sent a familiar tingle rippling over her skin.

Brandon pulled back. "Sorry I didn't get the chance to call you today."

"It's okay. I was on the phone with Mark most of the day." She stepped aside and motioned at the evidence of her efforts.

"Wow. You've been busy."

"Yeah." Kimber circled the couch and motioned to the whiteboard with Amelia's name on it. "With what we've uncovered so far, Amelia and Ramon are the two who have stayed at the top of our suspect list, but we can't find anything that specifically ties them to Labyrinth. Logically, Ramon would be the top suspect since we know for certain he was in Europe in October." She waved toward the whiteboards. "The only person we couldn't track through his financials was Conrad. He doesn't have a company credit card, and he rarely uses them personally either."

"He probably doesn't need a company credit card since he would only interact with clients when they're signing their contracts," Brandon said.

Another knock sounded at the door.

"I'll get it." Brandon answered, and Rafi rushed inside, closing the door behind him.

"We caught a break." Rafi opened the flap of his messenger bag and pulled out a file folder. Moving to the serving bar separating the kitchen from the living room, he spread out a dozen eight-by-ten photos.

Kimber moved closer. The one nearest her was of a crate of books. "What are we looking at?"

"This." Rafi picked up one of the photos in the middle and held it up for her and Brandon to see. In it, several boxes had been removed from the large crate to reveal a long, thin crate in the center. The inner crate was filled with automatic rifles.

"I assume this shipment was from Labyrinth," Brandon said.

"Yes." Rafi held up another photo revealing an open box filled with hardback books. "They were using the density of the books to hide what was really inside."

"Clever." Brandon took the photo from Rafi for a closer look.

"How did you find this?" Kimber asked.

"A routine inspection in Baltimore," Rafi said. "Apparently, the inspector didn't like how the X-ray images looked, so he opened several boxes."

"What happens now?" Brandon asked. "If the port authority seizes the shipment, Labyrinth and whoever is working at Monroe will know we're on to them."

"We're already ahead of you on that," Rafi said. "We inventoried the contents of the crate, copied all the documentation, and cleared it to continue on. We're working with the CIA to stake out the end destination for when the shipment arrives."

"Where is it heading?" Kimber asked.

"Somalia."

Brandon studied the photos in front of him. "Sounds like a simple weapon transaction rather than a setup for a Labyrinth attack."

"Agreed," Rafi said. "But uncovering their method gives us the ability to check each crate at customs. We'll do a more thorough search and follow these shipments to their end destinations."

"And hopefully shut down the business side of Labyrinth," Brandon said.

"That's all fine and good," Kimber said, "but I'm more concerned with the side of their organization focused on creating terror."

"We hope tracing Monroe Publishing's shipments will help with that too," Rafi said. "We already have two more scheduled to hit the docks in Baltimore within the week."

"What about shipments coming into the United States?" Brandon asked.

"One passed through Baltimore yesterday, but by the time we knew to search it, the crate had already been picked up."

"Any idea where it ended up?" Kimber asked.

"No, but we'll keep looking."

CHAPTER 39

ASADI HELD HIS mobile and shook his head at the screen. How his people had missed that Kimber Frost was really Kimber Seidel was beyond him. The woman was an open CIA employee, for heaven's sake, and had been photographed with her sister numerous times over the past three weeks.

An impatient knock sounded at the door, and Asadi answered it.

His associate stormed into the loft. "What is so important that I had to risk coming here?"

"This." Asadi held up his mobile.

"Kimber Frost?" His eyes narrowed. "What about her?"

"Did you know her real name is Kimber Seidel, and she works for the CIA?"

"What?" He shook his head. "No. Her check was made out to Kimber Frost. She wouldn't have been able to cash it if she'd been using an alias." He paused, a new understanding flashing in his expression. "Unless she set up the paperwork to do business under her pen name."

"She works for the CIA," Asadi repeated. "Clearly, she could work her way past that little problem."

"What do you want me to do?"

"There's only one thing to do." Asadi slid his hands into his trouser pockets.

"What?"

"Make sure our author friend disappears," Asadi said. "I'm afraid Kimber Frost's career is going to end before she ever sees a single book on the shelf."

"What about the advance money?"

"I'm sure you can find a way to funnel that money to wherever we need it." Asadi didn't care about such petty details. He only wanted results. "And check out the new employees at Monroe again. It's possible that we aren't the only ones who have more than one employee working there."

His associate swallowed. "I'll take care of it."

• • •

Something wasn't adding up. Last night and all of today, Brandon, Kimber, and Rafi had pored over intel reports, financial data, and travel records. Now Brandon sat beside Kimber in a cab that would soon arrive at John Webb's house, where they would be expected to pretend they knew little about the very people they had been investigating for the past several weeks.

They'd narrowed their suspect list down to Amelia and Ramon, but nothing tied either of them to Labyrinth, just as none of the evidence fully eliminated anyone else in the top echelons of the company, with the exception of Haseeb, John, and Jamal.

The cab pulled up to a Fifth Avenue apartment building, and Brandon paid the driver before opening the door and waiting for Kimber on the curb.

She tightened her grip on her clutch and slipped her other hand through the crook of his elbow.

The cab pulled away.

Brandon realigned his thoughts from investigative mode to boyfriend mode. He needed to look like someone who was simply here by chance, the man lucky enough to have caught Kimber's interest. "You ready for this?" he asked.

"What if I say something wrong?"

"Just keep things simple." Brandon put his hand over hers. "Anytime someone asks you a question, give a basic answer and ask them something. Most people like to talk about themselves."

She drew in a deep breath and blew it out slowly. "Okay."

A doorman opened the door as they approached. Inside, marble floors covered a wide lobby, a set of glass doors and another doorman separating it from the elevators beyond.

"May I help you?" the second doorman asked.

"Yes, we're here to see John Webb in 3812," Brandon said.

He lifted an iPad and tapped the screen. "Names?"

"Brandon Hale and Kimber Frost."

"Of course." He opened the door. "You'll want to take the elevators on the far side."

"Thank you." Kimber released Brandon's arm and passed through the open door.

He followed and waited beside Kimber for the elevator.

The door opened behind them, and Brandon turned. Ramon and a petite woman with dark hair entered.

"Good evening, Mr. Alvarez. Mrs. Alvarez." The doorman held the door for them, and Ramon and his wife reached Brandon's side as the elevator arrived.

Ramon looked past Brandon to Kimber. "You must be Kimber Frost." He extended his hand. "I'm Ramon Alvarez, and this is my wife, Natalia."

Kimber shook his outstretched hand before shaking hands with Natalia. "Nice to meet you both." They all entered the elevator, and Kimber continued. "Ramon, I assume you already know Brandon."

"Yes, of course." Ramon's eyebrows lifted slightly, his only acknowledgment that he hadn't expected Brandon's presence tonight. "It was good of you to make sure Kimber arrived safely."

Suspecting Ramon planned to dismiss him when they reached their floor, Brandon took Kimber's hand. "It was my good fortune that Kimber invited me to join her."

"How long have you two been dating?" Natalia asked.

"Only about a week," Brandon said.

"I see." A hint of disdain hummed through her voice.

The look of disapproval Ramon cast Brandon's way suggested both he and his wife had come to the same conclusion, that Brandon had chosen to date Kimber because of her newfound riches and fame.

Eager to move past their impressions and turn the conversation else-where, Brandon asked, "Is Whitney going to be here tonight?"

"I'm not sure she made the invite list," Ramon said.

"In that case, I'm happy to take photos for her to use on social media. No one needs me to be in anything Whitney and Haseeb will want to post."

"Haseeb may take you up on that," Ramon said.

"We certainly can't trust Ramon to take photos," Natalia added. "We went on a three-week river cruise last fall, and I don't think he took a single picture."

"I don't particularly care to watch the world through a camera lens." Ramon gave his wife's shoulder a squeeze. "Besides, you took enough for both of us."

"It's true."

Brandon's thoughts raced. Had the river cruise been at the same time they thought Ramon could have been meeting with Asadi Mir?

"When was your cruise?" Brandon asked. "My mom has been think-ing about going on one for forever, but she can't ever decide on when the best time would be."

"We were there in October. Really, I can't imagine a better time to go."

"I bet it was amazing," Kimber said.

The elevator doors opened, and all four of them walked toward the CEO's apartment. Brandon rang the bell, and a moment later, John an-swered the door himself.

He looked past Brandon as though he didn't exist and focused on Kimber. "You made it." He waved them inside. "Please, come in."

Kimber and Brandon walked inside.

The conversation from the elevator played through Brandon's thoughts as they made their way into the living room. If Ramon had been on a cruise in October when they thought he'd been meeting with Asadi Mir, that left them only one viable suspect—Amelia—and she was standing across the room.

CHAPTER 40

KIMBER WAS STANDING beside a terrorist. She struggled to remain calm as Amelia and Jamal spoke about a shipment that had been delayed in customs. Kimber suspected whatever one they were referring to had been held up so the FBI could search for more weaponry.

Beside her, Brandon asked, "Does this sort of thing happen often?"

"It has lately," Jamal grumbled. "This is the third time this month."

"Probably some new inspector in customs trying to make a name for himself." Amelia took a sip of her wine. "We'll need to build in an extra week or two in our production schedules for our fall releases."

Brandon put his hand on Kimber's back, a subtle reminder that she had barely spoken since they arrived. Grasping for something on topic, she said, "It's hard to believe how far out you plan in this business."

"Your day will be here before you know it," Amelia said.

Jamal tilted his head toward Amelia. "And as long as Amelia keeps you on schedule, Conrad will make sure those checks keep coming."

"Conrad?" Kimber spotted the man across the room, with his brown hair recently trimmed, his suit perfectly tailored. "What does he have to do with my advances?"

"Overseeing the contracts is only part of his job. He also runs our royalty department." Jamal leaned in and lowered his voice. "It drives Ramon crazy, but John seems to like having Conrad share in the financial side of things."

"I'm surprised one person would work with both contracts and finance," Kimber said.

"He has another attorney working under him to take care of the grunt work. That frees him up to takes care of the international side of the business." Jamal shrugged. "I guess it makes sense since Conrad has the British connection."

"British connection?" Brandon asked.

"He's a dual citizen," Jamal offered. "His mom's a Brit."

A dual citizen who likely had two passports. Kimber looked at Brandon, her new awareness reflected in his eyes. Conrad didn't have a company credit card, and with a British passport, he would be able to come and go without his US passport flagging.

Amelia stared at Kimber for a moment before she cocked an eyebrow. "Jamal, you're boring our guest."

"No, not at all," Kimber said. "I studied finance and international business in college, so all of this is fascinating to me."

"Finance and international business?" Amelia narrowed her eyes. "I thought your degree was in creative writing."

Creative writing. That was exactly what Kimber Frost's resume said.

Brandon took Kimber's hand. "Studying finance and graduating in finance are two completely different things."

"So true," Kimber said, grasping at the lifeline Brandon had thrown her. "My parents wanted me to study something practical, but eventually, my creative side won out."

Amelia lifted her glass. "Lucky for us that it did."

Kimber glanced at Conrad again. "Yes, very lucky."

• • •

All the pieces were falling into place. Conrad's access to the international funds for Monroe Publishing, his dual citizenship, his lack of credit card usage.

Brandon had texted Rafi right after learning this new information, but the man had yet to respond. Two hours and thirty-seven minutes was more than enough time to have the State Department run a passport scan on Conrad's British passport.

They'd already finished the elaborate meal John had catered for them, and now the guests were starting to leave.

Haseeb stopped beside Brandon. "Please make sure you send the photos from tonight to Whitney. Hopefully, she'll feel well enough tomorrow to put some posts up."

"I didn't realize she was home sick."

Haseeb nodded. "I'm sure she was sorry to miss this." He offered a wave to John and continued out the door.

"Thanks again for a wonderful evening," Natalia said.

"Always a pleasure to have you," John told Ramon's wife before shaking hands with Ramon. "Are we still on for golf tomorrow?"

"Ten o'clock." Ramon escorted his wife out the door.

Brandon slid his hand around Kimber's shoulder. "We should probably go too."

John focused on Kimber. "We look forward to great things in your future."

"Thank you."

Brandon took a step toward the door, but before he could follow Ramon and Natalia into the hall, Amelia moved into his path and spoke to Kimber. "Make sure you get some rest this weekend. We'll be starting on your edit next week, so the more you can get done on your next project before that comes to you, the better."

"I have every intention of sleeping in tomorrow." Kimber lifted her hand and waved to the room in general. "Good night."

Good nights echoed as she and Brandon left John's apartment.

Brandon's phone buzzed. "Hopefully, that's Rafi." He pulled it free of his pocket and opened the text. *Conrad Breslin entered Madrid October 12 on British passport. Returned to US on October 18.*

Brandon tilted his phone to show Kimber.

Her eyes widened. "Those dates are an exact match for the ones Evangeline gave us."

"Looks like our search is finally over." Brandon pressed the button for the elevator.

"Yes, but I'll feel better when Conrad is behind bars and Asadi Mir is in custody."

"Me too." But he didn't want to think about Labyrinth right now, not with Kimber standing next to him all dressed up. Unable to resist, he leaned down and pressed his lips to hers. He lifted his hands to frame her face, losing himself in the sensation of her kiss.

The elevator dinged.

He pulled back and escorted Kimber into the empty elevator with every intention of continuing their kiss once they were safely inside.

He hit the button for the ground floor. Hurried footsteps sounded, and someone thrust their hand into the car to prevent the doors from closing.

The doors opened back up, and Conrad stepped inside. "I thought I'd missed it."

Brandon sensed the way Kimber's body tensed as the elevator doors closed. Hoping to draw Conrad's attention away from Kimber's reaction, he said, "It was a nice party tonight."

"Yes." Conrad lifted his hand to reveal the pistol he held. "It was."

Brandon's gaze lowered. A gun in an elevator. Not again.

• • •

The moment Conrad hit the emergency stop button for the elevator, Kimber reacted instinctively. She thrust her hand out, knocking Conrad's gun away from where she and Brandon stood.

The pistol flew free, impacted the wall, and dropped to the floor by Conrad's feet.

Brandon reached for his own weapon, but he'd barely pulled it from the holster at his belt when Conrad grabbed Kimber around her throat and yanked her in front of him.

Limited by the small space, Kimber stomped hard on Conrad's foot, but he didn't release her. Instead, he tightened his grip around her, pressing on her windpipe.

Panic rose inside her, and she opened her mouth as she attempted to breathe.

"Let her go." Brandon aimed his weapon at them.

"And let you shoot me?" Conrad shook his head. "Not a chance."

Desperate for air, Kimber elbowed Conrad in the stomach. He groaned, and his hold on her loosened but not enough for her to break free.

Brandon's gaze flicked to hers briefly before he asked, "What's Labyrinth planning?"

"You'll find out soon enough."

"Where's the bomb?" Brandon pressed.

Kimber couldn't see Conrad's expression, but his body tensed, suggesting Brandon had confirmed their suspicions.

"I don't know what you're talking about."

"We know about the bomb," Brandon continued. "Just like we knew about the one in London."

Silence filled the elevator for several long seconds.

"You'll never find it." Conrad's voice was smooth and cocky when he added, "And if you kill me, I won't be able to help you."

Taking another approach, Kimber said, "Help us, and we can help you."

"I doubt that." Keeping Kimber between him and Brandon, Conrad squatted to retrieve his weapon.

Brandon fired at the floor, but the warning shot did nothing to deter Conrad.

Conrad grabbed his weapon and straightened.

Kimber's survival instinct kicked in, and she thrust her weight back, forcing Conrad into the elevator wall behind them. The gun fell to the floor again. This time, Kimber and Conrad both dropped to retrieve it.

Conrad was faster, and he straightened, swinging the gun toward Brandon.

Brandon squeezed off a shot and then another. Conrad stumbled back a step before crumpling to the ground.

Brandon kicked the gun clear of Conrad's reach, and Kimber leaned down and scooped it up. She stared down at Conrad's body, her breath coming in rapid gasps. The past few seconds replayed in her mind as though everything had happened to someone else. But it hadn't happened to someone else.

She looked up at Brandon, her pulse still racing. "He tried to—He almost—"

Brandon pulled her against him, holding her for a long moment. His hand stroked her hair, and he spoke in a low voice. "He can't hurt us now."

"Is he—" Kimber couldn't finish the question.

Brandon released her and leaned down. He pressed two fingers against Conrad's throat for several seconds. He repositioned his fingers, again waiting several seconds. Finally, he looked up at Kimber. "He's dead."

Conrad was dead.

Kimber struggled to comprehend Brandon's words. "What do we do now?"

Brandon straightened. "I'm afraid I have a bit of experience with this situation." He retrieved his phone from his pocket and dialed. "Rafi, I have another elevator problem." He paused. Then he grimaced. "Yes, there's a body."

●　●　●

Brandon approached the elevator in their apartment building lobby, not sure how Kimber would react to the idea of walking into an elevator so soon after being trapped in one with a gunman. To his surprise, she pressed the button and walked inside the moment the doors opened.

She hit the button for their floor. "This all feels like a nightmare or a scene that happened in some spy movie."

"I know what you mean." His queasy stomach had yet to settle, but he kept that to himself.

The elevator doors started to close, but in a repeat of what had happened with Conrad a short time ago, someone rushed forward and thrust their arm into the opening.

Kimber jumped back. Brandon grabbed his weapon.

The elevator doors opened, and Rafi stepped in. "Glad I caught you," he said.

Brandon resecured his weapon in its holster. "Are you crazy? You nearly got yourself shot."

Rafi looked from Brandon to Kimber. "What did I do?"

"You rushed into an elevator in the exact same way Conrad did two hours ago."

Rafi winced. "Sorry. I wasn't thinking."

Kimber leaned against the elevator wall and took several deep breaths.

None of them spoke until they reached their floor and made their way into Kimber's apartment. As soon as they were safely inside, Kimber asked, "Do the other people from the party know Conrad's dead?"

"Officially, he'll die in a car accident tonight," Rafi said.

"Why hide the truth?" Kimber set her purse on the counter.

One look at Rafi's face was all Brandon needed to find the answer. "You think Conrad wasn't working alone."

"We need to consider the possibility that he had help." Rafi motioned toward the ARC copy of *Countdown* that lay on Kimber's coffee table. "Conrad worked on the business side of the house. I don't know if he would have had access to the books that had the microdots in them."

"Which brings us back to Amelia." Conflicting emotions twisted through Brandon. He wanted this assignment to be over, but he also didn't want to risk being separated from Kimber.

"For now, the two of you need to continue as usual," Rafi said. "We'll work on figuring out the *where* and *when* of Labyrinth's planned bombing."

Kimber narrowed her eyes and crossed to pick up the book on her coffee table. "What if we already have the *when*?"

"How would we know that?" Rafi asked.

She held up the book. "The microdots are twenty-three pages apart. Maybe that's because that's part of the message."

The lightbulb went on in Brandon's head. "The number of instances could have been the month—three for March—and the number of pages could be the date."

"That's a stretch." Rafi shook his head. "I'm sure the people working in Labyrinth already know the date."

"Exactly. Which makes burying the code using the information they already have an easy way to share it."

"Maybe." Though skepticism still carried in Rafi's voice, he said, "I'll share that possibility with the rest of the terrorism task force." He paused. "Also, I received an update from London. Evangeline's condition has been upgraded, and she's expected to make a full recovery. The rest of her team is also improving."

"Thank goodness," Kimber said. "Did MI6 have any useful information for us?"

"They sent over their report. The bomb was C-4 based with a dual detonator," Rafi said. "They're still trying to piece together the details, but I'll keep you updated."

"Thanks," Brandon said.

"I'll talk to you both on Monday." Rafi headed for the door. "Try to get some sleep."

Brandon suspected he and Kimber would spend more time fighting nightmares than resting, but he nodded. "Thanks for your help tonight."

Rafi turned the knob. "Just do me a favor and avoid gunmen in elevators for me."

"Believe me, I do try."

•　•　•

A car accident. Asadi wasn't buying that story for a minute.

The woman on the other end of the call shared the details that had been distributed to the Monroe Publishing employees. As soon as she concluded her account, she asked, "Do you still want to move forward with your plans?"

"Yes." Asadi clenched his teeth and paced to the closet where the bomb was stored. "Have the movers pick it up tomorrow."

"I will. That will give me time to place it after dress rehearsal and activate it before opening night."

"Excellent. And after you've completed your duties, we should meet," Asadi said. "It appears we will need to find a way to improve your position at Monroe now that Conrad is no longer there."

"I look forward to meeting you in person."

"As do I."

CHAPTER 41

BRANDON GAVE KIMBER'S hand a squeeze as they rode in the back of the limousine to the Gershwin Theatre. One of the most famous actors in the country was taking them to opening night of one of the most anticipated Broadway shows of the year, and Brandon could only think about how close he'd come to losing Kimber.

For the past four days, the two of them had struggled together with the memories of their elevator confrontation while also searching for any clues about who might still be working with Labyrinth. So far, they didn't have anything useful.

Mark was still watching for intel that might come through his sources, Rafi and his team at the FBI were actively searching for Asadi, and a surveillance unit had Amelia's home and office staked out. So far, nothing in her behavior had given the authorities any clues regarding where Asadi might be staying or what the target might be. Now Brandon was starting to question whether Amelia was actually the person involved or whether it was someone else entirely.

The limo pulled to a stop. Ian and Phoebe climbed out first and then Greta, Tessa, and Kimber. Brandon came last.

Cameras flashed until Ian disappeared inside, and Brandon hung back in the hope that he could manage to stay out of the photographers' frames.

Kimber reached the doorway and turned to wait for him, the tension in her body evident.

He understood her current struggle keenly. Beyond the frightening memories they were still struggling to overcome, a terrorist attack could happen any minute, and they were going to watch a musical.

Ian showed his phone to the gate attendant, then led the way inside. Brandon caught up to Kimber and settled his hand on her waist.

Ian retrieved six passes from his inside coat pocket and handed one to each of them. "I say we take advantage of our backstage access before the show starts. Tyrone always does better when he has a bit of a distraction before he performs."

The moment the security guard let them into the backstage area, the energy of the cast and crew enveloped them. Several dancers stretched in the wings of the stage area, and crew members weaved past them as they prepared props for the first act. Two men dressed in shuka cloth sat beside four black trunks, three of them trimmed in gold, the fourth one larger and trimmed in silver.

"What's the significance of the one trunk being trimmed with silver instead of gold?" Brandon asked.

Kimber furrowed her brow. "There weren't any that had silver on them when we were here last week."

"They must have had to replace one of their props and couldn't find an exact match," Ian said.

"Does that happen often?" Brandon asked.

"Often enough. This one looks like a last-minute swap. Otherwise, they would have already painted it to match." Ian sidestepped one of the dancers and knocked on a door that had a gold star with Tyrone's name on it.

The door swung open, and a woman holding a makeup brush stood in the doorway.

"Hi, Hannah. How's our boy doing?" Ian asked.

"He's convinced he's forgotten all his lines."

Ian walked through the door. "Sounds like we got here just in time."

• • •

Kimber sat between Brandon and Ian, only three rows separating them from the orchestra pit and the stage. Tessa and Greta had taken the spots on the other side of Phoebe. Madison Peters and several others from her birthday party filled in the seats around them, everyone chatting excitedly about Tyrone's big night.

Kimber still couldn't believe Ian had invited her and that she was sitting among the who's who of the entertainment world. Somehow, she'd envisioned watching the show from the balcony, where the actors' faces were little more than distant blurs. And while Kimber loved the great view, part of her wished she were sitting somewhere where she wouldn't be noticed if she checked her cell phone for messages.

The possibility of a terrorist attack this week, maybe even today, had her on edge, and she hated that she wasn't doing anything to research Asadi Mir and Labyrinth. Logically, she knew the FBI was far more likely to locate the missing bomb, but sitting here tonight had her feeling both antsy and indulgent. She should be helping, but instead, she was rubbing shoulders with the rich and famous to keep her cover intact. And in so doing, she had dragged Brandon with her, potentially risking his cover.

Music swelled all around her before tapering off as Tyrone took center stage, his voice carrying through the entire theater on his wireless microphone. And despite Tyrone's earlier nerves, he was currently captivating the audience.

The orchestra conductor lifted his baton and cued the musicians. A new song began, and the entire cast danced onto the stage. Tyrone's voice rose as others joined in, the vitality of the entire cast rising with each word.

When the first act ended and the curtain came down, the applause was instant, and several people came to their feet.

As soon as the audience quieted and the house lights went up, Ian said, "If they're getting a partial standing ovation after the first act, this show is going to run for quite a while."

"Especially since the best part is the finale," Kimber said.

"You've seen the finale?" Brandon asked.

"We watched them rehearse it when we came to have lunch with Tyrone," Kimber said. "Of course, I haven't seen them perform in costume."

"I don't envy the dancers," Ian said. "Any time you have to carry props like those trunks, it's a workout."

"You're talking about the ones we passed when we went backstage before the show?" Brandon asked.

Ian nodded.

Phoebe stood. "I'm going to the restroom while I have the chance. Does anyone need anything while I'm up?"

"I'm fine," Ian said.

"Me too," Brandon said.

Needing to get up and move, Kimber pushed out of her seat. "I'll come with you."

"I will too." Tessa stood, and so did Greta.

"Don't take too long," Ian said. "You won't want to miss act 2."

Phoebe stepped past her husband. "We'll be back in plenty of time."

• • •

Brandon swiveled in his seat and looked at the rows and rows of people behind him. He'd been to the theater before, but this one had to be the largest he'd ever attended. At least a thousand seats spread out behind him, and that didn't include the hundred or more that lay between him and the stage.

He automatically searched for Kimber, but she'd already disappeared into the crowd of patrons heading for exits in search of restrooms and refreshments. Uniformed staff milled among the rows, guiding people to their various destinations.

"Quite a sight, isn't it?" Ian said.

"Yes." Brandon adjusted his position so he was once again facing forward.

"I have to admit, I miss the theater," Ian said. "A new crowd every night, the constant challenge of feeding off their energy and keeping everything fresh."

"I can only imagine." Brandon caught a glimpse of movement beyond Ian, near the door leading to the stage area. A sense of familiarity flashed inside him. He focused on the staff member standing by the door, and his eyes widened. Whitney.

The question of why she was here flitted through his mind at the same time a memory from Saturday night pressed forward. Ramon had said he didn't think Whitney had made the invite list, but Haseeb had said she'd been home sick. Whitney certainly didn't look sick now, nor had any of her financial information suggested that she would have need for a second job, especially one well beneath her skill level.

Brandon reached into his pocket and pulled out his phone and the backstage pass. "Would I be able to use this to go backstage during intermission?"

Ian's eyebrows rose, clearly surprised by Brandon's question. "The pass should let you back there any time tonight, but it's pretty chaotic during the break. They'll be resetting the stage and prepping all the props for the second act."

Props, like the trunk that didn't quite match the other three.

Brandon stood. "I'll be right back."

"Do you want me to come with you?" Ian asked.

"No, that's okay." Brandon didn't want Ian anywhere near the back-stage area if his suspicions were correct. Because if he was right, tonight was the night Labyrinth was going to strike, and the target was here.

He slipped his backstage pass around his neck and started toward the side of the stage where Whitney had been a moment ago, but a man now stood in her place.

Brandon showed his pass to the staff member and was admitted through the door leading to the stage. Then he quickly texted Kimber. *Whitney is working here.*

CHAPTER 42

KIMBER FOLLOWED PHOEBE out of the restroom and approached the spot across the hall where Tessa and Greta waited. The show so far had been incredible, but something kept niggling at her, an uneasiness she couldn't quite explain.

She drew a slow breath and fought to push the sensation aside. The FBI was looking for the bomb, and she was here with her sister, her boyfriend, and people who were not only important in their industry but who were genuinely kind and on their way to becoming true friends.

"I still can't believe we're here tonight," Tessa said, interrupting Kimber's thoughts. "Phoebe, thank you again for inviting us."

"It's our pleasure." She waved a hand toward the large banner to their left. "We should take a picture, just us girls."

"That's a good idea," Tessa agreed quickly. "Kimber, do you have your phone?"

"Yes." She pulled it from her purse. An alert for a text message from Brandon illuminated the screen, but she ignored it and opened the camera.

Tessa flagged down an usher to take the photo for them, and Kimber handed over her phone. As soon as they lined up and the usher took their picture, Kimber collected her phone and headed for their seats with everyone else.

Suspecting Brandon had changed his mind about wanting something to eat or drink, she opened her text message and read the four words: *Whitney is working here.*

The oddity of Whitney working at the theater when she already had a full-time job and a robust bank account confused Kimber until the pieces of the puzzle fell into place: An employee from Monroe. A bomb planned for tonight. A crowded theater. A large prop that had been replaced so close to opening night.

Kimber's chest seized, and her throat constricted. The seats so close to the stage no longer felt like a gift but rather a death sentence for her and her sister and her friends.

Kimber pulled out her wallet. "Tessa, would you mind grabbing me and Brandon something to drink at the snack bar?"

"Where are you going?" Tessa asked.

"I need to grab a tissue."

"Oh, I have one." Phoebe opened her purse.

Ignoring Phoebe's offer, Kimber focused on Tessa. "I'll be back in a minute."

Kimber did a quick analysis of her current position in relation to where Ian had taken them to the backstage area before the show. Then she rushed toward the stairs that would give her the quickest access to her intended destination.

As she rushed past people making their way back to their seats, she texted Brandon. *Check the trunk with silver trim. It might contain a bomb.*

She pressed the Send button, her heart racing. She could be completely wrong on her analysis, but if she was right, Conrad wasn't the only person Labyrinth had working for them at Monroe. Whitney would make two.

· · ·

After reading Kimber's text, Brandon made it only a few yards before a man in his early thirties moved into his path. "You shouldn't be back here."

Brandon held up his pass. "I'm allowed to be back here."

"Those passes are only good for before and after the show."

"That's not what I was told." Brandon stepped to his left. "I'll only be a minute."

The man opposite him countered his movement. "You need to go back to your seat."

"I will after I check something." Brandon stepped to his right.

Again, the other man moved to block him.

Beyond frustrated, Brandon held up his pass again. "I have this for a reason."

"Those passes are for people to come back here before and after the show, not during."

"And I promise, I'll go back to my seat before the second act starts."

"Sorry, sir." The man shook his head.

Not willing to be deterred, Brandon faked a step to his right. The moment the crew member moved to block, Brandon quickly adjusted his weight to the left and pushed past him.

"Hey!" The man grabbed for Brandon's arm, but Brandon darted out of reach and rushed toward the stack of trunks.

He stopped beside the one with the silver trim and squatted in front of it. Holding his phone up, he flipped on the flashlight and shone it along the hinges and the edges to search for any sign of tampering.

He made it only as far as the front corner before the man he had evaded grabbed his shoulder and yanked him back. "You need to go back to your seat, or I'm going to have you kicked out of here."

Rapid footsteps approached, and Kimber's voice carried to them. "Wait! Let him go!"

Kimber's command didn't carry any influence. Instead, the man turned to face her. "You need to get out of here too."

"We'll both leave as soon as we look in that trunk," Kimber said.

Brandon shrugged out of the stagehand's grasp, and Kimber immediately stepped between them before the man could grab at him again.

"Can you tell us when this prop was replaced?" Kimber asked, her tone placating.

"What does it matter?" he asked, tension vibrating through his voice.

"Just answer the question," Kimber pressed.

"It was a day or two ago."

Brandon shone the flashlight from his phone on the trunk again. No sign of any wires or booby traps.

"Who brought in the new trunk?" Kimber asked.

"One of the new hires. She said she had one that looked almost the same as the other three."

Brandon looked over his shoulder. "Was it Whitney?"

Now confusion illuminated the man's features. "Who are you?"

"That doesn't matter," Brandon said, focusing again on the information he needed. "Was Whitney the one who switched out this prop?"

"Yeah, but that kind of stuff happens all the time."

Brandon's gaze met Kimber's, her awareness matching his own. "You should get out of here."

Before Kimber could respond, a woman rushed toward them. "Trent, we need you to help with the statue."

Trent looked at the woman, looked at Kimber and Brandon, and then looked back at the woman. Then he hurried toward the stage.

Finally alone, Brandon focused on Kimber again. "You should go."

"First, let's see if we're right about what's inside there." She moved to the opposite side of the trunk from where he knelt. After checking for any sign of a booby trap or automatic detonator, she said, "It looks safe to open. Are you ready?"

Brandon drew a deep breath. "Yeah."

He gripped one corner while Kimber put her hand on the other side. Together, they lifted the lid slowly.

The backstage lighting filtered down, revealing what he had hoped not to find. C-4 filled the entire trunk, a detonator affixed to the top, four sets of wires connecting from the detonator and stretching out in every direction until they disappeared around the sides of the bomb.

"Oh no." Kimber's words came out in a whisper.

"Call the bomb squad." Brandon checked the hinges again, confirming that opening the trunk the rest of the way wouldn't cause the bomb to detonate.

Kimber made the call.

Brandon traced the wires, fighting to remember every explosive ordnance disposal course he'd ever taken since joining the agency.

Kimber spoke to the emergency operator. "We have a bomb backstage at the Gershwin Theatre." She fell silent, and the indecipherable buzz of a male voice carried over the line.

Two dancers rushed by, oblivious to the threat.

Kimber edged closer and peered into the chest. "It's C-4, remote and secondary detonators." Kimber hesitated. "Four connected circuits."

Brandon looked up at her. With the way she was talking, she sounded more like an operative than he did.

"He wants us to evacuate," Kimber said.

Brandon debated the wisdom of the emergency operator's suggestion.

"The bomb isn't active," Brandon said as a stagehand rushed by. "But if Whitney is nearby, she could set it off as soon as she's clear of the blast radius."

The words were barely out of Brandon's mouth when the fire alarm sounded. Brandon looked up at Kimber.

"I didn't do it." Kimber held out her hands. "Someone must have heard us talking and set it off."

Several people in the wings of the stage started talking at once. A man bumped into Brandon, knocking him hard into the trunk.

The detonator lit up, five minutes showing on the digital screen.

"Sorry," the man called over his shoulder, oblivious to his having just armed a bomb.

"It must have had a failsafe built in to activate once the trunk went into motion," Kimber said.

Brandon's heartbeat quickened. "How long until the bomb squad gets here?"

"Three minutes. Maybe four."

"This is going to be close." Brandon stood. "They might not have time to get through the crowd, much less disarm the bomb."

"I'll see if I can find any wire cutters or scissors," Kimber said. "Worst case, we try to disarm it ourselves."

"Kimber, this is an active bomb." Brandon stared at her. "And we'd need to cut all four circuits at the same time, or it will detonate."

"I know, and there are over a thousand people out there, some of whom won't be able to clear the building before the bomb goes off."

Before he could protest further, Kimber rushed out of sight.

CHAPTER 43

ASADI HAD NEVER watched before. He sat at the restaurant down the street from the theater, the corner of the building visible from his table by the window. He would have liked to have sat directly across the street, but the potential of the bomb damaging the nearby buildings was too high. No point risking himself to satisfy his curiosity.

His phone buzzed with an incoming text. *Leaving now.*

Asadi checked his watch. Right on time.

The second act would begin in a matter of minutes, and by the finale, hundreds of lives would end in an instant. Labyrinth would make headlines, and the Americans would learn that they were far from invincible. Finally, they would feel the depth of his pain.

A couple rushed into view, the man dressed in a suit and tie, the woman in a glittering dress, her coat hanging over her arm.

The oddity that the woman wasn't wearing her coat on such a cold night caught his attention. Before he could ponder the reason, several more people rushed down the street.

A police siren sounded, the flashing lights coming into view as a police car raced by.

Had the bomb been found? It couldn't be.

Asadi stood and moved to the restaurant exit. His waitress said something to him, but Asadi ignored her as he made his way outside.

The view before him was exactly what he'd feared; people poured out of the theater from every possible exit.

This wouldn't do.

Asadi reached into his pocket and retrieved the burner phone that had a single number programmed into it. One call and the bomb would detonate.

He pulled up the single contact, and hovered his thumb over the Call button. He looked out at the theater and returned to the restaurant. Best to stay out of the danger zone.

. . .

Kimber rushed through the now-empty backstage area toward the prop room. If she had any chance of finding what she needed to disarm the bomb, she would find it there.

Seconds ticked by in her head, the pressure mounting. At least with the secondary detonator active, remote detonation would no longer be an option. She supposed she should be grateful for that little flaw in the bomb's design, but at the moment, she was more concerned about surviving the next four minutes and nineteen seconds.

She reached the prop room at the same time her cell phone rang with Tessa on the other side of the call.

"Where are you?" Tessa asked, panic in her voice. "They're evacuating the theater."

"I'm backstage." Kimber headed for the corner where she'd seen a toolbox during her backstage tour with Tyrone, but it was nowhere in sight.

"What's going on?" Tessa asked. "Why did the alarm go off?"

"I'll explain later." Kimber pushed a stack of boxes aside. "Just go outside and get as far away from the theater as you can."

"But—"

"Just do it. Please." Kimber spotted a glimpse of red metal and leaned down. Success! "I'll call you as soon as it's safe."

Tessa's voice pitched up a note. "You're staying?"

With the seconds ticking off in her head, Kimber said, "Just go outside." Before her sister could protest further, Kimber ended the call and opened the toolbox. She rummaged through until she found a pair of wire cutters, then she dug deeper, hoping there would be a second set. That hope wasn't realized.

She turned and spotted a small desk in the corner. She rushed across the room and opened the center drawer. A pair of shiny, metal scissors lay inside. She grabbed them. Halfway there. Now she needed two more methods to cut a wire. She glanced at her watch. In less than three minutes.

Rapid footsteps echoed against the wooden floor. Tessa's voice followed. "Kimber. We need to get out of here."

Kimber's chest seized, and panic enveloped her. "What are you doing? I told you to leave."

"I'm not leaving without you." Tessa's gaze lowered to the wire cutters and scissors in Kimber's hand. "What are you doing with those?"

"Trying to defuse a bomb."

Tessa's face paled. "A bomb?"

Kimber checked her watch again. Two minutes twenty seconds left. Tessa wasn't making it out of here in time, which meant Kimber's only chance of saving her sister was to keep the bomb from going off.

Though it was a long shot, Kimber asked, "I don't suppose you have any scissors in your purse, do you?"

Tessa stared wordlessly.

"Tessa." Kimber snapped her fingers in front of her sister's face. "Do you have scissors?"

"No." Tessa's wide-eyed gaze met Kimber's. "I use my nail clippers when I need to cut something."

"Nail clippers," Kimber repeated. Those could work. She held out her hand. "Let me have them."

Tessa plucked a pair of nail clippers from the inside pocket of her purse and handed them to her.

Not bothering to thank her sister, Kimber sprinted toward the area where the makeup artists had set up.

"Where are you going?" Tessa asked, following behind her.

"I need another pair of nail clippers or scissors." Kimber reached the makeup table. Lipstick, powders, eye shadows, makeup brushes—the entire surface of the table was covered.

"Right there." Tessa reached past Kimber and produced another pair of nail clippers, only these were the nail scissors variety.

Kimber snatched them from Tessa as seconds continued to count down in her mind. Ninety-six seconds left.

She didn't know if nail clippers would be the solution, but there was only one way to find out. She pivoted on her heel and raced back toward Brandon and the bomb that would more than likely kill them.

• • •

Brandon held his phone out so the member of the bomb squad speaking to him could see the wires leading from the detonator to the four sides of the trunk.

The man on the other end of the call said, "The only sure way to defuse it is to cut the lead wire on all four circuits at the same time."

Which was exactly what he'd suspected. "I don't have anything to cut them with."

"Then, clear out of there."

"Is the theater evacuated?" Brandon asked.

"Almost," the man on the phone said.

Almost meant there would be casualties beyond him and Kimber.

Brandon glanced at the timer. A minute and twenty-eight seconds. "How close is the bomb squad?"

"They're on the premises and trying to get to you now."

"Brandon!" Kimber rushed to his side and held out a pair of wire cutters and scissors. "Here."

"We have to cut the four white wires at the same time." Brandon held up the scissors and wire cutters. "We need two more."

"I know."

Tessa appeared at Kimber's side. "What can I do?"

Kimber handed Tessa something. Were those nail clippers?

"When we tell you, clip this wire." Kimber gently ran her finger under the correct wire and lifted it to give Tessa easier access. Kimber looked at Brandon. "I'll take this one, if you can get those two."

It was a long shot, but time was running out. A minute sixteen seconds. A minute fifteen.

"We have to have perfect timing for this to work. I say we wait a few more seconds in case the bomb squad gets here," Brandon said.

"Get ready, just in case," Kimber insisted.

Brandon blew out a breath. He slid the scissors into place so he could cut the wire to his right. Then he put the wire cutters in position for the one on his left.

Tessa held up the nail clippers in her hand. "These are too small to fit around the wire."

A man and a woman rushed in carrying an EOD containment device nearly twice the size of the trunk containing the bomb.

They set the containment box down, and the woman asked, "How much time?"

Brandon was already staring at the timer. "Fifty-four seconds."

The bomb techs looked at each other. Now the man spoke. "We don't have time to wait for the robot."

Brandon didn't need them to expand on their comment. Their standard operating procedure would be to have a specialized robot place the bomb in the containment device.

"We're trained." Kimber stood and gestured to herself and Brandon. "We can help secure it. Or get out your wire cutters, and we can try to disarm it."

"Thirty-six seconds left." Brandon pointed at the timer. "We need to decide now."

The female bomb tech took a closer look at the device. "It's too risky to disarm it."

The male tech opened the lid of the containment device. He gestured to Tessa. "Hold this open. As soon as we have the bomb inside it, close it."

Everyone moved quickly, Tessa taking her spot by the containment device as instructed while the rest of them each took a corner of the trunk with the bomb. Twenty seconds left.

The male tech closed the lid of the trunk. "On the count of two. One, two."

Everyone lifted the trunk in unison, the seconds ticking off in Brandon's head. Fifteen, fourteen.

They lowered the trunk into the container. Eleven seconds. Ten.

"Close it!" the male tech ordered.

Tessa flipped the lid closed, and both bomb techs started securing the latches that would keep the lid in place when the bomb detonated. Brandon followed their lead, as did Kimber. Six seconds. Five seconds.

The female tech closed the last latch. "That's it. Everyone, get back!"

Three seconds. Two.

Everyone scattered. Brandon, Kimber, and Tessa rushed down the hall while the two techs headed for the stage.

A flash of light burst from the containment device, and the floor shook. Brandon turned as the unit filled with fire and smoke. His breath shuddered out as his heart continued to pound.

Beside him, Kimber had also turned. "That was close."

Beside her, Tessa stared wide-eyed at what was left of the bomb.

Kimber let out a heavy breath and looked up at him. "Did we really just do that?"

"Yeah, we did." And Brandon hoped he never had to face an active bomb again.

CHAPTER 44

ASADI CHECKED HIS watch again before looking out at the crowded streets and the emergency vehicles that had blocked off the nearby intersection. None of this was making any sense. The only reason for the remote detonation to not work was that the main timer had activated, but it had been nearly six minutes since he'd tried to detonate the bomb.

He texted Whitney, the woman who was supposed to make sure everything went flawlessly tonight. *What happened?*

The response appeared on his screen a moment later. *I don't know, but someone from work might have spotted me. I need help making sure he can't talk.*

Like Asadi had time to deal with these minor inconveniences. *You'll have to take care of him yourself. I need to get out of the country.*

What if I told you that by helping me, you can gain access to a quarter million dollars?

It would be easier to clear out of New York if he had an influx of cash. *What did you have in mind?*

I'll text you the address. Meet me there in two hours.

I'll be there, but first, find out who found the bomb.

Better give me an extra half hour then.

Two and a half hours. Plenty of time to get away from the police presence and make sure he wasn't being followed.

Asadi dropped a few bills on his table and stepped outside once more. With a last glance at the theater that should be in ruins, he turned in the opposite direction. It was time to make a new plan, but first, he was going to make sure whoever got in his way tonight would never be able to do it again.

．　•　•

Kimber climbed out of the back of the taxi, immediately looking up and down the sidewalk in front of her apartment building. A handful of people stood outside the Italian restaurant across the street. Others hurried past as though life were normal. Life was normal for them, but for her, she couldn't shed the fear of what could have happened tonight had they not succeeded. Her sister had nearly died because of her. She and Brandon had nearly died.

Brandon put his hand on her back. "Let's get inside."

Kimber let him guide her forward, her mind still racing. Maybe she should have insisted Tessa come home with her. She would have if Rafi hadn't shown up and whisked them away to debrief them on the incident. Thankfully, Ian had been kind enough to take Tessa and Greta home.

The story of an electrical fire had satisfied the other patrons at the theater. Only she, Brandon, and Tessa knew the truth. Well, the three of them and the police.

The phrase "the show must go on" had taken on a new meaning, the play suspended for at least a few days to give the police and the theater time to ensure Whitney and whoever she'd been working with had left no other surprises.

Kimber and Brandon made it as far as the elevator before she spoke. "What would have happened had we not been there tonight?"

"I don't want to think about it." Brandon hit the button for their floor, his hand not quite steady. "I also don't want to think about what will happen when Labyrinth finds out their plan didn't work."

"Do you think the police will find Whitney?"

"I don't know. New York has a lot of places to hide, especially when someone has unlimited funds."

"Labyrinth doesn't have unlimited funds anymore," Kimber said. "With Conrad in custody and Monroe's international accounts frozen, it's possible the whole organization is having cash-flow problems."

"I hope so," Brandon said. "Without money, the havoc they can create will be limited."

"It would be more limited if we could find Asadi."

"I know. I hoped we'd have him in custody by now."

They passed Trudy's apartment.

"Do you want me to come in with you?" Brandon asked. "If you want, I can sleep on the couch."

Though tempted by his offer, she shook her head. "It's okay." If Tessa could spend the night alone, so could she. "I'll see you in the morning."

Brandon placed his hands on her shoulders. "I hope you know how amazing you were tonight."

"I was terrified." She shuddered to think what would have happened had she not opted to refresh her bomb-disposal skills every year when she renewed her firearms qualifications.

"Hundreds of people are alive tonight because of you."

"Because of *us*." Needing more of the comfort of his touch, she took his hand. "The miracles that occurred tonight happened because we make a good team."

"We do make a good team." Brandon leaned in for a kiss, his hands caressing her arms.

A shiver rippled across her skin, proof that she was still alive, that she could still feel.

Brandon pulled back, his thumbs trailing over her wrists until his fingers grasped hers. "Call me if you change your mind about being alone."

"I will." She leaned in for one more brief kiss before she retrieved her keys from her purse and unlocked her door. "Good night."

"Night."

Kimber stepped into her apartment and closed the door as she reached out and flipped on the light. She made it three steps before she caught the scent of a floral perfume and sensed another presence.

A figure emerged from the office. Whitney.

"It's about time you got home," Whitney said.

Kimber started to grab for the doorknob, but Whitney lifted her hand, a pistol aimed at Kimber.

Whitney took a step forward. "I wouldn't do that if I were you."

Kimber froze.

"It's time you and I had a little talk."

"What do you want?" Kimber asked.

"Your money."

"Excuse me?" Kimber didn't know what she'd expected Whitney to say, but asking for money certainly wasn't it.

"My friend and I need cash to leave the country, and you're going to help us get it." Whitney motioned toward the office as a man walked through the doorway. "Asadi Mir, meet Kimber Frost." Whitney tilted her head toward the framed photo of Kimber and her sister. "Or should I say, Kimber Seidel?"

CHAPTER 45

BRANDON PULLED HIS keys from his pocket and fumbled them twice before he managed to slide the key into the lock. The possibility of sleeping on Kimber's couch wasn't the most comfortable option, but he couldn't deny that he'd prefer that to staying home alone.

He glanced down the hall. Even chatting with Trudy would be preferable to going into his dark apartment, where he would be alone with his thoughts, with the terrifying what-ifs that kept popping into his mind with annoying frequency.

The elevator dinged, and Brandon whirled around. The doors opened only halfway before Trudy rushed into the hall, a pistol in her hand, her grip steady, her weapon aimed toward the floor.

Brandon's instinct should have been to take cover, but everything in the older woman's posture suggested she was law enforcement.

Trudy reached him and spoke in a low whisper. "Where's Kimber?"

"In her apartment." Brandon narrowed his eyes. "Who are you?"

"Gertrude Evanston. Retired FBI." She jutted her chin toward Kimber's door. "Asadi Mir and a woman were spotted on surveillance cameras five minutes ago."

"Where?"

Concern flashed in Trudy's eyes. "Going into Kimber's apartment."

Pure fear rushed through Brandon, and he whirled toward Kimber's door.

He made it three steps before Trudy grabbed his arm and held firm. "You go rushing in there, she's as good as dead."

"But—"

"I have an idea." She waited until Brandon focused on her before she continued. "Are you armed?"

Brandon shook his head. "My gun's in my apartment."

"Get it. I'll meet you back here." She released Brandon's arms and grabbed her keys from her pocket. "Don't go in there without me."

Brandon shoved his door open and rushed into his apartment. If anything happened to Kimber—The mere thought of her with Asadi Mir clogged his throat.

He sprinted to his closet, where his gun safe was concealed, and he retrieved his weapon and three extra magazines of ammunition.

Leaving his safe open, he ran back through his door into the hall. He reached Trudy's apartment as she emerged, her gun gripped in one hand, a set of keys in the other, and a plate of cookies nestled in the crook of her elbow.

She handed him the keys. "Here. I'll need you to unlock her door."

Brandon didn't know how Trudy had obtained a key to Kimber's apartment, nor did he care. He took the keys from her. "What are the cookies for?"

Trudy cocked any eyebrow. "Asadi Mir and his friend are about to learn where the phrase 'kill them with kindness' came from."

• • •

Kimber stumbled as Whitney shoved her toward the serving bar, where her laptop now lay, a dialogue box open on the screen, awaiting her passcode.

"We took the liberty of retrieving your computer from your safe." Pure evil flashed in Asadi's eyes.

"What do you want from me?" Kimber was pretty sure she had already asked the question, but her mind hadn't quite caught up with her current reality. She'd narrowly escaped death only three hours ago by helping to contain a bomb with only seconds to spare, and now she was facing one of the most wanted terrorists in the world while standing in her own living room.

"We just want your money." Asadi gestured toward Whitney. "My friend here said you were paid a quarter million dollars for your first advance."

"My money?" If that was all they wanted, she would gladly give it to them. She and Mark could trace the funds to whatever bank they were using and help the authorities locate these two fugitives.

Kimber looked from Asadi to Whitney. Their expressions both told her the same thing: they weren't going to let her live. Once they had the money, they would kill her. The future she had begun to imagine with Brandon would never happen. Tessa would be left to grieve with their parents, and Kimber's accomplishments at the CIA would be reduced to a single gold star on a wall.

"Unlock the screen," Whitney demanded.

Kimber needed help, and she wouldn't have the chance to message anyone with Whitney and Asadi watching her every move.

"My banking information isn't on my laptop. It's on my cell phone."

"Where is it?" Whitney asked.

"In my purse."

Whitney took her purse and rummaged through it until she found it.

Kimber held her hand out to take it, but Whitney shook her head. "Oh, no. I'm not giving you a chance to call for help. I'll make the transfer."

Whitney tapped on the screen and then turned the phone toward Kimber so the facial ID would unlock it.

"The bank isn't even open right now," Kimber said, desperate to buy time. But time for what? No one knew she was in trouble, and she had no way to send a message to anyone.

Asadi's voice cut through her thoughts. "The banks don't need to be open to put the transfer in motion. A few keystrokes and the money will be on its way to my account. By the time anyone realizes you didn't initiate it, we'll be long gone."

And she would be dead.

Whitney tapped on the screen again, and her face lit up. "Found it."

Kimber assumed Whitney was referring to her banking app.

Whitney held it up and focused on Kimber. "What's your password?"

"I—" Kimber paused. If she gave it to them, they would kill her as soon as they had the money. If she didn't . . . What would happen if she resisted? "I have to look it up. My passwords are coded in a spreadsheet on my laptop."

Asadi crossed to her in two long strides. He snaked his hand out and grabbed her by the throat, his thumb and forefinger squeezing hard until she was gasping for air.

"No tricks." Asadi leaned closer, his brown eyes boring into hers. "Understood?"

Kimber couldn't do anything but blink.

A knock sounded at the door, and Asadi released Kimber and pulled out his gun, aiming it at the door.

Kimber drew in a ragged breath.

Whitney lowered Kimber's phone and focused on Asadi.

"Ignore it," Asadi whispered, answering Whitney's unspoken question.

The knock repeated, followed by Trudy's voice. "Kimber? It's Trudy."

"Who's she?" Whitney asked, her voice low.

"My neighbor. She drops by a lot," Kimber said. "She's usually just bringing by cookies or something."

"At eleven o'clock at night?" Whitney asked.

"She must have heard me get home."

"Kimber?" Trudy called again.

A key rattled, and the lock released.

Asadi lowered his gun to his side and leaned close, his gaze intense. "She has a key to your apartment?"

Apparently, but Kimber wasn't going to admit that this knowledge was new to her too. "She has my spare in case I get locked out."

The doorknob turned, and Kimber prayed her neighbor wasn't about to become another of Labyrinth's victims.

CHAPTER 46

TRUDY POCKETED THE keys she'd taken from Brandon and turned to him. "Ready?" she whispered.

Though Brandon hated the idea of Trudy going in first, he gripped the pistol in his hand and nodded.

"Go on the word *favorite*."

Again, Brandon nodded.

"Kimber? Are you home?" Trudy called out one more time. She pushed open the door a crack as she continued. "I have some cookies for you, and I wanted to see if you had any popcorn I could borrow." She peeked inside, leading with the cookies. "Oh, I'm sorry. I didn't realize you had company." Trudy continued forward.

"That's okay," Kimber said. "And sorry, I ran out of popcorn. Maybe Brandon has some."

Brandon visualized the room, noting Trudy had turned her attention toward the kitchen serving bar.

"I'll just put these on the counter. They're chocolate chip. Your favorite."

Brandon darted into the room and did a quick assessment. Kimber, alive and breathing but far too close to Asadi, who stood beside her. Whitney standing in the middle.

"Federal agents. Freeze!" Brandon said the words, but whatever fleeting hope he harbored that Asadi and Whitney would follow his orders disappeared the moment Asadi's gun came into view.

From where she stood by the serving bar, Kimber thrust her elbow into Whitney's stomach, knocking Whitney into Asadi as he fired a shot. The bullet whizzed between Brandon and Trudy, impacting the doorframe.

Whitney ducked behind the chair closest to the kitchen. Asadi dove onto the couch and rolled off it so he was completely hidden from sight.

Brandon darted behind the near side of the kitchen counter while Trudy took cover in the nook that separated the entry hall from the main part of the living room. Two on two with Kimber caught in the middle.

"There's no way out," Trudy said. "And our backup is on the way."

"They aren't here yet," Asadi said, his voice eerily calm. "And you don't know who you're dealing with."

Brandon knew exactly who he was dealing with: Asadi Mir, the man who created havoc and death wherever he went, the man who was responsible for Finlay's death.

Brandon peeked around the edge of the counter into the kitchen and spotted Kimber crawling toward him, a butcher knife clutched in her hand.

A lock of Whitney's blonde hair came into view at the same time her hand reached over the chair with a gun clutched in it.

"Kimber, watch out!" Brandon swung his gun in Whitney's direction and fired high to make sure Kimber didn't get caught in the crossfire.

Whitney jumped back, and Kimber scrambled the rest of the way to reach his side. He moved over to make room so the two of them were pressed against the end of the counter.

Relieved beyond words that Kimber appeared to be okay, he gripped her hand briefly before turning his attention back to the two threats on the other side of the room.

"Give it up," Brandon called out.

"I never give up," Asadi called back.

They were in a stalemate, and Brandon suspected that wasn't going to change until backup arrived. He glanced at Trudy. She held up three fingers. Three more minutes. All they had to do was stay out of the line of fire until then.

• • •

More shots sounded as Trudy and Asadi exchanged gunfire.

Kimber ducked her head, her shoulder pressed firmly against Brandon's. One hand clutched the knife she'd grabbed from the drawer, and she strained to hear sirens or any sign that help had arrived. If she was reading the signal from Trudy correctly, whatever backup she and Brandon had called would be here in less than three minutes.

"Let Kimber give us what we want, and we'll consider letting you live," Asadi said.

"What does he want?" Brandon whispered.

"Money."

Before Brandon could respond, Trudy said, "Last chance. Come out with your hands up."

"Last chance is right," Asadi said. "Too bad you didn't play nice."

A metallic click sounded with an accompanying thud. Kimber spotted the cylindrical object as it dropped just beyond her. "Grenade!"

Kimber kicked it toward the open door.

As though receiving a pass in a soccer game, Trudy booted it hard through the door and down the hall. She then slammed the door shut. "Take cover!"

With no place to go without exposing herself to gunfire, Kimber tucked her chin to her chest and covered her head with her hands. Brandon ducked his head, too, but he shifted his body to put himself between her and the door.

The floor shook; the door burst from its hinges and flew into the room. The force of the grenade's blast threw Trudy against the wall, and she fell to the floor.

A cloud of drywall plaster filled the air and clogged Kimber's lungs.

Brandon coughed, a welcome sign that he was still breathing.

Kimber wrapped her hand around his arm. "Are you okay?"

Brandon nodded.

She focused on Trudy again, who lay motionless on the floor. Trudy's pistol had dropped to the carpet and rested halfway between the door and the kitchen counter, where Kimber currently sat.

Kimber fought the instinct to rush to Trudy's side. She couldn't do anything to help her neighbor, and getting herself shot wouldn't help anyone.

If she could get to Trudy's gun, the odds would be even. Of course, that was assuming she could actually shoot another person. The thought made her stomach curl. No, she would wait until their backup arrived.

The shrill ring of the fire alarm sounded, and smoke drifted toward them.

"Can the police even get to us now?" Kimber asked Brandon, keeping her voice to a whisper.

"I don't know."

Asadi shouted to be heard over the alarm. "Transfer the money, Kimber, and all this will be over."

A new wave of panic washed over her. "I don't think I'll like his definition of *over*."

"Me neither."

She looked at the gun lying three yards away. There was no way to reach it without exposing herself, and no matter how much she didn't want to admit it, the odds of surviving the night were dropping fast.

CHAPTER 47

BRANDON COUGHED, THE smoke from the hall filling the air. Sirens sounded in the distance, but whether the police would come into a burning building remained to be seen.

A floorboard creaked, and Brandon caught a flash of movement the instant Whitney came into view, her gun raised.

"Watch out!" Kimber hurled the knife in her hand toward Whitney at the same time Brandon lifted his gun.

Kimber missed, but the flying knife was enough to force Whitney to duck.

Brandon took a second to aim and squeezed the trigger. He missed with his first shot, but when he fired again, the bullet hit Whitney in the chest, and she fell to the floor.

Asadi popped up from his spot behind the couch and fired two more times, both of the bullets thudding into the wood of the kitchen cabinets.

Kimber scrambled around the corner of the serving bar and into the galley kitchen. Brandon came behind her.

Kimber opened her utensil drawer and pulled it all the way out. It crashed to the floor, silverware rattling. She pulled the steak knives out, holding all eight by the handles.

A message buzzed on Brandon's Apple watch.

Rafi: *Trying to get to you. The fire alarm has locked down the elevators.*

"Last chance," Asadi said.

"The police are already here," Brandon said. At least, they were in the building.

"Another grenade will take care of them."

Brandon prayed Asadi was bluffing, but he couldn't take the chance. He looked down at the knives in Kimber's hand, then his gaze lifted to meet hers.

She held up the knives and used hand signals to show her intentions. She would go one way and throw the knives at Asadi in an attempt to flush him out of his hiding place. Brandon would go the other way with his gun.

She was offering to put herself out there as bait with no real defense. Brandon shook his head.

Kimber put her free hand on his and nodded. She leaned close and whispered, "We have to try."

She was right. If another grenade went off, they could very well end up in the blast area, and any reinforcements coming their way would likely be killed.

He clenched his jaw and forced himself to nod. Regardless of the risks, they had to stop Asadi. And they had to stop him now.

• • •

Asadi checked Whitney's prone body, hoping for a sign of life. He barely knew the woman and didn't particularly care that she might be gone, but if she was dead, that meant he was on his own, without backup.

He'd been here before. His fourteen-year-old self had survived worse scrapes than this after his brother had died. Surely, with a grenade in his hand and the ample supply of magazines for his Beretta 92FS, he would survive again.

Whitney didn't move, but a stirring on the other side of the room served as a reminder that he was currently facing two-to-one odds.

No matter. Kimber Seidel might be CIA, but she wasn't an operative. And the man with her clearly wasn't in a good frame of mind, or he never would have rushed into the room with only a middle-aged woman and a plate of biscuits for backup.

His fingers tightened around the grenade. The odds might be two against one, but they were still in his favor.

The muscle in his arm twitched as he prepared to throw a second grenade, but a new thought emerged. Three dead government agents might make headlines, but if they really had backup on the way, the body count could be far higher if he waited.

A slow smile crept across his face. Yes, the odds were in his favor, and he was going to make these Americans sorry that they had ever gotten in his way.

• • •

Kimber crawled the length of the kitchen, careful to keep the knives from hitting the floor as she went. If Asadi Mir really did have another grenade, the likelihood of her and Brandon getting out of here alive was fifty-fifty, at best. That they had survived the last grenade blast was a miracle. She envisioned Trudy sprawled by the front door—she hoped they'd all survived the last one.

Kneeling beside the last cabinet in the serving bar, Kimber glanced back at Brandon, who was peering around the corner of the kitchen island.

Kimber shifted a knife from her left hand into her right, gripping it as she envisioned her target. If she could pop up and throw the knife without getting shot, it would be a miracle in itself, but she had to try. Without the front door in place, another grenade would be deadly to all of them, perhaps even Asadi.

She looked back at Brandon. He was here because of her. He might die because of her.

He held up a finger, clearly asking if she was ready. She swallowed hard. He was trusting her to work with him as an equal. He was trusting her training, and she needed to trust both Brandon and herself.

Flushing Asadi out of his hiding place was the only sure way to give Brandon a clean shot, and it was their best chance at survival. They could do this.

She set the spare knives on the kitchen side of the counter, lining them up to make them easy to grab. She then opened the lower cabinet. Metal mixing bowls, skillets, pots, and pans. She added several to the empty space on the counter beside the knives. Then she lifted the knife in her right hand, picked up a skillet with her left, and nodded.

Brandon held up three fingers and began a silent countdown.

The moment his pointer finger lowered, he fired toward Asadi.

Kimber straightened enough to peer over the counter, and she lobbed the skillet over the couch at the same time Brandon fired off two shots.

Asadi let out a startled cry but didn't reveal himself.

Kimber grabbed a mixing bowl and sent it flying, followed by an omelet pan. This time, a thud followed, and Asadi yelped in pain.

Kimber followed up with a knife, aiming blindly as she tossed it high into the air toward the far side of the couch.

Brandon fired again. Kimber tossed another knife and grabbed a third.

A startled cry sounded amid the gunfire that sparked from Brandon's weapon.

Bullets shredded through the back of the couch, and Asadi scampered back, right into her view.

Kimber gripped the knife, took a brief moment to aim, and threw. Without waiting to see if she hit her target, she threw a fourth knife and a fifth.

Asadi cried out again.

Footsteps pounded toward them in the hallway, and a male voice called out, "FBI. You're surrounded."

Help had arrived. Finally.

That thought had barely formed before a grenade emerged from behind the couch and flew toward Brandon.

"Grenade!" Kimber shouted.

Asadi scrambled out of his hiding place and sprinted for Kimber's bedroom.

The door slammed as Brandon fired two shots into it.

Brandon dropped his weapon and scooped up the grenade from where it had landed in the center of the room.

The footsteps in the hall grew louder.

If Brandon threw the grenade into the hall, he would kill the men and women who had arrived to save them. If he sent it into the apartment, they would both die.

The only option was to get the grenade out of the room. With a crazy plan in mind, Kimber straightened and held up her hands. "Throw it to me!"

Brandon stared at her like she was insane.

"Throw it to me!" she shouted again.

Though his doubt was obvious, he threw the grenade to her.

She bobbled it once, the red glowing numbers ticking down. Seven, six, five.

Kimber took aim and hurled the grenade through her open office door.

"Take cover!" she shouted even as she scrambled back to where Brandon remained behind the far end of the serving bar.

She made it to within two feet of her destination before Brandon reached out a hand and pulled her to his side. In the same instant, an explosion rocked the apartment. Glass shattered, flames speared through the office doorway, and something heavy crashed to the floor.

Brandon put his hand on top of her head and pulled her tightly against him, using his body to shield her from the debris flying through the air.

The dust had yet to settle when Rafi and three other agents rushed through the opening where the front door had been.

One immediately dropped beside Trudy, checking her for a pulse. When he remained by her side, Kimber felt a glimmer of hope that the older woman had survived her injuries.

"Where's Asadi?" Rafi asked.

Brandon pointed. "The bedroom."

Rafi and the other agents continued forward, spreading out so they weren't going at the door head-on.

Though Kimber would have preferred to stay in Brandon's arms, she pulled back. The blast from the grenade may have burst out into the living room, but she had no way of knowing if it had broken through the wall into the bedroom.

Apparently sharing the same thought, Brandon said, "Wait here."

Though eager to know Asadi's fate, with no weapons at her disposal, Kimber nodded. Maybe this time, she would be wise to sit this one out.

• • •

Brandon's ears were still ringing from the explosion, but he wasn't about to sit back and wait for Asadi to send another grenade their way. He needed to make sure the man could no longer hurt anyone.

He expelled the magazine from his pistol and reloaded as he crossed the room.

Kimber's bedroom door hung drunkenly on its hinges, the top hinge attached to the wall by only a single screw that was two-thirds of the way exposed.

Rafi's two colleagues took the far side of the door. Brandon fell into position beside Rafi.

As Brandon had done just moments before, Rafi used hand signals to indicate he and Brandon would go through the door first. Then he counted them off using his fingers.

Brandon's stomach clenched. He would be the second man through the door, the one most often shot when going into a hostile situation.

Rafi's hand fisted, and Brandon responded instinctively. He raised his pistol and followed Rafi into Kimber's bedroom. He took aim at Asadi, but he needn't have bothered.

Rather than being poised to shoot at them, Asadi lay on the floor, Kimber's bookshelf firmly on top of him.

Rafi leaned down and scooped up the pistol that lay just out of Asadi's reach.

Brandon kept his gun pointed at the international terrorist. "Check him for grenades."

Without moving the bookcase, Rafi grabbed both of Asadi's hands, pulled them over his head, and snapped a pair of handcuffs on his wrists.

Brandon lowered his weapon, and Kimber appeared at his side.

"Did you get him?" she asked.

"We didn't need to." Brandon motioned toward where Asadi lay. "Looks like you're the one responsible for neutralizing our terrorist."

She looked past him, her eyes widening when she spotted Asadi surrounded by her books. "My bookshelf stopped him?"

Brandon nodded. "I guess insisting on that large one worked out after all."

CHAPTER 48

AFTER THE EVENTS of the past few weeks, Kimber doubted that she would ever struggle with material for her books again. The grenades Asadi Mir had discharged in her building had done enough damage to her apartment and the hall outside that all of the residents had been required by the fire department to relocate for the night. Once a structural engineer deemed the building safe, everyone else would likely be able to return to their homes. Everyone but Kimber.

Rafi had secured hotel rooms for both Kimber and Brandon for the night. How fast they would be able to make repairs, she didn't know, nor did she know if the CIA would want her to remain in New York now that Asadi had been captured and the two Labyrinth operatives working at Monroe Publishing had been neutralized. Based on the evidence thus far, it appeared that Labyrinth didn't have anyone else on the inside at Monroe working for them.

Now here she was, standing beside Trudy's hospital bed, still trying to reconcile the fact that her friendly neighbor had been looking out for them the whole time, and not just by feeding them baked goods.

From where he stood beside her, Brandon laid his hand on Kimber's back. "I can't believe you used to work for the FBI and never told us," he said to Trudy.

"You never asked." Trudy shifted slightly, adjusting the pillow behind her back.

Brandon glanced at Kimber, and she bit back a smile. The two of them could relate to how the lack of a question could impact their understanding of another person's true identity.

Kimber slipped her arm around Brandon's waist. "How long are they keeping you?"

"Just one more night." She motioned to her leg, which was in a cast. "Once they set me up with the basics of physical therapy, I'll stay with my daughter for a week or two until the doctors are okay with me being on my own again. By then, the repairs to the hall and our apartments should be finished." Trudy tilted her head slightly. "That is, assuming you two are staying."

Kimber tensed. Even though her publishing contract was binding, nothing in it required her to remain in New York. She didn't want to think about what life would be like if she and Brandon ended up in different cities. She rather liked having him living just down the hall.

His phone rang, and he pulled it from his pocket. "Looks like we're about to find out." He held up his phone. "It's Director Yarrow." He hit the Call button. "This is Brandon."

Kimber leaned closer in the hopes of hearing both sides of the conversation, but she managed to pick out only a word here and there. When Brandon's face lit into a smile, her heart lifted.

"Thank you, sir." He fell silent for a moment. "Actually, she's standing right next to me. Do you want to talk to her?" He paused for a moment and then nodded. "Here she is." Brandon passed the phone to her.

"This is Kimber," she said.

"I wanted to let you know that we'll have someone start on the repairs to your apartment within the week."

"Does that mean you want me to stay here?"

"I do. The access your author career is creating could help the agency in the long run, and I believe you and Brandon will continue to make a good team."

Her smile was instant. She was staying in New York with Brandon. "Thank you, sir."

"Keep up the good work." Director Yarrow ended the call, and Kimber looked up at the expectant look on Brandon's face.

"Well?" he asked.

"Looks like I'll be staying in New York."

His eyes lit up. "Then, we both will. The director wants me to keep cultivating my career at Monroe."

"And he said he likes the access my author career is creating," she said. Her author career. Those words crashed over her. Even though doubts still plagued her, somehow over the past few weeks, she really had become a writer. She keyed in on Brandon's current undercover assignment. "I hate that you'll have to keep working as an executive assistant."

"It is what it is. The director wants me to stay where I am for now."

"Working for Amelia?"

Brandon nodded. "I may not love the job, but I'm good at it. He wants someone on the inside to keep an eye on things."

"He wants you to make sure Labyrinth doesn't plant someone else?"

"That's exactly what he wants."

Trudy hit the button on her remote to adjust her bed. "I'm glad to hear I won't be losing my neighbors."

"Now that we know who you are, does that mean you aren't going to keep making us banana bread and chocolate chip cookies?" Brandon asked.

"Don't you worry about that." Trudy shook her head. "I may have retired from the FBI, but I still love to bake."

"That's a relief."

"Thanks again for everything," Kimber said. "I don't know if we would have survived without you."

Trudy winked at her. "I was just being a good neighbor."

"And we are very appreciative that you're the type of neighbor who keeps a pistol nearby," Brandon said.

Trudy lowered her voice. "No need to share that with anyone else in our building."

Brandon chuckled. "Understood."

Trudy waved them off. "We'll talk soon."

Kimber and Brandon walked out into the hall. "You know, if you can take the rest of the week off, we could go stay at Ian's place in the Hamptons. He offered to let me use it for a writing retreat, and it would give you some time to think through everything that's happened."

"That's not a bad idea." Brandon pressed the Down button. "We could use some time away from the city to reset."

"I agree. I have a few nightmares I'd like to leave behind for a while."

Several people stepped off the elevator, leaving it empty. Brandon took Kimber's hand as they walked inside. "You know, I have found one thing that helps with that."

"What?" Kimber asked as the doors closed.

"We need to create good memories to overshadow the bad." He smiled and leaned close.

Kimber's breath mingled with his. "Is that so?"

Brandon drew her close and kissed her. "Absolutely."

ACKNOWLEDGMENTS

THIS BOOK COMES from so many pieces of myself and so many people who have played an important part in my life. First, I want to thank the many people I served with at the Central Intelligence Agency. Many years have passed, but your impact on the person I am was profound.

I also want to thank the many people who have helped me through my publishing career, especially my incredible editor, Samantha Millburn. I don't know where I'd be without you. Thank you to Amy Parker and Bri Cornell for all your efforts to get this book into the hands of readers. Thanks as well to the members of the Shadow Mountain team who have done so much to get this book to this point: Chris Schoebinger, Heidi Gordon, Callie Hansen, and the members of the sales and marketing teams who have already done so much for me—Ashley Olson, Troy Butcher, Lehi Quiroz, Haley Haskins, and Mckenzie Bliss. And thank you to Halle Ballingham for designing such an amazing cover and Bre Anderl for a beautiful typeset.

Thanks to Sian Bessey for sharing your homeland with me, and to Sarah Eden for making our trip such an adventure. Thank you to Lara Abramson and Scott Abramson for your help throughout the writing process, from idea development to final edits, and to Mandy Biesinger for your invaluable help at the beta-reading stage. My deepest appreciation to the many critique partners who helped me through the early stages as I struggled to find the story: Ashley Gebert, Daniel Quilter, Eliza Sanders, Connor Olsen, Emma Jackson, Millie Hast, Jack Stewart, Steve Stratton, David Elliott, Brian Godden, Ann Feinstein, and Don

Saracen. Thanks also to Doug Grad for sharing your insights into the New York publishing world.

Thank you to the CIA Publication Classification Review Board for your continued support, and thanks to my family for your support throughout my career. Words cannot express the depth of my appreciation. And finally, thank you to the readers who continue to allow me to do what I love.

CAN'T GET ENOUGH?

STEP BACK INTO THE THRILLING WORLDS OF
TRACI HUNTER ABRAMSON WITH...

--- LUKE STEELE SERIES ---

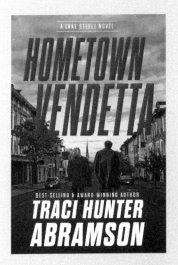

Available Now!

Coming October 2025

--- PEN & DAGGER SERIES ---

Available Now!

**PEN & DAGGER
BOOK 2
COMING 2026**